A Kind
of Shelter
Whakaruru-taha

A Kind
of Shelter
Whakaruru-taha

Edited by
Witi Ihimaera &
Michelle Elvy

MASSEY UNIVERSITY PRESS

Contents

He karakia ki a Papatūānuku
Hinemoa Elder   9

Introduction
Witi Ihimaera and
Michelle Elvy   12

Part one
The sheltered
curving side of
Papatūānuku

Woven triptych
Nina Mingya Powles   18

Ātea
Tina Makereti   20

We are family
Lisa Matisoo-Smith   24

Ka mua, ka muri
Kiri Piahana-Wong   30

Four Pacific shores
Paul D'Arcy   33

What the river said to me
Ben Brown   42

The lifeboat
Gina Cole   44

Our human and more-
than-human world
Craig Santos Perez
and Lana Lopesi   49

Way up south
Cilla McQueen   57

Hazel Avenue
Faisal Halabi   63

Tabula rasa
Siobhan Harvey   70

A long walk
Alison Wong   73

A canopy of cousin trees
Cybella Maffitt   80

This river of life
Ami Rogé and
Brannavan Gnanalingam   82

Peonies
Emma Neale 92

Our house at Staytrue Bay
Hinemoana Baker 97

Part two
From inside
the cave

Tree house
Ian Wedde 102

At the Kauri Museum
Wendy Parkins 105

Looking for boas in the
mangroves
Ashley Johnson and
Pip Adam 112

Tomorrow
David Eggleton 125

Every grain is careful labour
Renee Liang 梁文蔚 128

Ancestry, kin and shared history
Aparecida Vilaça, Dame Anne
Salmond and Witi Ihimaera 136

Dangeropportunity on the lake
Anne Kennedy 149

Come and see it all the
way from town
Laura Jean McKay 152

Ram Raid
Essa Ranapiri and
Michelle Rahurahu 158

Holding the line
Alice Te Punga Somerville 162

Overturning motherhood
Catherine McNamara
and Ghazaleh Golbakhsh 171

Finders, keepers
Sonya Wilson 177

The devil's coach horse
(*Ocypus olens*)
Serie Barford 187

The intentional community
Erik Kennedy   189

An invocation
Gregory O'Brien   193

Inside / Outside
Reihana Robinson   198

We should be
Witi Ihimaera   200

You'll never see unless you look
Janis Freegard   207

Standing tall
Louise Umutoni-Bower
and Apirana Taylor   209

Coracle at a confluence
Sudha Rao   222

The four limitations
James Norcliffe   230

Part three
Stepping out into the world before us

Before dawn
Victor Billot   234

Sailing to Aotearoa
Michelle Elvy   236

Not feeding the world today
Diane Brown   248

Ngā Rārangi
Whiti Hereaka   251

An appreciation of mentors
Aparecida Vilaça, Dame Anne
Salmond and Witi Ihimaera   261

On parenting during the
zombie apocalypse
Emma Espiner   272

To inherit
Ya-Wen Ho   277

Young god
Courtney Sina Meredith   281

Five photographic moments
Day Lane   284

On bushfires, blood
sugars and babies
Kate Rassie   290

One metre
Emma Barnes   297

Break the calabash |
discover and rejoice
José-Luis Novo and
Ruby Solly   299

If we give up flying it doesn't mean
we can't speak to each other as
if countries or scan our genomic
sequences for travel to the flats
Vana Manasiadis   306

Lōemis song cycle: 'Epilogue'
Harry Ricketts   309

You send me Seneca
Selina Tusitala Marsh   318

On writing humanity forward
Ru Freeman and Paula Morris   321

How am I going to make it right?
Chris Tse   329

I prefer sunshine
Helen Rickerby   331

taku taiao
Vaughan Rapatahana   334

Whakarongo
Patricia Grace   336

Dance me to the end of the world
Mohamed Hassan   340

Attend
Vincent O'Sullivan   346

Poroporoaki   348

Select bibliography   350
About the artists   355
Acknowledgements   358

Hinemoa Elder
He karakia ki a Papatūānuku

Dr Hinemoa Elder MNZM (Te Aupōuri, Ngāti Kurī, Te Rarawa, Ngāpuhi) is a Fellow of the Royal Australia and New Zealand College of Psychiatrists, and works as a child and adolescent psychiatrist at Starship Children's Hospital's Haumaru Ōrite Child and Family Unit and Mother and Baby Unit. Her Eru Pōmare HRC Postdoctoral Fellowship examined traumatic brain injury from the perspective of mātauranga Māori and developed resources for those affected as a whānau — approaches that are now used in rehabilitation. She writes forensic reports for the Youth Court and has been a deputy member of the New Zealand Mental Health Review Tribunal for more than 10 years. She is the bestselling author of *Aroha: Māori Wisdom for a Contented Life Lived in Harmony with Our Planet* and *Wawata Moon Dreaming: Daily Wisdom Guided by Hina, the Māori Moon*. Hinemoa had guidance from Professor Sir Pou Temara in writing this, her first published karakia.

E Whae, e Papa e hora nei,
te whaea o te tangata
whakarongo mai rā
ki te ruahine
ki te pūkenga
ki tō whakahina
ko Hina i te pō
ko Hina i te ao
ko Hina āmio ki runga
ko Hina whakarite tai
kia puta ko Tai Tamatāne,
ko Tai Tamawāhine
ko te Tai o Rehua e . . . i.

Rāhiritia atu rā te ūkaipō
kua hua ko te hiringa
te hiringa tapu
te hiringa ā Nuku
te wahine pū o te ao
hei ora mō te ao
hei mana mō te ao
tū i te ao
ko te tū nui
ko te tū roa
ko te tū tē ū
ko te tū tē ea
ko te tūrangawaewae
ko te tū oranga tonutanga.
Haumi e, hui e . . . Tāiki e.

Introduction

1.

When Ranginui the Sky Father was separated from Papatūānuku the Earth Mother, the landscape became a place of cyclonic dust storms and whirling debris.

Subterranean fires burst through Papatūānuku's skin. Solar winds rushed into the space between the parents, creating gaseous clouds. Sheet lightning crackled across the sky and shattered across a broiling sea.

This was the turbulent environment into which the 70 god brothers came, crawling and bloodied. Immediately assailed by the intense cold, they took shelter in a cave formed from one of the curving sides of Papatūānuku's body. Called whakaruru-taha, Māori still apply the term to a warm and cosy haven away from winds and cold. It was from this place that the god brothers finally moved out into a new world.

2.

This whare pukapuka is, similarly, a whakaruru-taha.

Here, 76 creative thinkers — poets and fiction writers, anthropologists and biologists, musicians and visual artists, and more — gather at a hui in the shelter, which you might visualise as a magnificent cave-like dwelling or meeting house.

In the middle is a table, the tēpu kōrero from which, from time to time, the rangatira speak; they converse with honoured guests, and their rangatira-kōrero embody the very tāhuhu, the over-arching horizontal ridge pole of the shelter. They provide the strong spine for *A Kind of Shelter*. Sitting around them, or on either side of the wharenui, are other members of the iwi. Every now and then they join the conversation, talking story, singing story, energetically contributing to the kaupapa or performing for the enjoyment of the iwi: this is who we are. Their audience listens in, laughing, singing along or pondering further when the talk gets serious: sometimes they agree, sometimes they don't.

What is this world we live in, and where is it heading?

3.

The title of this anthology comes from a poem by Craig Santos Perez. The book's contributors look out from the shelter upon our world in the second decade of the millennium. This is what they see.

It's not only about seeing but also a greater sensing. It's about the way we gather knowledge; the way we hand it down, or over, to each other; the way we accept and examine and hold that knowledge. It's about exploring for ourselves, and thinking critically about the world we inhabit. It's about the cave, going all the way back to Plato's metaphor in all its realities (understood and misunderstood), and the idea of emerging from it.

In this manner, the book you hold carries far-reaching goals, not in the way it delivers answers, but rather in the way it asks questions. We hope the contents can be thought of as a dialogue, from writer to writer, and between the written word and the visual works included here: story and poem weave together thematically and pull at the edges; fiction and non-fiction ponder climate change and political urgencies, historical weights and cultural challenges, family structures and race and class. Painters and photographers suggest realities and un-realities.

In dialogues across space and time we look from Aotearoa New Zealand outward to the world, inviting individuals from Hawai'i, Japan, South Africa, Brazil, Italy, Rwanda, Spain and Sri Lanka to engage in conversations that explore identity and change, motherhood and healing, war and legacy, ancestry and shared history, art and music and the natural world. Artworks from Ghana, Singapore, the United States, Sāmoa and Aotearoa call out with our histories and stories. And all this occurs during our continued isolations in this Covid world. As Singapore-based photographer Steve Golden strolled through the streets of Tokyo after the first intense lockdown, he observed teens posing in kimonos and a solitary man praying before an altar. He writes: 'It struck me that however much we have been locked inside, however much we have been stopped from travelling, however much we have been digitally tracked, vaccinated, nasally swabbed, masked and monitored, we will emerge with what was always there: our traditions. Our cultures. Our families. Our heritage.'

A print by Noa Noa von Bassewitz features on the cover of this book. In an interview about her work, she notes the relationship between the creator and the viewer, the energy that translates across the space between them: 'I have come to realise that what I see and feel in my creative process is my own story. I hope that the energy of it is what is conveyed to the viewer. Others do not have to see what I see, and I welcome the viewer's curiosity and personal connection. I write stories as a part of my completion process — it is when I become the viewer of my own work that I can see my stories reflected back at me. It's a circular process, a reveal not too dissimilar to the reveal of block to paper: the negative becomes the positive and something new can be seen.'

This cover print is called *Embrace*, which might be looked at, in the words of the artist, as 'two clouds that take shape and are seen as commingling creatures, dark and light entwined'.

4.

Which brings us to the final note: that this book also suggests dialogues between its contents and you, its reader. Seeing, reflecting, sensing more, seeing again: this is the art of creating. A circular shape, like the koru whose presence is also reflected in this book.

We are very grateful to the book's contributors for sharing their creative voices and visions. We are grateful, too, to Creative New Zealand for funding this project. We offer our heartfelt thanks to Nicola Legat and the team at Massey University Press for believing in the project and seeing it through. Finally, we remember our elder Moana Jackson (1945–2022), whose energy and sense of justice also rings out in these pages.

The cave is full of shadows and light. Reality and truth are fragmented at best, influencing our intellectual, spiritual and philosophical wellbeing. So it is with an anthology: the contents are fragments of individual views — it contains sparks of inspiration and serious questions that might help us consider our own wellbeing. We must keep asking questions to examine what we know and do not know; we must keep asking questions as we move, out of the shelter, forward towards tomorrow.

Witi Ihimaera and Michelle Elvy
May 2023

Part one

The sheltered curving side of Papatūānuku

Ko te pae tawhiti whāia kia tata,
Ko te pae tata whakamaua kia tīna.

Seek to bring distant horizons closer,
and sustain and maintain those that have been arrived at.

Nina Mingya Powles
Woven triptych
after Pema Monaghan

The sun is white.
The sea is woven.
Harakeke bend towards
the waves.

The sun is white.
The sea is woven
through with blue.
Harakeke bend towards
the waves.

The sun is white
and I can't see.
The sea is woven through
with blue.
Harakeke touch
my knees
above the waves.

At night I watch
the weaver's hands
turning her basket
through the screen.

She says,
if you look after the plant
the plant will look after you.

At night I thread
the needle,
hold two strands
in one hand.
I do not let
go.

Harakeke
bend towards
a distant sun.
The white waves
do not
let go.

Handwork
is the night work
of women
and memory.

My memory
is a stone fruit
cut into quarters
by her hands.

Nina Mingya Powles is a writer, poet and librarian from Te Whanganui-a-Tara Wellington and of Malaysian, Chinese and Pākehā descent. Her food memoir, *Tiny Moons: A Year of Eating in Shanghai*, was published in 2020. In 2021 her debut poetry collection, *Magnolia* 木蘭, was shortlisted for both the Mary and Peter Biggs Award for Poetry for the Ockham New Zealand Book Awards and the Royal Society of Literature Ondaatje Prize. Her essay collection, *Small Bodies of Water*, was also published that year. She lives in London.

Tina Makereti
Ātea

The first thing Aunty Ivy asks them to do is sit in a circle and talk about their previous experiences.

Leila is the first to volunteer. 'I've done it once. There was no one else, and Papa Ronnie asked me to, and helped me with the kupu. I can't remember what happened. None of it.' She grins, shakes her head, clearly horrified. The other women mirror her, wide-eyed.

After a long pause, Amorangi speaks. 'I started to last year. At the wā' it's something they teach us. But I feel too young to do it at home, and away from home. I'm not sure rangatahi should do it yet.'

Into the next pause, Lisa eventually says something, her voice shaky, uncertain. 'It comes up for me through my work more than any other situation. But I never know what's right.' She thinks then of the colleague at her office in Wellington, the loudness of that other voice. The quietness of her own. 'I'm the right age. I can feel the need — that I will be called on soon. But the whakamā is so deep. I don't think I'll have a strong enough voice.'

'That's it with our generation, eh? It takes so much to get through that whakamā. We're in between our nannies and these confident young ones, the last generation to be raised without kōhanga or kura.' Her cousin is right, although Lisa wouldn't have had access to kura even if it had existed when she was a kid. She feels the barrier almost as if it is physical. 'I just want to feel some ease around it.' Her words are urgent now. 'The karanga, the reo, all of it. I just want to feel like I'm OK, where I am.'

The aunties look on, impassive, nodding. Then they start coaching, but there are no instructions, no pointers, no methods.

They tell stories.

Their own first times. Without exception, they were put on the spot. Told when to do it and given a gentle shove. They'd been watching, sometimes for years, but that was all the training they got. Lisa understands then. There can be no easing into something like this. But also, they've all been where she is, these kuia who carry the whole hapū in their calls back and forth across the marae ātea: apprehensive, full of trepidation, daunted at the incredible responsibility. What if they make a mistake? What will befall the people if they screw up?

Aunty Ivy is the last to speak. 'Remember, you're at home. You can't be wrong when you're home.'

Something inside Lisa slides into place at these words. She has been feeling lesser than since she walked into the wharenui, not because anyone has made her feel that way but because they are all ahi kā, keeping the home fires burning, while she has been a city Māori all her life. It is her home as much as theirs, but they all have their roles, they know their place, they know each other. She is a latecomer, one of the few to return since her grandfather was forced north by the need for work, thrice estranged after her parents' separation and her removal from the family as a baby. And then there are the more recent blows: the constant tension at work, her ideas shot down by the only other Māori in the Compliance Team, who is fluent and confident in te reo.

Tension with Pākehā colleagues doesn't bother her, but she has only ever found allies in Māori co-workers, especially wāhine. Somehow her failure to earn the respect of this one woman has pierced the soft ball of shame that she hid long ago within many layers of thick defence. Lisa knows her own record, knows that she's earned her seniority — the long hours, the constant battles with a system that isn't built to help her people, or even recognise their needs. But none of it matters. In the public service world she feels herself defined not by what she has achieved but by what she lacks. Even the reo she knows fails her when the time comes: she chokes and stutters, the words strangled in her throat.

You can't be wrong when you're home.

They go outside. Now the practical instruction begins. They are given some words to call — some will be hau kāinga welcoming the visitors and some manuhiri replying to the welcome. Lisa knows her voice will be quiet, and she doesn't know if she can make the right sounds. Her voice disappears whenever she is called on to waiata by herself. Still, she feels no anxiety; she cannot fail even if she sounds terrible. Everyone is just as scared as she is. She has decided, for these few hours, to do only exactly as she is told, stepping into the safe circle the aunties have created, where nothing about her is wrong.

They stand in a literal circle, arms linked, facing outwards.

'We'll go around, one after another, repeating the same lines,' Aunty Ivy tells them. Lisa closes her eyes. She can't see anyone, but she can feel them through their linked arms, and suddenly, she can hear them. The voices calling, progressively getting closer to her. Finally, her cousin's voice directly to her left. She knows she is ready. She feels calm.

'Hāere mai e ngā manuhiri e-ii-eee!' Her voice is strong and clear, and *loud*. She had no idea she could make that kind of sound — so sure, so clean. This is who she is, then, someone with a voice like this. The call goes around the circle again and again, and each time, as the women's confidence grows, they begin to make different calls, adding complexity. A couple of times she stumbles, but that's OK, they all do.

Later, the men rejoin them and they organise a mock pōwhiri. Lisa joins the manuhiri side, where six novice women will karanga for the first time. They line up and decide the order of the callers. The nerves hit then. Will her voice disappear when she has to face the marae ātea and all the people?

'I don't know if I can—' She doesn't even finish the sentence. Aunty Ivy is immediately beside her, linking her arm through Lisa's.

'I'll go first,' she says. 'You call after. What are your kupu?'

Lisa takes a breath. She looks out at the expectant faces on the other side framed by the mahau of the wharenui, the tīpuna curling up the pou, the wide expanse of green in between, and thinks about what she's going to say.

Tina Makereti (Te Ātiawa, Ngāti Tūwharetoa, Ngāti Rangatahi-Matakore, Pākehā) is author of *The Imaginary Lives of James Pōneke* (2018) and co-editor, with Witi Ihimaera, of *Black Marks on the White Page* (2017). In 2016 her story 'Black Milk' won the Commonwealth Short Story Prize, Pacific Region. Her other books are *Where the Rēkohu Bone Sings* (2014) and *Once Upon a Time in Aotearoa* (2010). She teaches creative writing at Te Herenga Waka Victoria University of Wellington.

Lisa Matisoo-Smith
We are family

I am a biological anthropologist. My academic training and research for more than 30 years has focused on understanding human origins and diversity.

I started studying this subject at a very interesting time, just as scientists realised that we each carry the information about the history of our species in our cells, and DNA technology had developed to the point that we could easily access that information. In 1987 Allan Wilson, a New Zealand scientist at the University of California, Berkeley, and his students Rebecca Cann and Mark Stoneking published their revolutionary research on modern human origins. They focused on a small part of DNA called mitochondrial DNA (mtDNA), which is passed down directly through the maternal line, and, using DNA collected from women of diverse ancestry from around the world, they were able to reconstruct our family tree.

The results of that study, dubbed the 'Mitochondrial Eve' theory, shook the scientific community and the broader public, because it suggested that all humans share a common maternal ancestor who lived in Africa some 200,000 years ago. Perhaps more surprising was that the DNA also suggested that our modern human ancestors did not start spreading out of Africa, to disperse across the globe, until about 70,000 years ago.

Research undertaken over the subsequent years, including further DNA studies and archaeological research, has confirmed and clarified our global migration history. Within a few thousand years of leaving the African continent, humans had arrived in New Guinea and Australia, presumably by spreading across Asia, following the coastline until they reached the southern edge of the continent. At this point, they figured out how to create some kind of watercraft to cross the deep-water passages of more than 70 kilometres to reach New Guinea and Australia by around 60,000 years ago.

Our ancestors didn't start settling in Europe until about 40,000 years ago, and didn't cross the frozen land-bridge linking Asia to the Americas until about 20,000 years ago. Our own part of the world, the great Pacific Ocean, was not settled until the past few thousand years, culminating with the arrival of Polynesian voyagers on the shores of Aotearoa only about 750 years ago.

It is this last leg of the great human journey, the human settlement of the Pacific, that has been the topic of my research for the past 35 years. My own personal journey started in the Pacific. I was born in Hawai'i, grew up in Japan and moved to Berkeley,

California, to start university. After graduating with a BA in Anthropology in 1985, like so many other middle-class kids I decided to take some time off to backpack around Europe. I wanted to figure out who I was and what I really wanted to do with the rest of my life. I arranged to do some volunteer work on a couple of archaeological excavations in France but, before that, I decided that I wanted to reconnect with my own Estonian heritage.

During the first week of that voyage of discovery I met my New Zealand husband, who was also on an OE. After I finished backpacking, he flew to France to meet me at the archaeological site I was working on in Nice. We got married a year or so later, and moved to New Zealand in 1987, where I started postgraduate studies at the University of Auckland. For my PhD I wanted to see if I could use this newly discovered DNA technology, combined with archaeological and linguistic evidence, to reconstruct the settlement of the Pacific islands using mtDNA.

Instead of studying human mtDNA, I decided to study the DNA of one of the animals that travelled with the Polynesian voyagers as their canoes crossed the Pacific Ocean. In addition to carrying people, dogs and important food plants, the waka that arrived on the shores of Aotearoa beginning in the thirteenth century CE also transported the kiore, or Pacific rat. I realised that if we could look at mtDNA differences in the different populations of the rats in Polynesia, and determine, for example, which islands the New Zealand kiore came from, it would tell us where the waka came from.

During my research, I have been incredibly lucky to be able to visit many Pacific islands, and to meet people who were intrigued enough by what I was doing and my research questions that they were willing to talk with me. They knew where their ancestors came from, and they very kindly shared their stories. I was told that if I trapped rats from around the marae of Taputapuātea, on the island of Ra'iātea, for example, I would find the source of the rats in Aotearoa. And, indeed, I did. We found that the kiore here likely came from a large number of islands in the Cook and Society Island archipelagos, including Ra'iātea. None of this is a surprise to many Māori or other Polynesians I speak with. I was telling them something that they already knew from their oral traditions and whakapapa.

Over the next 20 years or so, I was able to continue my research, reconstructing ancient human migrations using the DNA of plants and animals carried by the people as they settled the islands of the Pacific. There was general scholarly interest in my research, but not too many people beyond academia would normally engage with the subject of DNA and human migrations.

In 2007, the biotech company 23andMe introduced the first direct-to-consumer home DNA ancestry test. In 2008 it was declared by *Time* magazine to be the invention of the year, as so many (mostly Americans) were willing to part with $100 to find out 'who they are and where they are from'. While the popularity of these tests may have reached its pinnacle in the subsequent 15 years, over 25 million people, including many from Australia and New Zealand, have taken a DNA test to find out 'where they are from' or to 'uncover their ethnic mix', and even 'to connect with relatives', and no doubt many more are still considering 'having their DNA done'. What has driven this mass engagement with DNA technology and the sudden need for information that it might be able to provide? Are we so unsure of who we are and where we come from?

In 2008 I was approached by the National Geographic Society and asked to join its Genographic Project to further investigate the dispersal of humans worldwide. I was to engage with Pacific communities to see whether they wanted to participate in the study. This project, of course, coincided with the development of direct-to-consumer ancestry tests, and the Genographic Project not only sampled DNA of Indigenous communities around the world, but also incorporated a 'citizen science' component — volunteers could pay to have their DNA tested and then have their data added to the Genographic study and database.

Tens of thousands of people bought the Genographic deep-ancestry tests, and of course many more bought other DNA ancestry kits. So, again, why were people suddenly so interested in 'doing their DNA'? What was driving this need to know, to reconnect to some location or group of people they have never known? I keep coming back to one answer — it is about identity. So many of us have lost our connections to people and place. Some, sadly, have had those connections and history stolen from them through colonisation and colonialism, but many have disconnected by choice or — perhaps even more commonly — they have disconnected without realising the consequences. We have been so busy trying to 'get ahead', to buy the right house or the right car, to wear the right clothes or send our kids to the right schools, that we seem to have come to a point where we think that these things project or even determine who we are. They have become our identity.

If we look back to our primate ancestry, we see that we are social animals. As humans we have, for most of our existence, belonged to a tribe. We knew where we were from and who our people were. When we eventually settled down in villages we lived in the same places as our parents and grandparents, or perhaps in the next village. But, as villages became cities and rapid transport became possible, we began moving further and faster than ever before. The result is not only the wonderful multicultural cities and nations that exist today, but also the threat of monoculturalism — the McDonald's-isation of the world.

In the quest for a better life, we often moved away from family. We are less likely to live in multi-generation homes, so family stories and histories are not being passed down. The more we move to cities, the more likely we are to become isolated. The more we are connected by technology, the more disconnected we seem to become. By focusing so much on the future, we have forgotten about our past. We need those connections to anchor our identity. People who are not connected to people and place are not likely to look after that place or other people.

Perhaps it is not too late for us. Recent events may have woken us up just in time. I would like to think that perhaps the lockdowns that so many of us endured during the first year or two of the Covid-19 crisis gave us the shake-up that we needed. When we weren't allowed to go out and socialise, we realised that we really wanted to do so — in fact, we needed to. We realised that if we were sick, we needed people who could provide meals or who would call to make sure that we were OK. We realised that our kids needed to be outside playing, and that spending all day on the computer was not good for anyone.

People did go out and spend time walking the dog or riding bikes with the kids. Instead of avoiding looking at the neighbours as we drove past their houses, we put signs and stuffed animals in the windows for people to see. We realised how much more time we had when we weren't sitting in a car commuting to our cubicle office in the city. We bought local, which we could see benefited not only ourselves, but our neighbours and our communities, too. Perhaps now, before we all rush to 'get back to normal', we can look back and learn from the past — from the past few years and the past 200,000 years. We need to reconnect and ground ourselves.

The 'Mitochondrial Eve', or 'Out of Africa', story surprised both scientists and the general public because it showed that, despite the physical and cultural differences we see in people from around the globe, our DNA is virtually identical. We all share a remarkably recent common ancestor. Her descendants undertook amazing journeys, whether it was crossing the desert 70,000 years ago, on a canoe that crossed the Pacific Ocean 750 years ago, on a ship that arrived 150 years ago, or on an airplane that landed 35 years ago. We can celebrate that tiny bit of DNA that connects us to some geographical location where one or more of our ancestors might have lived 10 or 15 generations ago, but we can also celebrate the shared history that is told in all of our DNA.

For some people, having their DNA analysed may be the only way that they can connect to lost family members or particular aspects of their ancestry. However, for most people, the information that they need to link them to a culture, a place, a history, an identity will be found not in their DNA but rather in the stories and the people close to them. If you are lucky enough to have family members around, talk to them about what they know about the family history. Make sure you pass that information on to the next generation. They may not be interested now, but they will eventually want to know. If you don't have access to those people or that information, start with today. Today will be history tomorrow. Get involved in your local community and celebrate that sense of belonging. Get to know your local history and the stories of the people and the place where you live. Reconnect, and together we will create the future.

Lisa Matisoo-Smith is a Professor of Biological Anthropology in the Department of Anatomy at the University of Otago Te Whare Wānanga o Otāgo. She is a Fellow of the Royal Society Te Apārangi, a Fellow of the Society of Antiquaries, London, and was the principal investigator for the Pacific Islands with National Geographic Society's Genographic Project. Lisa's primary area of interest is looking at the biological evidence for the human settlement of the Pacific, applying both ancient and modern DNA techniques to reconstruct population histories. She lives in Ōtepoti Dunedin.

Kiri Piahana-Wong
Ka mua, ka muri
Walking backwards into the future

My great-grandmother, Ethel Jemmett. She's 36 years old and on a boat with her eight-year-old son, my grandfather Lionel, journeying

My mother, Lois. She's reading *The Very Hungry Caterpillar* to her two youngest children, my sisters, their little mouths open and eyes wide

My father, David. He's diving for kaimoana, and there's quite a haul today: a bucket of scallops, four fat crayfish. Snapper caught on the line

Ethel again. She's washing dishes, scrubbing and rinsing sink after sink of hotel glassware, cutlery, plates, her back bent and her hands cracked and sore. In this new world, she is a maid

My great-grandfather, Te Hare Piahana. A man of pre-eminent mana, but in this recollection, he is taking a very young version of my father shopping for his first suit

My grandfather, Doong Lun Wong (known as 'Jack'). He's pegged my 12-year-old father up on the clothesline for misbehaving — hiding in a tree and throwing stones at the mayor's passing car

Doong Lun again, but he's much younger. It's 1927, and he's leaving China. Leaving his elderly mother, his village, his family. Leaving his first wife, pregnant with their son. In three years' time, she'll be gone and their child an orphan. At 10, this boy will sell panels of wood from the family home to survive

My grandmother, Alma Jemmett, in her sewing room. Overflowing jars of buttons, sewing machines, patterns, thread. I am measured in this room for dresses and skirts and even underwear. I am six

Her husband, Lionel Jemmett, leaving his young bride to go to war. It's 1940. When he returns, he'll never speak of it to her, and she won't ask him

My dad again. He's lying on the road outside our house, and he's staring at the sky. He is dead

My nana, Doong Lun's second wife, Sylvia Piahana Wong. She's making plum jam, with fruit harvested from her own tree. The house smells sticky and sweet

And then my son. He's running as fast as he can down the hill from kindergarten, away from me. His arms are stretched out wide, as if this world is to be longed for, as if it's to be embraced. He is laughing. He is unafraid

Kiri Piahana-Wong is a publisher, poet, writer and editor of Ngāti Ranginui, Chinese and Pākehā descent. She is the publisher at Anahera Press, which she founded in 2011. Her publications include the poetry collection *Night Swimming* (2013). She is co-editing an anthology of Māori poetry and fiction as well as a book of dual-language flash fictions and prose poems in te reo Māori and English, both forthcoming in 2023. She lives in Whanganui.

Paul D'Arcy
Four Pacific shores

I have always been drawn to beaches. They have become a metaphor in Pacific history for cultural interactions and as zones of transition. Four Pacific beaches have particular significance for me; each is associated with a particular time in my life and my development as a Pacific historian. Over time it has become hard to separate personal emotion from the academic associations that have accumulated.

Brighton Beach in Otago was the beach of my childhood, when I glorified my British heritage to distinguish me from other Kiwis as a prop for childhood insecurities. Waikīkī was my first overseas beach. It represented an island shore where I felt I could at last break free of small-town mentalities and the myriad self-imposed constraints that all New Zealanders carry with them. I discovered Waikīkī while studying Pacific history at the University of Hawai'i at Mānoa. This study, and a trip to Britain during it, made me aware that the grey Atlantic world of Britain was a foreign land. I longed for, and felt at home with, the intense blue of the Pacific's sea and sky.

It was not until I visited Pūko'o on Moloka'i, however, that I really began to see Pacific shores as ancient cultural landscapes and seascapes. The knowledge I had learned from books came to life there as never before. My sense of the Pacific as a vast culturally connected ocean space steeped in history reached its apotheosis at Iwan in southeastern Taiwan on a cold, misty morning in November of 2014, when my personal experiences and academic learning merged as never before. This understanding drew me closer to the Pacific and its peoples, and made me more at ease with myself. I feel at home on Pacific shores and thirst to find out more about them, and to share this Pacific with others.

Brighton Beach

I am a first-generation New Zealander. My English parents came to New Zealand in the late 1950s from Liverpool in search of a better life. Like thousands before them and many more since, they came to New Zealand to escape the post-war economic decline of the once prosperous industrial north, and a system where class and religion mattered as much as skill and talent. British colonies like Australia, New Zealand and Canada seemed so full of promise and opportunity by comparison. My parents opted for New Zealand because its government was offering assisted passages for skilled labour and its climate and landscape seemed less alien than the other two options.

The transition from rambunctious, gregarious Liverpool to the more cautious and understated interactions of New Zealand culture took some time, but my parents never regretted the move. I am also glad they moved. My childhood was spent in Mosgiel, a small rural service town with a large woollen mill, about 12 miles from the sea. Our family friends were a mix of European immigrants, consisting mainly of English, Irish, Welsh, Scots and Dutch. Two of our English friends were married to a Hungarian and a Latvian, respectively.

Summer holidays at the beach figure prominently and fondly in my early memories. Our favourite local beach was Brighton, about half an hour's drive south of Dunedin. The main beach consists of a broad expanse of fine white sand sheltered between two headlands. It was always crowded with people when we were there. Beachgoers parked their cars on the wide grass verge between the beach and the coast road. Brighton's one general store was located on this road, while its baches and houses spread out over the hills behind the road.

The township was merely a backdrop to the beach for us. It did not have a life of its own and seemed unimportant for our young preoccupations. The store was the only part of the township we ventured to — for hokey-pokey ice-creams that began to melt as soon as they were scooped out of their containers and relocated precariously onto wafer cones. Even today, I cannot think of anything that can match the taste of creamy New Zealand ice-cream on a summer's day.

Other memories crowd in: cucumber, tomato and cold meat sandwiches with lemonade for lunch on towels on the beach, or, more often, on a rug beside the car; cricket on the beach or the grass domain where anyone was welcome to join in — as long as they didn't bowl too fast at the smallest Bert Sutcliffes to step up and take their guard (all fathers were fair game, though); building sandcastles on the shore with moats for the incoming tide to fill; and wading into the surf, daring ourselves on past one more wave, and one more still. Less vivid memories also remain, particularly of mothers sitting chatting to each other most of the time, reminding us to cover up and put sunscreen on, and forever preparing food or cleaning up.

I was a friendly but quiet child and very self-conscious of my gangly, thin physique. My brother had a good olive complexion for the sun, but my skin betrayed my

English roots. Sunburn was always a problem. Often I would wander off on my own to investigate the stream that flowed into the bay, tracing its meanderings like an explorer following a mighty river. I was fascinated by the power of flowing water to shape the wet sand on its banks, and I loved to climb the small headland that jutted out into the right-hand side of the bay. I enjoyed the relative solitude of the promontory, from where I could look down on the crowded beach and then out to sea.

The sea frightened me, though. I could not swim and did not like getting into water much deeper than my rib cage. I inflated the achievement of scrambling over rock pools between tides to get on the headland. I dreamed of finding pirates' treasure in the surrounding caves, and perhaps the remains of a Māori pā. I never did make any great discoveries, though. Brighton Beach remained, and remains, a symbol of Kiwi rather than Polynesian culture.

While I told myself that 'we' British were smarter than New Zealanders, and certainly better association football players, the reality was that my summer experiences were very Kiwi — beaches, sun, communal cricket and a proximity to nature. I fought to resist this realisation into my teenage years. Although I did not recognise it at the time, the battle had already been lost.

Waikīkī

In 1985 I began postgraduate studies at the University of Hawai'i at Mānoa (UH Mānoa). I had specialised in Pacific and African history at the University of Otago. This was the first time I had left New Zealand, and only the fifth time I had been outside Otago.

Hawai'i presented a chance to break free and discover myself after living in a small community where too many people knew your past for you to find or re-create yourself. The cultural diversity of the UH Mānoa campus and the friendliness of locals were intoxicating. My 'English' accent set me apart and was enjoyed by Americans. My life centred on campus, and my passion was my studies. Only two diversions could lure me off-campus with any frequency: browsing through the wonderful second-hand bookstores of Honolulu, and walking along the beaches and tourist precincts of Waikīkī.

Most spoke of Waikīkī as a false place that betrayed and distorted the real values of

Hawai'i and the Pacific. In many ways this was true, but it was also what was appealing about it. At any time of the day or night, at any time of the year, Waikīkī is alive with people out to enjoy themselves and escape their mundane daily routine.

The beachfront at Waikīkī is alluring. I particularly enjoyed walking along it in the late-afternoon sunshine. It is a relaxed time of day when tourists have absorbed all the sun they can take, and thoughts turn to showers and dinner back at the hotel, while locals use the open-air showers in the beach parks and prepare to tuck into carbohydrate-rich picnics. Saturday was my favourite day in Waikīkī. Afternoons were spent looking for used or vintage books, particularly at Froggies, which boasted 500,000 books, before wandering down to Waikīkī to be first in line at Shore Bird Restaurant to secure a beachside open-air table. Shore Bird offered students a $5 all-you-can-eat deal every week, providing you brought your Shore Bird coupons from the student newspaper *Ka Leo O Hawai'i* with you. This included fresh meat or fish, which you cooked yourself on an open grill, and a massive salad bar.

Mahimahi was my favourite meal. Most of my friends were on the cheaper university accommodation package that did not include meals after breakfast on the weekend, so they would hold off all day and join me in line at Shore Bird when it opened for dinner in the late afternoon. We would heap our plates up, sit back and watch the sunset, enjoy the pleasures of a full belly, 'talk story', then proceed on to second or third helpings we really did not need or even want. The sunsets at Shore Bird were always stunning. We would look along the stretch of white sand protected by reefs or breakwaters that made Waikīkī so popular, watch lovers strolling arm-in-arm along the beach, or gaze out to sea past the flotilla of private boats and cruise ships and surfers just offshore to the vibrant sunsets over 'Ewa.

Gradually, I became aware of the marginalised existence of many Kānaka Maoli (native Hawaiians) as kama'aina (literally, the people of the land). They were disproportionately represented in low-paid jobs in the tourist industry. I met a few at university: Terry Kanalu Young, perhaps the most gifted Pacific historian of my generation; and Jon Kamakawiwo'ole Osorio, whose songs and prose are filled with poetry and passion, and whose elegant scholarship also left me in awe.

I would see other Hawaiians every time I ventured to the beaches of Waikīkī. My favourite stretch of sand was on the edge of Waikīkī, backed by Kapi'olani Park, with

Diamond Head looming in the background. The beach was always crowded with sunbathers, while just offshore crowds of Hawaiian youths bodysurfed for hours and only reluctantly came ashore when darkness descended. The sight reminded me of the missionary William Ellis's early nineteenth-century description of Hawaiians as 'almost a race of amphibious beings'.

I visited England for the first time in 1986 during the university summer break. I did not feel as English as I thought I would, and remember standing on the promenade overlooking their Brighton Beach sensing I did not belong. It was mid-summer, and I was wrapped in a warm jacket staring out at an unappealing and crowded beach, and beyond to a grey and foggy English Channel. I wanted to see more of my English cultural heritage, but also to return home soon to Hawai'i's sun and surf.

This ease of Hawaiians in the water enthralled me because it was such a contrast to my own seafaring heritage. The D'Arcys had been involved in various maritime occupations in Liverpool for generations up to the interwar years. Over time, those links with the sea had withered, and the only legacy I was aware of as a small boy growing up in New Zealand was my father's fabled — but now lost — stamp collection, enriched by stamps from ports around the world that had found their way to Merseyside. Many British seamen could not swim, simply reflecting the grim realities of the colder latitudes and waters of the North Atlantic. Only recent generations had learned to swim in the comfort of indoor swimming pools as part of their school education.

Waikīkī lost some of its allure for me in the late 1990s while I was researching the overthrow of the Hawaiian monarchy for one of my courses at Victoria University of Wellington. I came across a line drawing from a San Francisco newspaper depicting 'government' forces (white American residents who seized power with the aid of American Marines in 1893) bombarding 'rebels' (Hawaiian royalists) on Diamond Head from what is now the middle of Waikīkī.

Another hidden side to Waikīkī was the mystery of its fine sandy beaches. Generally speaking, leeward beaches should not have sand as fine as that at Waikīkī, as they are sheltered from the pounding waves of the trade-wind coast; offshore reefs shield them from Kona (leeward) storms that sweep in from the south. Friends who should know informed me that this uncharacteristically fine leeward shore sand was brought in from windward beaches on Moloka'i by barges and deposited along the Waikīkī shore, while every night the beach is combed by machines to remove litter and other 'unseemly' objects.

Pūkoʻo

I only really began to grasp the full complexity of Hawaiians' relationship with the sea when I travelled to the outer islands after reading about Indigenous Hawaiian culture in the Pacific Collection of the UH Mānoa Hamilton Library. On Molokaʻi, I finally began to imagine and realise that seas, like islands, were cultural mosaics. The sea was not a uniform void, and cultural spaces did not end at the beach.

Eastern Molokaʻi is a special place. A bumpy ride in a small 12-seater aircraft made our destination seem more remote from Honolulu and modernity than the half-hour flight, and landing at Kaunakakai on the parched west of the island made the southeastern Kona shore seem fertile and abundant. Hawaiian history was all around. I stayed within walking distance of the massive ʻIliʻiliʻopae Heiau (temple), near a gentle shore punctuated with stone fishponds that formerly produced prolific yields. These made Molokaʻi a sought-after prize and battleground for the aliʻi (chiefs) of both Oʻahu and Maui.

When Captain Cook's expedition passed Molokaʻi in the late 1770s, fires were observed along the shores, which crew member and diarist Lieutenant James King later learned were the result of fighting between the forces of Peleioholani of Oʻahu and Kahekili of Maui. I drove around to Hālawa Valley, the westernmost of the deep, eroded valleys that made up the windward shore. The sea pounded the coast, and dark, menacing rain clouds shrouded the upper reaches of the valley. I was already familiar with Halawa as the site of a famous study of 'prehistoric' evolution by archaeologist Pat Kirch.

The beach at Pūkoʻo is relatively narrow, with overhanging coconut trees. A gentle wash rather than surf brushed its seaward edge. It looked out onto the sheltered waters between Maui, Molokaʻi and Lanaʻi. The high-rise tourist hotels of Maui's western coast were clearly visible in the distance. Lanaʻi was just across the water, its wild eastern mountains contrasting dramatically with the low plateau covered in pineapples that made up the rest of the island. The most complete picture of Pacific

Islanders' perception of the ocean in the nineteenth century comes from Hawai'i.

Descriptions of the zones and moods of the sea recognised by Hawaiians are almost as detailed as their terrestrial equivalents. The nineteenth-century master fisherman Kahaulelio had described in detail the sea I now looked out onto. His writings reflect a comprehensive knowledge of fish and seafloor characteristics as deep as 200 fathoms. Kahaulelio knew 100 fishing grounds that were at least 10 fathoms deep in this area. It was only in Kahaulelio's lifetime that European science overturned the belief that water density caused sunken ships and drowned sailors to drift suspended at middle depths according to their weight, while all below remained forever dark, freezing and lifeless.

Iwan

The fourth beach in my journey lies at Iwan on the rugged east coast of Taiwan, home to the Austronesian-speaking 'Amis peoples, just north of the southeastern coastal city of Taitung. Steep, bush-clad mountains rise beyond narrow coastal plains, both shaped by moisture-laden winds off the Pacific. Typhoons are a regular threat. Although more tropical than temperate, the mist-clad mountains, gravel beaches and grey seaward horizon reminded me of visits to the temperate beaches of the west coast of the South Island of New Zealand, a rich source of nephrite jade, or pounamu in te reo Māori.

Taiwan's eastern mountains have been the source of prized nephrite jade since the first Austronesian-speaking inhabitants, who went on to colonise the entire Pacific, settled there. Taiwanese jade has been worked into highly prized pendants and traded across regional networks through much of South-East Asia for at least 3000 years. This link between the oldest and one of the last shores of the Pacific diaspora left a deep impression upon me.

My first visit to Taiwan occurred when I was invited to speak at the International Austronesian Conference 'Weaving Waves' Writings' in November 2012. The conference highlight was the awarding of Taiwan Government Life Sustainability Awards for nurturing and protecting cultural, spiritual and environmental sustainability to Papa Mape from Mo'orea in French Polynesia and Lifok 'Oteng from Taiwan. I had met Papa Mape a few years earlier on Mo'orea and had nominated him for this award.

Papa Mape was a quiet and humble man with profound traditional expertise on the natural world, and especially the sea, which he generously taught to groups of Māʻohi (Tahitian) students, schoolteachers, Western scientists and anyone interested in learning. Visiting Taiwan was his first trip off-island, and he had to get a passport to travel to the island, which, fittingly, is the homeland of his ancient ancestors. He was the first non-Taiwanese to receive the award. Sadly, Papa Mape died the following year on 30 October 2013, in his beloved home village of Papetōʻai.

One year later, I stood on Iwan's rugged shore looking southwest towards Moʻorea over 10,000 kilometres distant and recalled Papa Mape's long moment of silent reflection two years earlier in the southwest of Taiwan when I pointed towards where Moʻorea lay over the horizon. Further north on this coast lies Waiʻao Beach, a commuter suburb of Taipei renowned for its surfing. Its ancient history is now lost to most, but in Hawaiian, its name means water of dawn, the place where the sun rises every day to light up this Pacific coast. South from Iwan lies the scenic Taimali section of the South-link railway line, poetically called 'Sky and Ocean Merge into One Vastness'. Now a connected vastness links ʻAmis, Maoli, Māori and Māʻohi shores of history and understanding.

In 2015, I was adopted into the Langachu subclan of the Sor clan of seafarers and fisherfolk who inhabit the atolls of the Mortlock Islands of Micronesia. The Langachu are people of the sea, and their name means 'connecting people'. I feel increasingly drawn to the Pacific, both professionally and emotionally. I am fascinated by the depth and diversity of its interconnected cultures, and intrigued by their relationship with their oceanic environment. I also feel bonded to Pacific shores, although not yet with the intensity of my Pacific friends. For now, I remain content to be a less distant stranger.

Paul D'Arcy is a Professor in the Department of Pacific Affairs at the Australian National University, Canberra. He teaches and publishes on environmental conflict resolution, sustainable development and climate change mitigation in the Asia–Pacific region. He is general editor and coordinator of the seven-year project *The Cambridge History of the Pacific Ocean*, published in 2022. He lives in Canberra.

Ben Brown
What the river said to me

                    'Ko

                        wai

                        koe

                     taku

                  tama,'

              the river

            said to me

          as I crossed

      from one side

      to the other. It was

        not the interrogative

          'Ko wai koe, taku tama?

              Who are you, my son?' I

                could tell the river wasn't

                  asking me a question. It was

                    the assertive intonation that gave

                      it away. 'You are Water, my son!' said

                      the river. 'Ko wai Koe, taku tama!' Ae, Ko.

                      Wai au. I am water. How could I not agree?

                      And anyway, you cannot really argue with a river.

                      When I reached the other side of the river, Te Whenua
                      called out to me, 'Taku tama, i hea koe i ēnei wa katoa?
                      My son, where have you been all this time?' Within Te Whenua,
                      I was formed, just as Te Whenua was formed, just as you were
                      formed, he pūtahi, of a Mother's flesh and blood, a Father's fire and
                      will to laugh where Māui failed and Pīwaiwakawaka thought it funny.
                      Te Whenua that fed and fattened me and grew me into Te Ao Marama.

Ben Brown (Ngāti Mahuta, Ngāti Koroki, Ngāti Paoa) is a poet, writer and performer. His recent publications include the memoir *A Fish in the Swim of the World* (2006, updated edition 2022), and the poetry and performance piece *Between the Kindling and the Blaze* (2013). He edited the poetry anthology *How the F* Did I Get Here* (2020). He was appointed the inaugural Te Awhi Rito New Zealand Reading Ambassador in 2021. He lives in Lyttelton.

Gina Cole
The lifeboat

Bubu told me a seed grows from destruction. The idea lay dormant in my brain, buried in a neural substrate where she'd planted it, until the ferry incident. The ferry incident destroyed me in one way. Big ships terrify me now. In another way it led to my love of drua: double-hulled canoes. Bubu can steer drua by the stars, the sun, birds and currents. On the day of the ferry trip she hesitated on the gangplank, studied the sky.

'There's a storm coming.'

I just wanted to get on board and sail across the strait to see my cousin-sister. I spotted the captain at the top of the ship, also examining the sky. A maritime hat shaded his eyes against vault-grey light.

Halfway across the strait, gale-force wind and driving rain whacked into the side of the ferry. Someone shouted through a squealing intercom: 'Put on your orange lifejackets.' The ferry heaved up the face of a huge wave, smashed down the other side and capsized. Seawater crashed through the windows. Bubu grabbed me. Pulled me into the rush, bubble, choke, freeze, shock, pain, blackout. I woke *inside* the sea, a blue monster on my chest. My legs ballerina, ears drill, eyes speckle, arms claw, shutdown. I choked free, coughing seawater in the open. The freezing ocean tossed me about like a dead fish. Bubu held on, tethered me to her waist with thick rope. I was bone cold, gasping for air as wave after wave hit me in the mouth.

The captain's face appeared above the swells, his hat pulled tight onto his head, sticking to him even in big water, even in howling wind and needle-spray rain. He grabbed Bubu's hand, dragged us both alongside into the lifeboat. I crawled into a corner, sodden and cold, and collapsed into a dream of frozen silk sheets. Fiery sunlight woke me. My eyelashes were rimed with salt, like bees' legs laden with pollen. Someone splashed water in my face.

'Drink.'

I gulped from a tin cup the captain held to my lips.

'Bubu!'

I scrabbled about on hands and knees, the bulky lifejacket scratching my skin. I found Bubu lying unconscious on the deck. Her chest rose and fell in easy rhythm. I took her hands in mine, rubbed them warm.

'Bubu, wake up.'

'She's been out for a while.'

The captain proffered a pudgy hand in my direction. A silver-wrapped chocolate bar lay on his upturned palm. I took it, stared at him, dumbfounded.

'She'll come around.'

I counted 15 other people in the wooden lifeboat. All day we sat, lay, slept, leaned and bumped into each other. A plastic awning shaded half the boat. Water slap-slapped against the wooden hull. I stood up too quick, fell sideways into the gunwales.

A tall woman with green eyes caught my elbow. 'Easy.'

I steadied myself against her. The sea lengthened out in every direction to infinity, a barely discernible horizon meeting an ever-blue sky. The captain produced a device from somewhere like a magician pulling a rabbit from his cape. A thrown-together Frankenstein gadget — gold strip, arc, circle, handle, telescope. He held it to his eye, traced a finger along a laminated map, squinted through the gadget once more.

'We've been turning in a circle for an hour,' said Bubu. She levered herself up to sit.

I dropped down, hugged her with all my might, tears streaming down both our cheeks. I handed her a tin water canister. She drank carefully.

'Row the boat in the opposite direction or we'll be halfway to South America by tomorrow,' she said.

The captain brandished the golden device. 'We're on the right heading.'

'The currents are bouncing off an island over there.' Bubu pointed past my head towards the horizon. 'Bear north or the trench currents will take us east into another storm after nightfall.'

The captain stared at her, chuckled. 'What island? Āe, the wind's up a tad. But we're nowhere near the trench,' he said, tapping the laminated map.

Bubu's dark silence told me exactly what she thought of his map. Once again, he brought the weird gizmo up to his eye. No introductions, no exchange of pleasantries. Only side glances and frowns all around the boat. I rested my chin against a warm steel rowlock, tipped my head back, gazed up into wispy clouds high overhead. Bubu says clouds are land mirrors, light-gatherers, homing beacons. These ones dissipated into cold blue.

'The starboard current is taking us into the trench,' said Bubu.

The captain huffed and looked away. Night dropped on us like a thick blanket. Cold starlight rose and sparkled across an expansive sky. The full moon paved a pathway so solid across the sea, I wanted to step out and walk home. A chill wind ruffled my hair, told me to stay put. The moon went dark and torrential rain dumped on us. A brace of waving hands rose into the air like anemone fronds clutching at the awning, pulling it over to shelter us all.

'This is our last chance to get away from here!' Bubu shouted.

The wind ripped her words away. She pointed towards the island, a blob on the horizon. The captain shook his head, gesticulated in the opposite direction. Bubu grabbed an oar. He tried to take it off her. They struggled, a multi-limbed monster, jostling back and forth. The oar came loose. The captain took a blow to the head, fell back, sprawled onto the deck.

Bubu yelled over the pelting rain. 'Viti, grab the oar!'

I took the oar, clamped it into a rowlock.

'Pull!'

I dug the oar into the sea, leaned into its heaving resistance, rowing in time with Bubu on the other side of the lifeboat. The sea was too strong. The tall woman took over from me. She reminded me of my cousin-sister's mother. Her face was grim and determined.

'Stop!' yelled Bubu. The woman lifted her oar out of the water while Bubu rotated her oar and turned the boat. 'Pull!'

We took turns rowing, the tall woman and me in sync with Bubu. We followed Bubu's commands for hours. My arms went numb. Finally, the ocean resistance subsided. The current lost its power. I sat down, exhausted.

On the second day a shriek woke me. Seagulls flew overhead. I unfurled in the rising sunlight. The captain and Bubu rowed together, pulling through the water in unison. Their oars dipped into the sea with light splashes. Their arms moved in casual loops, pulling the lifeboat in little jolts through the water. The rest of us stood or kneeled at the sides of the lifeboat, our faces turned in the same direction, towards the island rising out of the sea off the starboard bow. A floating raft of green coconuts bobbed alongside, carried on the same currents taking us in to shore. They landed when we landed on the island.

We spent weeks on the island until a fleet of drua rescued us. I watched the coconuts' outer husks crack and decay. Their insides came out, sprouting new shoots from the rotting orbs. And when we pulled away from the island on board the drua, a field of small coconut fronds swayed in the breeze, waving us out to sea.

Gina Cole is Fijian, Scottish and Welsh, and works as a freelance writer. She holds a Master of Creative Writing and a PhD in Creative Writing. Her book *Black Ice Matter* won the Hubert Church Best First Book Award for Fiction at the 2017 Ockham New Zealand Book Awards. Cole's work has been widely anthologised and has appeared in numerous publications. Her science-fiction fantasy novel *Na Viro* (2022) is a work of Pasifikafuturism. She lives in Tāmaki Makaurau Auckland.

KŌRERO

Craig Santos Perez
and Lana Lopesi

Our human and
more-than-human world

A conversation on growing a better place

Two trailblazers in the Pacific region speak across the waters to each other with, as a starting point, the whakataukī 'Ruia te taitea, ka tū taikākā anake; shake off the old, reveal the new'.

Craig Santos Perez and Lana Lopesi explore ideas around decolonial thinking, which is central to both of their work, finding common ground between themselves and the greater world, and looking to the future. As Craig notes, it's important to seek 'reciprocity with each other and the more-than-human world, and to act with an ethics of interconnection'.

Craig Santos Perez is Chamoru-born, and was raised on Guåhan (Guam) in Micronesia. When he was 15 his family migrated to California, where he eventually studied poetry for his Masters and ethnic studies for his Doctorate. For the past 10 years, he has been a Professor in the English department at the University of Hawai'i at Mānoa, where he teaches and publishes creative writing, Pacific Islander literature, and eco-poetry. His work includes *Undercurrent* (2011); the four-book sequence *from unincorporated territory [hacha]* (2008), *[saina]* (2010), *[guma']* (2014) and *[lukao]* (2017); and *Habitat Threshold* (2020). Among his awards is the 2011 PEN Center USA Literary Award for Poetry.

Lana Lopesi (Sāmoa, Pākehā) is author of *False Divides* (2018) and *Bloody Woman* (2021). She has a background in art, and has taught art theory in the visual arts programme at AUT Te Wānanga Aronui o Tāmaki Makaurau. Her work focuses on imagining Pacific subjectivities in the diaspora. She is an Assistant Professor in the Department of Indigenous, Race and Ethnic Studies at the University of Oregon.

CSP: Håfa adai, Lana. We have much in common as writers, scholars, editors and educators.

LL: Kia ora, Craig. I have long been an admirer of your work and can't wait to get into *Habitat Threshold* — congratulations! It's great to see so many synergies between our work and our thinking.

CSP: I'm excited to think through with you some ideas on climate, history and growing a better place together, and to do this with the whakataukī 'Ruia te taitea, ka tū taikākā anake; shake off the old, reveal the new' in mind. When you imagine how to 'grow a better place' and 'reveal the new' through your work, how important is decolonial thinking and action?

LL: Good (and big) question, and, of course, decolonial thinking is central to any imagining of futures, including of that 'better place'. The world we all exist in is driven by capitalist consumption; and colonisation, one of its primary tools, has led us to a place where there is immense human suffering and the destruction of the planet right from under us. I believe decolonial thinking is a tool that offers epistemic ruptures to the entrenched capitalism which is so cemented in our contemporary worlds that there doesn't seem to be a way out. When we decolonise ourselves, we reject hegemonic colonialism. We remember our own ancestral societies. We activate a state of being, a critical consciousness from which action can follow.

So, long answer short, it's at the heart of everything I do, whether that be writing about Samoan womanhood, my academic work or even my editorial work for mainstream publications.

CSP: Decolonial thinking is central to my work as well. My homeland of Guåhan is one of the longest, continuously colonised places in the world. Since 1898, we have been a US colony, which has impacted everything, from the language we speak to the food we eat. US militarism has displaced us from our ancestral lands and contaminated the soil and water. Thus, decolonisation has been an essential way that I have imagined otherwise, whether it means revitalising my Chamoru culture, speaking out against militarism or advocating for environmental justice. Speaking more generally, we can only 'grow a better place' by decolonising the Pacific and imagining sustainable futures. My poetry helps me articulate and cultivate that decolonial consciousness.

But my situation is so different from yours, and I'm curious as to how you maintain connections to your Samoan culture while living in Aotearoa![1] How has migration and the reality of living in a Samoan diaspora influenced your thinking?

---

1 A the time of this kōrero Lana Lopesi was living in Aotearoa.

LL: From the outside looking in, I imagine decolonisation to be much more immediate, or perhaps urgent, in your context of Guåhan for all the reasons you mention. The experiences of Chamoru people, in many ways, have required a different kind of decolonisation from what I am thinking about.

My ancestral home Sāmoa (or the part not under US occupation) was formally decolonised in 1962. However, Sāmoa today is still underpinned by colonial thinking. The centrality of the church continues in a neocolonial way. Even in diaspora, Sāmoa as a colonial construct requires epistemic decolonisation, which can feel very hard, but the difference with Guåhan is important to mention.

And then of course we are uninvited guests in Aotearoa, a settler colony, and so any thinking or working of Samoan people toward decolonisation has to be with that front of mind. Samoans in Aotearoa are rather fortunate to have longstanding communities here, which in my case means that my kids go through a Samoan bilingual education (and can do so until the age of 12). Samoan language and culture are very easy to access if you choose, so in many ways I see myself as belonging to a different village: one here in Auckland that is ancestral to my kin villages in Sāmoa.

In fact, disconnection has never felt like something I've needed to worry about. Being part of the Samoan diaspora has made me aware that we have many homes, and that we have always been very mobile people, although the forces of our mobility are now undeniably different.

I find the word 'how' is tripping me up: the question of *how* to grow a better place. I'm interested to strip it back a bit. What actually is a 'better place' for you? What might that feel like or smell like?

CSP: The different political contexts throughout the Pacific inform how we think about and enact decolonisation, or how we address and reckon with neocolonialism. Because Guåhan is a US colony, we are American citizens; however, we were not invited guests on Native American lands. During the 15 years I lived on the North American continent, I was fortunate to meet and commune with many other diasporic Islanders, not only Chamorus, but also Hawaiians, Samoans, Tongans, Marshallese and more. While it was important to us to maintain our cultures in this new place, many of us also worked with and honoured Native Americans whose land we were settlers on.

I have now lived in Hawai'i for about 12 years, and I have continued to both connect with diasporic Chamorus here and to stand in solidarity with Hawaiians and their own struggle for decolonisation, demilitarisation and sovereignty.

Informed by my personal history of diaspora, I guess a 'better place' is a place that feels like belonging. And to belong to a place means to learn, love, respect and care for the deep stories, ecologies and peoples of that place. It means to be able to smell a flower or the rain and to know their names. And then, of course, in your and my cases, to engage with place in our artmaking, writing and editing.

LL: I feel similarly in terms of solidarities with those whose lands aren't our own but which we live in and even call home. The 'better place' we are talking about must surely have to be a world predicated on our relationships with ourselves, with others and with the environment, rather than a place driven by the forces of capitalism which push colonisation and climate catastrophe, for example. We have to be in good relation with this world, which means committing ourselves to a movement which goes against the matrix. In that world we have the chance to be vulnerable, to be open to what we don't know, to be led by others and — as you say — be in deep, respectful and caring relation with others.

In terms of my writing and place, it's super-important to locate myself; to be really clear about my specificity. In my first book, *False Divides*, I thought a lot about what it meant to write about the Pacific from my vantage point, and 'my specific vantage point' became this phrase which I held on to (at one stage, after the third use of the phrase in my manuscript, my editor told me: *OK, we get it!*). In some ways the phrase provided me with a kind of permission to discuss big ideas about collectivity, the internet and the Pacific Ocean, and also to locate myself, and really think through what 'place' is. I write from my office, which is in the suburb of Rānui, right next to the train station, and this really specific location is my vantage point. So me looking and thinking from this place is infinitely different from where you'll be writing from at any given time.

I think that when we all hold on to our specificity, and are really clear about that, we make space for everyone to live their own full specificity. And, of course, one of the places where we show our specific vantage point is in our work.

CSP: I appreciate what you say about being in good relations with the environment and with others in the places we call home. Your commitment to social and climate justice movements is inspiring. I, too, deeply believe in cultivating kinship. In my culture, our most important value is inafaʻmaolek, to always be in reciprocity with each other and the more-than-human world, and to act with an ethics of interconnection.

I try to embody this value in my own writing as a way of expressing my connection to my ancestral homeland, but also to the other places I have lived. I attempt to learn (and listen to) the histories, geographies and names of the places I live so that I can honour these places. Currently, I live on the Hawaiian island of Oʻahu, in the city of Aiea, not far from Puʻuloa, otherwise known as Pearl Harbor. While I have lived in different parts of this island for 12 years, I still have much to learn about this complex, diverse and beautiful place. Plus, the island's ecologies are changing due to the climate crisis, so I am also paying attention to these shifts. The following poem speaks to the difficulty of writing about place during a time of climate change:

A Sonnet at the Edge of the Reef
the Waikīkī Aquarium

We dip our hands into the outdoor reef exhibit
and touch sea cucumber and red urchin
as butterflyfish swim by. A docent explains:
once a year, after the full moon, when tides swell
to a certain height, and saltwater reaches the perfect
temperature, only then will the ocean cue coral
polyps to spawn, in synchrony, a galaxy of gametes,
which dances to the surface, fertilises, opens,
forms larvae, roots to seafloor, and grows, generation
upon generation. At home, we read a children's
book, *The Great Barrier Reef*, to our daughter
snuggling between us in bed. We don't mention
corals bleaching, reared in labs, or frozen.
And isn't our silence, too, a kind of shelter?

As you can see, my sense of writing place is also influenced by being a father and thinking about the planet that my daughter (and future generations) will inherit. When I wrote this poem, I wanted to remember the deep sense of wonder my daughter exuded when we took her to the aquarium, especially the coral exhibit, with my knowledge of how this wondrous place is changing for the worse. Poetry gives me a space to reckon with these emotions.

LL: I have to admit that climate change is not a prevalent theme in my work, but I share a similar concern as a parent for the planet my children will inherit, let alone the many generations after them. The final essay in my last collection, for instance, was a really vulnerable thing to write, but it helped to remind me why I was doing the work:

An open-letter 'to my future adult children'
(Excerpt)

Maybe this is a romantic dream, but I have always hoped that you two — and maybe your own families — will be able to find little messages of love or hope throughout my work when you're older, or later when I transition into the place of the ancestors. Little clues of how things were, or parts of family stories waiting for you until you're ready. Part of this is me wanting to keep the memories that I have of my grandparents and parents alive for later generations who can't know them like I do; part of it might be an act of vain self-preservation. I will leave that judgement for you.

Parents always want the best for their kids, starting with love, food, money, housing. And you two are lucky — those needs have been met, which is your absolute privilege as kids and ours as parents to be able to give all that to you. Your dad and I have picked up the diaspora dreams of our families and continued to work to give you the clichéd 'better life' that our parents and grandparents imagined for themselves. But there are other things that I want you to have, like an understanding of the world. This letter is a part of that. Being a diaspora kid involves each generation growing financially on the generation before them (or at least that is the aspiration), but it's also about growing the knowledge and understanding of the previous generation as well. About finding other ways to care for each other, once the basic needs are met.

I love the value of inafa'maolek. How you describe it makes me wonder if it's comparable to the Samoan notion of vā, which I understand as a way of relational tethering to everything around us that teaches reciprocity. Isn't it so telling that we have these values already with us that can guide not only how to be in the world but also how to grow a better one? I'm thinking back to the Māori translation of the proverb 'shake off the old, reveal the new', and I wonder if, in our context, when we shake off the layers of Western knowing in all forms the revelation is the other ways of knowing and being that have always been there — ways that are incredibly kind to the environment and which require us to understand our relationship to it, rather than power over it.

It's amazing how just being in conversation can suddenly make what feels heavy and hard seem possible. Maybe even inevitable, āpōpō — a tomorrow that, once this day or time ends, is guaranteed to arrive.

CSP: You speak so honestly to your children in the future, and perhaps to the future itself. The way you end on the idea of 'care' resonates deeply with me.

I see a connection between inafa'maolek and vā. Our Pacific cultures have embedded so much knowledge and wisdom in our languages. I hope we will continue to learn and enact reciprocity, relationality and kinship. With these environmental ethics, I hope we can shake off colonial ways of knowing and being, and instead embrace Indigenous and decolonial ways of living sustainably and respectfully. May our children help navigate us towards a thriving future.

Cilla McQueen

Way up south

Rare air, pale light, beyond   up south, old world,
Rakiura.   Step ashore
bush masks the way   watching blue shadows
whirring wings, waves   hush   wind stirs leaves,

I like to write on a veranda, between inside and outside
the house and myself   can see who's coming up the path
and when they leave   with a wave, words
flow back in to fit the poem.

Sunrise Cottage, old and sturdy, looking over Halfmoon Bay
where fishing boats at anchor   swing   sound of wings
Tūī come to check us out
from the overhanging fuchsia.

A red, white and blue striped hand-painted table made from a cable reel, with a
Perspex top screwed down; under the top in gold and black lettering: TODAY BLUE
COD,

old weathered timber as black as shadow, brass propeller tussock pāua shell stone
fern   quality of silence pervading (different birdsong from Bluff),

on the kitchen door the pokerwork message 'Gone Fishing' hangs from a long
wooden fish with chicken-wire scales.

I hear Tuwhare's voice, in the broad Scots accent
of his boilermaker workmate, who preferred his work-bench
'hard by' 'the big doors',   with easy access
inside and outside   space for a poet to think.

One Anzac Day, with Gwen, I read a poem at the Dawn Service on the beach at
sunrise. Another visit, for a poetry reading, brought the Foveaux Express crammed
with a whole symposium of poets.

A timeless village bay. Wharf, pub, fishing boats, church, school, museum
cling to the shore. Small blue islands dissolve in mist,
the horizon like thumbed chalk —

similar to Hirta perhaps, island of muttonbirders, fishermen, families,
loyal, self-sufficient, adaptable, obedient to weather,
canny, hospitable, tough, with discerning taste in fish and fowl.

Kākā comes down on the deck and sings a warbling song, having a good look,
hops on the sofa beside me,

interior narrative weaving through — my small inclusion, life's thread, history
making itself continuously even in small things, unique instances.

This is where I like to be — on the porch of a fisherman's crib looking out to sea —
have found my liminal space (to write) on the blue sofa — what's more, here come
Pauline and Geoff bringing fresh blue cod, in batter.

A holy island, Hone?
I'll not go in, but touch an edge
as the village keeps to the rim of the bay
so far and no further
the island keeps to itself, a vast quiet place,
untouched land's power.

A large brown bird with a hooked beak
comes to the fuchsia branch: Kākā.

History's quick, right here, deep-down
sensitive   in its privacy   covers its tracks
in layers   beyond the Pākehā, beyond the early
and the earlier people,   beyond the museum,
beyond these, something
elder   even
echoes
feels like something sacred is working
(do not disturb).

The island aware of itself in the museum;
that which is given to be seen   in plain sight
the history narrated by means of bones, stones, whale's jaw, shells,
artefacts, photos, stories. Concentrated power in an ancient anchor stone.

At the school there's a poetry class of lively young ones
who give the words their full attention, know their good fortune
in living here, loving Rakiura and its nature,

and in Pauline's class, act out how it must have been
to undergo the Dawn Raids of Muldoon.

Air-slicing wings all around, dawn chorus, ripping sound of Tūī wings
clicks and squawks   as they ply between the breakfast branches.
Last night I heard a Kiwi screech.
Geoff warbles to the Kākā, the Kākā warbles back.

News of a discovery at West Ruggedy:
the near-intact skeleton of a giant Moa, naturally deceased,
has been found lying 'in a granite bowl . . . exposed by wind',
its gizzard stones undisturbed.

The invisible past continues to exist is simply vanished
to my sight   I lack the senses to perceive so deep
renews its archive layer by layer.

In time, wind brings the bones to light.
So far, no further —

This history isn't mine. On one shoulder sits Hone, on the other an old St Kildan
grandmother; between them my English mother, who considered the importance of
Te Tiriti ō Waitangi equal to that of the Magna Carta.

Luminous greys in sea and sky, a memory of sealskin, feather, rock, rainwater;
white-chested Kererū, heavy on a branch, a slight bounce.

I felt relief to hear of the Moa resting in its granite bowl.
Alive once, those eyes would have gazed across the land-bridge
and gone there, over here, on foot.
Extinct yet extant, gizzard and stone.

Deep silence undisturbed by sound events — wings, strings of liquid notes —

I'm entered by this silence, in my writing place transported to this porch,
this end of the comfortable blue sofa   where I listen
to the Island   as if it were a consciousness telling itself

in Hone's voice, perhaps,
'something more real, more lasting,
more permanent maybe, than dying . . .'

With acknowledgements to Hone Tuwhare and his poem 'Monologue', from the collection *No Ordinary Sun* (Blackwood and Janet Paul, 1964).

Cilla McQueen is a poet and artist. She was the New Zealand Poet Laureate from 2009 to 2011, and in 2010 was awarded the Prime Minister's Award for Literary Achievement in Poetry. She has published 16 poetry collections, including *Edwin's Egg and Other Poetic Novellas* (2014), *In a Slant Light: A Poet's Memoir* (2016), *Poeta: Selected and New Poems* (2018) and *Qualia* (2020). She lives in Motupōhue Bluff.

Faisal Halabi
Hazel Avenue

About almost halfway down the middle of Auckland's Dominion Road sits a cul-de-sac called Hazel Avenue. At the bottom of it is a reserve, at the top of it a collection of shops, and in between is where my family's new life in Aotearoa New Zealand began.

I can still remember exactly our first journey to the street in the 1990s — all of us sitting in a taxi van driving under the bright sun, turning left from the Mount Roskill end of Dominion Road, and my uncle (who had arrived in the country a few months earlier) waiting there to welcome us. My dad had about $5000. My mother could barely string a sentence together in English. I was six years old and my brother had just turned two. We were 15,650 kilometres from home, and it was uncertain what would come next — but we were here.

Twenty-six years later and New Zealand has, along with much of the global community, endured so much. The War on Terror and its collateral. The rise of disinformation and conspiracies. Trumpism, Brexitism, climate change. The Covid pandemic. Our first-ever — and second-ever — terrorist attacks in Aotearoa. In early 2022, we watched as protestors gathered at Parliament, with flags flaunting messages ranging from violence against the prime minister to American presidential election campaign material. It makes for a painful list, each event lurching New Zealand closer to a cliff edge of uncertainty; each event asking of us to make a choice as to how to respond.

Throughout all this, New Zealand has become home to me and my family — I love this place, I'm proud to be part of its present, and I'm excited to grow with it into the future. But at this point, after two years of the pandemic and as a hangover from all the other events the country has had to endure, things feel uncertain. Uncertainty gives way to division and conflict. As an immigrant child growing up during this period, when faced with uncertainty one response was to look inwards for comfort and push away everything else. The strength of my parents and family during that time taught me that differences exist: acknowledging them and finding the common ground are the tools for responding to them — letting them wash over you is not.

As New Zealand looks to the future, the tools for responding to today's uncertainties are in finding and building on the common ground we do have, rather than giving power to that which we don't.

It's a lesson that I began to learn from my parents the moment I got out of that taxi van on Hazel Avenue.

I n the weeks, months and years following, I watched my parents navigate the uncertainties of the new world around them. Despite how often I was told I was the first Faisal somebody had ever met, or the number of times the question 'But where are you *really* from?' was posed to us, my parents never allowed us to feel as 'the other' in our new world. Instead, they encouraged us to look for the common ground between us and those we encountered on our journey. We were encouraged to sign up to sports clubs (karate and football were not a success) and get involved in our school productions (*Joseph and the Amazing Technicolor Dreamcoat* was). It's a journey so many immigrant families before ours will have navigated, and so many more after us will have, too.

The uncertainty of those early days was amplified by homesickness, language barriers and culture clash. In more recent years, my dad — a fully qualified engineer — shared with me that at that time he was told that to find work it might be a good idea if he changed his first name, and probably an equally good idea to get rid of his moustache. He'd never shared those stories with us during all the years he had driven my brother and me to karate practice or taken us on weekend trips to the zoo. Instead, my parents invited in the differences, acknowledged them and navigated them — showing us that if we're to coexist in a place where differences exist, then these were the tools that would let us move forward in this new place.

It didn't always go to plan. Sometimes cultural differences caught us off-guard. On one of our very first nights in New Zealand, Guy Fawkes Night was observed. The sheer confusion that soared through my mind is still seared into my memory. We all watched the flashes of light through my bedroom window together, wondering in equal parts whether we'd missed a crucial detail: that perhaps this was some form of entertainment provided for our pleasure — or perhaps New Zealand wasn't exactly as peaceful as we'd been told it was.

Of all the things I remember that bring a kind of pride in my parents, watching them interact comfortably with our new next-door neighbours on Hazel Avenue felt the most powerful. The relationship we formed with them represented to me a very real result from inviting differences in.

The new neighbours were a young family, with three daughters around the same ages as my brother and me. One day soon after we'd moved in, they walked down the road and waved hello, introducing their world to us and asking about ours.

Practically everything about the way they lived their lives was different, including their dislike of what we understood was the most universally acceptable of all Western cuisine: McDonald's. They described it as 'junk food'. This had me scrambling back to the drawing board of what was socially acceptable in this new place. In addition to their dislike of Big Macs, their dad cycled to work (especially novel in the mid-1990s), they had a mound of sand in the middle of their backyard (which they played in and termed a 'sandpit'), and all three siblings wore tie-dyed t-shirts (strictly forbidden for my brother and me).

And yet they became our newest best friends. They helped me settle into my new primary school, the same one the girls attended. They showed us around the neighbourhood, and let my brother and me spend afternoon upon afternoon playing at their house. We rode our bikes together, and our parents planned day trips through broken English. Once, we covered my entire body in sand in the sandpit. My favourite thing was the trampoline on their front lawn — the gold standard of being a Kiwi kid.

At around this time, my father taught me an English word ('Pass'), which I would use at school whenever I was asked a question to which I didn't know the answer — or didn't understand the English. At first it had felt painful to say the word out loud day after day at my new school. But by the end of the first summer of afternoons on the Hazel Avenue trampoline, I barely used that word anymore.

The quickest way to get onto Auckland's northwestern motorway from the CBD is via the Hobson Street onramp. One evening earlier this year I was in an Uber going home after working late. The driver was a friendly, chatty Malaysian man.

As we sped down the empty, dark roads, the driver joked to me that he was surprised that I was in his car — that when he was looking for the person who had ordered the Uber, he thought he'd see an Arab man instead. I explained that I am Arabic and that I'd grown up here. He laughed that I was more a Kiwi than an Arab in that case, and I chuckled politely in response. But my chuckle quickly trailed off; I wanted to speak up, and to tell him about tie-dyed t-shirts, to tell him about 'pass'.

We drove on in silence.

Recently, I met up for a drink with one of the Hazel Avenue siblings — Antoinette. In among the catching up on our respective careers and dating lives, we reflected a lot on the Hazel Avenue days. The following day, through Facebook Chat, she sent me a copy of a photograph taken at one of her birthday parties, which I must have gone along to shortly after we'd moved into the neighbourhood. Mum had sent me out dressed up in a three-piece suit, on the assumption that a Kiwi kid's birthday party was the same formal affair it was back home. In the photograph I am surrounded by several children in t-shirts and shorts, swinging at a piñata.

I stopped scrolling through our Chat window, looked at the photo and smiled. The colours of the birthday party and the determined faces of children staring down a piñata jumped out of my laptop screen. Antoinette and her family had been even more generous than I had appreciated those 26 years ago.

About two minutes away from the apartment block where I live is a thoroughfare called Asquith Avenue. It's a model example of an Auckland road: it connects two other very busy roads with narrow corners, and has several speed bumps and a rail crossing at one end for good measure. I drive down Asquith Avenue every weekend to see my parents, who live at the other end of the city.

I visited them on the same weekend that the protestors arrived at Parliament. These protests were a tangible representation of the conflict that had been building up in New Zealand over recent years. They revealed to many what the years of uncertainty had led to: a response that came from a crowd looking inward — or on the internet —

for answers. The crowd at Parliament didn't form overnight, nor will it disappear in the same way.

As I sat with my parents watching the news coverage, I felt strange seeing the footage of our fellow New Zealanders shouting over one another. I didn't know where in the room to look. I looked over at my mother. I recalled how her face had lit up when she chatted to the Hazel Avenue neighbours all those years ago. Now her expression was flat and wore a slight frown.

I wondered what she thought of this New Zealand now — this New Zealand, the same one that had welcomed her. In those earlier times of uncertainty, we'd formed together to find the common ground between us. Now, in this time of uncertainty, a family that had set its foundations upon that common ground was watching as it cracked apart.

When I think about the uncertainty that marked the first chapter of my family's life in New Zealand, it is accompanied by knowing that the fabric of New Zealand is made up of so many Hazel Avenue neighbours. Twenty-six years later, while the seams of that fabric might look like they're under strain, so many of us know that it is still strong enough to hold. Every one of us has a story like Hazel Avenue. It might not necessarily involve arriving from the other side of the planet on an aeroplane, but we all have stories that cross different islands, cities and families. It might be a story of comforting a friend on 15 March, or of dropping off groceries for an isolating neighbour as the pandemic settled in. Finding common ground will keep us connected 20, 30 or 50 years later, long after the grass on the lawns at Parliament has regrown. These words are written by a man who is the product of that.

On the drive home from visiting my parents, I pass through Asquith Avenue again. It's an obstacle course for traffic. On a particularly tight corner of the road, a row of drivers line up to let me and a few others pass. I give the first driver a half-wave and he promptly returns the gesture. As I drive past, I wonder what this driver thought of the protestors down at Parliament today. If we think differently about it and he knew that, would he still have given way to me? I wondered what he thinks about the conspiracy theories around the pandemic, or of the role of Te Tiriti or the impacts of climate change. If we'd discovered we think differently about one or all of these questions, would he have invited me across the road?

Across New Zealand today — down Hazel Avenue, up the northwestern motorway and along Asquith Avenue — each one of us crosses paths with another New Zealander who thinks, speaks and behaves differently to us. We might be heading in different directions and taking different turns, but let's remember to pause and look across the road. To wave hello to who is there. To ask them how far they've journeyed to be here beside us, as we look to share the future together.

Faisal Halabi is an Iraqi-born lawyer and writer. His works have appeared in various publications across Aotearoa New Zealand, including The Spinoff and *Paperboy*. Most recently, his work was included in *Ko Aotearoa Tātou | We Are New Zealand* (2020), an anthology of New Zealand writing exploring national diversity. He lives in Tāmaki Makaurau Auckland.

Siobhan Harvey
Tabula rasa

for Rae, 1941–2022

Do not mourn the past, it survives in us when we move on.
Whenua, whānau, whakapapa, friend, a house turned upon
its neighbours, dead end: these we thought lost to shadow-
selves mirroring our existences in absentia as we disappear
elsewhere. But what we leave far behind always resurfaces
in a place of escape, our minds dwelling upon reflections
tricked into chimeras of what was, what is, what might be . . .

When the pandemic came, doubt spread like a virus: Covid-
deniers, conspiracy theorists, misinformation influencers, fake
news generators, antivaxxers, anti-mandate occupiers, closed
borders, closed minds. Freedom of movement meant loss of
smell, taste, memory, employment, trade and life. Lockdown
and managed isolation enforced a separation we already knew.
Do not mourn the past, it survives in us when we move on.

Now the world seeks a resilience we already own, as we endure
oceans in dinghies, skies in wheel wells, and the trafficking of
our children and dreams. Detention centres and body bags hide
our persecution as Muslim, Kurd, Syrian, Uyghur, Rohingya, war
refugee, dissident, trans, lesbian, gay, bi, non-binary . . . always
survivors. Always this remains with us in place of passports:
do not mourn the past, it survives in us when we move on.

In us, the future is *tabula rasa*. We are yet to be realised
symphonies, songs, dances, films, plays, novels, poems
and paintings which will offer fresh ways to consider
intractable issues like disease and displacement. Erasing
fraught years others will forget, our legacy will endure:
art as solace and salvation; yes, art as our eternal refrain,
do not mourn the past, it survives in us when we move on.

Siobhan Harvey is the author of eight books of poetry, including *Ghosts* (2021), which was longlisted for the
2022 Ockham New Zealand Book Awards. She has been awarded the 2019 Kathleen Grattan Award for a
Sequence of Poems, the 2020 New Zealand Society of Authors Peter and Dianne Beatson Fellowship and the
2021 Janet Frame Literary Trust Award for Poetry. In 2019 she won the Robert Burns Poetry Competition.
She is a senior lecturer in Creative Writing at the Centre for Creative Writing, Auckland University of
Technology Te Wānanga Aronui o Tāmaki Makaurau. She lives in Tāmaki Makaurau Auckland.

Alison Wong
A long walk

I begin writing from my qigong class. I think we are meant to empty our minds as we breathe deeply and follow the teacher's gentle movements, but my grandfather was a Christian convert and I was not raised with Eastern spiritual practices. For me, this is a form of prayer.

I stand, knees relaxed, body upright, as if suspended by a string, breathe in stillness, breathe my body into poetic forms — *mist rising from the lake . . . parting the clouds . . . flying dove spreads its wings . . .* my mind drifting into the languid, creative space of contemplation — mind, body, spirit flowing, one being communing with God and the cosmos.

In this world of noise, anxiety, existential crises, *this* is what I need.

It's been over a month since I contracted Covid. I am no longer infectious, but there are lingering after-effects. Loss of smell. A sense of being — in every respect — less robust, less sharp, less energetic. A fraying of the nerves.

In a time of rampant Covid, colds, flu, any deep breathing carries risk from airborne aerosols. I wear an N95 mask and stand distanced from the rest of the class in the crossflow of the open doors. Open to the outside world.

Infection came at the end of a long walk, following in the footsteps of about 20,000 Chinese gold-seekers, who, to avoid the Victorian poll tax, walked in the mid-1800s from Robe, South Australia, to the Victorian goldfields. I had no ambition to walk the entire several hundred kilometres, nor to carry all the required gear on a shoulder pole or in a backpack. (Confession: At primary school I managed to get an E for Phys. Ed. May this give all of us hope — with time and determination, we can usually improve.) My ambition was to explore the history and landscape, the flora and fauna, the emotional and spiritual temperature, the stories. And I wanted to walk.

After a couple of years of lockdowns and long hours at my desk editing and promoting *A Clear Dawn: New Asian Voices from Aotearoa New Zealand*, I'd put on lockdown kilos. The walk would give structure and focus. I could walk out of a rut, improve my physical and mental health and add a new, broader and deeper dimension to my writing.

Four years ago, I moved out of what had been a series of rentals and into 'our own place'. Wadawurrung Country. Part of the Kulin nation. Unceded country. Now I walked. Over land where First Nations peoples were removed from country and each other; past massacre sites undocumented on tourist brochures; past towns, streets, landmarks with British (often Scottish) names, some after celebrated squatters/pastoralists who murdered First Nations peoples.

Names matter. Words, stories matter. Who are the narrators? What is revealed and what is hidden? Where on the walk were 60,000 years of First Nations history and culture? And how had so many myths of the Chinese walkers been perpetuated? How can we go forward if we do not understand and reckon with the past? I am learning, only beginning the conversation. Voice. Truth-telling. The Uluru Statement from the Heart.

When I imagined the walk, I had expected to identify with the walkers who came from southern China like my ancestors — their bafflement at the strangeness of the animals, the dull brown-green vegetation, the dry flat country. How I felt when I first arrived in Australia. Displaced. Unable to find my place.

As I walked, I was seeing much of this land for the first time. Yet now I realised I had changed. A temporary custodian trying for the first time to establish a new garden, I had been learning about Australian plants, about the native birds and animals I hoped would find a home there. And now everywhere I looked — magnificent *Eucalyptus camaldulensis*, river red gums with their streaked trunks of peeling bark, the most common eucalyptus species across Australia, growing to 45 metres and some nearly as old as Tāne Mahuta, their tree hollows refuge for native fauna; the ferny foliage of *Acacia mearnsii*, black wattles; the white leaf undersides and yellow candles of *Banksia marginata*, silver banksias; *Myoporum insulare*, common boobialla, everywhere used as a wind-hardy hedge; *A. paradoxa*, prickly wattles (great shelter for fairy wrens and other small birds, but not for me needing a roadside pee) — all these were familiar from walks through my neighbourhood.

As I walked into southern Gariwerd (the Grampians) I found, jutting from the soil and cut through for roads, the same orange-beige mottled sandstone I had chosen for feature rocks in the garden. Magpies, sulphur-crested cockatoos, yellow-tailed black-cockatoos, rainbow lorikeets, rosellas, willie wagtails, galahs. Unexpectedly, this country had lodged in my heart.

W hen I first arrived here to join my husband, I was so homesick I wanted to throw my arms around any Māori I saw walking towards me on the streets of Naarm Melbourne. I imagined a New Zealand garden here — lush ferns and tree ferns, tī kōuka. But ferns and tree ferns are not sustainable in the dry climate, and tī kōuka are highly flammable. The first summer of 40°-plus days, my bird's nest fern turned black and was slowly consumed by groundcover. My three $5 *Cordyline australis* 'Red Star' were decimated by the wind. Then I heard about karamū escaping residential gardens, overshading native understorey, outcompeting acacias and eucalypts. How was I different to those who introduced rabbits and possums to Aotearoa, rabbits and foxes to Australia? I needed to adapt, to see beauty with renewed eyes.

P hysicists question the notion of time. Whether time exists or not, we still bear the consequences of our actions, our inactions. Our rights and freedoms must be paired with responsibility. Yet the spiritual realm is not bound by notions of past, present and future. As I walked past vast sheep, cattle and cropping farms — and walked back with the Chinese gold-seekers of the 1800s, walked back further through ancient landscape under full traditional ownership — in the present, I saw signs for Landcare and land management groups: 'DO NOT MOW ROADSIDE: Regenerating native grasses'; 'CLOSED TO DUCK HUNTING (Description of area closed: THE WHOLE OF THE GREEN SWAMP STATE GAME RESERVE)'. I saw established and also, in their three-sided green plastic guards, newly planted indigenous trees and shrubs — landholders encouraged and given incentives to regenerate native bush.

Let us recover and learn from the past, from sustainable traditions, Indigenous and customary practices — in Australia, for instance, the First Nations' cool burning fire and land management practices, which not only promote indigenous flora and fauna, but also potentially lessen the intensity and spread of fires affecting not just Australia but, as smoke travels the world, Aotearoa and the whole Southern Hemisphere.

Yet in these unprecedented times, we also need to consider the Japanese poet Matsuo Bashō's advice: 'Do not seek to follow the footsteps of men of old. Seek what they sought.' How can we combine the wisdom of old together with scientific knowledge and technological advances? How do we adapt to climate change, to new ecological and societal threats? Are the old assumptions still valid? As our climate warms and weather patterns change, will some indigenous species no longer be viable? Just as we selectively grew kiwifruit from the Chinese gooseberry, will we need to selectively grow indigenous species to better adapt? Will northern species and variants migrate southwards, coastal species move inland?

How do we ensure that ethics and honourable values, accountability, rehabilitation and justice direct us in our research and applications, in our developments and endeavours?

On the outskirts of Djilang Geelong, within view of my stepson's home, years of restoration have come to an end, healing the land after a 'recycling' operator had stockpiled 286,000 cubic metres of toxic waste there. A catastrophic fire risk, when finally faced with compliance, the operator put his business into liquidation and bankruptcy. The entire asbestos-laced stockpile had to be transported to licensed landfill. The land had to be rehabilitated. It cost $71 million. After multiple cases of the taxpayer footing costly clean-up bills because of the negligent or fraudulent practices of 'recycling' and waste operators, only now is more stringent legislation and oversight coming into force.

Individuals, organisations, businesses often complain about bureaucracy and compliance costs. Unnecessary red tape is in no one's interest, but lax regulation, inspection and enforcement have had disastrous consequences all over the world. In Aotearoa, I could mention leaky homes, combustible cladding and the Pike River mine disaster.

How do we prevent greenwashing and negligent or corrupt practices? How do we limit the abrogation of responsibility? How do we counter self-interest and promote the common good?

It would be a mistake to base our strategies on the assumption that humanity is fundamentally good. Or fundamentally evil. We can be both, and our strategies need to reflect this. Education is crucial, whether in schools or directed at all ages within wider communities. A tipping point of informed, ethical consumer and voter behaviour can effect change. To deter the worst excesses of human greed and power, we need to combine incentives with adequate and efficient regulation, monitoring, reporting, inspection and enforcement, together with sufficiently punitive penalties.

From the garden of my Tītahi Bay home I used to watch tūī feed from the dark red flowers of the harakeke, listened to their creaks, clicks, wheezes, their joyous song, their heavy wingbeat overhead. Tūī are considered messengers of the gods, symbolising life fulfilment and spiritual harmony, and, like all songbirds, they have two voice boxes that can sing simultaneously. The wildlife sanctuary Zealandia has so enabled the flourishing of native birds that when I come back to Te Whanganui-a-Tara, to Pari-ā-Rua, my sheer delight in the abundant tūī is often met with 'It's just a tūī' or the grumpy 'They wake me up in the morning!'

Now from my desk in Djilang Geelong I watch a New Holland honeyeater, its black pupil within a round eye that gives it its starey look, black-and-white streaked feathers with yellow wing-patch puffed in the cold. It sits on a bare twig of the Bechtel crab apple, flies out and reverses in one quick motion, lands again on a twig one down. Metallic high-pitched tzeets and chattering tjit-tjit-tjits. It darts out again, now straight into the dense green foliage of the *Banksia* 'Birdsong'. Fine leaves tremble as it feeds from the profusion of orange candles. It will sit surveying the territory from the highest feathery branch of the *Agonis flexuosa* 'Lemon and Lime', bobbing in the strong westerly. Sometimes it will fly into the bushes, then come out again, undeterred by larger aggressive magpies, wattlebirds, mynas.

This small, plucky bird reminds me of Aotearoa. Quick to fly out; quick to reverse. Willing to take a more independent path than many of our larger traditional allies.

What is our path?

American theologian Robert McAfee Brown posited that where we stand determines what we see. If we stand in only one place, we have only one vision. We need roots, the security of a sense of ourselves, a celebration of our identities, heritages and cultures. But these identities and cultures are not static. We remember and honour. We adapt and undergo transformations.

Let us embrace our diversity. Listen to each other; see with renewed eyes. Let us work together with respect. As we share our diverse cultures, experiences and viewpoints, this could be a path not only to inclusiveness and justice, but to innovative solutions.

In *The Art of the Impossible*, Czech politician and poet Václav Havel said: 'We must not be afraid of dreaming the seemingly impossible if we want the seemingly impossible to become a reality.' Faced with existential challenges, may we calm our minds, breathe deeply. Care for one another. Live to give life. May we come together with grace to heal our land, our air, our water. Our relationships.

大家齊心跋涉
Koling wada-ngal
Kia haere tahi tātou
Let us walk together

Alison Wong is a poet, novelist and editor. In 2007 her poetry collection *Cup* was shortlisted for the Jessie Mackay Award for Best First Book of Poetry, and in 2010 her novel *As the Earth Turns Silver* won the fiction prize at the New Zealand Post Book Awards and was also shortlisted for the Prime Minister's Literary Awards in Australia. She is co-editor, with Paula Morris, of *A Clear Dawn: New Asian Voices from Aotearoa New Zealand* (2021). In 2022 she held a State Library of Victoria Marion Orme Page Regional Fellowship to work on a memoir. She was born and raised in Te Matau-a-Māui Hawke's Bay, Aotearoa New Zealand, has lived most of her life in Te Whanganui-a-Tara Wellington and Pari-ā-Rua Porirua, and now lives in Djilang Geelong, Australia.

Cybella Maffitt
A canopy of cousin trees

Family reunion, Russell's Lake, 2007

July heavy with the love of it,
when small feet upend stillness, heels
refracting off of eels,
in the rush from bank to water.

Here where the cattails hold grudges,
where we hunt down the chatter of sandflies,
cup them in our palms. Catch

the ripple as it babbles inwards, shower
ears against the wave. Dad
tells us how when he was young
the shore was alive

with the rhythm of tadpoles
and frogs, how trees grew
thick, close as the interlock of sticky fingers.

Let us burrow deep in silt as willow roots,
a canopy of cousin trees sheltering the shore,

finding small gods
in the minnows which settle
as a thick blanket across toes.

Listen closely.

Cybella Maffitt studies English literature at Columbia University. Her work has appeared in *Starling*, *Signals*, *Flash Frontier*, *The Telescope* and the anthology *A Clear Dawn: New Asian Voices from Aotearoa New Zealand* (2021). She grew up between Los Angeles and Tāmaki Makaurau Auckland, and lives in New York City.

KŌRERO

Ami Rogé and
Brannavan Gnanalingam
This river of life

A conversation on the healing power of words and music

'We're all part of a wider conversation with the past. . . and society at large.' Brannavan Gnanalingam engages the internationally known pianist Ami Rogé in a kōrero that looks at creative impulse and mystery. They explore music and language, and how both art forms invite us to listen. Here we learn how each, through their individual experiences, has gained new perceptions of the greater world and an understanding of healing. Creativity and embracing life: these two things go hand-in-hand. As Rogé says, we must learn to understand the flow: 'We should all be moving along this river of life.'

Of Japanese and Indonesian descent, Ami Rogé has travelled around the world as a classical concert pianist since 2005. With a Masters of Music from Mannes College and a Bachelor of Music from The Juilliard School, she has appeared in prestigious concert halls and festivals across four continents, including New York's Carnegie Hall, the Hong Kong Joy of Music Festival, the Australian Festival of Chamber Music, the Beijing International Piano Festival and the Salisbury International Festival, among others. She lives in Japan.

Brannavan Gnanalingam is a novelist and lawyer. He has written seven novels, including *Sodden Downstream* (2017) and *Sprigs* (2020), which were both shortlisted for the Jann Medlicott Acorn Foundation Prize for Fiction at the Ockham New Zealand Book Awards, and *A Briefcase, Two Pies and a Penthouse* (2016; longlisted for the same award). *Sprigs* also won the Ngaio Marsh Award for best crime novel in 2021. His most recent novel is *Slow Down, You're Here* (2022). He is a regular columnist for the *Sunday Star-Times*. He lives in Te Whanganui-a-Tara Wellington.

BG: Why music? I'm always interested in people's foundational reasons for their chosen art form.

AR: Honestly, I cannot really imagine myself doing anything but music. It was the thing I loved the most since I was little. I was not very brilliant in school in any other academic subject. Music was the only thing I was able to do, and loved. I never had to question my path. If I had excelled in science or math, maybe I would have done something else.

But probably not — I love music. And what of your creative ear? Where do you listen most? For me, it's music. For you . . . ?

BG: Music similarly forms a critical part of my day. I probably engage with music more than writing on a daily basis, from a creative point of view. I listen to music when I walk anywhere, when I'm on the bus trying to relax from the day, when I'm cooking, when I'm writing — I abhor silence, and music fills that role for me. It's funny because my parents weren't really into music. My mum listened to a lot of ABBA and Boney M, but otherwise not much else. I had the pleasure of being able to listen to whatever I felt like when I was growing up, and learned more about the world that way.

My initial entrée into artistic pursuits was music — I played saxophone, drums and guitar growing up, and I played jazz, classical and rock. I then felt that I didn't have the chops to really make it as a musician, but I ended up studying popular music as an art form. I was a music reviewer, did my MA in popular music studies, and then tutored and occasionally lectured in the popular music papers at Victoria University of Wellington. I've always thought critically about music, and that's helped me think about structure, tone and rhythm and, most importantly, history, power and society more generally.

Because of my background, I'm interested in the way music exists outside of performance, and, in particular, how you yourself use music outside of performance. When did you start to see music as having this broader/different function?

AR: I had always been into music, played the piano throughout my life, but a few incidents in recent years (within the past 10 years) have changed how I see music: not only as an art form, but also as a healing modality. Music of course always made me feel better, but in the past I hadn't given much thought to its healing power.

That all changed in August 2011, when I was diagnosed with breast cancer — stage 3, double mastectomy, and the full treatment of chemotherapy, radiotherapy and five years of hormone therapy. During that time, while enduring chemotherapy, I kept playing the piano, and I realised that music was actually giving me strength and helping me to heal. This was when I first started to be more conscious of the healing power of music.

Then, a few years later, my mother was suffering from dementia, and my father developed another serious cognitive illness similar to dementia. I played music to them, both at the piano and by singing songs from their youth, and I saw that this had a positive effect on them. It was around this same time that I saw a documentary called *Alive Inside*, a powerful movie that showed the effect of music on the elderly in seniors' homes. I started to be interested in music therapy. Going back to university for a degree in music therapy was not an option for me at the time, so I slowly studied on my own, read books and took workshops, etc.

In March 2019, my father had heart failure. I had to rush back to Japan from Switzerland, where I was living at the time. We almost lost him then, and I almost did not make it in time. Even after I had arrived, he was having multiple ventricular fibrillations, and his heart kept stopping; they had to revive him with an AED (automated external defibrillator). They advised me that the best thing was to let him go. I asked the doctors and the staff if I could put on some music, a few tracks of songs he loved, and a few tracks of beautiful soothing music. Miraculously, after putting on the music, I was stunned to see how his heart stabilised, and he never had attacks again.

BG: Was he conscious of the music at the time? I'm interested in the way the subconscious creates memories in this way.

AR: He was unconscious, yet his heart stabilised in the ICU. Music definitely helped him. It's possible that he heard on a subliminal level, and his heart entrained with the beats of the music. I'm not sure *how* it worked, but it *worked*.

I don't know if the subconscious creates new memories; I'm not an expert in that area. In some ways we listen more deeply when we are half-awake, when the brain waves are slower, and thus more receptive.

When my father regained consciousness, he was very much aware of the music. I kept the music going in his hospital room. I had the music on until the moment he passed on. It ended up being a sort of palliative care for him. He passed away very peacefully.

A year later, I came across a very special book called *The Healing Power of Sound* by Mitchell Gaynor. Dr Gaynor was an oncologist based in New York City. It's curious how I never met him or even came across his name during my cancer treatment in the city, but he unfortunately passed away, so I never had the chance to visit him. He was unorthodox compared to the mainstream medical world, in that he strongly believed that music — and not only music, but sound and soundwave — had a concrete healing power, sometimes even more powerful than orthodox medical treatment. In the book he offered a sound scientific explanation of how the vibration entrains with the cells in our body. He mentioned, particularly, crystal singing bowls, made from quartz which contain silica — which is also in our bodies, in our bones, and is responsible for cleaning our blood, for taking toxins out of the body.

After I read his book, I absolutely needed to search for these crystal singing bowls, get my hands on them and hear the sounds for myself.

In a similar way, I wonder how you see things developing for you outside the task of merely reading and writing — how for you does the creative process work outside this broader function?

BG: For me, the creative process is how I make sense of the world. Reading and writing is a small way in which I articulate what I discover, but I suspect I'd be using some form of creative process even if I didn't have an audience. I guess I've been fortunate to have had a bit of success with my writing, which has added a touch more public scrutiny to these wider purposes for me. I try to read widely, and push myself in what I read. I must admit, though, I had never planned to be a writer or for this to be my key creative outlet.

AR: It's curious how things turn out in one's life. As soon as those thoughts about the crystal bowls crossed my mind, opportunities presented themselves one by one. I went to Bali, and there I had the opportunity to hear the crystal bowls during a soundbath session in a yoga centre in Ubud, a meditative or healing experience where people lie, immersed, or bathed, in (often vibratory) soundwaves. Then, when I got back to Japan after that, I saw streaming on Facebook a lady who played crystal bowls and piano at the same time. I contacted her and went to visit her in Yokohama. It was an eye-opening experience, as I learned more deeply about the crystal bowls. One thing led to another, and that very day I found myself going home on the bullet train with four beautiful alchemy crystal singing bowls neatly packed in a single case.

I was living in Switzerland at that time, going back and forth from Japan. My father had passed away, and I had to find proper dementia care for my mother. But then my life in Switzerland ended abruptly as my marriage fell apart quite suddenly, and I was back living full-time in Japan.

Then Covid happened. We were all confined, but this opened up another opportunity for me, as things became available online. A reputed school in the United Kingdom called the Sound Healing Academy started offering online certificate courses. I was able to do a full certificate course on sound healing, specialising in the crystal bowls. Since then, I have had several opportunities to give soundbaths both online and live. I have also explored playing the piano and crystal bowls at the same time, and, I must say, the crystal bowls have changed, completely, how I approach the piano as well.

Has your life changed in unexpected ways? Has your creative response to events in the world led you to new places?

BG: You often don't realise that the turning points in your life are happening. For me, I can pinpoint a few. I was a sports-mad kid, whose passion far outweighed my talent. We had a compulsory music class, and my music teacher saw some spark in me and convinced my parents to enrol me in itinerant saxophone lessons (the itinerant music system was an affordable way for students to learn music). It led me to realise that I could have a creative outlet.

Then, when I was at university, a friend in my film class, who was the film editor in our student magazine, asked me if I wanted to write a review for him. I'm terrible at saying 'no', so said 'yes', and that is how I became a writer. Even then, I became a novelist by accident, too — I was doing a trip from Morocco to Ghana, and a friend asked if I was going to write about it. I hadn't planned on it, but then I did, and I got published, and that was it. My first two novels were in response to travel — and some horrible things, including the 2007 killing of French tourists in Mauritania (which I got caught up in), the precursors of the Malian War, and the rise of the Front National in France — while also dealing with the ongoing legacies of colonialism and xenophobia.

More recently, in 2019, I had a bad concussion, and it took a year to become OK. I hit my head at a playground, following my daughter up a rope. It wasn't a spectacular accident, but it had long-term ramifications. My sleep became terrible, and I had real issues with concentration, bright lights, headaches and communication. A couple of months ago, my toddler accidentally bashed heads with me while having a tantrum. It had much more of a physical effect: I was constantly drowsy, had bad headaches and insomnia.

One of the things I've been most worried about is the potential impact this could have on dementia. I'm a big rugby/football fan, and there are a lot of conversations happening in those spaces about the effects of multiple concussions and the later onset of dementia. Writing became even more of an imperative as a result, as a way of preserving my memory and making some small etchings in the world.

This in part also reflects my Tamil heritage. I left Sri Lanka at a young age, following the effects of the civil war. One of the key things that triggered the civil war was the destruction of the renowned Jaffna Library, a repository for Tamil voices and history. I was conscious about how our 'containers' for words can be so fragile, so vulnerable to externalities.

It's fascinating the way lives can change without realising. Can you explain how your recent circumstances have changed your performance approach?

AR: Crystal bowls changed the way I listen. I listen more carefully to the harmonies in the lengthened notes, and also to the silence in between notes. I am also more aware of the overtones created in the harmonies — something that is very apparent in the crystal bowls, but if I listen carefully, it's also there on the piano. I am less 'busy' at the piano, and more attentive. And every sound feels more beautiful than it had before.

I am still midway through my journey, but so far it has been very exciting indeed.

BG: Do you know where you might end up on this journey?

AR: No, I don't — but that's the beauty in life, isn't it? I'm 54 now, and I am finally starting to realise that, no matter how much you try to carefully plan out your life, it doesn't really always work out the way you had expected. You have to go with the flow sometimes, and listen (again, 'listen'!) to where life takes you. And the journey doesn't ever end, until you leave this Earth. It's also important not to hang on to things too much. Sometimes you need to let go and let life guide you instead.

I have this great image — I think I got it from one of the books I mentioned earlier. Say you are in a river with a rapid current, and desperately hanging onto a branch by the bank, scared to let go, afraid of being washed away by the river. But then you let go. The river takes you away. At first it's very scary, but then you get the hang of it, and learn to flow above and with the current. Then you start to notice that you are seeing lots of beautiful scenery along the way, which you would have never known if you had kept desperately hanging onto that branch. I think we should all be moving along this river of life.

What about you? Do you ever know where you are going? How can the creative process lead somewhere — as it must — but still remain so open-ended? How does that concept work for you — the idea of being determined along a path, but also open to change?

BG: I love that part of the creative process, that anything you do is a snapshot of a particular time and place. I'd always (rightly or wrongly) viewed music as having a kind of tyranny of the young, where the musicians who get celebrated tend to be young and raw. Writing instead has that ability to keep opening new worlds as you get older. I'm sure that's also the case with music, too. I love the idea of ensuring each book is different, and yet builds on what I've already done. I think the open-endedness of a novel becomes less intimidating the more you do it. I love wrestling with the nuances and ambiguity when considering my next project, but I'm also keen to ensure there's a strong current in my writing, that whatever I'm trying to explore is clearly articulated (at least in my head!).

I'm interested in the way you situate yourself with music — who/what interests you as a listener and as a practitioner?

AR: I am interested in all sorts of music. And I choose what I listen to according to how I am feeling at that moment. I am a classical musician, so naturally I have listened to lots of classical music, especially piano music. I love vocal music — opera, for example. I listen often to nineteenth-century repertoire, but I also love early music (baroque). But I do listen to other music. I love Lady Gaga, for example. She has uplifting messages in her music. When I want to feel inspired, I listen to more healing music, used for meditation.

BG: Does the healing power of music apply to all forms of music in your opinion? Or is it more likely to apply to classical music?

AR: Of course it applies to all forms of music! Most definitely! And musical taste is personal and different for everyone. I just happen to be a classical musician. In the movie I mentioned earlier, *Alive Inside*, we see the dementia patients going back to favourite music from their past. I think that's the best. If the patient loved oldies pop from the 1950s, by all means listen to that instead of a Beethoven sonata. For anyone, not only dementia patients, listening to some music from your past will conjure up memory. It can be very healing.

There are some studies, however, that show that certain classical music — Mozart in particular — has a special effect in music therapy care. There is something in the frequency of harmony. And that Bach is good for the brain.

And what of the healing power of the word? Can you also see how words are a way forward? With the idea of building a house for our future, the ideas expressed in this book, I wonder how you see the place of fiction as offering not only inspiration but also real structures for people to see and believe in.

BG: I guess a house is a collection of component parts. My day job is as a construction lawyer, and I have particular expertise in analysing seismic reports and providing advice to take into account Aotearoa's seismic environment. I see first-hand how the most incredible buildings end up being constructed by the smallest parts interdependently working with each other. If one system part fails, then the whole house, effectively, fails. So you can't build a house for the future without interrogating what has worked in the past. What failed, what ground was it built on, what did any failures look like?

I think fiction operates in a particular fashion — we're all part of a wider conversation with the past, other writers and society at large. Language similarly works in a component kind of way: books constructed by the seemingly arbitrary but ordered by how an author decides to place their words. Small parts creating larger worlds. I imagine it's the same with music — where a piece of music comprises how you order a note or silence.

Novels can point to the future through the way narratives can effect change — we can understand the world more through a narrative than we can through a polemic. They offer space for voices to be recognised and listened to. Narratives offer a chance for healing, by wrestling with ambiguity and nuance and alternative viewpoints — while at the same time providing a way of synthesising that world.

I'm conscious of not overstating things, given the word can do just as much damage as good, but there's real power in the word being used to construct houses for the future.

Emma Neale
Peonies

When Macey's husband left her his off-site vintage car collection, and the privately owned golf course that had been in his family for generations, she wanted to kill him. Which was confusing and shaming, because he was already dead and she missed him so bitterly that sometimes she forgot how to stand up out of a chair.

Dealing with the cars would be relatively easy. She'd sell them to support the girls. Yet even the thought of Breckenridge Fairway made her head haze with pointless, delayed anger: for the way Dougal's obsession with it had taken him away from her and the children; for the way he'd expected her to dazzle at functions with utter boars and loathsome bores. Hilltop Henrys, she called them: people who insulted or condescended, thinking they concealed it. 'Oh, you're a South Creek valley girl! You dirty devil, Dougie. A virgin in the valley is like four-leafed clover on Astroturf.' The men who said such things often had bulbous purple nose tips that looked vaguely obscene. Then there were those lines one particular pro-coach said far too often: 'A South Creek girl? Grow a woman there, she's surprisingly hardy and needs little care. Like a peony, they say. *Thrives* on a bit of frost and neglect.' Perhaps that made her so furious because she actually loved peonies: their large, secret, compound hearts, as ruffled as French cabaret petticoats.

Inheriting Breckenridge from Dougal — who died so suddenly — felt like being left yet another of his messes. His sweaty laundry, always dumped on top of, not *in*, the washing machine; his shambolic garage filled with junk he rarely used; his study, with its population of weird machine parts and electrical cables; his ongoing feud with an alcoholic couple across the street... Dear Dougal deposited little mounds of chaos and stress around the place as unwittingly as a giant cat shedding dander.

'Shut the door on it,' he'd say about each muddle, a boyish light in his eye. 'It's not your problem.' But there was no door to shut on his will. She had no interest in the Breckenridge behemoth: just wanted to carry on with her nursery. She grew flowers (peonies included) for local florists; she sold any less-than-perfect blooms from a covered stall she wheeled through the side gate of their home, the house Dougal had called 'our tuck-away'. Their old, renovated villa was small, discreet, as if even Dougal needed respite from the assumptions and ostentations of the jet-set.

Yet part of him remained bewitched by wealth. There was the American billionaire, for example: Kayne Dell, who toured international golf courses on the scout for investments. One of the rare clients Dougal brought home, he was a wiry, elegant man whose voice seemed transplanted from another body: it ground on and on, a front-end loader shifting gravel. The men had sat drinking all night, Kayne cascading with that scraping laughter, which left Macey uneasy, as if the flint in it might strike some spark that would blaze through the house.

When Dougal died, Kayne, whom Macey had met only that once, sent her such a massive, baroque bouquet that it had the air both of invasion and insult: y' think y' do *flowers*? When he left a voice message — far too glib, far too soon — saying, 'Macey, so sorry for your loss. Dougal. One in a mill. Can't imagine. Can't stop thinking about his peach of a place, either', it tipped her over into temporary derangement. She wanted Breckenridge off her hands; yet that Kayne also made her want to decapitate every one of her hothouse flowers with the ridiculously expensive ladies' driver Dougal gave her, the one whose marketing puff said was 'engineered for maximum speed and exceptional levels of forgiveness'.

She ignored Kayne's multiple texts. Then came a call with a direct offer. He wanted to buy Breckenridge, 'go more exclusive': hand-picked membership, luxury accommodation, silver-service restaurant. 'We'll have, like, local Indigenous themes,' he said. 'But, like, respectful. We'll get some cultural sensitivity guys in, do it right. We'll name the holes after great warriors. We'll use the Te Uri language on the bumpf.'

'Te *what*?' she asked.

He sighed. 'Oh, goddamn autocorrect on my notes.' He tried to tell her that no matter the geopolitics, *his people* would always be able to travel to leisure havens like this.

Did he think she was naïve, or was he delusional? The longer he riffed on future-proofing 'Dougal's sweet little number there', the clearer Macey grew. It arrived less as a thought, more like atoms of light teeming over her skin.

I t was a body memory of early autumn's lockdown. She, Dougal and their daughters, walking local parks, had wandered all the way to Breckenridge itself some afternoons; Dougal inspecting the greens with a mournful, lost expression, like a basset hound that can't find its favourite chew-toy. One mild Thursday, they took along a picnic. Dougal and his staff had placed signs up saying the public were welcome to walk the grounds during Level 4, but there were no other ramblers that day.

They sat on a rug in a sunny grove, listening to creek water running over trout-coloured rocks; smelling jasmine that fizzed over a walkway wall; watching fantails jazz and jink. Macey had never felt so at ease there. The girls and Dougal had talked in a way they hadn't for so long: the teenagers listening, as if his answers weren't cringingly dated, or dad jokes. Time felt as if it, too, lay down in warm butter-coloured pools on their throats, forearms. Only a Zoom meeting Dougal had scheduled forced them up off the rug. They walked back along the rough, then saw the unexpected sight of a young woman tucked in close to a hedge. She sat alone with diary, textbook, backpack.

Dougal's greeting seemed simultaneously proprietorial, wary and warning. Their girls were embarrassed by it; rang out their own pealing hellos, as if to smother the contrail of their father's. They pulled him away, arms looped through his.

Something in the way the young woman angled into the hedge's shadow made Macey hang back. 'Are you OK?' she asked.

'Yes!' The woman raised her eyebrows in mild surprise, diary on her tucked-up knees. 'Isn't it lovely here?' She looked into the distance. 'My student hall is hectic. I come here for some peace.' Then, with an earnestness Macey took to be swotty, diligent: 'Did you know that silence itself is almost extinct?'

'Extinct?' said Macey.

The student nodded. 'I read about it today. Apparently, the vibrations of human-made machines have even been detected in the Mariana Trench. Crazy.'

Macey wasn't sure what the Mariana Trench actually was.

'It's easier to study here, sometimes,' the woman said.

'And we've been so lucky with the weather!' Macey offered, feeling a trivial bore, but not knowing how to get her own sense of expansion from these golfer-free grounds into words.

The young woman smiled. 'My friend listens to a white noise app when she studies. Thought I'd make my own.' With her foot, she nudged her cellphone, which rested on the grass. 'I've been recording. The birdsong, the wind.'

They chatted more, about how the whole city was actually better without traffic, and with men either off the streets, or keeping their distance from solitary women.

'Turns out a fake cough works even better than pepper spray,' said the student, her earnestness turning sharp, sardonic. Perhaps Macey should have guessed from that: the woman, too, had grown up in the valley. 'Tihomira,' she had introduced herself: a Croatian name. Both grandfathers had emigrated here when young; she was the first of her family to attend university. 'Mum says we usually cook or garden for the golf types.' Then her head turned. 'Look!'

Masses of white thistledown poured across the course, startling against a gentian sky. The movement had the unity of a bird flock: as if the floss-borne seeds were shifting, adjusting, in silent, intuitive agreement.

Macey found herself listening, then. To the sift and whisper of the trees. To that paradox: the delicate thunk of a flowerhead falling. She imagined lying down, ear pressed to the earth, to hear grass blades unfolding from her footprints, the swell of toadstool cells rising like bread. She felt her heart cease its stirring-stirring: that constant agitation, as if it was a spinning-top set whirling in her chest the moment she woke.

When she caught up, a little later, with Dougal and their girls at the main entrance, he said, 'Stunning afternoon.' He looked a mixture of perplexed and amused. 'Think I heard myself think.'

His words returned when Macey hung up from Kayne, her skin still awash with goose-flesh. Golden goose-flesh. She would see her lawyer, ask how to donate the fairway to the city and local iwi under a conservation covenant. Motorised vehicles would be banned. Power tools, too, if possible, though there might be bylaws about grass height, pruning? Either way, Breckenridge would transform into a tree-filled reserve. She wanted one self-indulgence: peonies planted in four corners, one spot each for her, her daughters and Tihomira. She imagined Dougal, first reluctant, then wry, then warming to it, as she told him in her head, *Oh, two self-indulgences, actually. I'll also rename it. How do you like the sound of this? — The Quiet Keep.*

Emma Neale is a writer and editor. She is the author of six novels, six collections of poetry and one collection of short stories. Her short story collection, *The Pink Jumpsuit: Short Fictions, Tall Truths* (2021), was longlisted for the Jann Medlicott Acorn Foundation Prize at the 2022 Ockham New Zealand Book Awards. In 2020 she was awarded the Lauris Edmond Memorial Award for a Distinguished Contribution to New Zealand Poetry. She lives in Ōtepoti Dunedin.

We the custodians

If the written contents of this book are a call for conversation, an invitation to examine our world and ourselves as we look towards tomorrow, then the visual art provides equally powerful ways of seeing, feeling, thinking. Here, eight world-renowned artists share their work in our whakaruru-taha. Maureen Lander's *Aho for Hinetītama* provides threads to the first woman in Māori myth. Lisa Reihana's *Papatūānuku (pregnant with Rūaumoko)* reminds us of the power of motherhood. Noa Noa von Bassewitz's *He Kanikani te ora me te mata* evokes a morning dance celebrating life. And Yuki Kihara's evocative work positions the powerful silhouette of a woman in black garb looking out on a brooding world. What does she see? What do they all see, looking out from Aotearoa?

These New Zealand-based artists are joined by El Anatsui from Ghana, Steve Golden from Singapore, Oliver Jeffers from Northern Ireland and Alex McLean from the United States. What we take with us, what we leave behind, what we will lose if we continue to ignore Papatūānuku's warning — these are themes that intertwine with those of their fellow artists and writers.

Together, these artists provide a dynamic and moving panorama, perhaps even changing each time we look. Their work is textured and layered, ambiguous and suggestive. They push and pull on the themes in this book: memory, history, the perils of Covid, the realities of climate change, a shifting sense of connection and an elusive grip on control, and also the very notion of creation and an inherent joy of being alive. They cry out, they leap up, they reach across, they sing. They offer an ever-flowing, ever-changing view, with myriad questions around who we are, what our world is and the future to come.

Steve Golden, *Snow Flurries, Tokyo*, 2022. Photograph, 254 × 381 mm.

Steve Golden, *New Year's Day, Tokyo*, 2022. Photograph, 254 × 381 mm.

Steve Golden, *Karung Guni, Singapore*, 2022. Photograph, 254 × 381 mm.

Steve Golden, *Collectibles, Singapore*, 2022. Photograph, 254 × 381 mm.

Yuki Kihara, *Ōtamahua Quail Island*, from the series 'Quarantine Islands', 2021.
Lenticular photograph, 1050 × 1485 mm. Courtesy of Yuki Kihara and Milford Galleries.

Yuki Kihara, *National Biocontainment Laboratory*, from the series 'Quarantine Islands', 2021.
Lenticular photograph, 1050 × 1485 mm. Courtesy of Yuki Kihara and Milford Galleries.

Hinemoana Baker
Our house at Staytrue Bay

It was always daytime when
they had their biggest fights.
Good, I guess, to poultice all that
poison up and out into the sunlight
sanitise it like the spread out

bedsheet you left out by mistake
overnight, now it fills the room
with the smell of lost snails.
The flea-market *koffer* I bought
a globe away last Saturday

has that same smell: each time
I pass, I lift the weighty metal lid,
put my face inside it deep and
inhale. It was a sailor's trunk,
I decide: the frayed canvas

belt inside held down
that sailor's few belongings
while waves crashed over decks
and Mother Superior snapped
and cracked her leather strap

like a flag in high winds.
For now, friends, I must away!
I'm sailing down the line
to harbours with improbable names
striding on the wide feet my father gave me . . .

It's always a risk, bringing old
luggage into new quarters.
Opening it wide in the still
air of your home as if it won't speak.
As if there's nothing inside but stars.

Hinemoana Baker (Ngāi Tahu, Ngāti Raukawa, Te Ātiawa, Ngāti Toa Rangatira, Pākehā) is a poet, musician and recording artist who is completing a PhD at Potsdam University in Germany. Her latest book, *Funkhaus* (2020), was shortlisted for the Mary and Peter Biggs Award for Poetry at the 2021 Ockham New Zealand Book Awards. She lives in Berlin.

Part two

From inside the cave

The tapestry of understanding cannot be woven by one strand alone.
Only by the working together of strands and the working together of
weavers will such a tapestry be completed. With its completion let us look
at the good that comes from it. In time, we should also look at those stitches
which have been dropped, because they also have a message.

— Kukupa Tirikātene

Ian Wedde
Tree house

The stroppy, garrulous, flighty inner-
city dwellers assembling around the
leafy tree outside our window or else
under the shelter of the barbershop
eaves over the road or along the work-
stained footpath outside Car Tune Auto whose
insistent radio cannot compete
with their chitter-chatter nor ever quell
their flirty displays, impervious to
the testosteroned gearshifts of souped-up
racers daring orange up at the lights
with Jervois, tolerant to the point of
oblivious to the plodding nodding
pigeons who share their asphalt and shade, their
sun and rain and the insistences of
their persistent young who flutter and
need to be noticed and fed beyond need
except the need to be there too when dusk
announces the sweet hour of gathering
in the fading light beneath the tree where
we scatter the bowl of leftover rice
and torn-up crusts of stale bread, a meagre
charity but good enough to summon
the miscellaneous inner-city
survivors, the bright-eyed, beak-stropping crowd
of sparrows of course and the pigeons yes
but also the dapper black-necked mynas,
their mates the mouthy Aussie magpies and,

from time to time, a pair of show-offy
rosella — on the roadside beneath their
leaves they gather, these quick-talky flaneurs,
nifty acrobats of air, branch grippers
and asphalt hoppers, feasters upon scraps,
the lone tree outside our place their forest.

Ian Wedde is a novelist, poet, anthologist and editor. His books include nine novels, 16 collections of poetry, a collection of stories, two books of essays, a memoir, several art catalogues and a monograph on the artist Bill Culbert; his edited work includes two Penguin anthologies of poetry. In 2010, he was appointed an Officer of the New Zealand Order of Merit (ONZM) in the Queen's Birthday honours list, and he was the New Zealand Poet Laureate from 2011 to 2013. His most recent books are the novel *The Reed Warbler* (2020) and the poetry collection *The Little Ache — a German notebook* (2021). He lives in Tāmaki Makaurau Auckland.

Wendy Parkins
At the Kauri Museum

After the first easing of lockdown, Grace and Ned resumed Sunday drives — Ned called them that, even if it wasn't a Sunday — just like when Rebecca was small. They would drive to a beach or a nature reserve on the fringes of the city where they could stretch their legs and have a coffee, preferring places they hadn't been before. When restrictions relaxed a little more, they took the ferry to a Waiheke winery. And today the suggestion to drive north to the Kauri Museum had turned from a half-joke into a serious plan.

They had spent many previous wedding anniversaries in distant places, like Granada for their thirtieth, where it had been so hot that Grace had craved ice-cream by 10 in the morning, taking refuge in a cave-like heladería near their hotel each day. A far cry from their honeymoon in Taupō, all they could afford then. This year they had talked about a short break in Sydney, assuming they would be free to fly to Australia by the end of June, but like everyone else in the team of 5 million they would be staying put this winter.

So on Saturday morning, under a cloudless blue sky after days of rain, Ned and Grace turned off State Highway 1 at Brynderwyn to wind west between impossibly green paddocks and crisply outlined hills. Small towns with halls advertising badminton, line dancing and quilting classes. A row of leafless poplars, knocked over by a storm and leaving exposed root balls stuck with clods of thick chocolate-coloured earth.

The museum carpark at Matakohe was largely empty and, inside, an elderly man behind the gift shop counter greeted them warmly, as if glad of the company. Handing a guide to Ned, he said, 'Make sure you don't miss the Gum Room, downstairs.'

Grace misheard him, thinking he had said 'Gun Room', and imagined the kind of room she always avoided on visits to stately homes: muskets and rifles lining the walls, perhaps a fan of broadswords. Ned had no more interest in historic weaponry than she did, although Grace could never be entirely sure what might take his attention in a museum. Or anywhere else, for that matter.

Ned approached things aslant, not in the expected way. That was one of the things she had loved about him from the beginning. Words, especially: Ned liked to turn words around or repeat them over, to discover their strangeness or tease out their absurdity. He should have been a poet or at least a professor of English rather than law. But it had been Grace who had gone into publishing, perhaps more clear-eyed than

Ned about words that might hook a reader in ways that could be quantified, *monetised*. A word Ned hated, of course.

She followed her husband into the museum's first room, filled with Victorian wardrobes, sideboards and desks, all decorated with intricate inlay or fretwork, their polished surfaces shining under strategically placed spotlights. On the walls were sepia photographs of dour-faced men — standing, sawing, digging, driving wagons — dwarfed beside felled logs and soaring trunks. The space was chilled after the warmth of the car, the massed furniture oppressive in a stillness broken only by the sluggish tick of an antique clock. While Ned studied the photographs, Grace walked on ahead, and it was then she realised her mistake about what the man had said: a sign pointed to the Gum Room.

Downstairs, in a low-ceilinged room, honey-coloured lumps of translucent gum were piled high in glass cases. Along one wall, altar crosses, model ships and lighthouses looked as if they had been shaped from glistening toffee.

> *Kauri gum has a special warmth. To touch, it is never cold like stone. It gives a variety of optical effects in different lights. It is found in a wide range of colours — from black to clear. Kauri gum is fascinating.*

But some of the exhibits told another story. Exploitation and industrialisation. Dispossession and depletion.

Grace turned to a cabinet containing gum jewellery, along with more sculpted models, and a plait of golden hair. Just another jumbled display, like you find in regional museums all over the world. A saint's fingernail next to a finely laced christening cap in Limerick, for instance. But then she noticed another coiled length of butter-yellow hair, tied at each end with a faded grosgrain ribbon, with a typewritten card in front of it.

> *Hair could be made from kauri gum by heating it and then drawing out fine strands, like threads of spun sugar. While still warm, the 'hair' could be plaited, but once cooled it became very brittle and could not be handled.*

What were you supposed to make of that? Ageless lumps, dug up from the earth to be turned into varnish and linoleum, could instead also become something as fragile, as useless, as kauri gum hair.

'Just as well we didn't miss it,' Ned said, chuckling as he came up behind Grace.

She laughed, too. 'You have to see this,' she said, pointing at the ribboned hair.

Ned brought his face close to the glass. 'Don't you have a length of your hair at home somewhere?'

G race had not thought about that for years. At her first haircut after Rebecca's birth and almost dizzy with sleep deprivation, she had asked to have it all cut off.

'Are you sure?' her stylist had asked, a hand resting lightly on each of Grace's plastic-draped shoulders as he faced her pale reflection in the mirror. He had probably learned the hard way to be wary of clients making dramatic decisions, desperate to be free of whatever was weighing them down.

'Yes,' Grace had said. *One less thing to worry about*. 'I'm sure.'

So he had pulled her hair back into a ponytail and tied it with an elastic before removing the entire length in a single cut, the scissors making a sound like shears through a width of thick fabric. He gave her the length of hair, saying, 'You might want to keep this', and she had sat with it in her lap for the remainder of the appointment, not knowing what else to do, while he shaped her remaining hair into a smooth wedge cut.

Years later, a startled-looking teenage Rebecca, who had never known her mother with long hair, brought a large unsealed envelope to Grace in the kitchen.

'What *is* this, Mum? It was at the back of your make-up drawer. I was looking for a nail file.'

In the envelope was the length of brown hair still held by the elastic, the neatly cut edge like the fine bristles of an artist's paintbrush. Grace had smiled at her daughter's discomfiture, but Rebecca was right: there was something unnerving about keeping this former part of herself. Grace had taken the envelope and dropped it in the kitchen bin.

Now she could not recall telling Ned about the envelope of hair, or what his reaction had been to her short hair. That first year of motherhood was mostly a blur.

She turned away from the glass case. 'Not anymore,' she said. She placed a hand briefly on Ned's arm. 'Come on, let's keep going.'

Back upstairs, they turned into a large gallery devoted to the cutting and milling of timber. Ned was soon absorbed, but Grace walked through into the next wing, where a full-size replica of a boarding house was peopled with glass-eyed, pasty-faced settlers — *unsettlers*, Ned would probably say — in Scenes of Pioneer Life. They made Grace uncomfortable, like stumbling on an amateur-dramatic performance of a play that had not aged well. She moved quickly on to some display cases, where her attention was caught by a pair of eau de Nil silk shoes with French heels and ornate silver buckles.

Made in Norwich. Found in a truck on a farm in Matakohe.

Had they been treasured, these shoes that had somehow made their way from Norfolk to Northland? Maybe they had belonged to a woman who only wore them once or twice, kept them wrapped in tissue paper, out of sight. Too precious to risk exposing? Or a shameful extravagance? From behind the glass, the Edwardian shoes called out to be touched. The silk would be smooth, the curve of the heel pleasing to trace with your finger.

Ned called her name and Grace turned back to where he was looking into one of the boarding house rooms.

'Reminds me of Alison, back in the day,' he said, indicating a mannequin of an adolescent boy in tweed trousers and a striped shirt. The boy's wig of extravagant black curls did look a bit like her friend Alison's mushroom perm, *back in the day*. When had they started to talk like their parents?

'The eighties have a lot to answer for.'

'I don't know,' Ned said. 'You always looked great.' He rubbed a thumb lightly over the nape of her neck, where her hair still formed a tapered V-shape above her collar.

Grace had thought of Alison only yesterday. Alison had been her sole bridesmaid even though, in the first flush of her sociology PhD, she had disapproved of all things matrimonial. At the reception, Alison had said to Grace: 'This is the one day — today and for the rest of your life — that you will be expected to have sex. It's the foundation of patriarchal marriage, after all: conjugal rights.'

Grace had laughed at the bad-fairy prophecy, but after Alison had dashed off in an awkward swish of apricot chiffon, she stood alone for a moment amidst the hubbub of the celebration. She recalled it so clearly: staring out through French doors to a sheltered courtyard with a single magnolia tree, gashes of pink petals just emerging from split, furry-lipped buds, and thinking about a future where sex might become something she and Ned owed to history, like an annual wreath-laying ceremony.

In fact, though, Grace and Ned *had* had sex last night, the eve of their thirty-seventh anniversary. They had gone for dinner at their favourite restaurant, a night early but the only time they could get a booking, and Grace had arrived straight from work, still preoccupied with the day's annoyances and complaining about the editor in the Melbourne office.

'That man is the bane of my life,' she had said.

'I thought the bane of your life was the precocious prize winner who takes herself too seriously?' Ned asked.

'Can't I have more than one? *Banes*? Why does that sound odd?'

'Banes is actually an obsolete synonym for banns, as in wedding banns,' Ned said, tracing a furrow in his soup with his spoon.

'Are you trying to tell me something?'

'What do you mean?'

'Banes and banns. A bane is a cause of ruin or trouble. It seems an odd thing to say on our anniversary. Well, our almost-anniversary.'

Ned looked bemused. 'You know me. It's just an odd word, as you say.'

She had said nothing further, but between their first plates being cleared and the main course arriving they had fallen into a conversation of half-articulated grievances and vague regrets. Her fault, probably. It was as if she had suddenly looked down and seen no net beneath them, unsure when it might have disappeared. This was not how she had wanted to spend the evening. If this year had taught her anything, it was the comfort of the known, the reassurance of grasping a familiar hand.

Then, back at home, Ned had opened another bottle and lit the fire even though the night was mild. Grace found flowers on her bedside table. They had talked about the planned drive north, joking again about the modesty of the excursion. Later, when the rain returned, they had reached for each other in the dark as they had done countless times before.

Kauri gum is a resin which bleeds from the tree. If the bark is damaged, or a branch is broken by the wind, the resin bleeds out and seals the wound. This prevents rot getting into the tree. The resin can build up into a lump which goes hard. Over time, the gum is forced off, falls to the ground and is covered by forest litter. This has been happening for millions of years.

Thirty-seven years. Grace set no store by the achievement of metallic anniversaries — silver, golden. A long marriage might be simply force of habit, the triumph of routine over desire, when it wasn't something far worse. She and Ned had their share of habit and routine but had escaped the far worse. Touch wood.

What traces would they leave behind? Rebecca, of course. No grandchildren yet. Everything else was intangible but no less valuable for that, surely? When you least expected it, there was a warm presence in the bed beside you that could still make your heart quicken, your breath catch. It left no visible trace, but it sustained. She could summon a day, a mood, a memory for Ned with just a word, a name — Tekapo, Vézelay — and he could do the same for her. *Remember that day when . . . ?* It was enough.

Wendy Parkins is the author of *Every Morning, So Far, I'm Alive* (2019), as well as scholarly monographs and numerous journal articles from her previous life as a Professor of literature in the United Kingdom and Aotearoa New Zealand. She divides her time between Ōtepoti Dunedin and the Tomarata Valley, north of Tāmaki Makaurau Auckland.

KŌRERO

Ashley Johnson
and Pip Adam
Looking for boas
in the mangroves

A conversation between essay and fiction

Canadian artist Ashley Johnson collaborates with New Zealand fiction writer Pip Adam to explore the symbiotic relationship between humanity and the environment. This conversation begins with non-fiction elements offered by Johnson and fictive imaginings from Adam; then it continues as Johnson invites us further into a discussion about looking and seeing.

Ashley Johnson's metaphorical paintings explore socio-environmental issues such as the state of the ocean. The identity of forms is 'loosened' through overlays and omissions to generate an uncertain perception. This creates a zone for viewers to reimagine existence. Originally from Johannesburg, South Africa, he now lives in Toronto, Canada.

Pip Adam is a novelist, short story writer and creative writing teacher. She is the author of the short story collection *Everything We Hoped For* (2010) and the novels *I'm Working on a Building* (2013), *The New Animals* (winner of the Acorn Foundation Fiction Prize at the 2018 Ockham New Zealand Book Awards), *Nothing to See* (2020) and *Audition* (2023). The reviewer Briar Lawry probably came closer than anybody to capturing what it's like to peer into the writer's mind when she described 'the gobsmackingness of Pip Adam'. Adam lives in Te Whanganui-a-Tara Wellington.

Gliding effortlessly through the tangled branches of the mangrove trees, the boa moves to a fork and pauses there to coil and wait. In the mangrove swamps a constant ebb and flow of salinity ensures all creatures, including plant life, coordinate within this brackish ecosystem. We pause and look up at the coiled boa, not more than 2 feet above us. Almost within reach and, certainly, if we were prey, it could drop. But, somehow, nature knows at a very deep level.

Mangrove trees look like squatting men, with their outstretched limbs descending into the dark pools of mystery. There is a vulnerability and nakedness in this position, which suits neither the charging brigade nor the occlusion of flight. We are all in this together.

The mangrove swamp is a metaphor and a lesson for our own survival in a society that has grown increasingly brackish. Artists hang on to any part-time job they can get in the hope that they will endure and have time to make art. I am reminded of the two grey storks I saw standing on the bank. They wait all day for the salinity to reach a certain level and then they can drink for 20 minutes.

In the end, it is quiet. Like when an adult takes a toy from a toddler just as they are giving up on it. We woke up one morning and things had been put to right. Like a decentring. A change of heart. A giving up to the natural order of things. An understanding that we had made a mess of the whole thing and a willingness — within this shame — to hand it all over. But even those words 'hand it all over' are an illusion. The plants and the animals and all the non-human things gently loosen our grip and take the planet from us. And we stand. Looking at the new shape of us all, the web of us all. Like, Surprise! at a party, that was of no surprise to anyone — not even to us. Because you can push it down — and we did, but it is always with us. As we move paper and have arguments about small things, the small, almost silent, static of it is inside us. If you, the people of the past, listen now, if you are quiet just for a moment, if you stop reading and just sit, you'll hear it — the small uncomfortable noise that we now know is leading you in the right direction. Preparing you for the quiet shift that is coming. Because, in the end, it is quiet. We hear the plants. The animals walk our streets. Not threatening us, just moving in. They chose our houses. We are not accustomed because we have laid ourselves over everything — but we see the conversations now, taking place without what we would call voice. A look, a feeling, one animal grooming another toward a decision about who will live where. And the night comes and we stand outside our houses and as the cold comes one of the animals comes to us and invites us in, with a push, with a pull, with a bark or a whelp and we are inside again, incorporated into a pack or a shrewdness or a swarm and we are of no concern and we all sleep together.

The crabs have a more successful strategy. They exude water from an orifice at the top of their carapace. The water runs down their back and gives off carbon dioxide while taking on oxygen. Then it drains back into the shell and is recycled endlessly. What can we do as artists to emulate the crab in our society?

When decisions need to be made. When an emissary is sent. They don't look for the politicians. At first, they walk and fly and swim past us, looking at us as we stand — there is nothing for us to do anymore, we are awaiting instructions. And then they find the ones that are most plant-like. The ones that feel to them like mangroves, like fern, like Amanita or twisted stem agaric. And as they gravitate toward these plant-people it becomes clear more and more that they are the dancers and the singers and the painters and the people who are always telling jokes and these are the ones they return to and a conversation starts. And we use the word conversation, but it is pointless to try and use the words from the old way. These words don't work here. Because the things the words stand for are gone, or meaningless here. Because the animals and the non-humans teach us that we have been wrong the whole time. When we said 'Alive', we had no idea. When we said 'Inanimate', we were wrong. When we said 'This has to go', we got rid of the most important things. And when we said 'This has to be here', we supplanted them with the useless things. The animals show the plants to us what food we can eat. Once the fruit has fallen from the tree, taking it causes no more harm. When we eat it we help move the seeds around. And we are fine. Better than we have ever been, but our words are breaking down because we are living beyond them now. We are living in a new place, everything has changed. Our words will be gone soon and we will be only gestures and sound.

Varieties of mangroves order themselves according to their capacity to handle salinity. The red mangroves can occupy positions closer to the ocean, while the black mangroves are found deeper into the swamps. Trees get rid of the salt by exuding it through their leaves and sending it to the old leaves, which drop off into the water. Their roots develop tubules that protrude up above water to take in additional oxygen.

Their seeds are long, weighted, missiles that drop, lodging themselves in the clay as miniature trees, ready to sprout and grow. No waiting around for special conditions! One can only be dumbfounded at nature's capacity to adapt.

Mangrove swamps are also incredibly important as carbon sinks. They absorb 10 per cent more carbon than the rainforests do, yet are constantly destroyed to make way for shrimp farms and other construction. Certain vulnerable societies that are dependent for survival on these swamps have realised this to their cost. The shrimp farms did not perform well, and the water quality was altered. In addition, fish became scarce. The fish spawn in the ocean near the swamp mouth and swim into these protected zones to mature, before venturing back out into the ocean. The best place to fish is near the juncture of swamp and sea. Destroy the swamp and you decimate your own food supply.

Some of these affected societies have been managing their swamps and gaining a renewed appreciation for them as a necessary partner in the struggle to survive. The capitalist idea 'survival of the fittest' has no place here. Instead, environmental communalism prevails. If someone wants to chop down a tree, they have to plant five trees to replace it.

There are many kinds of art with different needs, but I don't think any of it is particularly successful at generating a living. Galleries and auction houses thrive on exclusion, which drives the price and profit. Grants are also exclusionary, due to paucity of funds, bias towards forms or even shades of nationalism. Art theory creates power structures within institutions so these can hold sway over what gets exposed or validated. Like the storks, we wait for our 20 minutes!

I walk through commercial pine forests being overtaken by pūriri, kahikatea, kawakawa. My cousin walks in the depths of a boreal forest in the North West. Walking in turn through forest tundra, open lichen woodland and closed forest. White spruce, black spruce, then spruce, balsam fir, jack pine, white birch and trembling aspen. We stay in touch through the ground. We stay in touch through the roots and the mycelium. He is a painter, I am a writer. We walk. Dropping our own seedlings, fully formed, into the mud like a mangrove tree. Our work has changed. We work ephemeral, immaterial.

*Leaving no trace but painting and writing nonetheless. He describes colour to
the plants, landbirds and caribou — talks them through what he sees, but we
leave no trace. Nothing is surplus in our new art. We have become the crabs.
The balance of what we drop and the oxygen we produce is perfect. This is our
footprintless art. This is the way we make without making. I hum the story
out. In the new shape of things, words hold very little stock. We are past that.
As I walk, my walking makes the story. My body language, the way my face
changes as I think. Sometimes I dance in the thick mud, and as I lift my foot
each time the mud rushes in and there is not a trace of me and all that remains
is the memory of the dance and the displacement in the air. The way, for a
moment, the tiniest flying things adjusted their path and off me, out of my
breath, came the biome, the bacteria that I make in me. The gases, the heat, the
shimmer. And this is the art we make and it is unlikely we could have got here
without the large disruption, without the massive readjustment because we
loved money and fame and now I walk and call out with a step, Cousin. Cousin
what colour is the sheep laurel? What wavelength is the Sphagnum bog in the
light you are in right now?*

I think we need to alter the paradigm. Instead of trying to mould existing, dysfunctional structures to our needs, we should find ways of support within our own community. I don't mean artist-run centres so much as finding a commonality among artists generally. If art was no longer primarily about selling or getting gallery representation but about showing, discussing and trying to link with one another in a broad conversation, I wonder whether it wouldn't begin to generate a discrete identity. Perhaps Art, as a definition of a certain activity, has to go. At the moment we are being defined by the system and we are passive within that, embracing failure, rather than actively making our own system.

Democracy is a shredded beast right now, with threads hanging down where the holes are. Yet we can see a surge in popularity for certain social ideals, despite the reigning ideology or oligarchical despotism. I believe in the theory of critical mass that predicts change once a certain point is reached. It's painfully obvious that something has to change and that the prevailing society has to be dismantled. How do we reimagine ourselves within and without our surroundings?

Could we artists change the world of art? Change the definition, change the venue, change the whole idea? We validate the system by endorsing its presence, participating in its particular fantasy, thus negating our ability to adapt. Could we drop our own seedlings, fully formed, into the mud like the mangrove trees? I would like to present art that functions as a mode of thought and whose point is to engage the public and world with ideas about environmental coexistence and the human condition. There are many other creative manifestations that remain unrealised because there is no vehicle. What did the Dadaists do to stamp their character into existence, despite it being anti-art?

Eventually, the words of the old world fall from us completely and we flap to ascent and shuffle to ask to be let through. We sing back at the wind in the shift of our hair and the raise of an arm. Hollow framefort establishnot humbug and the shape of a duck we think back at each other and when we think each other now or make the hum in our sinuses of the idea we mean everyone. Art is politics now and food and shape and the action of bring a baby to walking homing wilding not consistent and we remember an okd wey wif keeboreds n taz gu-ing afaa thrm us ⟩e ★ ⚚ ℛ ♻op♯ Ψr ♂⚲ ♀⚑⚐⚐ ⚓⊕ ⚘❀✿❋
❋❋❋❋❋✄✂✪❋✿❋

The key is probably a collective surge of support for an alternative way of showing and disseminating work. Artists need to inhabit a metaphor that can build a unified identity. Perhaps I am being naïve, but I can't help feeling that there must be a way of reimagining our collective destiny. The concept of good and bad art is the least helpful polarity. Creative divisions should fall away and a sharing economy should be established. The strength of open-source technology and a free internet is inspirational here. If artists gave voice as a totality and simply moved to occupy the tree, we could shed our gnarled skins and maybe become boas in the mangroves.

Uno?!?

Yumpot,

surrounum

min flamé je.

Senti jet scent

butu hudu you soup?

Emp-ty barrels, emp-ty caskets.

Entimati ilonga paulum beech.

Wineded down dadornda walkum.

Illgeree, berifriez, frikkle aday,

agorn splitzeree.

Agar hoeget agarven.

Oëgeeia,

Yumpot.

Abstruck Oxpress

The Resurrection of Looking
Ashley Johnson

On this Easter Monday as I write, we stand on the brink of several catastrophic scenarios. Our world goes up in a puff of smoke as a murderous kleptocracy seeks to eradicate a neighbour in an act of unwarranted genocide. The war is another petrochemical act of greed that decimates the planet while elevating a small minority to indescribable riches. We swallow the thick air and wonder when this will be radioactive, too. How do we change this?

In our 'thinking' and actual 'seeing' we have certain anomalies, so the prevailing idea is that we are unfortunately 'hardwired' to 'see' incorrectly. We take in the clues and interpolate what we think we see. The shortcut we take to conceive reality is supposed to reflect efficiency for moments of resolution, like hunting or reacting to fear stimuli quickly. Hence all the illusions we fall for, and yet are unable to stop seeing.

Consider the café wall illusion by psychologist and leading figure in the scientific study of visual perception Richard Gregory. We can't help 'miss-seeing' the illusion because we have primed our vision to be cued by our *a priori* prejudice about how buildings in light look and we interpolate perspective into that. This is a cultural way of looking, and cultures that have not imbibed the same assumptions will have difficulty seeing the illusion. For instance, the Egyptian manner of transcribing visual objects eschewed perspective in favour of narrative, so the symbolism overrode the literal view, leading to a different kind of image. My big question is whether we are really 'hardwired', or whether we have merely accumulated habits of looking with concomitant assumptions?

How do we see?

Technically:

> When we look at an object, information about what we see travels through circuits of neurons beginning in the retina, through the thalamus and into the brain's visual cortex. In the visual cortex, the information gets processed in multiple stages and is ultimately sent to the prefrontal cortex — the area of the brain that makes decisions, including how to respond to a given stimulus.
>
> However, not all information stays on this forward moving path. At the secondary stage of processing in the visual cortex some neurons reverse course and send information back to the first stage of processing. Researchers at Carnegie Mellon wondered if this feedback could change how the neurons in the visual cortex respond to a stimulus and alter the messages being sent to the prefrontal cortex.[1]

Our brain–eye coordination affects everything, so all our prejudices that define our society and way of looking at life get influenced by what we choose to see. The question, then, is: Could we change our way of seeing to allow for new prejudices and possibly find a new way of interpreting reality, which we are inventing anyway?

Consider dot illusions. We choose to 'see' or 'not see'. Could we acquire some

---

1 'Explaining the Mechanism Behind Optical Illusions', *Neuroscience News*, 30 March 2016: https://neurosciencenews.com/visual-system-optical-illusions-3941

new visual habits that would allow us to 'look' in a quantum field manner rather than the de facto classical Newtonian object–space–time paradigm, which is so obviously moribund?

We choose to 'see' or 'not to see' — as dot illusions demonstrate. Sometimes we insert dots that aren't there, or we decide 'not to see' dots that are there. How can it be that the one instance is true and the opposite is also true?

What is Truth? This value is endemic in our society, to a life-and-death point in jurisprudence. I have experienced being a witness and asserting a distant memory of a murderous event as true. The defending attorney asked me how sure I was, and, true to my nature, I said 90 per cent, which is considered doubt enough to avoid conviction. In reality, the entire fiasco is a metaphor. Metaphor is a crucial concept to me because we invent our reality. Metaphor asserts that 'something' 'IS' another 'thing', so one might say: 'He is a lion!' To me it's the foundation of our 'experience', whether we call it literal or not. We do not see 'truth' at all, and reality is entirely made up.

To illustrate the depths of our mistake, we can indicate the interpretations and assumptions incarnated by the meeting of Europeans and Indigenous Native Americans. The artist George Catlin, who lived among these people and engendered the mythical idea of the 'noble savage', had an exhibition attended by Charles Dickens, who subsequently wrote an essay titled 'The Noble Savage' (1853), from which this quote is drawn:

> To come to the point at once, I beg to say that I have not the least belief in the Noble Savage. I consider him a prodigious nuisance, and an enormous superstition. His calling rum fire-water, and me a pale face, wholly fail to reconcile me to him. I don't care what he calls me. I call him a savage, and I call a savage a something highly desirable to be civilised off the face of the earth . . . [H]e is a savage — cruel, false, thievish, murderous; addicted more or less to grease, entrails and beastly customs; a wild animal with the questionable gift of boasting; a conceited, tiresome, blood-thirsty, monotonous humbug.[2]

---

2 Readers can find Dickens's essay in full at https://w3.ric.edu/faculty/rpotter/temp/noblesav.html

'Civilised' in these words translates to eradication or genocide. We struggle today as Russia attempts to strangle Ukraine with much the same attitude.

What are the differences? As artists we are trained to discriminate between sections and elements within a design. We note shapes and positioning within the picture plane that evoke differing tensions. Things in the middle inspire stasis and symmetry, but move them off-centre and tilting makes our mind want to reassert stability, so we engender visual dynamics. Corners and centres have a 'magnetic' attraction that can 'kill' movement. We negotiate to find the appropriate resolution. It is useful to consider the form in a simplistic abstract structure so that elements can be arranged without content getting in the way.

Rudolf Arnheim wrote *Art and Visual Perception* in 1954, which is the Gestalt manner of explaining how art is constructed. He considers the psychological forces engendered by balance. Then there is the importance and simplicity of shape, which eliminates ambiguity and ensures clarity of perception. Despite actuality, we can conjure qualities such as symmetry where it does not exist. Consider, for example, 'The Spinning Ballerina' illusion on YouTube: a dancer can spin and we can see their figure as spinning clockwise or counter-clockwise by choice.

Our sense of gravity is projected onto the image, and we already have a visual concept of solidity, which will confirm the assumption. We foreshorten and engage perspective to describe objects in space, in a somewhat culturally biased perception. Growth is a visual sensation, so we 'feel' a plant pushing up through the soil. We extend the logical binary progression to complete the form.

Overlapping and excluding parts of the image is the Western way of looking to create 'space'. We can adhere a sense of time to the geometry of space. This adds a sense of distance that is augmented by differing sizes of 'objects' in the perspectival 'space'.

Light cues us to positioning and creates 'space'. It enables the illusion of form in space. Shadows aid in this, although in the Japanese Notan style of composition shadows are eschewed. Georgia O'Keeffe follows these dictums in her paintings so there are no shadows. She credits Arthur Wesley Dow's book *Composition* (1899) for enlightening her.

Light can be as symbolic as colours. We associate emotions and feelings with them. However, all colours are apprehended only in their particular contrast. Many illusions show how we can assess the identical colour as variant depending on what it is contrasted with. Certain colours harmonise and are called complementary, such as red and green, blue and orange, and yellow and purple. These attract one another and vibrate if at similar tones, while analogous colours — those of a similar derivation, such as yellow, yellow-orange and yellow-green — repel one another and expand.

All art inspires movement, and the viewer's eye is encouraged to wander along a path set up by the artist, working within the confines of our pictorial predilection. Art also expresses a sense of time and timelessness. There is a dynamic interaction taking place overall, and the viewer interprets a multiple of interacting features. This is what makes art such a magical and engaging experience. Arnheim's book is a very important read for artists wishing to understand what they are doing.

We have two visual systems. Peripheral vision uses greyscale with rods, while there are three cones that accept certain wavelengths and allow us to see colour. When we turn to look to the side, we interpolate colour into our greyscale vision. You can test this for yourself by being aware of the tone of an object in your peripheral vision, and then seeing how the brain interpolates colour into the scenario when you turn to look at it directly.

There is a need to revisit our innate blueprint (as I imagine it). I think we are the sum of all possibilities and that we can activate biological changes by adopting new behaviours. Ambiguity and contradiction are qualities that I think would be present in our actual 'seeing' if we upgraded our way of seeing from classical Newtonian to quantum field. So I wonder if we are really hardwired, as they say, or merely expressing ingrained habits of looking. Can we 'see' a completely new reality that exists in a symbiotic relationship? Can we come into a quantum state of mind and leave behind our classical conditioning?

I create these abstract images to teach colour to students, but the images have another 'rationale' for me in that I base them on ambiguity and contradiction. They are still created intuitively, but I go against expectation wherever I can, building on ambiguity and contradiction. I see that as an *a priori* expectation. This flies in the face of treatises like Arnheim's *Art and Visual Perception*, which elevates 'simplicity' as the yardstick for seeing. The expectation is that the vision will become inchoate if confused.

But something else happens: I create a strange depth and unity that in many respects is more like our natural act of looking. The identity of forms is loosened so they have a shifting personality. As the viewer becomes aware of a section and follows it, it leads the eye into a completely new expectation. A section that is 'read' in one instance to be expressing a certain identity and movement, changes to become something else in a switch reminiscent of the Spinning Dancer illusion. Our capacity for imagination burgeons and the artwork becomes endlessly fascinating. In writing parlance, it has changed from a noun to a verb, resulting in action and flow.

The concept of quantum mechanics has its own complications, with differing interpretations. The prevailing Copenhagen interpretation by Danish physicist Niels Bohr considers the anomaly of whether something can be both a particle and a wave, which changes according to whether it is being measured/observed in the double-slit experiment. American-Brazilian-British theoretical physicist David Bohm presented a concept of electrons floating on an electromagnetic wave with various pulsing movements, which became the pilot wave theory. As an artist I identify ambiguity and contradiction with a loosening of identity and as a way of considering what 'quantum looking' would feel like.

It strikes me that we might be able to revolutionise our very way of 'seeing' and rescue our planet if we adopted those qualities among a new set of habituations. We have to stop eulogising 'truth' and 'reality' as immutable so we can embrace the world in a more complex way, hopefully opening up the dark windows of our perception. The abstracts I create are also imbued with animal qualities, so they are a bit removed from geometrical shapes. Perhaps we could learn to see as a tree might if we have made ourselves open to a new way of looking within a new symbiotic identity that eschews the 'individual'. Perhaps our planet could be resurrected.

David Eggleton
Tomorrow

Tomorrow, every now and then, the world might end,
but we will carry on.
Tomorrow, the whistle blows for the start of the week,
and that's where you come in.
Tomorrow is tomorrow, in aroha and sorrow.
Tomorrow is the spice paladin's heated aromas.
Tomorrow is the green flag of hills above window-sills.
Tomorrow is petals, proud and bright on magnolias.
Tomorrow, everything goes in the rumpus room:
the spillage, the abandoned card game,
the unemptied ashtray, the sticky whisky-glass.
Tomorrow is golden chimes, lighting up the lemon tree.
Tomorrow is wild mountain hail, and snow gentle to sea-level.
Tomorrow is tomorrow, in all its iridescence and mesmeric beauty.
Tomorrow, I got your back, and I want to hold your hand.
Tomorrow, we go as inseparable comrades, through the years.
Tomorrow will press you to coal, and then to rough diamond.
Tomorrow, the world is as blue as an orange.
Tomorrow, the world is going micro.
Tomorrow, each of us will follow,
backwards, sweeping the trail clean with a branch.
Tomorrow, see you on the flipside, sistah, in vinyl.
Tomorrow, from drist, rain will dringle and drumble
to form evanescent balms, rinses and vapours.
Tomorrow, more bafflegarb, gobbledegook, bumpf,
officialese, taradiddles and blatteration.
Tomorrow, never give in, never give in, never;
in nothing ever give in, except to accede to sense

and deeds of honour, for the sake of others.
Tomorrow, out of black: ka awatea, daybreak,
the ocean immense, eels crossing dark waters;
and above, a mollymawk's glide, tomorrow.

David Eggleton is a poet, writer and critic whose book *The Conch Trumpet* won the Poetry Award at the 2016 Ockham New Zealand Book Awards. In 2016, he received the Prime Minister's Award for Literary Achievement in Poetry. He was the New Zealand Poet Laureate from 2019 to 2022. His latest book is *Respirator: A Laureate Collection 2019–2022* (2023). He lives in Ōtepoti Dunedin.

Renee Liang 梁文蔚

Every grain is careful labour

憫農
鋤禾日當午
汗滴禾下土
誰知盤中飧
粒粒皆辛苦
李紳

Li Shen (772–846)

I'm taking my father out to lunch. His hand holds firmly to mine; I'm surprised how warm it is. I know he's trying not to lean on me, but he's getting more unsteady these days.

Our family loves to eat together. My father is a jump-in-the-full-glass kind of person, and it's never clearer than when he's around food. As a child I remember him coming home with buckets of freshly caught fish. My mother would sigh and start scaling while my father darted around, splashing water into pots in preparation for one of his big dinners. He used every implement in the kitchen, which he would then leave for my mother to clean. Nothing was wasted — leftover flesh was carefully extracted from bones and used for congee, the heads later boiled for creamy soup served with plump pillows of tofu.

On trips to Hong Kong to see family, my father would head for the wet markets within a few hours of touchdown, taking us kids with him 'because you need to learn these things'. We'd navigate the steep concrete steps of the Mid-Levels, placing our dusty sandals beside dogs panting on the narrow sidewalk, old ladies selling buttons and incense planted in tin cans waving their lazy messages to the sky. I remember the smell of animal sweat and the look of the chickens waiting in their cages; the flapping of the fish in too-shallow polystyrene boxes. My father would show us how to pick the liveliest meat ('it tastes better, it has to be as fresh as possible'), but he never let us watch the chickens having their throats slit. I sneaked back once when he wasn't looking. I wanted to know I could watch something die and not turn away.

Although my father liked to show off his chef skills, it was my mother who did the 'everyday' cooking. It wasn't her way to let us help, but she wanted us to see what she did. Marvellously, she performed every fine movement wearing oversize yellow gloves. 'Slice the meat against the grain, watch your fingers. Always strip this part out and throw it away, it's no good.' My mother was suspicious of plastic wrap, and even today she sniffs when I suggest using the microwave. Under her busy fingers, Cantonese-style cooking followed an easy logic: fresh food, enhanced with simple aromatics and a hot wok. I took in these lessons without even noticing. The smell of ginger slices hitting hot oil fills my kitchen now and brings me back to when I stood on a stool looking over my mother's shoulder.

Nup nup gai sun fu, my parents repeated often as we finally sat down to eat. Every grain is careful labour. My father explained that the line comes from a poem about farmers toiling to grow grain. To respect the labour of the farmers, we needed to eat all the rice in our bowls. We learned to chase down every speck with the points of our chopsticks, gathering little piles, sweeping them upwards to the lip of the bowl and into our mouths. Making loud slurping noises helped. The term 飯 *faan* in Cantonese refers to both the cooked rice and the meal as a whole. Rice is nourishment, a feast. Rice is needed to have a good life. It's why when we Cantonese greet each other, we say, 'Sik jor faan mei?' — 'Have you eaten rice/a meal yet?'

I think of this now when I heap rice into my father's bowl. These days, I am the one who takes him out in search of the freshest food. Our hunting grounds are the restaurants dotting the landscape of Tāmaki Makaurau. Our favourites glow like giant food bowls in my mental map of the city, and when I think of them my belly grows warm.

It's not the same as the wet markets of Hong Kong, but the thrill of the chase remains — I make food treasure maps wherever I go. My dad's maps cover his lifetime of travel: Vancouver, Tokyo, Beijing, Bangkok. He can still recall many of the places and their dishes. Once, when he found out I would be in Vancouver, he sent me on a wild goose chase to find restaurants that he'd last dined at 40 years ago with strict instructions: 'Try the fresh geoduck!' The mouth memories remain, even if the brick-and-mortar places have long since closed.

*N*up nup gai sun fu. My father smiles. 'That's enough rice,' he says, holding up his hand to stop me. But then he helps himself to more 餸 *sung*, the tasty dishes of meat, vegetables and seafood cooked to accompany the rice. In Cantonese culture, all the dishes are placed in the centre for sharing: we help ourselves to as much as we need. Young kids and seniors get the first pick. I watch my dad as he reaches for a prawn: his chopsticks are still steady. He's happy though when I sit beside him and make sure his plate is full. It means he's taught me well.

In our family, the love of food is the last to go. While my grandmother spent two decades sliding slowly under the surface of dementia, she continued to smile and open her mouth wide so we could slip in her favourite foods. Watching my father slide the same way, I hold on to him with food. At first I would ring him just to boast that I'd scored a treasured rare ingredient. I would ask him for details on how to cook a particular dish. But now, as more names and times slip through the widening sieve of his memory, I just talk about food, recalling past incredible meals eaten with his siblings or with us, name-dropping his favourite dishes. He's passed his mouth memories on to me.

*N*up nup gai sun fu. I can't remember how old I was when I found out this isn't just a line my parents used on us: every Chinese kid I know has heard this. I guess 'think of the poor children in China, finish what's on your plate' isn't very convincing for us actual Chinese children with our rich tradition of eating.

'Pity the farmer' by Tang Dynasty poet Li Shen is one of the classics still memorised by Chinese schoolchildren today. It's a brief poem: each of the four lines of five characters is succinct but carries a multiplicity of meanings. This explains the many varied translations available. None of them hit home for me, so I asked my friend Henry Liu, a professional translator, to help.

I am a baby Cantonese speaker, by which I mean that I stopped speaking my mother tongue fluently when I was three, when I started kindergarten in Auckland. I'm stuck with the language ability of a toddler. Henry grew up in Hong Kong, so he's fluent. When we first worked on a translation of Cantonese text for a different project, something magical happened. As Henry read the Cantonese to me, the seeds in my brain woke and started sending up shoots. I connected with ideas and concepts in a language I didn't know I still had. I *felt* the meaning of the words instead of having to translate them.

The half-remembered sounds acted like a plough, loosening the soil, letting the ideas breathe. Words, after all, are imprecise. They are marks representing memories and experiences unique to an individual, an attempt to imprint that feeling and pass it on to others. Words are swelling fragments of pluripotency, waiting to be dropped into someone's brain. Poetry knows about this multitude of meanings and harnesses it.

It's even more complex when those words are in a different language. If words are seeds, language is an ecosystem, reflecting a collective history. How can a translation accurately capture all these meanings when even the frame of reference is different?

The answer, Henry proposed, was to do my own personal translation. One that speaks to just me, for my time and place and experience. He's able to help me this way because of the history we share: we've been friends for a long time, and whenever we talk we can't help sharing about our delightful, frustrating, traditional fathers. We've resonated over their set habits and the way they prioritise certain qualities, such as hard work. We sympathise when our fathers don't understand our own priorities, which with bilingual children of migrants arrives from a place of being in-between. So much translation is needed when we try to communicate with the members of our own family. And now, Henry is about to become a father himself.

So we work collaboratively on the Li Shen poem translation: Henry speaks the text and explains the meanings of the characters, then he records the passage so I can listen to it over and over and let the word-seeds germinate. His voice becomes part of my experience of this poem, reminding me of the time I translated another poem this way with my father.

It's said that the Chinese unlocked the secret of immortality long ago: they live on through their children. As words fall through the cracks in my father's brain, I try to be there to catch them. I feel my steps take on the quickness his used to have. I see my daughter go faster yet, and fast-forward to the time when I hope she'll be there to hold my hand. When I use the cooking tricks my mother showed me, I call my son over to watch, but unlike my mother I encourage him to take the wok paddle in his hands. Not all lessons should be passed on unchanged.

I'm proud when my kids show signs of the food obsession my parents nurtured so well. My daughter dances when she discovers tofu jelly in the fridge, and I tell her about how my father used to go to a particular staircase in Hong Kong's Mid-Levels to buy tofu jelly from a monk — because 'Buddhist monks make the best tofu'. After dinner my daughter and I slurp tofu jelly, warmed in the microwave because the monk's version was always warm, and I wonder if she'll pass on the monk story to her kids.

I think of how my children's bodies hold parts of myself. It's been a long time since I fed them my milk, but maybe some molecules of that remain, wrapped around a neuron or ensconced as part of an eye. They have some of my DNA, of course; that's apparent in the way they wipe their noses or have an obsession with Googling information about parasites. But it's really the stories that I want them to absorb. I want them to understand that knowledge is adaptable. I want them to know that they help themselves by helping others. I want them to know that they can risk everything, as my parents did, to enter a different ecosystem. That although they won't always feel they belong, they can grow passable new roots.

My parents already spoke English when they migrated to Aotearoa in the 1970s, but they had to work hard to be understood. While my father worked 14-hour days as a paediatric registrar at Princess Mary Hospital in Auckland, my mother conquered her fear of driving and made the acquaintance of local women while out shopping. When I arrived a year later, my mother had to navigate the advice of Plunket nurses, advice that must have seemed deeply strange to her as they advised on the best cereals to start feeding solids and the importance of having a routine. I think of this now as I encounter new parents in my consulting room, equally confused, as our health system has barely budged from its monocultural foundations despite the aspirational rhetoric. I imagine echoing the thoughts of my parents as I say out loud that this has to change.

My parents worked hard to nurture the seeds they wanted to grow. I'm coming to realise that they didn't know what they were doing most of the time, just like me now as a parent.

I'm a paediatrician by training; parents often ask me for advice. Before I became a real-life parent I used to blithely quote from the research 'evidence'; these days I prefer to meet their eyes and tell them that whatever they're doing, they're doing well. It's hard to nurture seedlings; even harder to imagine the full-grown plant.

I wonder how differently I turned out from what my parents envisioned. I'm certain they still see me as a seedling. *Nup nup gai sun fu*. I'm teaching my children this phrase.

In Cantonese culture, time is circular. Our ancestors remain after they pass, in our bodies, in our minds and, most importantly, our actions. Our descendants are already seeded within us. As I hold my father's hand, I am holding the hands of his parents, too. As my father's time grows short, I feel a sense of urgency, wanting to spend time so I can inherit more of him. Have I got enough to sow his seeds into the future?

Looking into tomorrow, I can see the past. Looking into the past, I can see the future. Not all traditions need to be discarded. Some are soil for future growth. I am grateful to my parents for managing to teach me this, despite the difficulties in translation.

Nup nup gai sun fu. As I look at the characters of the poem, with my notes on meaning scribbled beneath, I see my possibilities. I find the meaning that speaks the most to me at this moment. I fill the spaces between the words with myself. And I make sure to eat every grain.

鋤禾日當午

at noon plough grains deep

汗滴禾下土

sweat drips to ripen seeds

誰知盤中飧

who knows the pain of nurture?

粒粒皆辛苦

every grain is careful labour.

With acknowledgements to Henry Liu for the creative translation of 憫農.

Renee Liang 梁文蔚 is a poet, playwright, paediatrician, medical researcher and essayist who has collaborated on visual arts works, film, opera and music; made theatre works; dramaturged; taught creative writing; and organised community initiatives such as New Kiwi Women Write, a writing workshop for migrant women. Renee has written, produced and toured eight plays, including *The Bone Feeder*, which was later adapted as an opera, one of the first Asian mainstage works in New Zealand. In 2018 she was appointed a Member of the New Zealand Order of Merit (MNZM) for services to the arts and she was also named the NEXT Woman of the Year for Arts and Culture.

KŌRERO

Aparecida Vilaça,
Dame Anne Salmond
and Witi Ihimaera
Ancestry, kin and
shared history

A conversation on whakapapa as a philosophy for the world

Aparecida Vilaça, Dame Anne Salmond and Witi Ihimaera have each demonstrated a lifetime of commitment — professional and personal — to indigenous environments around the world, both political and cultural. In this conversation, these three humanitarians talk to each other about whakapapa and shared histories, the relationship between humans and animals, and the possibility of hope.

Aparecida Vilaça is Professor of Social Anthropology at the National Museum, Federal University of Rio de Janeiro, Brazil. She has been a leading advocate for the Wari' people since 1986. She is the author of *Strange Enemies: Indigenous Agency and Scenes of Encounters in Amazonia* (2010), *Praying and Preying: Christianity in Indigenous Amazonia* (2016) and *Paletó and Me: Memories of My Indigenous Father* (2021), and co-editor, with Willard McCarty and Geoffrey Lloyd, of *Science in the Forest, Science in the Past* (2020), among other books. She lives in Rio de Janeiro, Brazil.

Dame Anne Salmond is a Distinguished Professor of Māori Studies and Anthropology at the University of Auckland Waipapa Taumata Rau. Her award-winning books include *The Trial of the Cannibal Dog: Captain Cook in the South Seas* (2003), *Aphrodite's Island: The European Discovery of Tahiti* (2009) and *Tears of Rangi: Experiments Across Worlds* (2017). She is a Foreign Associate of the National Academy of the Sciences in the United States, a Corresponding Fellow of the British Academy and a Fellow of the American Philosophical Society. In 2013 she was awarded the Rutherford Medal and selected as New Zealander of the Year. In 2019 she was awarded a Carl Friedrich von Siemens Award for lifetime achievements in research by the Alexander von Humboldt Foundation. During 2021–2022 she hosted two series of *Artefact* on prime-time television. She lives in Tāmaki Makaurau Auckland.

Witi Ihimaera (Te Whānau-a-Kai, Te Aitanga-a-Māhaki, Rongowhakaata, Ngāti Porou, Tūhoe) has had careers in literature, diplomacy and academia. He was Aotearoa New Zealand's first Māori novelist with his novel *Tangi* (1973), and maintains an active career as editor, essayist, filmmaker, playwright and critic. His latest book is *Navigating the Stars* (2020). Parallel to his work as a writer, he served for 16 years as a New Zealand diplomat, serving in Canberra, New York and Washington, DC. He is also Emeritus Professor of English at the University of Auckland Waipapa Taumata Rau.

Recognised as one of the world's leading Indigenous writers, his international awards include a Premio Ostana, 2010, and a Chevalier de l'Ordre des Arts et des Lettres, 2017. He is patron of Kotahi Rau Pukapuka Trust and, in 2022, was made President of Honour, New Zealand Society of Authors. He lives in Tāmaki Makaurau Auckland.

WI: Kia ora, Anne; kōrua ko Aparecida. Perhaps we can begin with the Māori and Wari' approaches to whakapapa — genealogy — and the worldviews that two sovereign Indigenous peoples have developed to determine their relationships with the world.

I like to think of whakapapa as being, actually, a framework; it provides a way of unifying the world and of ensuring our connectedness and, for Māori, the connections go all the way back to mythic origins — to Papatūānuku, the Earth Mother, whose name is embedded in that word, whaka*papa*. From her the framework was widened by her 70 sons, all gods, who populated all the natural, animal, supernatural and spiritual worlds. What's interesting for us as humans is that our god, Tāne, was also the creator of trees and birds. So in the mythology we immediately get this connection through one god. And through all Tāne's sibling relationships — for instance Tangaroa, god of the sea — were developed contractual and complementary relationships with the whole of existence, the entire world we live in.

My personal image for the potential that the whakapapa gifts to us is the double helix: the structure of the DNA molecule. It's able to take a shape — what scientists call the 'I-motif' shape — and in this state scientists are trying to figure out what its purpose is. Well, I think Māori might say that the I-motif offers us a way not only of looking at resourcing ourselves from the past but also of conceptualising the future. Thinking of its gifts not only as an inheritance but as an investment. In your case, Anne, I know you see immense potential of whakapapa providing a guiding philosophy in establishing principles of kaitiaki-ship in all our bureaucracies — legal, corporate, free market and so on — looking after all our environments for the benefit of all.

AS: Kia ora, Witi. The thing I love about whakapapa is that it's not anthropocentric. It's a philosophy that doesn't put humans at the top of the cosmos, or at its heart. The entire cosmos is linked through kinship and through reciprocal exchange. I was fascinated, Witi, to hear about this I-motif and the double helix, because Pei Te Hurinui Jones says that the double spiral represents the successive stages of the emergence of the cosmos — and humans come quite late in the story. When you read those cosmological chants, or you hear them chanted, humans show up quite late.

And so, when thinking about something like climate change or water, or waterways or forests, or indeed how we treat each other as people — for me they're all linked and we're all kin on some level. When we think about the fate of the forest, or the fate of another human being, it's a planetary thing — the whole cosmos is linked up through this philosophy: our fates are tied together. It works against the alienation you find in so much neoliberal philosophy, where humans are just resources, along with rivers and oceans and plants and animals, and we take everything we can from them without returning, to make a profit. That's a tragic way of viewing our existence in the world.

I love this idea of reciprocity and exchange that goes beyond the human, that says other people are at the heart of it as well. Witi — right from the time we were young: that fellow feeling was there. And I'm thinking about my mother, too — I'll talk about her when we talk about our mentors.

So, Aparecida, I think for us, there's a kind of hope, a vision of hope, and a way of thinking about the world — where we're not here just to rip each other off or bomb each other into extinction, as they're doing in Ukraine — and how we can survive as well. So over to you — ki a koe!

AV: Thank you for so many good ideas. I have worked for 30 years, or almost 40, with Wari' people, who live in southwest Amazonia, Brazil, close to the border with Bolivia. They are around 4000 people, scattered in seven villages, and their first contact with non-indigenous white people happened in the middle of the 1950s, so not a long time ago, for us. So they've been through massacres and more.

Usually Amazonian people don't have ancestors. They collectivise the dead. They try not to relate to them because they are afraid the dead will take the living to go with them. To them, the dead are always looking for their relatives, and sometimes they want to take them to live with them in the world of the dead. So: no ancestry — a huge difference. This is not just the Wari', but most Amazonian peoples: they have no ancestry.

But in mythic times, animals and humans, the future humans: they are all humans.

There were no animals, and there was no creation time. The Wari' say things always existed — they just transformed. There was a kind of people, and then something happened and they became another kind of people. So what happened from mythic times to present times is that humans differentiated from animals, but just their bodies; they have a common soul, or spirit. So the Wari' see themselves as humans and the animals see themselves as humans, too.

But the Wari' cannot see the animals as humans, of course, except for the shaman, because they do not have special eyes. So the Wari' are able to kill and eat other human forms, because they just see them as animals. But the common human-ness means that they have to treat the animal forms well. When they are about to kill them, they have to behave well, to follow rules, they have to cook them carefully and very fast — because for them, the animals are immortals. When you kill an animal the animal's spirit goes back to his house, to his family — and again and again he'll be close to the human, he'll be killed, and then he'll come back to his own relatives. So the Wari' say they are the mortal people — because when they die, they will not come back to their relatives; they go to the world of the dead, the place that was traditionally the underwater, where they are young again, and they marry again and have kids.

So if I can think of some philosophy of life, it's that everyone is human; they live in a world populated by humans. But there are barriers: you cannot always see animals as humans — only the shamans are able to mediate, to negotiate between the two forms. And the animal forms, if not treated well, can take revenge: they can harm or kill a human. In doing this they take the human being to live with them, as the animals are always desiring human beings. They want to make them their kin. They want to bring them to live with them. So that's the balance the Wari' have established in their lives. Although they live in a world populated by human beings, they have to eat. Their shamans exist as mediators to negotiate with the animal forms.

WI: It's an amazing worldview. In many ways there is no real difference between this and the way Māori have approached existence — except that instead of thinking of everyone as humans, Māori think of everyone in relationships, and in terms of connectedness, and with animals and fish and birds, and with our conduct with one another.

AS: I am intrigued to know how the forest figured in the Wari' world. You're talking about Amazonia, one of the great forests of the planet — the lungs of the planet, people often say. This relationship between peoples and animals: how does the forest work in with that?

AV: The forest is the heart of the animal forms. So while the human forms might see a forest, the animal forms see a village — they have houses and they live with their families. Amazonia therefore exists in two different perspectives — not as one world or one nature, but, in fact, as several different worlds or natures. It all depends on who is seeing and acting. A human form might drink fermented maize beer. Similarly, although the jaguar's drink is blood, he will call his drink by the same name as the maize beer.

There is no kind of given universe. Rather, there are different perspectives that do not add up — they are just different. The world is populated by different beings that *see* things differently. In the forest, the Wari' might see a papaya, but the jaguar sees a rodent, an animal. Whose perspective do you have to negotiate? If you go to the forest and you see a papaya, and someone says, 'Oh, I like this rodent', then you have to figure out it's from the view of the jaguar, and not a human being, like you. Then you *understand*: the jaguar sees the blood, so this 'person' must be a jaguar.

So the forest is forest just for us. We think that when we die, we don't see anything, but it's populated by people — lots of houses, lots of people. We look at these people and we see fish, for example, but they are human beings. Life is permeated by this idea of 'Who am I talking to?' and 'What kind of being is this being?' — it's very delicate and you have to pay attention all the time. You can be distracted easily — and become a jaguar's prey, if you don't pay attention.

AS: So in a way you're talking about shamans and I'm talking about tohunga, the knowledgeable experts, and some of those people were matakite — some of them had eyes that could see, but usually they see into the past and future, and the world spins around them in a way, but they can go to the realm of the ancestors. It's a bit different, but there is that fact that it's not just one world.

WI: My brain is going into overdrive right now, Aparecida, thinking of all the connections and disconnections between Māori and the Wari'! While Māori history arose out of the Pacific oceanic world, in Aotearoa the forest was also our home. And while we might not have considered ourselves as the one type of being, I hear echoes of Māori thought in the ways, for instance, in which we always had to negotiate whenever we were navigating the various domains of Te Waonui a Tāne, Tāne's forest. The bark of a kauri tree was thought of as being similar to the skin of the whale, and so on.

I have to be mindful, however, that we're talking about people in two different timeframes. We're two Indigenous tribes but the Wari' are more primal, having only been discovered by the rest of the world in 1950.

AV: Yes, the historical time is different. I've met people who have lived most of their lives in the forest without ever meeting a white man, without ever knowing anything about European civilisation or culture. My Wari' father, Paletó, until he was 35 he never met (well, just for war, for killing) a white man or had any kind of talk or relationship or exchange with a white person. So it's different. When I began my fieldwork in 1986, there were lots of elders who had lived most of their lives in the forest — they were monolingual, they spoke only their own language. And even until now the elders do not speak Portuguese.

WI: I think that for our world to start considering, today, that animals and humans are all humans would be revolutionary. Although, when I think about it, it's only the reverse of how medievalists classified humans — but as animals. They defined humanity as 'animal rationales', and Jonathan Swift, the author of *Gulliver's Travels*, satirically defined humankind as animal *rationis capax* — capable of acting rationally. Swift didn't actually believe this, and the evidence has proved devastatingly otherwise.

AV: I think there is something very interesting in this, because in our scientific and evolutionary thoughts we think we are connected to animals through our body, in an evolutionary chain, but the Wari' are not connected through their bodies but through their *souls*, because the bodies are radically different. Their souls are connected because they are human through their souls. The animals see themselves as humans,

142

but nobody else sees them as humans except the shamans. So what the Wari' see is a radical difference in body between them and the animals, but they know they have a human soul and they know the animals see themselves as humans — that they have houses, rituals, etc.

AS: You've referred, Aparecida, to your close relationship with your Wari' father, Paletó, and yet you're a white person. So how did that work?

AV: Paletó was a very curious man. Curious and open-minded. The white people killed all his family. In the 1950s they used to go into the villages while people were sleeping — with guns. They'd kill a whole village, and in one of those attacks they killed the whole family of Paletó — his wife and daughter.

I used to ask Paletó: 'Aren't you mad at me, because those are kind of "my" people?' And he would say: 'Oh no, you live in the south, far away; you have nothing to do with those people who killed.' He was very generous with me, and, being curious and open-minded, he wanted to know me, too — he extracted as much as he could from me, too. It was a kind of balanced relationship: he told me a lot and had many questions about my culture. And for the first time he came to a big town like Rio de Janeiro with me. It was fascinating for him, and he took advantage in a way — in an intellectual way, and in an emotional way.

WI: So maybe this would be a good moment to widen our kōrero and to look at Māori, at Wari', at all Indigenous peoples, from a global perspective. There are estimated to be more than 476 million of us in the world, which is about 6 per cent of the global population.

We are to be found in over 70 countries, we come under the United Nations Declaration on the Rights of Indigenous Peoples, and there are other instruments that preserve our rights to equity, equality and justice — but we don't have the power to even think of establishing any kind of recognition for, for instance, the whakapapa rights of human people. There are all sorts of mechanisms, but we've never been able to, internationally, create a force that would allow, for instance, change around some of the issues we have been talking about.

One of the reasons for this is that we account for some 19 per cent of the world's *extreme* poor. Another is that we have been historically impoverished and — I can't help saying it — racially profiled. Man's inhumanity to man (we hear that phrase all the time) is one thing, but man's inhumanity to Indigenous man, woman and child is something else. The systemic denial to us of an identity that acknowledges our equal worth, scientific, cultural or otherwise, and which continues to close off our political options for advancement has been tino whakamataku.

AS: It's interesting. Looking at the history of our country — our shared history — I've tried to understand its ebbs and flows. And we've had moments at which almost everything seemed possible. When Te Tiriti o Waitangi was debated and signed, for instance, promises were made that were *very* significant: between the Queen and the rangatira, the leaders, but also the hapū, the kin groups, and the ordinary people of the land. It was phrased as a gift exchange, which is really interesting.

And so that first ture, the rangatira gift to the Queen, was this thing called 'kāwanatanga'. No one really knew what it was at the time. Māori knew there were governors, or 'kawana'. They knew that there were governors in New South Wales; they'd been there, they'd met them and some had stayed in their houses. And Māori agreed to give kāwanatanga to the Queen — in perpetuity. It's quite absolute, the way that gift is phrased. But in exchange, the Queen agreed with the rangatira, the chiefs, the leaders, the hapū, and *all* the people of New Zealand — in the plural — to their 'Tino rangatiratanga'. That is, to their absolute chiefly authority: their self-determination over their lands and their dwelling places, and all of their lands and their ancestral treasures.

So that was agreed by the Queen — it wasn't a gift. She agreed that it was already there, it wasn't a matter of doubt; it was agreed and ratified. And in the last ture, the last law or clause of Te Tiriti, the Queen agreed to 'tiaki' — to look after — 'nga tangata māori', 'indigenous', 'ordinary', 'everyday' — just normal — people, as opposed to the incoming strangers, and that nga tangata māori, in their personal capacities, should have *exactly equal tikanga* with those of her subjects, the people of England.

Academic and historian Charles Royal talks about what he calls an indigenously inspired democracy, in which everyone is equal — absolutely equal — along with their tikanga. There was a lot of hope, but also a lot of doubt, if you listen to the speeches of the rangatira when they were debating Te Tiriti.

The people with the hope swung the day. At that moment, on 6 February 1840, a lot of things were possible. And then the government came in and smashed the promises — so many of them — almost immediately. And you're right, Witi, it was monstrous, because these promises were made in the name of the Queen. And when they began to be broken, well, people like William Martin, New Zealand's first chief justice, and a fluent speaker of te reo, was furious — he protested at every step when people were smashing the law, and there were governors who just seized land. Martin said that the honour of the Crown was at stake. He said as long as we benefit from the agreements that were made in Te Tiriti, we must uphold them. For me, that's still true in our country.

We have this history that turned from a moment of hope to moments of darkness and bitterness. What happened in the New Zealand Wars was terrible: villages smashed, children killed, people burned in their homes . . . And that history was hidden for a long time and is now being brought to light, in the school curriculum.

So yes, enlightened at times, and the hope is there. The promises were made, and still can be fulfilled. I endorse Charles Royal's idea of an indigenously inspired democracy. Equality of humans, as persons, is a fundamental principle: the dignity, the mana of each of us — but with our different tikanga. And we haven't done that; we are trying, but we have these big debates, for instance on whether mātauranga Māori is a science — some people say, no, it's not; the respect is not there. We still behave badly day by day, hurting people, harming them. But it doesn't have to be that way.

AV: With the situation in Brazil, well, the Indigenous people are several — nor do they speak a related language, so you have 200 different countries inside what we call 'Brazil'. It's not easy for them to relate. They have organisations but local ones, because they do not speak the same language and they have different ways of being — and they are not considered by the non-indigenous people as part of our society. They have their own villages, and they are not part of the rest.

So this is different from what happens with you, and different to you today. For instance, there are no more than a handful of Indigenous people who have a PhD, and this is only from three years ago. Indigenous people did not use to go to university, they did not have political voice. Now, though, they are organising themselves, and some of them are studying law. But this is really recent — just now happening. And they are not strong enough in this moment to battle, to face the kinds of atrocities that are happening to them.

I don't know about hope — I'd like to talk about hope, but really we are desperate; we don't know what to do — because everything is subtle — and the laws are passed by the majority, and Indigenous people are losing what they were guaranteed in the 1980s.

It's not only the government affecting the Indigenous people, but also the missionaries — the evangelical missionaries. They are everywhere and they are destroying souls, because what they say is that the Indigenous views that animals are humans is something that came from the devil, and it's because they are ignorant. And the missionaries say this explicitly — they do not hide their thoughts. They are there converting people, convincing them that their beautiful worldview — their whole set of thoughts, their way of life — it's a lie and it's malignant; it's bad. These missionaries are everywhere. And they are of course very close to the actual government, which allows those evangelical missionaries to go deeper and deeper into the forest and contact even uncontacted tribes. We still have tribes here in Brazil that never — never *ever* — had any contact with the whites. So now the government is allowing the missionaries to reach even those tribes, so it's not just a kind of physical danger for the Indigenous people because of new viruses and bacteria, etc., but a danger for their thoughts, their lives . . .

I hope things will change.

And you know, Witi, I was thinking of you as I was, by chance, studying Indigenous literature, here in Brazil. There are no Indigenous writers from the past, just young people writing today. And they seldom write fiction, because when they do write fiction their books go to the children's book category. Because when you talk about magic and transformation and things like that, people immediately classify their books as children's stuff. That's something to think about — people do not understand that there is Indigenous magic in the world, and it's not just for children.

WI: I find it fascinating that, throughout history, we've tended to compartmentalise our way of looking at our existence, and in that compartmentalisation has been created a lot of division in the way in which we look at what is really complementary: we talk about the environment being different to everything else; we talk about animals being different; we talk about fish as being different. But the Wari' seem to be offering us an alternative way of looking. It's almost like an arrow coming out of the past. And I enjoy arrows coming from the past! Can such an arrow coming from a small Amazonian tribe make any difference to our future? I don't know, but in many ways that's a metaphor for what Indigenous people in our world have been doing: attempting to upset the current Western European way of thinking, and saying, *Well, look at this in other ways. Find a new whakapapa for the future.*

So, as far as Aotearoa is concerned . . . Once upon a time, although the binary in New Zealand was very entrenched — Māori on one side, and Pākehā on the other — and we went to war with each other, the irony was that over time that Treaty Anne referred to earlier began to be seen by Māori as offering conflict resolution. People in my day used to say the Treaty was a fraud, but, as its status as a legal document began to be acknowledged, Māori and Pākehā began to use it to establish institutional change. Out of that, for instance, came the Waitangi Tribunal, which was established in 1975, based on the objective of healing the past. I'm cutting corners here, because it's been a huge task to set up a restitution process, as well as a change process. But why I am mentioning this is that I am thinking of the Wari' people and I want to tell you, Aparecida, that there was a time in our history when it was thought that Māori were a dying race and that all that could be done for us was to smooth the pillow so that our death would be comfortable.

Between the Waitangi Tribunal's establishment and up to 2014, it has settled 68 major land claims. And when the Tribunal settled the claim of one of my iwi, Rongowhakaata, in 2011, it acknowledged that Tūranga-a-Kiwa Gisborne grievances were significantly worse than those of any other tribe in New Zealand, including the illegal execution of 122 people by Crown forces. The Treaty negotiations minister, Chris Finlayson, apologised on behalf of the Crown for Treaty breaches, including the unjustified use of military force at Tūranga, the detention without trial of Rongowhakaata prisoners on the Chatham Islands, the summary execution of prisoners at Ngātapa in 1869, and the effective confiscation of a large area of Rongowhakaata land.

Fast-forward to 2022, and a three-year exhibition celebrating Rongowhakaata iwi and culture ended its showing at Te Papa Tongarewa, subtitled 'a story of shadow and light'. So what I'm trying to say here, Aparecida, is that it's been a very long journey for us. Whether we are Māori or Wari', we must not let the compulsions of history trap us.

Anne Kennedy

Dangeropportunity
on the lake

The throat of the planet is unlocking.
Mudfish bubble in the magical Fantalake.
The sun goes down and the sun goes down.

We were sunbathing on the plastic lotuschairs,
our meds mixed with the orangedyed pollenspores.

In the queue at the twinpeak supermarket,
we acted nonchalant, packetmules to the landfill.

Okay the throat of the planet has come onstage
in its polyester tanglegreen. The loaded whitemen
in the circle are studying their programs.

The lakes's gonna blow and sea's gonna blow.
Give it up for the lake, the sea, and for you and me.

Meanwhile the grey research of the scientists
floats among the toys in the children's rooms.

In the aircondished houses among the trees
the trees pray through their carbon mantillas.

It's one minute to the moment when
it's not over till the throat of the planet sings
but the dead-faced dictator is raising his baton

the button is the button connected to de
weather forecast for the foreseeable future.

We must wake from our petroljourneys
where we knocked our heads on the flyovers
of the *Monopoly* winners. It's time to

da-da-*da*-da, it's time to stop being leftpolite.
It's time to rush through the aperture,
the last catdoor, can you tell me how to get to

the soggy cardboard polling booth floating
in no matter no matter vote vote vote

for where the air is sweet, for the silence
of the swan on the water.

Anne Kennedy is a poet, fiction writer, screenplay editor and creative writing teacher. Her most recent books are *The Sea Walks into a Wall* (2021), shortlisted for the Mary and Peter Biggs Award for Poetry at the 2022 Ockham New Zealand Book Awards, and *The Ice Shelf* (2018). She was the recipient of the Prime Minister's Award for Literary Achievement in Poetry in 2021, as well as the New Zealand Post Book Award for Poetry (2013), the Montana New Zealand Book Award for Poetry (2004) and the Katherine Mansfield Memorial Award (1984). She lives in Tāmaki Makaurau Auckland.

Laura Jean McKay

Come and see it all the way from town

Always rocks, just rocks. Random through the mid paddock and hard to get to over the ridge. Dad said it was bad farming, bad riding. These rocks cropped up at angles and seemed to shift. Dad hadn't been in the top paddocks since he did his hip. Stayed on the porch shining his spotlight and muttering at us to keep our voices down.

'It's weird.' Sam followed the light with their eyes, through the sheep paddock to the top of the hill.

'Don't worry about Dad. He just likes the quiet.'

'The rocks, I mean. There's an edge.'

'A stolen edge.'

'He'll hear you.'

OK to steal land, apparently; not OK to say it. I hissed about colonisation, but Sam kept their eyes fixed on the paddock.

'Last time I was up there I heard voices,' they said. 'Not outside my head. Strange thoughts.'

'Maybe go up there before you check your crops next time.'

Sam wouldn't go on the quad bike with me after that, not for nothing.

Dusk time. Lonely time. I howled over the ridge wanting Jacko to howl with me. The dog just looked very sad about the howling. Sun lit up the rocky side — that orange way — and I tipped the quad over the edge, rumbling down on the other side: a golden green with dark grey slabs sticking out of it. The rocks bigger there, trees and gorse sparse.

'We lost you in this — you were just a little pup,' I told Jacko. 'Didn't we? Didn't we?'

The dog toured the base of one of the upcrops where the dirt had been disturbed — like a giant mushroom had pushed through, except the mushroom was a cloudy hunk of granite. Speckled up close like a skylark egg. He came around the other side sniffing at the base. Then he said something.

'What?' I turned my gaze on Jacko: always was convinced there was more to that mutt than terrier.

Back down the hill I told Sam that Jacko could suddenly talk. I didn't say I'd also seen Sam in the valley, torchlight flashing around. Not very stealth.

Sam grinned at me, red-eyed, from the couch. Said, 'Of course he can', and started singing 'On Top of Old Smokey' until Jacko reluctantly wrinkled his lips, wailed along, too.

'But I heard Jacko say *What's up?*,' I yelled over them.

'What's up with you? What about you?' Sam jostled Jacko's ears until the dog moved away.

'Actually, he just said *What.*'

Sam squinted at me. Got up and shut the door because Dad was out on the porch with his lights and notebook — a spotter, was Dad.

'You think Jacko said it?'

'Well, not like I saw his lips move or anything, but—'

'For me it was *bloomin'.*'

'Like, swearing? Jacko!'

Sam shook their head. 'Jacko wasn't even there that time.'

We wanted to camp up on the hill. Sam had done a survival course last autumn that I was apparently too young for, so they know how to pack a tent, a mat and cooker, and the best food like cans and things. How to replace the wool blankets with camphor-smelling sleeping bags. Dad nodded approvingly from his chair. The sun was doing some late-afternoon things so he didn't need a spotlight for a direct view to the rocky top. 'Take lamps. Lots of lamps.'

I said, 'Got it!' and pushed Sam out of the way. I was going to drive the damn quad at least.

'It's not a competition,' Sam said, climbing on the back with extra torches and headlamps. I whistled. Jacko pretended not to hear me. But when I started the quad, the dog jumped up and settled next to Sam.

Sam yelled how I should go the goat track because of all the gear. I took the lip. They swore and clung on when we tilted over the top, but then got to see how great a spot it was.

I switched off the bike. The voices were immediate.

'Jacko!'

Sam shushed me. The seat was so comfortably worn with Dad's bum dents I didn't want to leave anyway. Sam seemed contented on the back under the gear, too. Wind hummed around us. Jacko started digging the base of the nearest rock. Sam edged off the bike to where Jacko was muttering away.

'That dog's been pretending he can't talk this whole time,' I called. But Sam pressed close to the rock.

'Up.'

I climbed off the quad muttering how I wasn't a dog.

Sam looked at me. 'That was the word.'

'What?'

'Up. The rock said *Turn it up*.'

'The rock said *Turn it up*?'

Sam nodded, listening still. I wriggled into the small ditch Jacko had made, face against the stone — scratchy, freezing. My ear cold and my steadying hand.

Sam knew how to make a fire and had brought stale cinnamon buns from the bakery they worked at in town. Toasted up, the icing melted and the sweet bread was lovely, burnt. Jacko liked it, too. We didn't talk, we stayed quiet. Collected repeated rock words like we once collected river stones. From the house veranda came a series of flashes from the spotlight. Sam had learned Morse code in the survival course.

'What's it say?'

'Nothing. It doesn't even make sense.'

Still, we flashed back, longer and longer with the lights until Dad was either satisfied or fell asleep at the switch.

Sam could still make out the words over the quad engine when I wound down the morning hill.

'*What*,' Sam shouted from the back. '*Up.*'

Even in the house, where Dad had made toast, we could hear it. We took the peanut butter and plates out to the porch.

'Go on,' Sam whispered, taking a big bite.

'You tell him,' I whispered back. Sam pointed at their mouth. Full. Impossible to talk.

'Shithead,' I said.

'Excuse me now?' Dad heard that.

'But Dad, the rocks are saying *bloomin'* and—'

'The rocks aren't saying *bloomin'*,' said Dad.

'It's not swearing if Sam heard it, too . . .' I waited for Sam to tell me I was being a whiney bitch, but Sam looked stunned — like the possums we catch in the torchlight. Dad up and left. Finally done with us, I thought.

He came back again with two old exercise books, some pens.

'Never thought you two would be still long enough. Well, you're in for it now.'

'We don't have homework,' Sam told him, giving me a Dad's-losing-it look. 'It's holiday—' Sam broke off. Another voice. We all heard it and looked up the hill, still dark against the brightening sky. Dad motioned Sam to write the rock words in their book, then made corrections.

'Not *what*, but *watt*. Not *bloomin'* but *lumen*. They're after our light. They reckon there's light — electricity — coming from our bodies and they're asking about it. Took me ages to understand that. At first the words were in te reo — but I don't know much about that.' He coughed and hid his face, adjusted his glasses, turned on the spotlight again. 'Now they've switched to English. I'm showing them a stronger light here. They're not much keen on it, though.'

'How long have you been talking to them, Dad?'

'Since your mum. She's the one told me about it. Said they've been doing it forever. I didn't listen to her either.'

'Mum was ages ago.' We all went silent thinking about her in our separate ways.

How she went around the place with so much energy, so bright. 'Well, what else have they been saying?'

'That the people who were here before us were better at sharing.'

D ad made us wait until night, and then it took ages to get him up and settled on the quad.

'You drive,' I told Sam, but they gave me a little push towards the wheel. 'You're better at it.'

I edged up there so slow, the quad light picking up every pothole. I was sure we'd lose Dad, but every time I glanced back he was there on the rear seat with Jacko on his knee and Sam beside. When I got to the lip he told me to turn off the quad beam so we tipped over into darkness — broad shapes of the rocks below. We all heard the word — as though someone had flicked a switch — but Sam said it first.

'*Light.*'

Laura Jean McKay is the author of *The Animals in That Country* (2020), winner of the Arthur C. Clarke Award, the Victorian Prize for Literature, the ABIA Small Publishers Adult Book of the Year and an Aurealis Award for Best Science Fiction Novel. She is an adjunct lecturer in creative writing at Massey University Te Kunenga ki Pūrehuroa. She was awarded an NZSA Waitangi Day Literary Honour in 2022. Her latest book, *Gunflower* (2023), is a collection of short fiction. She lives in Meeanjin Brisbane, on unceded Turrbal and Jagera Country.

Essa Ranapiri and
Michelle Rahurahu
Ram Raid

Taane stands in front of the plate glass
sees their reflection move when they do
roots fingering the cracks in pavement
they hold a hammer in their right hand
& a great hunger in their left, they're searching
for a weakness in the cleaned surface
they've stretched their legs in preparation

the children are often on the street,
it is the only flat that welcomes them,
it offers its grit for sleeping & underneath Papa
listens to their uneven breathing,
in the world of dreams their ancestors
kick against their Mother
or toss restlessly like worms muttering
there is more in store for us than cages.
when the children wake, this new night has
many barriers, bars, bollards, barricades;

look at how the grown-ups have cling-wrapped
their goods with moral panic,
they lock their Nissan Navaras & their
Toyota Aquas with a *woop wop*
& eye any kid in a hoodie with suspicion,
muttering,
O it must be Taane! radicalising the youth!
driving a wedge between the generations!
— some people become accustomed to air-
conditioned breezes —
like there isn't something wild they've caught
inside their class insulation

the bubs are young yet recall when Rangi
watched over them all, eyes wet as the sea
now security cameras laser into their backs,
they're stung by the buzz of anti-loiter alarms
in this place you're not even allowed
to just exist in idle, on their own land
spikes grow under bridges & on park benches
gotta keep them moving like kiore
in a Cookhouse
& when the oceans rise they'll swim
till exhaustion or land
but they don't know where they'll end up
after the fall
they could have sworn they'd been under
this tremendous pressure before

the grown-ups have their legislation
stapled to the back of their eyes
each line compressed into the cartridge of a taser
each clause crouching inside the barrel of a gun
in this just a regular random checkpoint stop
O you youth have nothing to be afraid of!
except for being locked up & locked up &

the bubs are young but recall when Taane
pressed their legs against the weight of the Sky
& te Ao shattered,
they yearn to decorate the pavement with stars
Rangi's pain just raining over them but
Rangi's pain is what keeps the lights on
& Taane knows this
if everything here is built on shit

on top of shit on top of Papa
then how do you get it out without
razing their cities to the ground
Taane got revolution in a lockgrip
on the steering wheel
foot pressed hard against the accelerator
a lurching motion then
bull bar into glass
the children all *whoop whoop*
as the vehicle smashes past any barrier
& opens up the world
for them

Essa Ranapiri (Ngaati Raukawa, Te Arawa, Ngaati Pukeko, Clan Gunn) lives on Ngaati Wairere whenua. Author of *ransack* (2019) and *ECHIDNA* (2022). Co-editor of *Kupu Toi Takataapui / Takataapui Literary Journal* with Michelle Rahurahu. They have a great love for language, LAND BACK and hot chips. They will write until they're dead.

Michelle Rahurahu is a writer living in the cradle of Ngaai Tuuaahuriri, but heralding from Te Moana-a-Toi. She has a Master of Arts in creative writing from the International Institute of Modern Letters, where she won the Modern Letters Fiction Prize and where her manuscript 'Pōhara' was shortlisted for the Michael Gifkins Prize.

Alice Te Punga Somerville
Holding the line

you're not at the centre; there are no centres
you're just standing there
one node in a massive network
like the rest of us

In 1994, the foundational Māori writer J. C. Sturm spoke in an interview about a metaphor she engages in her poem 'Splitting the Stone'. She describes the 'green space' as the space of artistic production that can be found, for her at least, 'between the roses and the taupata'. Taupata — a plant that grows as a shrub or tree and has very shiny, fat green leaves — stands in for the Māori side, while the roses are the English side. She means the plants to refer to cultural background but also respective literary traditions. Her point is about the productive creative work that can take place when one manages to find space between the two.

Taupata has been used strategically as a 'pioneer' plant (in conservation speak #facepalm) because it is extremely hardy and salt-resistant, and so is one of the first plants in a process of gradual replanting and rejuvenation of Matiu Somes, an island that was almost completely cleared. Matiu Somes is a very small island in the middle of Wellington Harbour. You can walk around it in about 45 minutes, and that's if you stop to enjoy the view as you go. After being acquired (to put it politely) by the Crown in the nineteenth century, the island has been used by Europeans as a prison, a human quarantine, an animal quarantine and a scientific laboratory. Over a century of these various uses left it completely barren and in dire need of life. Over the past few decades, the island has been gradually replanted. But . . . what does it mean to restore something?

One day I sat with my cousin outside the iwi house on the island (it's a three-bedroom suburban-style house that looks like it has been Photoshopped in from Epuni), when someone connected with replanting stopped by for a chat. We talked about plant removal, and how some of the trees and other plants that had arrived on the island weren't actually indigenous to it. We asked about which plants didn't really belong here, and the person mentioned pine trees, which didn't surprise us, but then she said there were also some pōhutukawa. We were confused. Well, the person explained, pōhutukawa doesn't naturally occur south of a horizontal line about halfway up the North Island. We know what foreign means (pine!), but naturally occurring in this case meant without any human meddling. Restoring nature to its most natural form, according to this logic, prefers an ecosystem free of human intervention. Free of human action. Well, free of Māori actions. But achieved, propped up and maintained in the twenty-first century by non-Māori actions.

We may wish to turn back time, as Cher would say, but turn it back to when?

Fine lines

There are rocks and hard places. Chickens and eggs. Devils and deep blue sea. Knife edges. When we talk of rebuilding our world/s, what are we aiming for? Which worlds are we talking about? Who gets to inhabit them? Whose absences do those worlds require?

When we think about the past months, years, decades, centuries of oppression, how do we decide about which practices and values we see in our pasts that we want to continue, revitalise, reproduce? Or do we seek to make something new? It can feel like the two options are equally tricky.

When we imagine Māori futures, and futures of Māori, do we wish to *Make Aotearoa Great Again*, borrowing the frame of a Trumpian dystopia? While this rallying cry pretends to be about hope, its obsession is with returning to a past that never existed. It attempts to retrofit a version of the nation that excludes, violates, undermines and disregards the many people whose very presence is both sign and symptom of the unequal power structures of the past to which it advocates a return. There's a danger that, in the wrong hands,

When we imagine Māori futures, and futures of Māori, do we need to *stop living in the past* so we can prepare to walk with confidence into the future? It sounds good in theory to live beyond the legacy of the past two centuries — but so much of the present is structured by those two centuries that it is like when my daughter is nearly at our front door, turns back to call out to me (as I walk along the corridor loaded with our bags and jackets) 'OK, I'll race you to the door!' It's cute when it's a four-year-old and her māmā — but it's less cute tradition and 'the past' can be wielded as a weapon to keep familiar power structures in place. There is not enough room (or safety) in narrow versions of MAGA to challenge the insidious ways that patriarchy, homophobia, anti-blackness and capitalism have crept into some versions of 'Aotearoa'.

when it's people calling back at us: stop bringing up catalogues of grievances and insults and slights and massacres and thefts, stop moaning because other people in other places (or in this place) have it worse, stop trying to make it about race when we're all New Zealanders anyway!

The rock and the hard place leave us perched on a precipice. Neither option is OK: not the one where we selectively resuscitate a version of our pasts that serves to reinforce the effects of two centuries of inequalities and humiliations, and not the one that values neither the riches of the past nor the lessons learned the hard way.

A muri, a mua

There's that old saying about walking backwards into the future. I remember my first year at Auckland uni, when I was 18 and (to provide chronological markers) I was wearing 'No Fear' t-shirts with coloured baggy jeans. I was learning te reo Māori from a Pākehā lecturer and English from a Māori lecturer, and my friends and I kept confusing which one was mua and which one was muri. In the end, we came up with a phrase that would make a true-speaker-with-macrons-in-the-right-places blush: 'Put your kurī in the muri!' The dog goes in the back yard. Which means mua, the other one, is in the front. Got it.

A few weeks later, we learned the phrase 'i ngā wā o mua'— the Māori equivalent to 'once upon a time' that refers to the days ('ngā wā') in the front (o mua — not where the kurī is) but with an 'i' at the beginning that put the whole thing into the past tense: the days already gone by. How many earnest history essays I wrote, explaining how the 'i' and the 'mua' in 'i ngā wā o mua' taught us about the nature of Māori temporality. Got it.

I'm not sure I really *get it*, though. I understand it intellectually — well enough to write about it and explain it and even teach it — but that's not always the same as *getting it* getting it. After all, I'm so deeply colonised. It's so much harder to unlearn and relearn than to learn things in the first place. Decolonisation isn't a process of reversal: you don't understand Māori theories of the relationship between space and time by putting your dog in the front yard instead of the back.

A few years (OK, many years) after those first university years, when I was teaching a class on Pacific genre fiction in Hawai'i, I asked students to work in groups to present on a particular genre. The options — each of which connected to different texts we were going to read by Indigenous Pacific writers — were romance, mystery, fantasy and science fiction. As part of the presentation, students had to share a description of the first day of semester rewritten in the style of their genre. The 'science fiction' group started their presentation with this:

> 'Kia ora, class!' A woman carrying a tablet computer came into the room,
> the doors swooshing closed behind her. She introduced herself as being
> from Aotearoa, or as it was once called in the 20th century, New Zealand.
> New Zealand, she explained, is a sector in the Federation of Oceania that
> retained independence, despite violent restructuring experienced in the
> region during the global economic recession.

The idea that 'New Zealand' is a name used only in a particular time period with a clear beginning and a potential end is something I argue for, teach about and write on — but colonialism runs deep in all of us, and it runs in unconscious 'factory settings', instinctive places, so I still felt startled when I heard it presented back at me. Some things were continuities of what they'd already learned about me and the class in the first few weeks of semester: me walking in and saying 'Kia ora'; my preference to arrive on time (rather than early) for class so theirs are the first voices in the classroom each morning, me being from Aotearoa.

After hearing their presentation, I realised I could already make one aspect of their vision happen: I started to use an iPad for lectures and presentations, something that had just never crossed my mind but seemed incredibly obvious once I started doing it. But . . . what did the students' imagining of a 'Federation of Oceania' make possible? What made such a federation require, in their minds anyway, a phase of violent restructuring before it could exist?

Āpōpō

It is tempting, when writing about the relationship between the past and the future, to start imagining a future that's better than the present. Writing about āpōpō feels like an invitation to create something heroic: a manifesto! A plan! A map for how to find treasure! A How-To (or How-Not-To) list! A version of the future in which the sins and hurts and yuck of today no longer shape the lives of our collective mokopuna the way they continue to shape us. A version of our collective selves that has moved on — not in the sense of avoiding justice (as in 'Why can't you Mowries just get over it and move on?') but in the sense of experiencing and enacting justice so our collective and individual and intergenerational wounds are allowed to scab over, then scar, and heal, rather than gaping and oozing as they currently do.

Some of these hopes are expressed in the form of things desired: speaking te reo Māori from the wahakura to the grave; living with a sense of purpose and deep connection. Others are expressed in the form of things not wanted: I don't want my daughter to be told, as I was, that she shouldn't take physics at school because she's a girl. I don't want my great-grandchildren to be forced, as I have been, to leave Aotearoa because of speaking up against structural racism, *but more than this* I don't want them to experience structural racism (or any of its intersectional friends) in the first place.

It feels like an act of generosity for future generations to wish for them a world that is better than our own. But . . . it risks being a little narcissistic. It risks recentring ourselves and restricting what's possible for coming generations to the shape of our imaginations in the here and now.

When I started university there was a long list of required history textbooks, and I went to my high school to do a deal with a teacher: he would loan me the books, and at the end of the year I would come back to speak in his class about what I'd learned in history at university and he would write me a reference letter I could use when applying for jobs and scholarships. I used the books, visited the class and got the letter. But . . . when I read the letter, I found he had written it as a recommendation for teachers' college.

This unnecessary focus on a particular career choice meant I couldn't make any use of the letter. Like many Māori people, I come from a teaching whānau — so it's not that I looked down on being involved in education. Sure, I ended up being an educator after all. And I get that he meant it to be generous and encouraging.

But this isn't about that. It's about how the aspiration we might have for some future person may, if it is too closely bound to the here and now, clip wings rather than enable flight.

Lines

What does it mean to hold the line?

There are lines that connect, but there are also lines that are not to be crossed. While personal boundaries can enable us to care for ourselves and others, lines on maps imposed from outside (raupatu lines, 'allocations' of land and sea to colonial powers, nation-state borders) can be the first step towards oppression, genocide and dispossession. There are lines used for fishing and lines we stand in to wait for something to happen. Maps with lines tracing areas removed from Indigenous control are eerily overlaid with maps with very similar lines tracing sites of environmental devastation. Lines for clean washing can also display dirty laundry.

What does it mean to hold the line?

It is surely impossible to know this place without knowing the long history of holding the line: of people standing, sitting, marching, walking, speaking in order to publicly point out that a line has been crossed.

What does it mean to hold the line?

Personally and professionally, the injuries that hurt the worst have been inflicted laterally: our analysis of power in relation to linear vertical hierarchies fails to explain — to even make visible — the ways we become accessories to crimes committed against us for fear of putting ammunition into white hands. We draw lines (what we won't mention, what we won't call out) even as those same lines press into our own flesh and draw blood.

What does it mean to hold the line?

Whose line do we hold? Who decides where the line is that we're holding? If we sign up for holding the line in relation to a particular kaupapa, have we unknowingly committed to standing firm for other kaupapa to which we feel less committed — or totally opposed? How do we make sense of — how do we relate with — those who are standing alongside us, holding the line?

I overheard a powerful white man say to a room of Māori people that there's no such word as 'intersectionality', and, to me, that's all you need to know about intersectionality. He's known for being a beautiful speaker of te reo Māori — does that make his claim correct? Or does it make us less likely to challenge him directly? Or is there an ethical or cultural arithmetic equation that means the reo (our reo) somehow 'makes up for' his claim, as if perfect accuracy in the ā and ō categories was a 'get out of jail free' card in matters of racism, sexism, homophobia, etc.?

Writing lines can be a form of punishment: writing lines can also be a pathway to liberation.

A line on a whakapapa

In my line of work, a pathway to liberation is found in lines already written. It has been my privilege for the past two decades to both labour and feast on writing by Māori, Pacific and Indigenous peoples. I will hopefully never get over the buzz of reconnecting students to the writing of their own people and to the writing of people they haven't had the opportunity to know. I have favourite novels and poems for sure, but the work of my heart is not simply a book club. Instead, I turn to these written texts in order to engage with the sheer diversity and dynamism of Indigenous worlds — I turn to them as evidence of, and sites of, who we have been and therefore who we are.

It can feel trite to say that when we hold the past in our hands we can move confidently into the future. But . . . in my world, the past is literally held in hands when people pick up manuscripts, publications, books, archival documents and — because we are the embodiment of our ancestors — pens of their own.

The easiest story to tell of Māori, Pacific and Indigenous writing is the version that starts with a singular ancestor or couple, and then, as the generations pass, the lines spread out to form a pyramid that expands and extends and pays visual triangular homage to the ones from whence the descendants have all come. This isn't a Māori way of thinking about whakapapa, though, so why would we make use of it to trace the work of Māori writerly hands?

In her poem 'At the museum at Puke-ahu', J. C. Sturm describes whakapapa as a context in which individuals become: 'A mark on a page / A notch on a stick / A mere speck / Of historical dust'. Sturm's vision of genealogy is not about diminishment or irrelevance; it is about multi-nodal connection.

What is made possible by refusing a singular or evolutionary account of our collective past? What is made possible by tracing nodes and hubs and networks rather than imposing assumptions based on a progress narrative of movement from narrowness to breadth?

What if the lines we hold when we are 'holding the line' go in all directions and can stitch together, catch giant fish and keep people and environments safe?

When we find out more about our expansive multi-directional pasts, we realise that what we hold in our hands as we face āpōpō is not an authorised copy of cultural To-Do lists or bullet points. We don't need to insecurely bleat about Making Aotearoa Great Again, but nor do we need — or desire — to abandon the lines that connect.

What we hold, instead, is a set of questions about power and memory and relationships that can be posed in all directions: towards the dog in the front or the back yard, towards ngā wā o mua, towards pōhutukawa and the Māori people who moved them, towards shelves and shelves of unremembered pages, towards intersectionality, towards an imagined Federation of Oceania, towards wounds, towards roses and taupata and more besides.

Alice Te Punga Somerville (Te Ātiawa, Taranaki) is a leading Indigenous academic who specialises in the politics of Māori and Pacific literature. Her books include *Once Were Pacific* (2012), *Two Hundred and Fifty Ways to Start an Essay about Captain Cook* (2020) and the poetry collection *Always Italicise: How to write while colonised* (2022). Scholar, poet and irredentist, she has a PhD from Cornell University and has held academic appointments in New Zealand, Canada, Hawai'i and Australia. She teaches in the Department of English Languages and Literatures and the Institute for Critical Indigenous Studies at the University of British Columbia. She lives in Vancouver, Canada.

KŌRERO

Catherine McNamara and
Ghazaleh Golbakhsh
Overturning motherhood

A conversation in five parts

Catherine McNamara and Ghazaleh Golbakhsh offer their deeply personal meditations on life, death, sex, motherhood, birth and rebirth. They move from reflections on their teen years to other decades; they contrast changes and continuities. They share ideas of rebellion and liberation, of sex and love, of dreams both realised and shattered.

Australian writer Catherine McNamara is a novelist and short story writer. She studied modern African history and French at Sydney University before moving to Paris. She worked in an embassy in pre-war Mogadishu and later lived for nine years in Ghana, where she co-managed a bar and art gallery. Her short story collections include *Pelt and Other Stories* (2013), *The Cartography of Others* (2018) and *Love Stories for Hectic People* (2021). She now lives in Veneto, Italy.

Ghazaleh Golbakhsh is an Iranian-New Zealand writer, filmmaker and academic. She has made various award-winning short films, including the recent documentary *This is Us* (2020), which centres on Muslim New Zealanders. Her written work is widely published, and is included in the anthology *Ko Aotearoa Tātou | We Are New Zealand* (2020). Her publications include the essay collection *The Girl from Revolution Road* (2020).

1. Revisiting Simone de Beauvoir and Forugh Farrokhzād

CM: I made a declaration to my mother in our kitchen at age 19. *I will never make you a grandmother*. Completely adamant, rude even, my hopes set on study in Paris in the shadow of the great existentialists. I remember my mother was chopping vegetables, string beans perhaps, with an eye on the TV in the corner of the room. I was reading Simone de Beauvoir at the time. I knew my mother came from Simone's same dutiful generation — crippling stilettos and cinched waists — and probably thought I was merely a new-generation audience from a serene country, who'd never fought a battle in her life.

In Paris, I strutted about Simone's world 40 years too late. Years afterward I read in Hazel Rowley's biography that Simone popped pills to cope with rankling, straying Sartre, lost Nelson Algren when she shouldn't have, 'mothered' a few of her open-eyed

172

followers. Years afterwards I popped four bilingual kids who grew up on long-haul flights, and made my mother a distant grandmother who never brought up that afternoon.

GG: Some Fridays ago, in her beautifully decorated and cared-for three-bed home in a ritzy area of Tāmaki Makaurau, a friend confessed to me that she had finally said goodbye to her old dreams. Taking a giant gulp of her mid-shelf shiraz, which she no doubt had swiped from her actual wine cellar, she said: 'I'm 41 and single. I'm not going to have a child and I've made my peace with my mourning.' She was quite blasé and matter-of-fact, no doubt using her financial and materialistic success as approval. Part of me was jealous that she had made a decision, part of me was terrified because I was now on the cusp of that next stage of life. It reminded me of one of Iran's greatest poets of the twentieth century, Forugh Farrokhzād, who described her collection *The Rebellion* as being 'between two different stages of life, the last gasp before a kind of liberation'.

Farrokhzād left her first husband for a famous filmmaker, and her husband would not allow her to see her son. She had a breakdown, attempted suicide and was admitted into an asylum to undergo electric shock 'therapy'. It was during production of her only film, the documentary about a leper colony, *The House is Black* (1962), that Farrokhzād adopted a boy, Hossein. She died prematurely in a car crash on Valentine's Day, 14 February 1967, at the age of 32. Her legacy lives on in her adoptive son (who translates her works) and in her powerful works, which, during the 1979 revolution, were passed around in secret. Looking solely at the titles of Farrokhzād's books, we can trace a type of progression of a woman accepting herself: *The Captive* (1955), *The Rebellion* (1958), *Another Birth* (1964). If saying goodbye to motherhood means a type of death, then perhaps my next stage will indeed be a (excuse the pun) rebirth. *Another birth.*

2. One-night stand(s)

CM: We were disco babes. Out the back, we travelled. New Guinea was a pash, Moscow was going all the way. Anywhere in between had to be geography. We wore our love bites with pride and sculled Ben Ean in the toilets. And when one of us came home pregnant we gave her all the support in the world to get rid of it. We had rights. There were clinics. But she wanted to keep that baby. Against all of our earnest advice. We watched it push out her belly, and she wore pushed-out Indian dresses with wonky hems. She went through the horrid splitting apart of birth and brought home a doll in a basket. Those cells we wanted flushed out of her became a tall, lanky girl, prettier than any of us.

GG: A friend had a medical scare a few years back, and there was a risk that they would have to remove her womb. She'd never thought about having children, but here in this moment, the idea of the possibility being taken away so swiftly and coldly sent her into a slight craze. 'I want the choice,' she would say. 'I don't want it snatched from me.' Another friend had an abortion after spending years entangled in a web of lust with a terrible man. As I doom-scrolled through Instagram on yet another restless night through the pandemic, I would see this man's pictures — of his new wife and young daughters. I wondered what my friend would think every time this grim reminder would pop up, like unwanted DMs in your inbox from mysterious creepy men who think it preposterous that you don't reply to their unwanted virtual advances.

3. The time I wept

CM: After yoga, three red drops. The next morning, *le déluge*. Full-on miscarriage at 12 weeks. The doctor says, *Non c'è battito / There is no heartbeat*. There is a dead soul in my gut. After the embryo is carved out, I ask another doctor for reasons. He says, *Like a chicken, Signora. Uovo marcio / bad egg. Go home and try again*. Great, that. So I go home and we produce a new son, a beautiful, enquiring, mop-headed boy. I have never stopped wondering where that destroyed soul went, and by whose hand I was delivered this new soul, this new being. And where would he have gone if not for the annihilation of the first?

GG: Every Sunday, the beer garden at a local British tavern overflows with young (white, affluent) families. They gather in big groups around plain picnic tables. Toddlers climb over and run around like free-range chooks. It's organised chaos. On such a day I find myself cuddling little Matteo. A one-year-old ball of mush with giant blue eyes and a soft cascade of blond hair — making it sadly obvious that he is not mine. A mother near me complains about how tired she is and how lucky I am not to have kids. This uninvited statement and the comfortable way I am holding Matteo are constant contrasts I have begun to live with. That night, images of friends and their new 'lockdown' babies infiltrate my phone and make me cry. I weep openly and loudly like a baby myself, purely because I can't have what I want.

4. What to expect when expecting to be expecting but not expecting

CM: Scene 1. Accra. Private Gynaecologist's Rooms. Baby No. 3. A new French expat has arrived, expectant with her fourth child. She's heard on the grapevine that I'm expecting, too, and asks to come to my gyno. Of course I bring her. In the waiting room we agree that she will go first. The doctor steps in and motions her forward. The doctor is Ghanaian, something I had not mentioned. The woman stands up, backs out of the room, says *I didn't know, I can't do this*, and she is gone. The doctor shrugs, as if he has known women who are this way.

Scene 2. Accra. Ghana. Police Hospital. Baby No. 4. I'm up early with my bump and my new man and we reach the line of ladies waiting along a breeze-block corridor for pre-natal ultrasounds. In unison, these ladies raise their heads. I am a guest in their country, and I am pushed to the top of the line; no woman will accept my reluctance to take their place. My belly is patted with endearing smiles.

GG: Last scene: Seated at a faux Spanish restaurant opposite the beach. It's the type of superficial joint that only tourists go to because they don't know any better. The kind of place where the menu is far too long for anything to be a speciality. A giant paella dish is put out to attract more punters in from the sizzling sun and torridly windy beach. A bunch of seniors, enticed by the paella, take a seat behind us, each cradling their tiny lapdogs. The holiday is grand and I don't want it to end.

But it did end. Because he didn't want to have a child.

Him: If this is a dealbreaker, then *you* need to think hard about it.

Him: You know what? I don't think there's a spark anymore.

Sparks fly, sparks die. The anger I felt raged at the fact that he doesn't have to think about these things, because for him there is no final off button. I hate my body. At that moment, then and there, I hated the expectations I had for it and for me.

5. A religious (mis)explanation

CM: My aunt had an illegitimate child, and that was the first I heard of it because it was shush-shush until he was three years old. Out of wedlock. No husband. Father unknown. (Years later my aunt told me she would have given him up for adoption, but for a bumbling nurse who placed him in her arms.)

My aunt and cousin flew out from London for holidays when he was five and again when he was eight. On the second trip a bus hit the back of our car when my dad had turned back home to get his sunglasses. The sun was a low winter spear that flared in the bus driver's eyes, so he said. We were going to the country to ride horses, and I had put my seatbelt around my cousin so he would be safest, among our bickering selves. At the moment the bus hit, my cousin's neck was twisted around and he died on the side of the road, blood running from an ear and pupils dilated. None of us was injured but for bruises and howling shock and the wreck of the car. After the burial my grandmother said he had been chosen because he was fatherless, because he was illegitimate, and had he lived his life he would have been marked.

GG: Two days after I turned 40, my aunt passed away. As someone with the greatest sense of empathy I had ever known, her biggest worry was not the fatal pneumonia that was spreading through her lungs, but that she would ruin my birthday. When we fled Iran, we fled the things and people that would keep us stable and rooted for the longest time. I barely knew my grandparents, and so the closeness I felt to my aunt was immeasurable. When she passed, I believed that she would visit again. People would forever tell me about these great visions they'd have of their loved ones giving them a sense of final closure. My aunt never came. While others visit her gravestone, I refuse to, as it represents a sense of nothingness that I cannot attribute to her. This mourning has continued, and, alongside this literal death, I feel a more metaphorical one coming, too. The death of expectation. In a more selfish sense, I am also preparing to mourn an identity that I may never earn.

Sonya Wilson
Finders, keepers

My grandmother once glued 3000 seashells to a wall at her house.

The house sat one paddock back from the Invercargill racecourse: two-storeyed, brown brick, with a cracker view of the track from the upstairs balcony, and the wall, downstairs, measured about 4 by 4 metres.

She began with a simple trim of ostrich foot shells along the wall's bottom edge. A border of bivalves followed, a line of limpets, then hundreds of tiny clams to fill in the gaps of her white, wide-walled ocean. Outside, tides rolled in and out, moons waxed and waned, seasons passed, but on and on Nana plastered: cockles and cat's eyes, pīpī and pūpū, scallops and sea snails.

It took her an entire year to complete her grand mosaic of molluscs. It was the feature wall of a mermaid's palace, the seaside galloping in from across the paddocks, an ocean of art indoors.

My nana is a collector. Principally of shells, though she has many other fine assemblages: souvenir teaspoons, garden gnomes, pink stones and, lately, a burgeoning collection of meerkats.

It's the shells, though, that are her masterwork. This is no casual weekend gatherer we are dealing with here, like those people who take home the occasional pāua shell to sit on the windowsill next to the bath, or like those kids who pick up cat's eyes only to abandon them later, smelling like salt and death, in the footwell of the car; no, Nana's shell-gathering has been sustained, prolific, mercenary.

When we were young, my sisters and I were her seasonal workers on the sands of Southland, digging our fingers in at Ōreti, bracing ourselves against the southerly at Riverton, sifting through oyster shells abandoned between the barnacled piles at Bluff.

My cousins were employed up in the Bay of Plenty, plucking pink-fanned scallops and yellow-brown takai from Waihi Beach, shapes from the sea we mainlanders thought were terribly exotic when the tide, or Air New Zealand, brought them south.

Nana went out collecting, too, of course — in between Organ Club conventions and aquarobics sessions and Meals-on-Wheels volunteer deliveries — every time the salty sea breeze called her.

It is always Grandad who answers the phone when I ring, always in the same way.

'Halloo!' he chimes.

'Hi, Grandad: it's Sonya.'

'Sonya! So it is!'

Grandad, 91, a trainer of horses well into his eighties and long-term Trackside devotee, puts me on speakerphone because Nana's hearing aids have been playing up. I've called to talk to her about our family history; Nana is 88, and I've had the sudden urge to collect it. But I also want to talk about the shells. It is one of the abiding memories I have of Nana from my childhood: the things she carried, those treasures she kept.

It is late January 2020. The coronavirus is still just a vague nothing-much, happening on shores far, far away.

'When did it start?' I ask her. 'Your shell collecting.'

'In Wellington,' she says. 'When I was about six or seven.'

It was 1938, she thinks. Her family had moved north chasing work and washed up at Lyall Bay, back when Wellington Airport was just a strip of grass beyond the far end of the beach.

'Why did it start?'

'I don't know. I suppose it's just . . . always my love of water and the sea.'

In the background the old pendulum clock chimes, one ding for half-past the hour. That clock, mounted on the sitting-room wall of their Invercargill retirement village bungalow, has rung its way through four different houses now, and 30-odd years. *Ding!* Another half-hour has passed. *Ding-dong!* And another.

'Now, shall we start from the start?' Nana says.

Nana was born in 1932 in Invercargill, where an optimistic town planner had ordered the streets built four lanes wide but where there wasn't much around of anything at all. She arrived into a world still suffering the effects of the Great Depression and the First World War, but it was the Second World War that really troubled her — when her family couldn't buy enough butter or sugar or meat, when she feared the arrival of the Germans, when they had to run and hide in the trenches dug around the primary school if the air-raid drill sirens went off, when her uncle got man-powered to Cairo, and her father, too old to go to war abroad, got marched north to Christchurch to be trained up for the Home Guard.

'Us kids were absolutely petrified because we thought we were going to get bombed,' she tells me.

It was Nana's job to hold the classroom door open when the siren went. She was always the last to get out, and was terrified she was going to be left there when the shells (of the weaponised variety) started falling. They were still living in Lyall Bay when the war broke out, and Nana remembers the whole family marching down to the wharf in the wee small hours of the morning to see the departing of the First Echelon for Egypt.

'I was only six or seven,' she says, 'and I wondered why all the big people in the crowd were crying.'

Did I know that once, during the polio epidemic, they weren't allowed to go past their front gate for weeks? Maybe even months? Nana can't quite remember the timeframe.

'I was eight. That was quite a long time ago, you know,' she says.

When the clock chimes again, a full 10 cacophonous dongs for 10 o'clock, Nana says: 'I've realised I keep going back to myself in the olden days.'

'But that's good,' I tell her. 'I want to hear it. The world was so different when you were young.'

'Oh, wasn't it ever, yes.' Nana's 'yes's lilt, they always have, coming out as a gentle ye-es, as if she's slightly unsure halfway through the word.

All through her childhood, whenever the war or the polio epidemic or her grumpy father would let her, Nana went to the beach. She loved the beach. And she loved the shells the beach provided. She would run there every day after school to swim and search for shells, then trudge up the hundred steps to home. Even when her family returned to the wind-lashed south, Nana's shell gathering continued. Her collection grew as she did, a rising tide of sun-bleached carapaces gathered from the beaches of her youth: Lyall Bay, Ōreti, Riverton, Dunedin's St Clair.

She was dedicated, too. Once, when she left her clothes in a pile on the beach to swim, she returned to find them all on fire. Poof! There they were, up in flames, as she collected shells in her togs further down St Clair beach. Some cad had flicked his cigarette into them. Nana is pragmatic: 'Lucky my undies weren't affected,' she says.

Her family didn't have much. The dress for the school dance was made out of old curtains, the biscuits made with dripping, toilet paper made from cut-up squares of newsprint. Nana longed for things: a doll's pram, a trike, a garden gnome or two like the wealthy lady who lived down the street. There wasn't enough money for any of them.

'Nobody had much back then,' she says, 'way back in the olden days.' There's a wistful tone to her voice, as though she's sauntered all the way back to the beach, to that time she saw a handsome young chap sitting on the sand singing 'Mexicali Rose' to his girl, to that time before the war, and before Trackside TV, and before granddaughters ringing on cellphones.

'I just had a real fancy for all these shells. They used to fascinate me, the different shapes and colours. Those ones you could hold to your ear and hear the sea roaring . . . ye-es.'

Shells, unlike prams and trikes and garden gnomes, were free for the taking. The ocean just handed them over, gratuities from the sea.

'Halloo!'

'Hi, Grandad: it's Sonya.'

'Sonya! So it is!'

It's February. Nana's just back from getting her new hearing aids turned down. At a concert at the local church yesterday they gave her a heck of a fright, blasting her ears with a loud screech.

'I've never really thought of myself as a collector,' she tells me. 'Not until you started asking me about it.'

Oh, but she was. She is. It wasn't just shells. There were also stones.

'Oh, yes. I suppose now that you say it . . .'

When my grandparents bought a little crib on the edge of the Arrowtown camping ground in the 1980s, Nana's collecting moved inland, to freshwater. The bed of the Arrow River, full of schist and gold dust and miners' ghosts, also held a collection of sparkly rosé-tinged rocks. We called them by their scientific name — pink stones — and Nana decided that she must start amassing those, too.

My sisters and I went on collecting missions for her every time we visited. Some days there were none, but other days, perhaps after a storm had forced the silvery braids to change their course, perhaps on a day our young eyes were more alert thanks to our being jacked up on sherbet from the Night 'n Day, the valley's ghosts and the snow-fed river obliged us, sending pink stone treasures down from the mountains and depositing them at our freezing pink feet.

How many pink stones are too many pink stones? We never found out. Nana never saw a pink stone she didn't want to keep. Some of them were — are — huge. Pink boulders.

'You'd probably get told off for doing that now, wouldn't you?' I ask her. 'Taking big rocks from the river like that?'

'Oh help, I don't know. I never got caught anyway.'

They've survived through all the years and all the moves, Nana's collection of pink stones, shifting with her by wheelbarrow and sons-in-law to each new house smaller than the last.

'I'm the only one here in the retirement village with pink stones,' she says proudly, and I imagine a flock of jealous pensioners peeking through their net curtains, coveting Nana's rocks. And when she says, 'The one I've got at my door now, I want that to be my headstone', my heart thuds a little harder, just for a beat.

She never really thought of herself as a collector.

Pffft.

She also collected souvenir teaspoons. Hundreds of them dangled from purpose-built racks, rattling their kitsch hellos in the westerly wind. And garden gnomes: I remember Snow White and the full complement of seven dwarfs, a Cinderella garden gnome, ducks, chickens, geese; an entire concrete Disney village populated her front garden.

'Oh, ye-es,' Nana says, 'I had them all, just about.'

She also had a collection of miniature cups and saucers (far too small to be of any use for all the teaspoons), a wide assortment of things coloured lavender, thousands of copper coins kept in old beer flagons, and meerkats. Meerkats are her latest thing. She has meerkat garden gnomes, calendars, wind-up toy meerkats and statuettes. She has seasonally specific meerkats, too; at Christmas time, little Santa-hat-clad meerkats poke out from the indoor plants.

'I've got a movie of them now, too, a DVD. Have you seen it?'

'No?'

Her voice sounds like a smile. 'Oooh, you'll have to come and visit me and I'll play it to you!' (The implication being that I don't come and visit her enough.)

Does anyone collect things anymore? Like people once collected stamps and model cars and Royal Doulton china? Like my nana collected shells?

I collect books, I suppose. Rather, I keep books. The biography on Kate Sheppard I got for my eleventh birthday, an ancient little tome of Christina Rossetti poems I bought from an op shop during my first year of university:

What are heavy? Sea-sand and sorrow;

What are brief? To-day and to-morrow;

What are frail? Spring blossoms and youth;

What are deep? The ocean and truth.

In one of my other books, *The Songs of Trees*, David George Haskell writes:

An affinity for savanna-like landscapes is one of the neurological quirks that we humans carried with us as we spread across the world. Another is the desire to collect curios, especially pieces of the past. We're a storytelling species, so perhaps these artefacts are anchors and touchstones for the tales from which we find our reality.

Nana and Grandad lived on 80 acres at Kennington, out where the road away from Invercargill becomes the road towards Dunedin. They collected five daughters between 1953 and 1963, and they all have the gene.

My mum once collected cow-based paraphernalia, but now it's fabrics and stationery and old maps. My Aunty Sheryl collects vintage knitting patterns. Aunty Andrea: matchboxes. Aunty Jenny has extensive collections of hairdryers, sunglasses and approximately 54 sets of salt-and-pepper shakers. My cousin Kerryn has a pencil collection and a shoelace collection and a vintage apron collection. My other cousin, Anna, admits to 16 teapots, 57 teacups and 92 different types of tea — at least that's how many she had last time she counted them, which was back in 2017. When my sister Nikki confirms that she owns 15 vintage retractable builders' rulers, I start to wonder if there's some sort of group therapy we should all be doing.

'I've always wondered,' Aunty Jenny writes on our family group Messenger thread, 'what is bigger? A selection of collections or a collection of selections?'

We've started chatting more often lately, my aunties and cousins and me.

'Halloo!'

There's some sort of chamber music concert going on. 'Hi, Grandad: it's Sonya!'

'Sonya! 'Tis too! The very one!'

'It sounds like you've got an orchestra in your lounge!'

'It's Nana, playing the organ!'

It is late March. Nana plays on, but the world outside has stopped.

She says, when I ask: 'We are doing very well.'

She says she's keeping busy during lockdown with her organ and her crochet and her knitting.

She says: 'Oh, I've always got something to do. I'm knitting dishcloths at the moment. Real flash ones! I might knit you one actually.'

'I'd love one.'

'Oh, right, well I'll put your name on my list.'

'And how are you?' Grandad asks.

Thanks to Covid-19, my husband and I, both freelancers, have lost all our work. We are not sure how we are going to pay the mortgage. The tide is out.

'Oh well, a lot more than you's got troubles,' Grandad says, and he's right.

Nana's shell wall has lasted more than three decades. The Great Shell Wall! While I was watching *Fraggle Rock* and listening to Kylie Minogue and roller-skating down the driveway outside, Nana crouched and stretched, crouched and stretched, dabbing and pressing, dabbing and pressing, week after week, month after month.

It took a bit of organising, to get all her scallops in a row. A bit of trial and error to get the consistency of the grout just so. The family weren't that impressed, she says. But I remember, as a nine-year-old, being full of admiration. I thought of it as the wall of a great sea creature's palace, gilded in royal clams.

'It's been there thirty years,' Nana says, 'so it must've been alright.'

It's still in the family, in fact, albeit not nearly as big as I remembered. My aunty and uncle live in the house now. Many things have been removed or repainted, many things have changed, but the shell wall stays put.

It is April now; the virus is claiming lives, but Nana plays on.

'Do you feel frightened?' I ask her. 'About the virus?'

'Not one bit. I'm eighty-eight. The thought of dying doesn't worry me one bit.'

'I'm busy hooking a rug to put over my organ,' Nana says. 'In between knitting dishcloths. I've got yours nearly finished.'

'Fantastic.'

'And it's pink.'

'Excellent.'

'Have you ever had a pink dishcloth?'

Nana hasn't asked for shells for years, not since the shell wall got finished. Not since the pink stones and the garden gnomes and the meerkats took over. But I have continued to pick them up. So have my kids, though they're not as excited as I am when we find the perfect specimen, one of those ones that Nana would have loved: complete shells, the perfect shape for the waiting gap, wall worthy.

Pāua, mussel, scallop: sea creatures' abandoned armour of myriad colours and luminescent pearl, gifts that come from that special unseen place below the waves, they dull a little when you get them home to the lawn, with their ocean washed away. But like Nana, my shell gathering has always been more about my love of the sea than the shells themselves. It is about my collection of memories, those ones that stoke an ever-increasing nostalgia for home: of finding crabs and watching waves and being properly bitterly cold, of the southerly pushing us forward, me and my red-cheeked sisters, out in pursuit of the ocean's treasures.

When I pick up shells from the warm pōhutukawa-fringed beaches of Auckland where I now live, what I am remembering is Nana and the rest of my family at Riverton's back beach, where divers collect pāua from between the bull kelp and the rocks, and the wave-pressed sand where pīpī shells are left by the tide along Taramea Bay, and that view all the way back towards Bluff, where fishing boats dock at salt-stained wharves and the sun rises out over the Awarua Plains.

I left that place many years ago, for brighter lights and bigger cities, for the wide-open water, but increasingly, and particularly at times like these, I have the urge to make my way home; back to the source of my family's stories, to the wind-rushed beaches of my grandmother's childhood and of my own, like a shell returned to the sea.

Sonya Wilson is a writer, reporter, television producer and the founder and executive director of Kiwi Christmas Books. She has a Bachelor of Broadcasting Communications and, more recently, a Masters of Creative Writing from the University of Auckland Waipapa Taumata Rau. She is the author of the children's novel *Spark Hunter* (2021), which won the NZSA Best First Book Award at the 2022 New Zealand Book Awards for Children and Young Adults. She lives in Tāmaki Makaurau Auckland.

Serie Barford
The devil's coach horse
(*Ocypus olens*)

The devil's coach horse pre-dates dinosaurs. Beds its sinister
reputation in debris. Chews and spits the skin of earthworms.
Faces threats like a dancing scorpion — tail up with pincer jaws
ajar. Activates stink glands. Smells like fish.

Invertebrates couldn't outride Reactor 4's ruptured core.
Survivors size up worms. Bite off more than they can chew.

These days radioactive worms have sex with each other.
The flick of a switch flipped asexual reproduction
into coupling.

Reactor 4 was the site of the nuclear accident that occurred at the Chornobyl Nuclear Power Plant,
26 April 1986.

Serie Barford was born in Aotearoa to a migrant German-Samoan mother (Lotofaga) and a Pālagi father.
She held a 2018 Established Pasifika Writer's residency at the Michael King Writers' Centre in Tāmaki
Makaurau, performed at the 2019 International Book Arsenal Festival in Kyiv, and collaborated with
filmmaker Anna Marbrook for the 2021 Going West *Different Out Loud* poetry series. Her poetry
collection, *Sleeping with Stones* (2021), was shortlisted for the Mary and Peter Biggs Award for Poetry
at the 2022 Ockham New Zealand Book Awards. She lives in Tāmaki Makaurau Auckland.

Erik Kennedy
The intentional community

Before we started the commune, the first thing we did was solicit advice from old hippies who had lived the commune life back in the day. We got lots of great insights. 'You can change work, but you can't change human nature.' 'Everyone will be fucking everyone.' 'You'll probably wind up selling drugs, because it's easier than farming.'

Dorotka and Martin and I knew what we wanted from our community of about two dozen people. A tiny carbon footprint, like at Findhorn or Twin Oaks. Vegan living. 'No politics' (but we were all communists or anarchists). Art, culture, and then more art.

None of us knew how wet that first spring and summer would be, though, and how the water would colonise our minds. We came up with new words for rain. Every possible view of the farm looked the same, like a Constable painting glimpsed through a filmy plastic shower curtain. But the work had to go on. We had to grow *something*, because 1) we had to eat, 2) we needed veg to sell and 3) we had our pride and we didn't want to hit up our networks for loans yet.

The mood in Honey House, the cottage that Dorotka and Martin and I lived in, was fractious. I was being blamed for the community's shitty location, probably because I had chosen the location. Dorotka and Martin had been together for eight years; they'd met me only two years ago, but our mutual chemistry had taken us all by surprise and we were now a committed polycule. Dorotka and I were both sculptors, and I'd thought Martin was a bit of a hanger-on until I realised that he had actually run entire arts festivals, but he didn't feel the need to be a smug tit about his accomplishments like I did.

Dorotka was questioning the thoroughness of my initial research. 'All I'm saying is that these old stoners told you about the rain, the interminable fucking rain, and you insisted on here anyway,' she said.

'It was cheap,' I said. 'We had people cashing out of their supers. We needed to buy *something*.'

'We should have waited. We all should have waited. Martin and I should have waited until we were sure you weren't the sort of jackass who ruins people's lives.'

Martin, during this, looked high and flat, like northern Argentina.

'None of this helps us now, Dorotka. It's easy to assign blame—'

'Yeah, that's what I'm doing. I blame you.'

'—it's easy to assign blame,' I continued, 'but that doesn't fix anything. We need to talk next steps. Take advantage of all this water, if we can. Grow rice or something. Is it warm enough for rice here?'

'Does it *feel* warm enough?' Dorotka put some venom into that question. 'I can't remember the last time I felt my feet. It's just as well, though, because I think I've got trenchfoot or cabbage-pox or something. My toes are itching like a street dog's balls. I hope yours are, too.'

'Nope,' I lied, annoyed to be reminded of the unbearable itching in my wet socks.

'I came here to decompress and smoke and work on my pieces,' Dorotka said, 'and I haven't been in the studio for two weeks. I'm either in the fields or on the phone with pissed-off stockists wondering where their turnips are. I also came here because I believe in the collective. I believe in what we stand for together. You are destroying that belief. It's like you've set us up to fail. We don't have enough money, enough people-power, or enough know-how. There are twenty people who aren't us living on this farm, and a lot of them are struggling with this rain gulag vibe more than we are. Way more than *you* are. Do you even know that?'

I didn't know that. And I didn't know what to say, so I said nothing. Martin was also silent. He continued to watch our catfight aloofly, assured in his serenity.

'Not everyone wants challenges all the time. Not everyone can handle 100 per cent change all at once,' she said. 'We don't have "leaders" here, but you are a leader, whether you realise it or not. In a collective, a leader needs to define the terms of the possible in a way that makes sense to everyone. We need to aspire but also occasionally achieve things. And you've made things too hard.'

'It isn't too hard. It's just unfamiliar,' I said.

'The art is in attempting something that seems too hard,' said Martin suddenly, his first contribution to the discussion. 'If it isn't too hard, it isn't art.'

Wow. In that moment, if aesthetic theories were weapons, I could have clubbed Martin to the floor in cold blood. How dare he try to out-art me?! And not only out-art me but also be wrong! I was about to reply with some long-winded, incandescent sputtering, but Dorotka got in first. She was cold and clinical.

'Martin, we've been over this. We don't talk about art like that in this house. Art is for everyone. There's no intellectual entry fee. Difficult isn't better. Check your classism, you creep. Don't be a snob. It's disgusting.'

God, I loved it when she was like that. Like an electrical storm sitting on a couch. I looked at Dorotka, radiant in her contemptuousness, and she looked at me looking at her. I gave a little smile, and she gave an even smaller one. Yeah, we all hated each other. But everything was going to be OK.

Erik Kennedy is the author of the poetry collections *Another Beautiful Day Indoors* (2022) and *There's No Place Like the Internet in Springtime* (2018), and he co-edited, with Jordan Hamel, Rebecca Hawkes and Essa Ranapiri, *No Other Place to Stand: An Anthology of Climate Change Poetry from Aotearoa New Zealand* (2022). His poems, stories and criticism have been widely published. Originally from New Jersey, he lives in Ōtautahi Christchurch.

Lisa Reihana, *Papatūānuku and Rūaumoko*, 2021. Crystal flex on aluminium, 880 × 880 × 40 mm.

Oliver Jeffers, *Before My Time*, 2011. Oil on linen, 717 × 863 × 50 mm.

Oliver Jeffers, *Fluorescent Protracted Landscape*, 2016.
Oil and cut fluorescent paper on canvas, 565 × 717 mm.

El Anatsui, *Wade in the Water*, 2021. Aluminium bottle caps and copper wire, 2490 × 2260 × 178 mm. Photograph courtesy of Brandywine Workshop.

Gregory O'Brien
An invocation

After Elizabeth Thomson's 'Lateral Series'

> For Earth which is an intelligence hath a voice and a propensity to speak in
> all her parts.
> — Christopher Smart, 'Jubilate Agno'

This world in sun- or moon-light, in shadow, star-encrusted,
  enclouded, thunderstruck, rain-washed . . .

This lenticular world, through which other worlds are observed.

This world in the variety of its movements. This world and its
  theories.

This world from which you fall, as from a great height, into the
  arms of one or another.

This world you hold but not in your hands.

This world which is cured, spoiled, seasoned, sanded, fermented,
  polished, tainted, cooled, ripened, ornamented, steamed,
  composed, aged, augmented, refreshed, dusted, percolated,
  warmed and weathered . . .

This world as described by its topography, hydrology,
  meteorology and cloud physics. As it finds itself in a tangle
  of latitudes and longitudes, and somewhere else entirely.

This world marked RETURN TO SENDER.

This world in which we are polar opposites but somehow find
each other.

This world part soap, part cloud, part birdsong, part aluminium
smelter, part foxtrot . . .

This world spinning on the axis of the present tense.

This world a part song. In part leaf, in part descending heron, in
part flashing lightbulb, in part plucked lyre, in part a towel
wrapped around the head of someone loved.

This world this blazing hemisphere. This world and its poetry,
'that winged, fickle, sacred thing' (Plato).

This world as a thought bubble. This world or what else?

This world a satellite of another world, each a pomegranate held
in an outstretched hand.

This world and this 'sense sublime of something far more deeply
interfused, whose dwelling is the light of setting suns, and
the round ocean and the living air, and the blue sky, and in
the mind of man: a motion and a spirit, that impels all
thinking things, all objects of all thought, and rolls through
all things'. (William Wordsworth, 'Tintern Abbey')

This world on the brink of another world.

This world and its gods. A risen sun. Water molecule. Moonfish. Starfish. A line from Thomas Aquinas: 'God is intelligible light.'

This world as a map of another, far distant world.

This world as it is described and left undescribed.

This world left out to dry.

This world in which London is a city of palm-trees, in which redbird and peahen sing and preen. This world in which such things are recorded and archived, but only in dreams.

This world a quickening of another, long-forgotten world.

This world you liken to a peacock feather, sea egg, nautilus, wineglass, teardrop.

This world in its many harmonic parts, in its rigorous counterpoint, in its cacophony.

This world that once swallowed the moon and was itself then swallowed by a fish.

This world in which each day is its own Renaissance.

This world a glass eye, a telescope trained upon itself, a mirror-
 pond.

This world but only for now.

This world in its own season, a profusion of sage, melon-thistle,
 globe amaranth, prickly poppy, may apple, blood flower,
 water lily, sun flower . . .

This world at the hour of our death.

Gregory O'Brien is a visual artist, poet, essayist and curator. His collection of poems and paintings, *House
& Contents*, was published in 2022. His recent projects include a monograph about the modernist bird
painter Don Binney and an exhibition that he is curating for the New Zealand Maritime Museum Hui
Te Ananui a Tangaroa extrapolating on the themes and imaginative leaps in his 2019 book *Always Song
in the Water*. He lives in Te Whanganui-a-Tara Wellington.

Reihana Robinson
Inside / Outside

Inside — what to see

A swift transition to an iPhone she's holding
Holy cow — the latest Bollywood images.

The iPhone belongs to a random fighter — 17 years old
Door kicked in at 3.00am
Dragged off his mattress by death-dealers
Mother and sister shoved, shamed
Foreign-trained fellow Afghani humiliate him to life ever-after.

And the returned soldier tweets
After handing him over
After opening his phone
How she hates this war
This nonsensical war
And she tweets *No more pretending it meant anything*
It didn't
It didn't mean a fucking thing.

Outside — what to see

Let's start with the rusted trailer still in use
Chooks resting in its shade
The shadow cast is short right now
It's late morning on the South Pacific coast
Far from towns and villages
The sea clasping a quiet sky, filling half the picture
The chooks beginning to get 'in the zone'
Dazed and post-coital
Conjuring an egg into Te Ao Mārama.

Reihana Robinson (he tamaiti whāngai) is a writer, artist and environmental activist. She is the author of three poetry collections: *AUP New Poets 3* (2008), *Auē Rona* (2012) and *Her Limitless Her* (2018). She received the inaugural Te Atairangikaahu Poetry Award and has held two artist residencies, at the East–West Center, Honolulu, and in Red Wing, Minnesota. She lives near Moehau.

Witi Ihimaera
We should be

1.

The poet Chris Tse and I are separated by one, perhaps two, generations. I've met him only two or three times, on all occasions briefly. The time that is most vivid in my memory is when his book *How to be Dead in a Year of Snakes* was shortlisted for the Mary and Peter Biggs Award for Poetry at the Ockham New Zealand Book Awards in 2016.

Chris is everybody's poet crush, and he also happens to be a really smooth dresser. On the awards night he was wearing a fabulous jacket from WORLD (dark grey with holes in it) onto which his friend Kirsten had sewn wings of tufted shimmering grey feathers as epaulettes. He looked like a swan prince, totally dangerous. Of that night he notably said: 'I was certain Witi Ihimaera was going to knock me out with his trophy and steal my jacket.'

As it was, a week later I went into WORLD and bought the same jacket. I wore it once and then put it in the back of my closet. I was frightened that I would wear it to some dance party and Chris would enter with his feathers and, well, I would look like I had moulted.

I'm not writing about Chris Tse, or even his brilliant fashion selections, actually, but rather about his poem 'like a queen' (2017).

I should be king
I should be torn from your stuffy pages

I should be monster
I should be undeterred by scars on shoulder blades

I should be tempted
I should be blackened, cum-stained and bleeding from love

I should be everything
I should be twenty-something with no heel

I should be wanton
I should be leaning over ledges with my fortune

                                                    I should be happy
                                I should be that bottle that never empties

I should be mirrored
I should be blanketed in folds of rolling silk

                                                    I should be child
                                I should be tender at their protests

I should be ready
I should be volume up on open roads

                                                    I should be paper
                                I should be leading you all into war

I should be visible
I should be on every street corner as is

                                                    I should be bold
                                I should be the reason you know my name

I should be spill
I should be more than enough

                                                    I should be queen
                                I should be your closing credits

2.

I am transported back to New York on 9 July 1986. It was there, in the Big Apple, that I heard the Homosexual Law Reform Act had passed back in Aotearoa.

I had been working with the Ministry of Foreign Affairs since 1973, and I went to New York as a career diplomat, as consul. My then partner, Murray, was already living in the city, having had an offer to work at the American Field Service headquarters close to the United Nations. We didn't plan it, but it happened that way. Just before I departed for the US, Prime Minister David Lange received a letter signed by '27 concerned New Zealanders' telling him not to send me — saying I would contribute to the spread of AIDS in New York. At the time, homosexual acts in New Zealand between men were illegal, and the ministry could not be seen to be condoning such a relationship or contributing taxpayer money to supporting it. However, the ministry agreed that I could go, with the warning that any hint of anything untoward and they would pull me out.

We found an apartment on the thirty-third floor of Broadway and West 67th Street. It was a fabulous place — we got the apartment over others who were in the queue because the man renting it out thought I had the same birthday as his favourite movie star, Kathryn Grayson.

And so, Murray and I were the first New Zealand gay couple, unofficially anyway, to serve overseas.

July in New York is the hottest month of the year. On the 9th, I went to take some sun in Central Park. The day was so hot that the sky was almost white. There were lots of runners about, and families with children by the lake. Lovers, too, kissed and fondled each other in the grass. In New York everything was so public: you could watch people through their apartment windows in the building next door, or, if you were gay and went to certain places, people had sex in back rooms and invited you to join them. Sex wasn't safe yet as the AIDS epidemic was still around.

The whole place was like theatre: you were on stage and always part of some amazing party that was going on. Of course, not all of it was glamorous. Drug deals happened while you were walking along the street. Death was public, too: one day I saw a man gunned down by police on 5th Avenue, and, on another occasion, I joined a group of New Yorkers clustered around a young drug addict who had overdosed on the steps leading to the 42nd Street subway station. Never think that New Yorkers are uncaring. For 10 minutes or so, until a couple of policemen came along, we stood respectfully with our heads bowed in tribute to the life of a boy we had never known.

Murray and I had eaten dinner with friends at a Broadway restaurant. We returned home around midnight and sometime around 5 or 6 a.m., the telephone rang. Murray got up to answer it. I was half asleep with the pillow over my head when he poked me in the ribs, jumped on me, and forced me to wake up. He had a huge grin on his face as he said, 'Anne's phoned from home. The Bill's just passed.'

He pulled me out of bed to dance around the apartment, singing like a little kid: 'We're le-gal, we're le-gal!' And my first thought was of nursery rhymes. Now Jack and Bill could go up the hill, or that Boys and Boys could come out to play, or that I could ride my Cock Horse to Banbury Cross wearing bells on my fingers and bells on my toes and making music wherever I go. Ding Dong, the Witch was Dead and, now that the Big Bad Wolf was gone, I could go Into the Woods.

3.

When I read 'like a queen' I was totally shaken.

It's been 36 years since the Homosexual Law Reform Act was passed in 1986, and 27 years since I wrote my 1995 novel *Nights in the Gardens of Spain*. The Property Relations Amendment Act 2001 had given *all* de facto couples the same property rights as have existed since 1976 for married couples on the break-up of a relationship. Civil unions were legalised in 2005. The Marriage Amendment Bill, allowing same-sex and transgender couples to marry, was passed in 2013. The New Zealand military is regarded as the most inclusive in the world.

And still this yearning.

To be.

Simply to *be* let be.

To express openly gay thoughts, desires, stories, dreams and ensure that they can be implemented judicially, equitably and equally in a country where one in 20 adults identifies as being LGBTIQ+.

This was the result published in the Household Economic Survey for the year ended June 2020. The survey also had another interesting statistic. Of the total adult population, almost 0.8 per cent identified as transgender or another gender/non-binary.

Back in 1986, there had been as many gay men and women as there were Māori in Aotearoa New Zealand. It was the reason why it was so easy for me to flip from Māori politics to gay politics in 1991. In that year a group of gay friends and I, mainly Trevor

Herewini and Bunny Thompson, established Te Waka Āwhina Tāne, aka Te Waka Āwhina Takatāpui Tāne. Although the AIDS Foundation funded a Māori education group for gay Māori throughout Aotearoa, ours was the first for Māori and Pasifika gay men and women in Auckland.

Te Waka Āwhina Tāne found office space with the Isherwood Trust, raised money privately, and we were soon in business. I like to think that we were a practical organisation. We didn't just sit at a desk in an office; our main work was going out into the community to talk to Māori men, bisexual as well as gay, specifically about using condoms. We weren't exactly welcome, and we got into physical fights with some men who were angry when we bailed them up about their sexual practices, safe or not.

Those with HIV were often too frightened to see a doctor, so we set up home visits for them. Most heart-rending were the times when some members of the Auckland community died. Some whānau, knowing their boy was gay, had not recognised them in life and had no intention of acknowledging them in death. But we took them home anyway, and that meant more battles. At one place we were denied entry until the boy's mother came out, let loose with a karanga and, well, we couldn't be stopped after that.

Later, Mama Tere Strickland — who worked with the transgender community as well as with vulnerable sex workers — came to see me and asked if she could bring some of her girls into the collective. I said yes, expecting that our current membership would be OK with that. But gay politics was still somewhat restrictive at the time, and supporting transgender, let alone sex workers, came with different sets of challenges. We began to have organisational problems that were solved only by splitting up into separate groups.

We did double duty — not only as Māori, but as gay Māori. And, reflecting on those times from the vantage point of 2022, I find it fascinating and important that there are LGBTIQ+ writers who are doing the same double duty today. Chris Tse, for instance, appears elsewhere in this anthology in his representation as the Asian Other; in 2021, he co-edited *Out There: An Anthology of Takatāpui and LGBTIQ+ Writers from Aotearoa*. Essa Ranapiri appears as the Māori Other; in 2022, they co-edited *No Other Place to Stand: An Anthology of Climate Change Poetry in Aotearoa New Zealand*. We hold up these important examples of Racial Other and Gay Other but also Gender Other.

Every generation must keep telling its stories.

Importantly, every generation must keep telling its generation's stories, opening the space for more diversity, more individuality.

Every generation must keep the watch.

In the past we may have been the last to come out of the swamp or, if you like, from that dark cave where we were abused or assaulted or killed or used by those who preferred to not let their desires be seen in the light. That's still happening today, despite the significant shifts in politics.

That's what must still be spoken to.

Today, we don't need to hide like some of us did in my day. The identities of this generation are clear; most don't hide any longer. However, there are still some who do because of societal pressure. Being gay in any shape or form can get you harmed or even killed.

But they are strong. They are shapeshifters, divinators, with skills and knowledge amassed from all the people in the dark before them, allowing them to look at how to change the future.

For all those who keep bringing us out of the long darkness, I echo Chris Tse: You should all be king, and all those things. Monster, wanton, happy; that bottle that never empties. Visible. Bold. The reason everyone knows your name.

You are more than enough.

You *should* be queen.

The poem 'like a queen' is included with the poet's permission. The second part of this essay is extracted from an interview with Witi Ihimaera, filmed at the Isherwood Trust's Auckland office, in 1996.

Witi Ihimaera (Te Whānau-a-Kai, Te Aitanga-a-Māhaki, Rongowhakaata, Ngāti Porou, Tūhoe) has had careers in literature, diplomacy and academia. He was Aotearoa New Zealand's first Māori novelist, with his novel *Tangi* (1973), and works as editor, essayist, filmmaker, playwright and critic. His latest book is *Navigating the Stars* (2020). He served for 16 years as a New Zealand diplomat, in Canberra, New York and Washington, DC. He is Emeritus Professor of English at the University of Auckland Waipapa Taumata Rau. His international awards include a Premio Ostana, 2010, and a Chevalier de l'Ordre des Arts et des Lettres, 2017. He is patron of Kotahi Rau Pukapuka Trust and, in 2022, was made President of Honour of the New Zealand Society of Authors. He lives in Tāmaki Makaurau Auckland.

Janis Freegard
You'll never see
unless you look

Your head sinks into the pillow, you pass through the tunnel where sometimes, briefly, voices speak words that don't quite make sense, where there are shapes and patterns you only ever see in this state, then you're through to the other world, the sleep world.

It's different here. Life happens in fragments. Time means nothing. A friend can become a cat and then your cousin. You see someone you know but they are wearing a stranger's face. Electrical appliances will not work. The dead were never dead.

Try to wake up inside this world. This way you can influence events. Flying is a good option for you. It may take a few tries. To start with, you might be hovering just above the ground, worrying about crashing down. Don't. Don't think about that. Concentrate on levitating above rooftops and trees. Get as high as you can because the view from here will be better. See? Drink it in. Now you are a kārearea. Or a spaceship. The city, with all its city concerns, is far below.

If you're not flying, and find yourself in a large house, and you are very afraid of what is in the basement, go on down there. Descend those cold, concrete stairs. The house is you. Open the basement door and say hello to yourself.

Janis Freegard's novel *The Year of Falling* (2015) was recently translated into Bulgarian. She is the author of several poetry collections; the latest, *Reading the Signs* (2020), includes themes of climate change and gender fluidity. Her short stories and poetry have been widely published in Aotearoa and beyond. She lives in Te Whanganui-a-Tara Wellington.

KŌRERO

Louise Umutoni-Bower
and Apirana Taylor
Standing tall

A conversation on racism and war, survival and healing

Louise Umutoni-Bower and Apirana Taylor speak across oceans from Rwanda to Aotearoa to look at the pain we carry from deep historical wounds, and how healing is possible. Umutoni-Bower says: 'We have made all of these advances in different ways, in different places, but we haven't quite moved beyond what we'd call archaic perceptions of humanity, of who's human and who's equal.' Apirana Taylor comes to the conversation with his multicultural history, and between them these two writers ponder the common ground of loss, trauma and, ultimately, what it means to be human.

Louise Umutoni-Bower is a Rwandan writer and the founder of Huza Press, which publishes contemporary literature by African authors. The press supports literary events on the African continent, and created Rwanda's first literary prize, the Huza Press Prize for Fiction, in 2015. An anthology of the best submissions was also published in 2016. In 2022, she was the African Region judge for the Commonwealth Short Story Prize. Ntsika Kota was announced as the winner, the first writer from Eswatini, Africa, to have won this prestigious award.

Apirana Taylor (Te Whānau-ā-Apanui, Ngāti Porou, Ngāti Ruanui, Te Ātiawa, Pākehā) is a poet, playwright, novelist, short story writer, storyteller, actor, painter and musician. He has published six collections of poetry, four short story collections, two novels and three plays. He writes for children and the theatre, brings poetry to schools, libraries, tertiary institutions and prisons throughout New Zealand, and is involved in acting and teaching drama. His recent publications include the poetry collection *The Breathing Tree* (2014) and a novel, *Five Strings* (2017).

Understanding
a poem by Apirana Taylor

understanding grows out of healing

healing grows out of life

life grows out of pain

pain grows out of feeling

fear grows out of not knowing

light grows out of knowing

healing grows out of understanding

love

LU-B: Apirana, it's quite interesting, listening to you — thinking about how does healing come about? Where does it come from? And I'm reflecting on some of what you're saying because, coming into this conversation, some of the things at the back of my mind are that we're currently going through the commemoration of those whose lives were lost in 1994 in the genocide here, in Rwanda, against the Tutsi, and thinking about what I have observed in the past few years. When I encounter family members and friends who were here at that time, I realise that the healing I thought we had all experienced isn't quite where I hoped it would be. I see the scars — they're so apparent now. I think that there was a period — and maybe it's me becoming much more aware of it, or maybe it's that people are a little less anxious about baring their wounds because it's not too close to when it happened — but I see the pain now much more than I did years ago, which was closer to the event. And I think I worry about those people who walk around with those wounds that have refused to heal, that have refused to close up . . .

These people who continue to carry around this pain, they seem quite incapable of moving past this period. They continue to live within this period. And there's quite a lot of what I would describe as PTSD that's been transferred to younger people — and you see them walking through life with that experience as well. And it's very worrying, because these experiences, these harmful behaviours that we inflict on others, have such long-lasting effects; it's not one generation that is going to have to deal with the issues, and then move on — it is passed on.

I lost my grandparents; I lost quite a lot of people on my mother's side of the family during the genocide here. And I actually walk around with this sense of 'Am I truly secure?' You know, there's a sense of: Could this just go up in flames? Should I be thinking about options for my children to have a place to run off and hide in case something like this were to happen again? This sense of *nowhere is safe* is quite . . . It's constantly there, and yet I wasn't even here during the genocide: I was not here. I was quite young — I was seven when it happened — I did not experience anything first-hand. It's interesting to see what's been transferred to my generation, but also even more complicated, to younger people — what's been transferred . . . There are children who were not even alive at the time, because it's been 28 years since the genocide. It's interesting to see these children, who are now teenagers, walking around with the same wounds, the same perspectives, and the same view of the world. And you wonder: How do you deal with some of these issues? I feel like the challenge is that the impact is so long-lasting — *so* long-lasting — it's waves and waves of it . . .

AT: Yes. Because 1994 isn't long ago. In places like Rwanda the blood is fresh. The blood that was spilled is still wet, sticky — hot and still there. It bleeds through generations. We can only try to stem the flow — and in time try to create some kind of healing.

How do we build a better world? Life seems in such peril: climate change, world wars, epidemics, totalitarian states. We've always had wars, we'll always have epidemics, and racism. These evils don't go away. How do we live within this dark world?

We hear of economic recessions, but the real evil behind the world's problems is a spiritual recession. How do we change the world? We need to change within ourselves. We need to strive for a 'higher' level of existence. We may have the technology to put people on the moon and to send spaceships to Mars, but psychologically and spiritually we live like savage gorillas and seem incapable of rising above this. Gorillas are probably more civil to each other than we are to one another. When I think about it, racism plays a major role in every war I've ever heard of, and it's part of our inhumanity to each other.

This is my poem called 'Parihaka', which explains some of the colonial injustices and racism visited upon my peoples.

Parihaka

we never knew
about Parihaka
it was never
taught anywhere
except maybe

around the fires
of Parihaka
itself at night
when stories
are told
of the soldiers
who came
with guns
to haul us up
by the roots
like trees
from our land
though the prophets
called peace peace
it was never
taught at school
it was all hushed up
how we listened
to the prophets
Tohu, Te Whiti
who called peace 'Rire rire
Pai mārire'
but the only
peace the soldiers
knew
spoke through
the barrels
of their guns
threatening
our woman children
it was never
taught or spoken

how we

were shackled

led away to the caves

and imprisoned

for ploughing our land

The sadness is that there's only one race, and it's the human race. Some of us are darker, some of us are paler, some of us have blue eyes, green eyes, brown eyes, etc. But we are the same race.

So to speak with you is significant — it's the same problem. Fear of someone who looks a little bit different. We have to rethink this. And it's not just on a small one-on-one basis — a man and a woman killing each other — but on the wider one also, the human race, which is on a journey of mass slaughter and global destruction.

LU-B: But even in the one-on-one — that's the bit that I think I sometimes want to focus in on: that one-on-one encounter where you have this person, this human, looking at another human, and deciding in that moment that the other person does not have the humanity that is required to continue to exist. How does one navigate that in-between space? How do you make up your mind, within that moment, that *this* human who's across from you actually isn't human, and doesn't have the qualities that you have, which are described as 'human', and because of that you have the permission to take their life? What gives you that permission to do that? How do you get there?

That's something that I'm constantly aware of. It was Maya Angelou who said that in dehumanising you're killing yourself as a human; you actually do not win in that process, because when you take the life of another you do not become victorious, actually. I found quite a lot of comfort in those words, because I had always felt like in a way there was a bit of victory on the side of the perpetrator because they got what they wanted. But now I realise that in that moment of depriving my grandmother or my uncle or my aunty of their lives the perpetrator actually deprived themselves of their own humanity, of their own ability to see themselves as a human. So then the question is: What does it mean to be human?

AT: Well, there's a link between the words 'human' and 'humane'.

LU-B: Yes. Yes.

AT: I think I know exactly what you're saying, because in order to wipe someone out you have to come up with justification; you have to make them seem like savages. You have to make them seem not quite human — which therefore gives you justification to go in and wipe them out, rape their women, take their land and kill the children — because they're not human. And this, I think, goes back to the fact that we have to realise we are *all* human. There's only one race, the human race. We have our differences, and so it should be — what a boring life it would be if we were all the same, all square boxes! And we should learn as much as possible to work with each other and appreciate people's differences, to grow together and learn from one another. I've had some wonderful experiences in my life as an artist, working with other artists from different cultures. It works well when there is a sharing of power — each has equal power and can come together to learn from each other, and they can create beautiful work, from their backgrounds, their stories. And this is how it should be.

LU-B: I think when you started this conversation and you were talking about the fact that these things have happened here, for a very long time — that there is a sense of the 'other', and wanting to depict the other as contrary to your existence, as *counter* to your existence. If you see other people as enhancing your experience of the world, and see that it's their *difference* that enhances your experience of life, that's beautiful, and you don't want to get rid of them. But if you see them as taking up your space, if you see the other as going against who you are, they are challenging what you perceive as yourself. This is what we see in racism: *I'm superior; I cannot treat you like me, because then that means that I am no longer superior and we're equal. But I have to be superior because that is the sense of who I am, and I've defined myself through that lens of being superior to you.* And so you have this constant engagement through that lens. And that's been the case for quite a long time.

But what I worry about is that we haven't moved as far as I thought we should have. We have made all of these advances in different ways, in different places, but we haven't quite moved beyond what we'd call archaic perceptions of humanity, of who's human and who's equal. In the past decade (and maybe this is what other generations that have come before have also felt), there's almost been a cementing of the fact that actually these things are here to stay. We haven't had a world war, but we've had many wars, and many wars that are rooted in these perceptions and these ways of thinking. We haven't had physical wars, but we've had *structural, systemic* wars that have solidified these perceptions — new types of wars that have reinforced the same perceptions that are in place about who is more important, who matters more.

I was reading something on the issue in Ukraine, and the fact that the reception of refugees from Ukraine in Poland is quite different to the reception of other non-European refugees into Poland. It's interesting to observe how certain lives are perceived as being more valuable than others, and just how pervasive this is in society. Ukrainian refugees are being received by unusually kind military personnel. They are carried if tired, and treated with such kindness, because the Polish see themselves in these people. And they receive them and say, 'You can settle in Europe for three years'; they give them residency permits without even a formal request. Whereas you have people who have more Asian heritage who are completely shut out, and the same military personnel are sent to keep them out at all costs. When we see this stark contrast in how people are treated, we are reminded of that sense that, actually, the world is not equal, and we've not evolved beyond these backward perceptions of who is human and who isn't. The superiority complex that is very much driven by Caucasian, Western humans has lasted and sadly gained salience over time.

AT: Racism, institutionalised and in all its ugly forms, often leads to war because of the madness of different cultures and ethnicities trying to dominate and oppress each other. The following poem is about the First World War and its madness.

rat a tat tat

who's that knocking

rat a tat tat

rat a tat tat

it's machine-gun Johnny

chatter chat chat
chatter chat chat

sweeping the field

rat a tat tat
rat a tat tat

looking for the boy in a man-sized hat

for a chatter chat chat
chatter chat chat

for empire adventure and all that

rat a tat tat
rat a tat tat

the bullets spat
from the nostrils of the gun

rat a tat tat
rat a tat tat

mothers weep
there lies your son

rat a tat tat

rat a tat tat

16 years old
fancy that

rat a tat tat
rat a tat tat

freedom's not cheap

rat a tat tat
rat a tat tat

do we remember

chatter chat chat
rat a tat tat

who's that knocking

rat a tat tat
chatter chat chat

LU-B: This weekend, I went away for a few days with my family, and there was this gentleman who runs a bed and breakfast in Muhaunga. He is a Rwandan Belgian. And he reminded us of an issue we have ignored for many years, which is the issue of what happened to the 'métis', the children who were born from sexual encounters between Belgian men who had gone off to the colonies and the women they found within those countries. So there was already this power divide: these women were raped, they were treated badly. The men were priests; they had their own families back home — and they went and sowed their oats throughout the continent . . . and then left. These men never wanted anything to do with the children who were birthed out of these forced acts. But the strange thing is what the Belgian government did *after* this: they went to these countries where the Belgian officials had been placed, and took the children who were born out of these encounters away from whatever families those children had — usually the African families they were born into. They took them away, changed their names, changed their identity . . . It was almost like a forced deportation from the countries — they basically took them and then placed them in foster families, mostly with Flemish families. The government would give a certain amount of money to these Flemish families to take care of these children in foster families.

I keep thinking of the impact of that — of that basic deprivation of who you are, what you are, what you stand for — and also to be told you were not wanted by your father, and you're never going to find your mother (because they tried really hard to distort any information that would lead you to finding out who your mother is). It's such a dehumanising experience. And to see the repercussions of that on this gentleman we met, and also quite a few other people I have encountered . . . The level of trauma that lives with a person is hard to see, but it is there. And, again, here we see this divide, this idea of 'Who is human? Who deserves to live a human experience?'

AT: Māori history is very similar in many ways. I think that to a certain extent when the colonisers came here the thrust seemed to be twofold. What drove them was piety and greed. Two strange things that came out of it: 'missionarise' us and take the land! And to take someone's land or subjugate them, oppress them — you have to justify it by saying they're not human.

It all goes back to what we've already said here, what we have to remember: We're all human. We have our faults, but we have to try and go for a higher form of human being. It's very difficult because we live in this world which so often draws us away from that. We are threatened by people who are different; we don't like them. And I often think this is because we don't have respect: men don't respect the women; women don't respect the men. We don't respect the sky; we don't respect the Earth. There's no respect. No respect for God, if you believe in God. No respect for these things.

We must learn respect for others and have some respect for ourselves — because, as you said: if we kill another human being, we become inhuman ourselves. And that begins here: the soul — the wairua, as we call it — this needs to go to a higher level.

LU-B: One of the things I struggle with is this need for us to rise above what's been set as 'the bar' to our encounter with those who choose to treat us as lesser than we are, or choose to see us as lesser than we are. We've got to rise above that and first of all not be reactive to it, and try to get into this place where we're saying we're all equal. Because we could do the reverse, we could say *Well, you don't think I matter — well, you don't matter either!* And then we're in this weird position whereby we're not affirming anyone's humanity or the basic sense of who they are, and we end up in this space of *I'm not affirming your humanity; you're not affirming my humanity.*

But what we're doing a lot of the time is coming in and saying: I affirm that you're a human and you matter, but I also want to affirm that I matter, and I'm human, too. It's quite a lot of pressure and expectation from the one who has been the victim to rise above this, and be this super-human. There is strength in that, but it's also exhausting because you're constantly having to rise to a level that is difficult. Because you're already the victim, you've already experienced repression and yet are required to rise above that, to be a better human, to create the space for the two of you, for both your abuser and yourself to coexist.

It's interesting — this coexisting in this world, and the challenge of it. I find it strange that we arrive at this point, choosing to pursue Christianity. I wonder if you can talk about your spiritual upbringing.

AT: I had strong spiritual upbringing from my father's side of the family. He's a Pākehā — 'Pākehā' is what we call European white people. His parents were missionaries and Salvation Army officers. So we had that, and my mother — my Māori mother — had her own spirituality. And I'm lucky I was born with both of those cultures, and I got the best from both. But I steered away from Christianity for a long time, because my mother died when I was young and I thought: *If God loves me, why has He taken my mother?* But I always felt that there is a spiritual side to things. And 11 years ago my baby sister Haina got killed in a road accident, which pulled me back to the Church: it didn't solve the problem, but it helped me to cope.

We get trapped in the darkness, but it's not a good way to live, carrying around hatred, anger, sorrow and pain, either on a personal level or a global level.

LU-B: No, it doesn't make you any better, and it doesn't make the place any better. Again, we're back to that place where you have to rise above — this automatic reaction that you get to these sorts of things. The question of coexistence, and the courage we need.

> You may not control all the events that happen to you, but you can decide
> not to be reduced by them.
> — Maya Angelou

Sudha Rao
Coracle at a confluence

Prologue

The first time I saw
a coracle was the last
sight of my father
sliding off a riverbank
in a small elegant box.

Shouldered by his sons'
calm and focused grave faces
the boatman pushed off
a riverbank glistening
and below the coracle.

Water a-swirling
green silk saree, unfolded
a climbing ancient
certain sun over grass
losing dew by sun rising.

The monsoon had gone
leaving a wake of flora
like a ritual
path slow and deliberate
for my father turned ash.

My father's journey
was his last with family
on a coracle
to join his parents at the
holy rivers' confluence.

The photograph showed
a simple box paddled down
a silent river
leaving my mother behind
but not captured by the shot.

There are no pictures
of my mother on the day
my father journeyed
leaving her banked alone
edged by the fright of it all.

Thirteen years ago
she was at a confluence
standing on her soil
harnessing timidity
to rise from his ash new-born.

Confinement

A tiny beast brought
her world to a standstill
as an invasion
on boundaries she called
calling on her loved ones.

Thirteen years later
we crossed the air between us
on a flat screen
to unwind her history
on her coracle for me.

Confined by her space
my ninety-year-old mother
nodding with white hair
spoke like a black bird at night
waiting to rest at sun-up.

From her enviable
Wellington harbour outlook
tides glistened and peaked
shadow free from shipping boats
but bearing daring seagulls.

An accidental
storyteller displays her
open memory
pad with magical wonder
as the sun dapples her walls.

Mother mother

She, of her mother, says
Eshtu chenage idhlu
Sudha, when she died
I was second-time unmoored
from my umbilical cord.

Composed again now
she becomes that precious stone
in a black and white
picture framed by her white hair
transformed into a young girl.

Here she is singing
long plaits pale face hesitant
eyes looking into
her deprivation, her void
'Oh Mother! I bow to thee.'

Her song celebrates
a gathering of warm smiles
draped in sarees
an ocean of recipes
an invocation to life.

Here she is married
a punctuation altered
by a new goodbye
bucketing expectations
when a red mantle turns blue.

She watches herself
opening a locked door
for unfamiliar voices
to surround and bind her path
to mothering and loving.

When she breathes

Bound for New Zealand
a cyclone hit the east coast
before she left home
the wind whistled adventure
and the forest was damaged.

Her tales are many
with commas falling as leaves
for the wet soils torn bark
growing children losing tongue
while she breathed out her joy.

Our genealogy
she recites back urgently
wrapped in silk thread
the flat screen vibrates felling
words yet freedom comes skipping.

Her lifetime weaving
carried by ether, carries
her song to bury
deep and play with memories
dropping unearthed gold stars.

Epilogue

How was I to know
this was a curtain raiser
on my mother —
she was plaiting for me
a coracle for our births.

At the confluence
she took me into a time
where time stopped for her
and I blinded and muted
connected to her big smile.

She made me see youth
before unexpected loss
sowed a deep sense
of longing for her mother
who dared the river crossing.

How this drives her
ferocious love for her four
how she feeds talk
with a banquet of spices
celebrated vanished.

When she speaks of us
we become her extensions
but she is computing
our paths away from struggles
she cannot bear to grasp.

This is my mother
emerging from a screen
talking laughing eyes
appear on screen as if
for the first time she breathes.

My mother floats above
the currents of her long life
I turn into a
parallel conversation
she, herself I inherit.

I am two women
one-time child one-time awed
by a small beast
unravelling yet binding
us, spinning silver thread.

The phrase 'Eshtu chenage idhlu', in Rao's mother tongue, Kannada, translates literally to 'How beautiful she was'.

Sudha Rao is a poet, dancer and teacher. Her first collection of poetry, *On Elephant's Shoulders*, was published in 2022. Her work has appeared in the anthologies *Breach of All Size: Small Stories on Ulysses, Love and Venice* (2022) and *Ko Aotearoa Tātou | We Are New Zealand* (2020). Originally from South India, she grew up in Ōtepoti Dunedin and now lives in Te Whanganui-a-Tara Wellington.

James Norcliffe
The four limitations

What you must know, said the dancing master, is that there are four limitations.

The first is the floor.

The second is the ceiling.

The third is the walls.

The class waited.

But I must confess I have forgotten the fourth, lost it completely.

The question in the air buzzed like a fly.

Is it gravity? hazarded one student, who wished to dance to the moon.

Is it light? asked another, who feared the darkness.

Is it imagination? asked one who dreamed wonder and wondered dreams.

Is it movement? Mobility? asked another, frightened of arthritis.

Is it the audience? asked the one who desired fame.

Is it memory? asked another who was slightly ambidextrous, always a bad thing in a dancer.

Rhythm? asked one, who occasionally missed a beat.

Cooperation? asked one ever fearful of being dropped or of dropping.

Is it the other? asked his friend. There must be deux to tango.

It is music, of course, said a smug one. What is dance sans music!

There was silence.

Put us out of our misery, master, the class begged finally. Which one of us is right?

The master shook his head.

No, it wasn't a trick question. Not at all, he insisted. I was telling the truth. I have genuinely lost my fourth limitation. Although, he added, it seems each one of you has found yours.

James Norcliffe is an award-winning writer of poetry and fiction, including nine collections of poetry and 11 novels for children and young people. His latest books are *The Frog Prince* (2022) and the poetry collection *Dear 'Oumuamua* (2023). He has co-edited major poetry, short fiction and essay anthologies including, most recently, with Michelle Elvy and Paula Morris, *Ko Aotearoa Tātou | We Are New Zealand* (2020). He has been awarded the Burns Fellowship, the Iowa International Writing Program residency, the University of Otago College of Education Creative New Zealand Fellowship for Children's Writing, and the Randell Cottage Writing Fellowship residency in Te Whanganui-a-Tara Wellington. He received the Prime Minister's Award for Literary Achievement for Poetry in 2022. He lives in Church Bay, Banks Peninsula.

Part three

Stepping out into the world before us

Te tōrino haere whakamua, whakamuri

At the same time as the spiral goes outward
it is coming back; at the same time as it spirals
forward it is returning.

Victor Billot
Before dawn

In the night of rain, bright jackets flash
against solemn hulls and wharves.
In warehouses where there is no night,
where call centres murmur ecstatically,
where an evanescent glow leaks from screens,
and networks are restless with cold energies.
Where nodes are sprinkled across dark plains
humming with latency, numinous and sinister,
where querulous alarms cry in shadows
cast by a sodium glare on concrete hectares.
The hours stripped of time, the heat drawn from youth,
and we are formless, divided and scattered
by the dialects of power and capital,
by invisible lines, by resources, by exigency.
This Devil and God enmeshed:
on the heaving fevered chest of the world,
a wing'd creature squats unmolested,
summoned from the complexity of our needs.
Yet there is great confusion, agitation.
Reefs bleed away their dream of colour.
Typhoons thrash humid coasts, relentless.
The monster grins, inhales. World eater.
Everything consumed, leaving foul silt.
Parasite tendrils curve cruel, barbed,
teeth affixed to the world's arteries.
The gates of Paradise are sealed. Just the maw
of arriving dawn remains, as a strange
and terrible day unfolds into being,
to make us what we must become.

Victor Billot's most recent book is the poetry collection *The Sets* (2021). He writes a weekly satirical ode on current affairs for the Newsroom website. His own website is victorbillot.com. He lives in Ōtepoti Dunedin.

Michelle Elvy
Sailing to Aotearoa

I. Two steps forward, three steps back

Pacific Crossing Log Notes, Day 25 — At the equator, almost
N 01° 08.8' W 124° 38.7'

We've been hovering near the equator for days. First it was those 48 hours up at 4 degrees north — seems like ages ago, and 3 degrees away seems a fair distance. In reality, it's only around 200 miles, but at our present rate that is quite a distance. We've been around 1 degree north all day today. In the middle of the night now, we are at 50' north, but we'll be north of there, and south of there, before morning comes.

Presently we are going a half-knot in a northeasterly direction, but a while ago we were managing the same speed on a southerly track. With no wind, we are at the mercy of the swells and current. We should start placing bets when we go to bed about the spot of ocean we'll find ourselves in the next morning. It might be a fun guessing game to play with the kids.

Lola and Jana gave up asking about the equator ages ago. Only today was their interest renewed when I announced that we were now at 1 degree north: only 60 more miles to go, theoretically.

We search in vain for their blow-up plastic globe, and settle instead on an orange and some pens. The orange has been in the fridge, and the Sharpies have smeared; instead of any rendition of North and South America and the islands of the Pacific, we end up with an orange that looks like it's been in a fist-fight. Orange and black and blue.

But the kids get the idea: the line I draw for the equator, while neither precisely in the middle nor straight, is the most effective part of my rendition of the world.

'So the equator is on the Earth to show us the halfway line?'

'Well, yes, but it's not actually *on* the Earth.'

'But it's there to divide the Earth *equally* in halves?'

'Yes. Did you figure out that *equator* divides *equally* all by yourself?'

'Yeah; why else would it be called that?'

I still have to explain that the equator is not a line that we'll actually *see* when we cross it, but Lola gets it intuitively. I suppose that, after all these miles at sea, she would not expect to see a great big line drawn on the ocean surface.

We haul out the paper charts and have a lesson in latitude and longitude, which is harder to explain to a six-year-old than you might think, even if she's eager and immersed in a world where latitude and longitude matter. We muddle our way through, talking about graphs and pencilling in lines on the chart for the Îles Marquises until we establish where we are going. Sometime during my not-so-effective explanation of minutes and seconds, both girls lose interest. Jana wants to draw her own pencil markings on the chart. Lola has moved on to Jell-O.

Seascape: swell

A calm sea is mirror still. On windless days you can't distinguish the line between sea and sky. The horizon is a shimmery mirage: blurred and beckoning.

But there is movement.

You are lifted and set down gently between waves: the height of a hill, when you can see almost round the world, then the deep trough, the surrounding blue.

The Earth is breathing.

Breathe with her: a reassuring rhythm.

Inhale, reach up and out. Stretch to the sky — you can almost reach it. Now open your arms to the sides and hold them above the Earth. Look out over one outstretched palm: where you come from. Turn your head and gaze across the length of your arm, out over your fingertips extending forward: beyond today and tomorrow. A longing you send out across the lower atmosphere. A gentle lift: optimism down through your spine. You stand tall and a line extends from the crown of your head down through your tailbone to the centre of the Earth.

Everything is connected, down to the core of things.

Exhale, relax into the deep. The deep of your insides, the deep of the ocean. Your view is obstructed by water rising up on all sides. You reach the bottom and there is no horizon, no backward and forward, no past and future. Nothing to see but this *here*. Nothing to feel but this moment, between breaths. The next will come and you'll reach up and out again; the Earth will inhale and hold you.

But before that happens, before the next inhalation: fold into yourself.

This is the now world: only water.

How will we celebrate the equator crossing when it finally comes? Some people mark such occasions with a celebratory plunge. Over the side you go: leap high and away from your boat, straight into the great big blue. I have tried to remain open-minded about this, but I cannot imagine that you'd willingly lower yourself into the water while offshore. For some, this mid-ocean plunge is a highlight of a long sailing trek. Me? I think, most emphatically: *No, thank you.*

Even if I consider rationally all the ways that this could be fun, I cannot convince myself to do it. Nor can I imagine chucking my children overboard into the wide abyss. I have a constant and pervading fear of them jumping in and being swallowed up. This fear is probably a good thing — it is the very thing that keeps my guard up at all times when we are out on deck, the reason the children have harnesses, the reason they are never outdoors without us while at sea, the reason I track their every movement all around the boat.

That's not to say I don't share the sense of awe at all that blue. Miles Hordern says it best, describing the moment he dives in (out of necessity, note) for an offshore repair: 'There is only blue, and silence. Blue to America, blue to Asia, blue to both poles . . . This place is limitless. Endless. But so short. Just one breath.'[1]

Pacific Crossing Log Notes, Day 27 — Fog
N 00° 47.0' W 124° 29.8'

We've set a new record for ourselves today: we've gone 16 miles in the wrong direction in the last 24 hours. The other day I was looking at the chart of Captain Cook's meandering off the windward side of the Big Island

---

1 Miles Hordern, *Sailing the Pacific: A Voyage Across the Longest Stretch of Water on Earth, and a Journey into its Past.* St Martin's Press, 2004, pp. 140–41.

of Hawai'i, and wondered how on earth they could have spent a month in one place. I'm not wondering anymore. We're just trying to get to the equator and then south of it — and we know where it is.

But knowing where it is doesn't make it any less elusive. It draws nearer on some days, then recedes again in the night. Yesterday we hand-steered all day in an attempt to keep us more or less tracking in the right direction.

By the late afternoon, we are forced to concede our failure; the current is pushing *Momo* once more in a steady northeasterly direction with no breeze coming to our rescue. It matters not what direction we point her bow — the sea is having her way with us, stealthily dragging us backward, allowing us the occasional illusion of facing the right way.

Our 24-hour period, despite our efforts at the helm: *minus* 16 nautical miles.

doldrums (n.)
1: a spell of listlessness or despondency
2: often capitalized, oceanography: a part of the ocean near the equator abounding in calms, squalls, and light shifting winds
3: a state or period of inactivity, stagnation, or slump
— *Merriam Webster Dictionary*

Latitude: 0000

Pacific Crossing Log Notes, Day 32 — Equator Crossing
S 00° 00.00' W 124° 53.209'

After two weeks just north of the 00 line, *Momo* ambles across the equator.

We drifted at an easy 2 knots all morning and therefore had plenty of time to plan for the moment when our GPS would read that line of zeros.

We showered, blew up balloons, baked a special batch of fluffy angel biscuits, broke out a new jar of Oma's strawberry jam, unwrapped our carefully stored pottery wine cups and twirly straw cups for Lola and Jana.

We savour the moment when we pop the cork on our bottle of Champagne Esterlin Brut and unscrew the bubbly apple cider for the kids. We run out a tape on our video recorder, documenting the gorgeous blue skies and calm sea state (barely a noticeable swell) and capturing our children. Jana is converted to Champagne: one sip and she announces, 'I love it!' Lola questions the tradition of offering libations to the god of the sea; she is confused as to why we'd pour a perfectly good drink over the side, especially given that her parents are the least superstitious people she knows. And it's true, really; there are few sailing traditions we follow: we have bananas on board, we sail with women, we leave port on Fridays.

But there's fun in this moment of crossing the equator, and the offering to King Neptune is a tradition that has endured to the present day. We don't dress up as Neptune, or bathe in bilge water, or humiliate our lesser crew. We don't get drunk for days on end. We mark the occasion by drinking a modest bottle of Champagne and taking photos of our kids holding the GPS at 0000. For over an hour we sit up on the cabin top as music by Great Big Sea blasts out our ports, marvelling at the fact that we have crossed the equator and appear, finally, to be heading southwest.

A perfect equator crossing, really — full sails up, no heel to our movement. And plenty of sunshine with a cooling breeze.

Fatu Hiva is 1033 miles away.

Earlier today, Lola and Jana thawed cookie dough from the fridge and made equator cookies: a bright yellow sun, a glowing white moon and a 12-inch planet Earth, decorated with four different colours of icing, mostly lots of blue: limitless, endless. An ample number of sprinkles make up the band across the middle. The sprinkles are generously dispersed, taking up about 20 degrees of latitude on the cookie-map. But you can't skimp on sprinkles.

And there, on the cookie planet Earth: the tiny dot of a sailboat making its way west across all that blue.

II. Between me and my sorrow

In her book *Searching for Steinbeck's Sea of Cortez: A Makeshift Expedition Along Baja's Desert Coast*, Andromeda Romano-Lax notes the difference between the micro and macro view of what we learn. How we can learn minute details about one subject but then know nothing at all.[2] Her book is semi-scientific, but more a reflection. In the end she has a moment of clarity where she realises that, after travelling the length of the Sea of Cortez, she knows *nothing* at all. And this feels just right.

I started out as an academic. Teaching German history and working towards my PhD. You start out with a general love of knowledge itself, sucking up as much as you can, believing that in some way all this learning is broadening your mind. Which might be true — the more you learn, the more you know; the more you know, the more you understand; the more you understand, the more you want to learn more. Then comes the specialising. And once you specialise, your learning takes on a different focus. With a study of German history in the 1990s, I was moving towards focusing on details. As you go deeper and deeper into one subject, you hazard to lose perspective on everything else.

I'm far removed from that life now. And perhaps I know nothing at all. Except for the startling blue of the tiny floating dragon-like creatures surrounding our boat one day at the equator. Or the weightlessness of holding my breath in a vast quantity of blue while reef life mills around me. Or the feel of my daughters' hands in mine. Or the feeling of time stretching between my life back then and my life now.

Out here, there's nothing between me and my sorrow. No other people or human-made objects to change my path. Reality as real as it gets.

I think it was Joan Didion who wrote that mourning is what you do in the face of a death and grief is what you feel.

A sudden death is abrupt. Everything else we do in life is gradual. There is a learning curve, a way of easing ourselves into new situations. New skills, new loves, new places — they do not come on all at once; you have to develop the skills, feel

---

2 Andromeda Romano-Lax, *Searching for Steinbeck's Sea of Cortez: A Makeshift Expedition Along Baja's Desert Coast*. Sasquatch Books, 2002, pp. 225–30.

the new love washing over you, come to know new places. You acquire habits and navigate step-by-step.

When my two older brothers died, taken from us when a Cessna fell out of the March sky over the mountainous northern New Mexico, I had a recurring dream. They were alive, with me, and we were always in the middle of something, involved in each other's lives, talking or laughing. Then I would wake up and realise all over again that they were dead. Gone forever. Those dreams were the best I ever had, but the reality — those waking moments — was a nightmare.

There is a fragile state in surviving — the long-term grief never leaves you.

But there is renewal. Time, the great changer. Life, the equaliser. What remains between then and now: grief, yes, but also more. My daughters' voices. The sound of rain on the deck.

> **doldrums (n.)**
> A place to get stuck, as in:
> People who don't pay attention often get stuck in the Doldrums.
> — Norton Juster, *The Phantom Tollbooth*

> **Origami**
> a white page unfolded
> no creases, no shades
> but look closer: quiet lines,
> memory marking ages upon ages

III. And on the 44th day

Pacific Ocean Crossing Log Notes, Day 44 — Arrival in Fatu Hiva, 17 March 2008

Daybreak. Fatu Hiva is a dark lump 10 miles off our starboard side. I play Jacques Brel on the stereo.

1600. Squalls. The biggest yet. Main is reefed down to its smallest;

forward sails down. Big waves rolling over us, breaking across the cabin top. 30–35 knots of wind. I hand-steer in the downpour — saltwater spray mixes with rain on my face, my chest, my legs. Pelting, intense. I think it must be gusting to 40 — I can barely see into the wind coming over the starboard side.

I am exhilarated.

~

And now, anchored.

Today is much like every other day, and yet it is spectacular in its singularity. Today we see the towering peaks of Fatu Hiva, the dramatic squally clouds overhead, the shining spots of blue sky in between.

Today we have 30-knot gusts whistling through the valley and down into our anchorage.

Today Lola wants to climb the top of the hills to touch the clouds. Today Jana says she's happy.

Today one thing happens for the hundredth time, and something else happens for the first time.

Seascape: squall

Squall

Strong wind characterised by a sudden onset in which the wind speed increases at least 16 knots and is sustained at 22 knots or more for at least one minute.

— National Oceanic and Atmospheric Administration (NOAA)

You try to predict the weather in cycles: 12 hours, 24, even 72. A squall is an area of strong localised convection, impossible to foresee longer-term. But even as they race your way, there are signs — there are always signs. In the distance (*Is it coming our way or moving off to the south?*): clouds will build in towering heights, Wagnerian, touching down on the horizon; the line between blackening sky and purpling sea will nearly disappear; where there is rain, a sheet of grey will connect them; the air will become acid, anticipation electric; from behind the magnificent skies the sun may shine through, glowing like a god.

As the squall approaches (*Batten down the hatches; reef the main; dowse the yankee!*): the sea top will become disturbed, wavelets whipped into action by the oncoming wind; everything turns grey, Rachmaninoff rain pounds the sea flat; you will hear it, especially at night, moments before it lands on deck. When the squall is upon you (*Steady course; here comes the heel!*): clashing wind and water, fugue-like acceleration in speed, lasting three minutes up to an hour.

When it's over (*Did we collect water in our buckets?*): silence. Then: slatting sails; sloshing sea; directionless drifting as the boat tries to regain balance and find her way again. And (French horns, Sibelius): tender kisses of colour across the sky, pastel whisperings of a rainbow. And: sails up, onward.

Forty-four days is a long time for an ocean crossing. The days are long, the nights may be even longer. For single-handers, time stretches, becomes indistinguishable. Some single-handers talk about how they glide from one day to the next, nights creeping along until the earliest grey streaks in the sky indicate that they've successfully passed another night alone at sea. For someone racing around the world, from Sir Francis Chichester to Ellen MacArthur, each day presents a hundred challenges to overcome.

Crossing the ocean, for me, is a slow unfolding of days with small bursts of enlightenment in the midst of necessary routine. Because everything you do is so basic, even your thoughts can evolve into the most elemental processes. Life at sea is an enforced slowing down, a necessary one.

It took days for us to settle into a routine of resting through the night — after an ocean crossing, we're in the habit of being on alert 24/7. We were tired, exhilarated, inspired and thankful for all our history that has brought us to this point. The choices, the chances, the determination, the luck.

Sea stories almost always end with landfall. Castaway sailors become more developed once they wash up on distant shores; they evolve. Miles Hordern writes about this: in the tradition of the sea story, 'voyaging itself becomes an act of baptism, as the sailor inevitably finds himself struggling for survival in stormy water, the ship and all the certainties of his old life destroyed'.[3] And then he inevitably arrives.

Arrival in Fatu Hiva

You arrive after a month at sea
and it is a grey morning but you
anticipate the pink of papaya flesh,
rust of earth blood, bananaforest smell,
pineapple hellos

You are surprised by the cathedral peaks
not because of their jutting irregular
beauty which you remember from the first time
you arrived ten years back but because you've forgotten
this kind of green

You emerge from a world of salt
and touch dirt, climb the nearest hill
and find yourself short of breath but going
further because among the mangoes and palms
you float on cushioned blue

And this feeling is a crisp something
you inhale and keep close, for when you float
across an ocean or up over the tall hills of Fatu Hiva
you occupy a world of in-between, a white cotton place
where you long to stay

---

3   Hordern, *Sailing the Pacific*, p. 208.

But as far as I can tell, there are no certainties, even after we reach shore.

IV. The beach and the wind

When we arrive in New Zealand in December 2008, I quickly acquaint myself with the literature and poetry shelves in the Whangārei library. For my birthday, I am given Graeme Lay's *The New Zealand Book of the Beach*, which introduces me to a selection of short story writers of Aotearoa and further connects me with the coastline — my entrée to any new place.

The sand slides between my toes, soft and warm. I feel an immediate affection for this place. More than that: a sense of connection, a place my children will feel safe as they grow up. A place I could come to call *home*.

The beach is our point of arrival. For years, this is how we've moved in the world, travelling with slow forward momentum. The wind driving power in our sails, the sense of connectedness with nature.

The beach is also a place beyond us — beyond human connection, beyond human tread. Here in Aotearoa, I come to sense that the beach, more than anywhere else, is where sea and sky and land meet in collusion, shoulders shored in symbolic protection, eyes looking out to the horizon.

Michelle Elvy is a writer, editor and teacher of creative writing. Her books include *the everrumble* (2019) and *the other side of better* (2021), and she has co-edited, among others, the anthologies *Ko Aotearoa Tātou | We Are New Zealand* (with Paula Morris and James Norcliffe, 2020) and *Breach of All Size: Small Stories on Ulysses, Love and Venice* (with Marco Sonzogni, 2022). Founder of *Flash Frontier: An Adventure in Short Fiction* and National Flash Fiction Day, she is also co-series editor of the annual *Best Small Fictions* anthology and is currently editing, with Vaughan Rapatahana, a collection of New Zealand multilingual microfiction. She grew up on the shores of the Chesapeake Bay and now lives in Ōtepoti Dunedin.

Diane Brown
Not feeding the world today

Hens don't get a toehold on our small inner-city plot
only a worm farm with secretive tiger worms,
requiring me to poke under the layer of food scraps
making sure they are still alive in the same way
I prod my husband if he is late to wake.

I suggest we could dig up the field at the top
of our neighbourhood park for fresh vegetables
now so costly for families. I really mean
someone else could dig it up. My husband says
the kids play football there and isn't that important?

There are, I guess, many ways of feeding.
He shows me how soft the bark of the tall
Wellingtonia redwood is. We need fields and trees,
exotic and native, as well as vegetables, he says.
It is difficult to know how to feed the demand

for so much: food, shelter, love, calls more insistent
every day. I could write a poem which might connect
with a lone soul but thin gruel to someone forced
to live on it. Perhaps my mother and grandmother,
less ambitious, had the right idea, growing

what they could, sharing it around without making
a deal of it, getting in the neighbour's washing if it looked
like rain. Making vegetable soup on lean days, preserving
autumn fruits for winter. Never any talk of feeding the world,
just noticing what needed to be noticed.

Diane Brown is a poet and creative writing teacher. Her eight published books range over poetry, novels and memoir. Her latest is the long poetic narrative *Every Now and Then I Have Another Child* (2022). She has held the Buddle Findlay Sargeson Fellowship, the Michael King Writers' Fellowship, the Beatson Fellowship and the Janet Frame Memorial Award. In 2013 she was made a Member of the New Zealand Order of Merit (MNZM) for services to writing and education. She is working on a collection of poems and a long poetic narrative of her female ancestry. She lives in Ōtepoti Dunedin.

Whiti Hereaka

Ngā Rārangi

Atā mārie.

> I mean, is it? It's still 'Pō mārie'
> from where I'm looking, nē?

Atā or pō, there's not a lot of
'mārie' with you around . . .

> Oh, should I just go back to bed then, eh?

C'mon, you grump, let's get going.

> I just don't see why we, as a culture,
> schedule everything to happen
> at the break of bloody dawn.

It's magic that time though,
when te pō gives way to light.

> Āe, but around 10.30 in the morning
> can be just as magical . . .
> Where's the car?

Thought we'd walk.
A good place won't be far away.

> Feels like it will take an eternity . . .

Well, we don't have an eternity, kia tere!

> Why are you so chipper?

Do you think I'm chipper?

> Well, *awake* then.

I kinda like this time of the day.

> I only like this time
> when you think of it as the *end* of a night.

Not the beginning of a day.

It's just so still and quiet . . .

That's because everybody is still bloody asleep!

And they're missing this!

What are they missing?
Because I'm missing my bed.

All of this. The sky will never look like this again.
Everything is moving. Constantly moving.
Tomorrow, it won't be exactly the same,
and neither will we.

The sky doesn't even look like this now.

What do you mean?

Light years and stuff. The stars aren't really there.

They've already moved?

Yeah. We're looking at an illusion.

It's funny to think that
people navigated to their future by the light of the past.
Kinda comforting, really.

How?

That the light endures.

God. Please. No inspirational quotes
until I've had at least one coffee.

One day the sun will collide with the Earth
and swallow us.

                                                        Like that movie?

What movie?

                                                The one about the Earth ending —
                                                    and they're on a golf course.

Caddyshack?

                                                No . . . it has that woman that I like.
                                                    And that man — very tall.

Oh, I know the one. That wasn't the sun.
It was a planet.

                                                        It was a big ol' metaphor.

Isn't everything?

                                                        Even this conversation?

Probably.

                                                        What is it a metaphor for?

I don't know. That's for the critics to decide.

                                                Don't you hide behind postmodern nonsense.
                                                        Say what you mean.

If I knew what I meant,
I wouldn't have to talk about it.

                                            That's just vacuous enough to sound profound.
                                                        Well done.

Shall we stop here?

                                        Well, I don't think we can get much more out of that bit.

I mean to wait.
To watch.

                                    Yeah. Here's good. Ground's wet though.

I brought this to sit on.
I grabbed it from the car before I picked you up.

                         You went to your car, picked this blanket up,
                                  and then *left* your car behind.

Yes. So we could walk.
And talk.

                              Are you regretting your choices now, e hoa?

Spending time with a hōhā like you?
Never.
Perhaps one day our mokopuna will be out here
waiting for the sun to rise.

                                    I hope *they* have coffee.

Probably not.
They reckon we've only got maybe
thirty more years of coffee, tops.
Then the plant won't be able to grow.
And y'know, who knows how much time *we've* got left?

                                 About half an hour, I reckon.

No. As a species.

                                           Oh.

Yeah.

                                           . . .

. . .

              . . .

I brought a thermos.

              Of coffee?

Of course.

              Did you make it?

Of course.

              Hmm.

Hey. This is a precious resource!

              Which makes what you do to it even more distressing . . .

Do you want a mug or not?

              Can't let it go to waste, I s'pose.
              Drink 'em if you've got 'em, nē?

You don't need to pretend you like it.

              You know me.
              I don't pretend.

Straight shooter.

              A spade is a spade, me.
              And this is all right.

The coffee is good?

              I said all right. Not good.
              Ah, nah. It's good, e hoa, it's good.
              We good?

Yeah, we're good.

                        I feel like before I have a coffee, my brain is like a dried-up old sponge.

That's . . . gross.

                                    Like all my thoughts are all compressed,
                                    and there's no room for anything new.
                                    But that first sip hits
                                    . . .
                                    and it's like my brain can absorb things.
                                    There's gaps and connections.
                                    There's room in there, y'know?

So now you've had your coffee,
we can actually have a conversation?

                                    Yeah. I can have big thoughts now.
                                    Meaning of life. Go!

I don't know. 'Be excellent to each other'?

                                    Another movie reference?

That's all we have, isn't it —
flickering shadows on a screen?

                                    Geez, all right. Back to your cave, Plato.

I've always fancied myself as a bit of a Diogenes.

                                    'Behold! A Man.'

Are you calling me a chicken?

                                    If the cluck fits, e hoa . . .

Diogenes Sun, Socrates Moon with Plato Rising, I reckon.

                                        Again, with the sun and the moon . . .

And the rising.
The rising is the important bit.
That's how the world sees.

                              Is the light changing, or is it just my eyes?

I think it is getting lighter.
Yeah, it *is* changing . . .

                                                          . . .

. . .

                                                        What?

What?

                        It just felt like you wanted me to say something.

That's generally how conversations work.

                              No, like something about change and us and . . .

. . . And?

                                        . . . And how we're different now.

Aww. Is that what you wanted to say?

                              It's what I thought *you* wanted me to say.

But don't you feel a little bit different?
The whole world has turned,
and for a short time
we lived
through time and light compressed . . .

I mean . . . wow.

Yes. WOW!

No, I mean *you*. Wow.
It happens literally EVERY DAY.

Just because it happens every day,
doesn't mean we should be blasé about it.
It's a *miracle* that happens every day
and we saw it. Not everyone will.

Yes, because they were asleep.

Here I am trying to show you
the wonders of the universe
and you'd rather be in bed.

I told you what I'm like before coffee . . .

I brought you some coffee . . .

I think it's best we agree to disagree on your 'coffee'.
I'll shout you a real one.

Just a few more minutes.
While it's still and quiet.

. . .

. . .

. . .

. . .

It *is* magic, nē?

Yeah, magic.

Did you hear the tūī?

Yeah. . .

Magic, all right.

Let's get that coffee.

Hey, do you think we can get an Uber out here?

What happened to 'it's not far to walk'?

What can I say? I've changed . . .

Whiti Hereaka (Ngāti Tūwharetoa, Te Arawa, Pākehā) is an award-winning novelist and playwright. She is the author of four novels, including *The Graphologist's Apprentice* (2010), and numerous YA novels. *Legacy* (2018) won the Young Adult Fiction Award at the 2019 New Zealand Book Awards for Children and Young Adults, and *Kurangaituku* (2021) won the Jann Medlicott Acorn Foundation Prize for Fiction at the 2022 Ockham New Zealand Book Awards. She lectures in creative writing at Massey University Te Kunenga ki Pūrehuroa. She lives in Te Whanganui-a-Tara Wellington.

KŌRERO

Aparecida Vilaça, Dame Anne Salmond and Witi Ihimaera
An appreciation of mentors

Following on from the kōrero on 'Ancestry, kin and shared history', Aparecida Vilaça, Dame Anne Salmond and Witi Ihimaera continued to talk about more personal matters: family and, in particular, their mentors. This part of their conversation, shared here separately, is like a koha, a gift or extra offering to remind us all of the elders in our lives and their roles in preparing us, their mokopuna, to stand in their place as the elders of today and tomorrow.

AS: I was thinking about this in relationship to whakapapa. Like you, Aparecida, when you met Paletó, I met an elder, Eruera Stirling, when I was quite young. I was only 17 when I met him and his wife, Amiria, who also became a mentor.

Reflecting on whakapapa, Witi, I also keep coming back to my mother, Joyce, whom you knew, because my mum was the link to my Scottish heritage. I have a great-grandfather, James McDonald, who was very involved with te ao Māori; he was a filmmaker-photographer, the acting director of the then Dominion Museum, and he had a close working relationship with some eminent Māori leaders at the turn of the last century — Apirana Ngata and Te Rangi Hīroa among them. Apirana Ngata was from Te Tairāwhiti, from the East Coast, a visionary, somebody who tried to make sure that his people didn't lose everything — their lives, their tikanga, their reo — and he fought with all his heart and soul to that end. And Te Rangi Hīroa, from Taranaki, the other side of the island, became a medical doctor. They were both brilliant. Te Rangi Hīroa's passion turned from a lifelong study of Māori material culture to include the whole of the Pacific. He became a professor at Yale, eventually.

So my mother, Joyce, through her whakapapa to James McDonald, is the link to that particular part of my genealogy that goes back to Scotland and the small island of Ulva off the west coast of Scotland. And our daughter, Amiria, who Witi also knows, is working very closely with the people there.

Eruera used to say, 'Study your whakapapa like the thousands of hairs on your head, and then you can talk in the gatherings of the people' — and our daughter has taken this advice, more than me, and she's been working in Scotland most recently and discovered that our ancestors there were the keepers of genealogies and histories for the Lords of the Isles. So there is a kind of deep resonance: a love of land, of ancestral stories and pūrākau and whakapapa, if you like, through that link, through my mum.

But equally, Mum knew Apirana Ngata's daughter-in-law, Lorna, and Peggy Falwasser, Lorna's best friend. And when I was 16 they gave me my first entrée into te ao Māori through teaching me some action songs, because I was going off to a high school in the United States as an American Field Scholar. When I think about whakapapa, it links back to my mum, and through her back to Scotland and, through her friendship with Lorna, to Apirana Ngata.

It's interesting how these relationships link up, because Eruera Stirling was mentored by Ngata. He looked up to Apirana Ngata — idolised him. He took part in Ngata's projects of cultural revival and renaissance. So when I think about whakapapa it's very personal — and increasingly so as I get older, and as I get to know more. That passion of connection, and of equal exchange of feeling that really matters — that love of land — is something that grows out of the land, but is probably also tied up with whakapapa in a deep way.

My life as an anthropologist has been born out of those kinds of links, and Witi is part of that story — we were at university together as young students, both from Gisborne, we come from the same town. Our parents knew each other — I've got a beautiful photo, Witi, from when we launched two of our books together, of my mum and your dad, Tom Smiler, sitting together, sending our two books off into the world. We've lived, and still do, in an interconnected cosmos.

WI: We three were talking earlier about this concept of te ao Māori. In our day there used to be te ao Māori and te ao Pākehā. And so, my mentors, including my grandmother Teria Pere and great-aunt Mini Tupara, thought that their role was to make sure I had the opportunity to know who I was in te ao Māori, even though our world was te ao Pākehā. So as a child what they did was take me everywhere with them — and I mean everywhere! — to every marae they visited. (Well, it wasn't as if they could leave me with a babysitter at home, as they were the babysitters.) I guess they tried to stabilise me in te ao Māori because they knew that when I went over into te ao Pākehā this same sense of identity — and whakapapa, of inheritance, because it was always surrounding us in the kōrero on the marae — wouldn't survive.

My upbringing was lacking in male mentors. I was brought up by grandmothers, by kuia and not kaumātua. But I have to say that my father, Te Haa O Rūhia (who you knew as Tom, Anne), was highly influential in his grounding of me into our lives as shearers. But, you know, our leaders in those days wore gumboots and Swanndris during the day; they wore suits, ties and hats when they went to the marae — that was Dad.

The irony is, Anne, with Eruera — the wonderful man whom I was related to through my mum, Julia Keelan — he and his generation saw my parents' generation physically locating themselves in cities where they went looking for jobs. I think Eruera and Amiria were among the very first elders to say, 'Oh, somebody better go where they go to look after them', and relocate from the East Coast to Auckland. Eruera saw we were all growing up there, truly going into te ao Pākehā, and that's where the basis of Pākehā knowledge was. You know, he truly lived by Apirana's dictum about Māori in the future living in both worlds, tender children with both wisdoms.

But to get back to Teria and Mini, they actually pushed me further. They were also showing me that, even though te ao Māori was my inheritance, I had to do something with it — be active in promoting it, become a mediator. In my generation we always said: 'When I grow up I will work for the Māori people.' And that's why I have gratitude for them.

AV: My story is really different. In fact, thinking of this genealogical line: my maternal grandparents were from Amazonia, and I think in a way I went to Amazonia to follow my memories of what they'd been talking to me about during my childhood. I had all the memories of the names of fruit, for example, and I could almost sense the smells, shapes, tastes simply by conjuring the fruit in my mind. But when I arrived among the Wari' as an anthropologist, I was doing my Masters, not yet a PhD. I was 20-something, and I was there, could not speak the language — I arrived there with my suitcase, lots of notebooks and so on. And this man came to me, and people said he was the one who knew everything.

This man was Paletó, and he tried to talk to me and I could not understand. Nor could he speak my language, Portuguese, which was his colonised language. He was speaking and speaking, and I could not understand. His son, who could speak some Portuguese, began to translate some of what he was saying.

Well, of course, I decided I had to learn the language! So I learned it as much as I could. And in three months I could understand the Wari' tongue and what Paletó and the people were saying. They said I could understand what they were saying not because I was taking notes but because I was eating their food. Because eating the same foods is a way to make your body similar — and if you make your body similar, of course you have the same language. So Paletó taught me everything that I know. I owe him my anthropological training. And he gave me lots of love. He took me among his family, to feed me and everything. He said we became 'real' relatives, not 'fake' relatives.

The Wari' do not care about genealogy or ancestry; they say you make yourself kin by being close to people, eating with them the same food, sleeping close to them, going with them and doing things with them, and that's the way your bodies become similar, and becoming similar you become kin. So, by the end of his life, Paletó was always saying: 'You are my real daughter — not fake daughter, my real daughter.' I understand because he was my real father.

WI: In many ways your relationship with Paletó sounds similar to the ones Anne and I had with our mentors. I think that maybe my grandmothers, and Mum and Dad, too, thought that if they did not give us any capital in terms of their investment in us, as young children and as young adults, then we would not be able to survive in that other world that we were going into, which was the inevitability. But I think the most profound thing I ever got from the people who brought me up was that they never thought of the world as being without hope; they always had this tremendous amount of hope. It didn't matter that we had been through the New Zealand Wars, that we were poverty-stricken. None of that mattered. What mattered was to keep going and looking at the future, with hope and the expectation that we would create a better world. Not that the world would be better, but we had to make our way through it in such a way that hope would be blazed like a trail.

AS: When you were talking about Paletó, Aparecida, and about eating together and sleeping together . . . In my case, Eruera and Amiria were godparents to our children, they named our children. They used to write me these letters when I was in Cambridge that began, 'Dear mokopuna' — they used that term. I had my own grandparents, of course.

The thing that astounds me is their sense of hope, not just with Eruera but with Amiria as well. She was my friend. We were very different ages, but we were really good friends. We laughed a lot, and we loved a lot of the same things, including growing flowers. We had a lot of fun together — she was a magnificent raconteur and full of humour, and great company. Eruera? That was different; that was the tohunga. In a way, quite austere, deeply, deeply knowledgeable. That mana. I was in awe of him when I was young. I always looked up to him. It was never the case that he was my informant or anything like that; he was my kaumātua; he was somebody I looked up to, all the time we were together.

Eruera's way of teaching me was very direct. I was invited to their house, and he started teaching me whakapapa on big sheets of paper on the floor. Quite early on! When we went to marae, he wanted me to understand the relationships between the different groups we would meet up with. But more than that, I think . . . I was fascinated by te ao Māori — like falling in love — and he warmed to that. He loved teaching, and I was a passionate learner. So he talked about the history of the country and his ancestors; the things they had gone through, the wars, the state of affairs when he was young. What he saw in our country at the time when we did our book together.[1]

And he was like Witi's tīpuna, I think; he had a sense that we might, together, create a better world, especially for our children and for our grandchildren. Very much focused on the future for ngā uri whakatipu, the descendants who are still coming. We had to make a better world for them, from the one we had inherited ourselves. And we couldn't do it by ourselves; we had to do it together somehow.

AV: I think that's what Paletó taught me, too: making kin is something you can do; it's not something you are born with, with relations. Relations and kinship relations can be done, by action. This is something important that I understood.

And another thing he taught me: different worlds can get together, but they do not have to meet. I can have my own thought, and he can have his own thought, and we do not need to agree, but must be together, to listen to what the other has to say. And I think this was very important. He never, never tried to impose some worldview on

---

1 *Eruera: The Teachings of a Māori Elder.* Oxford University Press, 1980.

me — never. He was just talking; that's what I know — what I learned. It's respect for other beings, other ways of thought. This is very important to me.

WI: What my kuia taught me was aroha ki te iwi, but it was not just some lovely 'we love each other' stuff. Oh no, they taught me in terms of the intellectualism of the Māori world; I mean te ao Māori has this highly complex construction that reaches beyond the physical. I like to say, actually, that I grew up in a world 'drenched in the divine'. I grew up with the idea that there was a mauri — a life force; there was an eke — an energy; there was a mana — a strength; there was a wairua — a spirit; there was a tapu — a sacredness; there was a wehi — a dread; and there was an empowering hā — the breath of life. Karakia was a way of accessing the divine.

Teria was the one, though, who kept me at the wero: challenging ideas, whether they were Pākehā or Māori. She left me with an armoury that I would never have been able to get from the Pākehā world, ever. It was a Māori armour. But, as Anne says, it was not to be used to defend myself, but, rather, ngā uri whakatipu.

AS: When I look at how I learned from Eruera and Amiria — a lot of that was the same as for you, Aparecida, and Witi. Travelling together, for example. I had a little VW for a long time, for about 15 years; from the time I came back from the States to do my PhD, I had this little blue car, and I was their driver for a long time — and Jeremy, too, my husband. We used to go to hui together. Eruera would ring me up and he would say, 'Oh . . . there's something or other . . .' — a tangi, a hui tōpu, or a hui about land with some important kaupapa, some sort of political matter. It could be Parihaka, or it could have been up north at Waitangi, it might have been in the heart of Tainui. And we would go there, and we would drive.

In the car, Eruera would be thinking his way into the kaupapa of this particular gathering. Because he was a well-known orator, and a genealogist, he'd be thinking about what linked him to these people and what he might end up saying on the marae. And when we got bored, Amiria would tell stories. I was always driving and soaking all this up. I don't think I talked much on those trips; I think I listened nearly all the time. And then we'd get to the gathering and Eruera would say to me in Māori: 'Ani, tīkina mai ngā pēke (go and get the bags)!' And I would trot off and go and fetch the luggage, and people always wondered who this girl was — they thought it was very funny. The people were never quite sure whether I was one of his grandchildren from one of his boys, and he did it for fun.

And then I'd be in the thick of this hui listening to the exchange of speeches, and I'd be sleeping in the meeting house at night, listening to the talk — and a lot of it just came through my skin. It wasn't really an intellectual exercise. It was sometimes, but a lot of the time I was absorbing it, by being in those places. And Eruera and Amiria did that for me: they took me to these places and put me in these places that were Māori places. Most Pākehā at the time didn't go to marae, didn't share those experiences.

And why did Eruera do that? Hmmm. I still don't know, to be honest. He was a great orator, a great tribal expert. He was one of the elders who was looked up to by many in his generation, including other kaumātua and tohunga. Perhaps it was just that thirst for knowledge we shared. He was a great scholar, like some of those professors we both know, Aparecida. Geoffrey Lloyd in Cambridge, for example: a great scholar of Greek science and Chinese science and the origins of the Enlightenment. He reminds me of Eruera, funnily enough — that love of knowledge, and that intellectual curiosity, that questing mind. I was so lucky. How lucky. How fortunate.

WI: That questing mind, eh? I like to explain it all in that image of the double helix. Te tōrino haere whakamua, whakamuri, at the same time as the spiral is going forward it is returning, at the same time as it goes out it comes back. When I think of the returning place on my spiral, it's always to Waituhi or to them, my grandmothers. But then they say, off you go again, Witi, and so, haere tonu rā.

AS: Can I be cheeky and ask you, Witi — because when I knew you at varsity, you were already talking about being a writer, I remember, so I wonder: how did that happen? To come from Waituhi and, as you say, that whole experience of yours as a kid with those kuia: how did that turn you into the sort of person you became?

WI: I still think of myself as that boy from Waituhi; that has always been my basic identity. What I inherited, I guess, was this ability to be organic, to be holistic, to organise ahead. I mean, we are sitting here talking, but I'm really not here: I've sent myself out five or ten years ahead and I am doing the mahi there; I've already done it here.

Another interesting thing. My father was different to Teria (his mother) and Mini (his half-sister), because, unlike them, he only thought of the world being one world: te ao Māori. So, because he thought that way, I felt I had no problem negotiating with Pākehā. That was empowering, too; not thinking of the divisions between all our different worlds. So I never had any inferiority complex or felt I was second class and couldn't do it.

I also spent 16 years as a diplomat in Foreign Affairs, and the same amount of time as a professor of English. If I didn't do my best to represent our people, just as they did, then I wasn't really doing sufficiently with and by their legacy. Really, that's what it's all about: legacy building. And I'm sure, Aparecida, that's what your elder wanted you to do: not just to use that information that he gave you, but to use it to build a legacy. Because I do see in it some dilemmas — that if those people are to survive, just how are they going to do that within the band of their skills and partnerships at the moment?

AV: I agree. I think that Paletó's legacy was a way of saying that I can do whatever I want to, and when Paletó died in 2017, I decided, thinking about this legacy, that it was my duty to talk about Paletó and his people, not just in academic books or words or ideas, but about his life, because he was such an extraordinary person that people should know him. That's what made me write a book about his life[2] — as part of my life, too, but really about his life. And then I think afterwards I felt like talking to other kinds of people; not just academics, because he has positioned me to do it, you know? We are living in Brazil in a catastrophic time (as is the whole world, really). Brazil is really, really dangerous, so I feel, as academics — and my legacy from Paletó tells me, too — that we have to talk to people. I have to talk about who the Indigenous people are, why they need to be where they are, why they need land, why they need to be respected. Their lands are being destroyed. We have a far-right government nowadays, and they are destroying everything — they are invading, letting people invade the reservations. They are allowing mining in Indigenous, sacred territory. Lots of Indigenous people are from families whose lands contain mercury and, because of mining, their resources are being looted.

---

2 *Paletó and Me: Memories of My Indigenous Father.* Stanford University Press, 2021.

Politics — Indigenous politics — is a very new thing here in Brazil, going back maximum only 30–40 years. We only have one Indigenous deputy, one Indigenous person in government. They are not well represented, and they are really in the weak part of our country, meaning they are susceptible to all kinds of bad things. I've never seen anything in my whole life similar to what is happening here in Brazil. We feel like we are in a blind alley, that something will just fall down.

AS: Wari' didn't know white people until the 1950s, but I guess things were [by then already] happening in the Amazon forest, and the river. They've had to deal with white people in a very compressed timeframe. And maybe they are at a stage now where the Māori were when the Land Wars were happening, when troops were occupying their lands. I was just re-reading the correspondence from a particular governor who decided to take a block of land in Taranaki, and he was told by William Martin, who had been the chief justice, that this was completely illegal: you can't do it; the people have not consented. But he did it anyway — he sent in troops. And you see this in our history time and again: there are people who argue the case for justice, and there will be somebody who comes in and smashes all of that.

I guess that's what Wari' people are experiencing right now, this smashing. I spent a very short time in Brazil; my daughter Amiria was there for a while. It's a country of extremes. The little glimpses I had of it showed extreme wealth, extreme poverty. I didn't get to anywhere near the Amazon jungle and the people there, but you're living in a world that's different from ours, that's for sure.

We're fortunate in many ways, but I think Māori are still in a battle for survival — not demographically so much as spiritually, and with tikanga. I look at what's happening with one of the things about the Treaty process, which is in a way insidious, and we might see it as a great betrayal, eventually: the requirement that in order to take these Treaty settlements, the kin groups have to turn themselves into corporates. And the fundamental tensions between corporate philosophies, which are ruled by a balance sheet, and the kind of tikanga we have been talking about — whakapapa and so on . . . Which philosophy will win? That corporate philosophy strikes right to the heart of te ao Māori — that only money matters, only the person matters, with its hyper-individualism. We saw it on the steps of Parliament with the February 2022 protests

— with some Māori demanding to be let into a marae, but without respecting tikanga, and some Pākehā behaving abominably at the same time — white supremacists. A war of the spirit, a battle for the soul of the country.

But I remain hopeful for the Treaty and for our relationships. We're a small country, an intimate society, and our whakapapa have entangled for a long time — there are many leaders who are fighting for a way to survive. And for me it's potentially our saving grace, that philosophy of connectedness and equal exchange and a deep respect for the mana of others. I imagine, in Brazil, it must look very bleak, but perhaps the philosophy could be your saving grace, too — and that's something worth fighting for.

Emma Espiner
On parenting during the zombie apocalypse

'I'll still love you, even if you're the Ashtray Murderer.' This is what Dad said every time I left his bachelor pad in Newtown on Sunday to return to Mum's house in Waiwhetū for the start of the school week. The Ashtray Murderer was an imaginary fiend whose crimes were as advertised. Dad could have said, 'I'll love you no matter what', but that isn't his style.

They really meant it, Mum and Dad. They never tried to influence my life choices, even the ones that would have benefited from some adult direction. Cocooned by their benign disinterest, I considered different careers like a toddler rummaging through a toybox; picking the one with the most glitter and wearing it down until it faded and I became bored, returning to the toybox to start the cycle again.

If you have a child, you become intensely interested in the backwards trajectory of your life. How did I end up here? Do I want this for them? How can I distil the good and eliminate the bad? There is a moment in every dystopian movie I've ever loved where the characters agonise over the morality of bringing a child into a horrible and cruel world. Children invariably represent hope, and in the movies it's a bright, fragile act of folly.

My daughter changed my life's path before she was born. It was 2013. I was finding it harder every day to pretend to care about my job in executive recruitment. I was six months' pregnant, hungry, angry and bored all the time. My molars lost height as I ground them down with every pointless task I had to feign enthusiasm for. I was the only brown-skinned person all the time, in every room. For a living I talked to people about their lives and their jobs, and most of the stories were colourless, the aspirations irrelevant, and I felt malnourished slotting square pegs into boring square holes.

Initially I was going to begin my maternity leave just a week out from my due date, then a fortnight, then four weeks, and eventually I thought fuck this, I'm taking six weeks off just to get away from you lot.

It started out as an exercise of desperation. What am I going to tell this baby about my life? She's going to come out, shit herself, and then laugh at my CV. I couldn't have a baby disrespecting me like that, so I got a piece of paper and listed all the things I wanted in a career. On another piece of paper I wrote down all the things I didn't want. The only thing on that piece of paper was 'my current job'. After a lot of thinking, LinkedIn trawling and perusal of online job adverts, medicine seemed to be the one thing that fitted the bill.

My most recent experience of learning science had been failing Chemistry 101 for not turning up to lectures, labs or the final exam during my misspent first degree at the University of Otago, which eventually became a half-hearted BA. Not a strong recommendation for a career as a doctor. 'You should use that Maowree entry pathway,' said my boss encouragingly.

None of my friends dared to have an opinion to my face. I was earning $110,000 a year, we had just bought a house in Auckland, we were about to have a baby, and I was suggesting to my husband that I spend six years not earning anything at all, for a career gamble that showed absolutely zero chance of paying off. 'You'd make a great doctor,' was all he said.

Recently that baby for whom I changed my life asked me if boys could be doctors, too. I found my purpose and my people because of her, and she's indifferent to this because it's the only version of me that she knows. Eight years old, her world is full of women doctors, many of them Māori, who drink wine with her mother at the dining room table and talk about unspeakable things that would make even the Ashtray Murderer turn pale. She glanced up from writing in her notebook during one of these sessions and looked me straight in the eye: 'I hear everything that you say.'

Some well-meaning person once asked her: 'Do you want to be a doctor like Māmā, or a journalist like Dada?'

'Neither,' she said. 'I want to grow up and do nothing.'

This week she has decided she wants to make ads. She forces us to keep the volume up during the ad breaks on the rare occasions that we watch free-to-air TV. They're mini movies in her eyes. This little curly-haired girl of mine gets a calculating look when we explain that you can tell stories that are so compelling that people will go and spend their money on something you're trying to sell, that sometimes you can even change the world with a story.

She speaks te reo Māori so well that she has decided she's too good to speak to her barely proficient parents. Her school exercise books are full of stories in our Indigenous language, carefully wrought in pencil in a child's large, expressive handwriting. It's irrelevant to me what she chooses to do for a job, because, whatever it is, she'll carry our culture and language as a korowai around her shoulders. I'm humbled by the work of previous generations that has gone into making that a possibility.

Right now, she is waiting on a letter from the prime minister. My daughter wrote to Jacinda Ardern about the cost of housing, and when she hears on the news that the average price of houses in Auckland has gone up again, she narrows her eyes, falcon-like, and mutters, 'She obviously hasn't gotten my letter yet.'

One night she was too scared to go to sleep because she had found out about the lifespan of our sun, and she was worried about the world ending. Every generation thinks they are living through the end of days, and our present includes a daily diet of real-time catastrophe delivered through social media. No wishful thinking of mine will shield her from the existential reality of climate change, inequity and terrorism. She is still changing our lives; our decisions as a whānau are now viewed solely through the lens of aspiration to support the creation of a liveable, just society for her to grow old in. This is the practical expression of love, no matter what.

In *Kurangaituku*, Whiti Hereaka's kaleidoscopic resurrection of the fearsome bird woman of legend, a whare tapere of the mind is constructed in the middle of te pō. These houses of storytelling, play, music and community were ubiquitous in ngā wā ō mua, the old days. Now, every time a Māori artist puts their work into the world, I imagine it finding a place in Whiti's whare tapere.

If I was the prayerful sort, I'd offer thanks every day to our Māori philosophers and creators, past and present, who have breathed life into the foundation for my daughter's tomorrow. The American writer Saidiya Hartman says that 'The loss of stories sharpens the hunger for them', and my generation came into the world starving, but I can see that our children will be well fed.

One Friday during Matariki in 2021, my first year of working as a doctor, I finished work on time and drove home from the hospital, revelling in the prospect of a weekend off. I smoked my vape with the window down,

7 degrees outside. I listened to waiata Māori celebrating Matariki. I picked up my daughter from home in her tiger suit. We drove into the twinkling city and sat in a room full of rangatahi Māori imagining indigenous futures for Aotearoa. She took it all in, took it for granted, knew it was all for her. She picked the clean white potatoes out of everyone else's hāngi and fell asleep on the drive home.

Dr Emma Espiner (Ngāti Tukorehe, Ngāti Porou) is a junior doctor at Middlemore Hospital, and an award-winning writer and podcast host. Her writing features in the *Guardian*, Newsroom, Stuff and The Spinoff, and in academic and literary journals. She lives in Tāmaki Makaurau Auckland.

Ya-Wen Ho
To inherit

傳承 *chuán chéng* (v.) to inherit, to pass on a legacy

I think about how to talk about whakapapa in my mother tongue. I watch the sunset bruise. If only the winds could sweep away hurts like clouds. I speak the two characters 傳 *chuán* and 承 *chéng* like a spell. Each character is a locus of meaning, the nuclei of a word cloud formed of bonded pairs of characters. I learned about molecular bonds from my father: ionic, covalent, metallic. I wonder how he might have described our bond. In Mandarin, intergenerational bonds comprise of two verbs: 傳 *chuán*, to transmit, and 承 *chéng*, to bear. Blood tastes metallic. Sometimes, we are handed heavy shit. Sometimes, we refuse the torch for 'personal reasons'.

傳説 *chuán shuō* (n.) a fable, a legend

Once, my Mandarin-speaking therapist told me that filial piety is one of the most damaging aspects of Chinese culture. Horrors have been committed in its name, she said. I think about the story of the Taoist boy-god Nézhā (哪吒), who vivisected himself to pay his parents what was due — 拆骨還父, 割肉還母 *chāi gǔ huán fù, gē ròu huán mǔ*, to his father went his bones, to his mother, his flesh — and how much that must have hurt. I think about my younger self watching *Nezha and the Dragon King* (1979) thinking *oh a cool animation about a boy battling dragons* without a second thought to the suicide–resurrection arc. I think about how I have thought all the second thoughts now. My therapists are legends.

傳紀 *zhuán jì* (n.) a biography

This is a choose-your-own-adventure story without any adventure. You married the first girl you dated and had your first child before you were 30. Your daughter was born the year martial law was lifted. Your son was born the year an incinerator was built on the other side of town.

You were not unhappy, but you thought yourself responsible for your children's happiness. One day your daughter came home from school crying because the rigid world had cut her. You saw you had to do *something*. You decided to immigrate to

New Zealand, because it was within reach, and your in-laws knew people who knew people there, and because of the way your daughter's eyes lit up when she tasted the milk on your visit to test the waters. It's so much better, she said. *The land of milk and honey.*

You sold your house in Hsinchu. You bought another house in Howick. You rehomed your dog, then they called to say the dog had run away. You worked two jobs while doing a second Masters of Chemical Engineering. Your new employers would not recognise your existing qualifications; you qualified as a skilled migrant. Your mother-in-law lived with you for a while. You made sure you had sex quietly. You worked late into the night. You were tired. Petrol was 99 cents per litre, but still too dear for you to get to where you wanted to go. You were always tired. Sometimes, you yelled at your wife, who told the children that you worked very hard and were not to be disturbed. Sometimes, you yelled at your children. You stopped having sex. Or maybe you didn't. Once, you slapped your daughter for waking you up from a nap.

You never told your children stories of your life. What they know, they know from other people. They have heard it told that you grew up in state care, that your father had *a temper*, that it was wrong of your mother to leave you behind in the separation. Only later, after your funeral, did your children hear about your father having threatened to kill your mother. *It runs in the family.*

承認 *chéng rèn* (v.) to acknowledge, to admit

Once, you tried to kill your children and then yourself. You loved them too much, and the world too little. You wanted, desperately, to spare them from suffering. Your children do not remember you putting down the hoe, or getting off their knees, or how they sat at the dinner table with you that night. Your children remember you picking up the hoe.

承擔 *chéng dān* (v.) to shoulder, to be responsible for

I declined to speak at my father's funeral. I did make his memorial slideshow, colour-correcting each photo to show his life in that flattering golden-hour glow. In the photos, I saw my father hold me on his shoulder at my first athletics day, and me holding him right back, more tightly than my prize. I saw him as a young man whose life precedes my existence. I saw him as a person making other people laugh at parties, and was haunted for having seen him when he stopped laughing. I automated the programme to open, edit, save and close picture after picture of his life, and could not cry.

承諾 *chéng nuò* (v.) to promise, to pledge

When I used my father's life insurance payout as a deposit to buy an apartment with my boyfriend, my mother told me *your father would have been proud of you.*

Then, I cried.

Ya-Wen Ho is a letterpress researcher, graphic designer and poet. A Taipei-born New Zealander, she works bilingually between Mandarin and English, merging the two languages in performance. Her first book of poetry was *last edited [insert time here]* (2012). Her literary awards include a Horoeka/Lancewood Reading Grant (2015) and the Ema Saiko Poetry Fellowship at New Zealand Pacific Studio (2016). She is restoring a unique collection of Chinese letterpress type, once used to print the *New Zealand Chinese Growers' Journal* (1949–1972), for future public use at Wai-te-ata Press, Te Herenga Waka Victoria University of Wellington. She lives in Te Whanganui-a-Tara Wellington.

Courtney Sina Meredith
Young god

on my way to a field across town / the road stitched with milky pearls /
    there stands my son /

young god I prayed for you / crowned in liquorice curls /
    I shaped you from giraffe stars /

quicksilver threaded shadow cloud / you wear the cloak of the warrior /
    salt black sparkle /

in the light of the niu moon / my son runs through wet grass /
    shiny with sweat and knowing /

he climbs into the car into my arms / here lie the wishes sown into my spine /
    I dig into the marrow /

morning and night I mine / blush and shade I thread /
    his love around my neck like shark teeth /

few and sharp the boat words of my son / small as grains of sand /
    sail the sweet vā between us /

I have no blood to hold him with / I have no laws to wrap him in /
    I am the action of a mother /

he is the motion of a child / huddled by leaf blade fronds /
    he never asked for but was meant for /

on my way to a field across time / the path stitched with pearly milk /
    here stands my son /

Courtney Sina Meredith is an essayist and poet whose work delves into issues such as racism, sexism and poverty and draws on her Samoan roots. She is the co-owner of MyGeneTree, the world's leading platform for turning ancestry into art. Her books include the play *Rushing Dolls* (2010), the poetry collection *Brown Girl in Bright Red Lipstick* (2012) and the story collection *Tail of the Taniwha* (2016). In 2021, she was named the University of Auckland Young Alumna of the Year. She lives in Aukilani with her visual artist partner, Janet Lilo, and their children.

Day Lane
Five photographic moments

1. Photo

There are two girl-children in the photo. The   outside the photo
has a complex relationship with the idea of   a child but none at
all with the reality. For a long time

        The   photo   was   taken   in   France   and   is
more   than   twenty   years   old.   There   are   two
girl-children in the photo. They laugh and   a
background of leaves. The adult outside the photo has
        the idea of itself as a child and none   with
the reality. One child didn't speak French until soaked   to
overflowing and the other was uncomfortable in English until
a graduate degree   many years later.
Outside this frame,   little brother never learned
        no one came to his
birthdaythatyearexceptsomefriendsofourparents   werethereonan
unrelated errand.

        he remembers many things I do not.

   I convinced him   without making
a sacrifice of my   . But back   to the girl-children;
        one grew up and
the other   I am unfamiliar
        child's French, all its
layers and   relearn
     I hear   close on the street

2. Cloudscradle

There is a red barn to the left of a tree, one of the low squatting pines that's wider than it is tall, above a white house whose roof just barely lines up with the top of the hill when seen from my window across the harbour.

There are two power poles, their cables invisible except on those rare days where fog lies heavy on the sea but has yet to roll over the peninsula.

The road lies so precisely along the hilltop that everything on it is on nothing but space from here, from my window.

This tableau sits on a gentle curve of grass, the lowest point of the ridge, cradling its little piece of the southern sky.

Once a white pick-up passed the first power pole and I saw it on the curve exactly halfway between the edge of the squatting pine and the edge of everything else, where the peninsula's quilt of houses and trees begins, and at the same time a black-backed gull flew over it back towards the barn — so it seemed, a trick of perspective matching the sizes of bird and truck —

Every configuration of clouds I know to be the one; soon this house will be another I cried to empty out and soon I will be at the other end of my life and will still miss the red barn and the tree and the perfect curve of the hill against the sky and this will be the way the clouds look in my memory.

In all this time I haven't touched my camera, not even on the day when the clouds reared up behind the red barn and the squatting pine as raw columns of dream and the sun rose directly in front of the far-off harbour mouth so the clouds shone like molten metal and the whole scene reflected muzzily in the morning sea.

3. Sea sigh

No silver in the Pacific up here.
Outgrown selves scatter the beach, the
waves like bodies on bodies on bodies, the
foreground sheets of new mudstone.

Gull chicks on the cliffs, tourists with their vans, seal skulls on the beach.

I'm crying, or about to, or just finished and the rain is hammering down, fuzzing the
hard line of the horizon. Winter this year was the usual except *everyone* was afraid to
go outside, everyone hid their face.

I worry often that I'm better at loving from a distance. I'm not ready and not at peace
with it. I'm trying to get a sense for the size of things; I want to line up the gaps in me
with what made them. I want this to be more than a list of unremarkable things. The
year has been small and still. The year has been yawning massive.

I want this to be more than it is, but the year has been so strange in scale. I have a
new job. My grandfather is dying. It feels as though the world is ending, none of our
tomatoes fruited all summer and the sunrises are breathtaking and a royal spoonbill
has taken up residence in the tidal pools where I walk, further south than he should
be. Time stopped and started, came and went; I wrote until I didn't; I cooked us
dinner until I didn't; I heard my voices until I didn't. The water in the harbour has
been unusually warm all year, maybe encouraging the spoonbill. There's more raptors
than I remember from childhood but fewer insects. My grandfather has been at it so
long I don't remember a time I was sure I'd see him again, and I am young enough
that this all has been happening forever.

4. Last gig, Ōtepoti

Ten years to the day since my parents folded me + Fraser + our bags + our boxes into the car, delivered us to the halls where we'd spend our respective first years of university, mine at the top of the hill + his at the bottom. Now it's me and Fraser again in Leith Valley Bowls Club; they keep closing the music venues so the settings keep getting stranger. Club presidents on the wall stretching back to the wars, all old men + tūī coughing outside. First album release for Human Susan, exclusively on tape of course, the gig itself a line-up affair + I buy a t-shirt for — who now to me? She didn't want to come + I bought her a t-shirt anyway.

First guitarist: twelve-gallon woman in a ten-gallon hat + shift dress + house slippers + plastic glasses + dress so thin the tattoos show through, plays hunched over her guitar like it hurts her. The other guitarist has a missing tooth in his grin and I wonder if I am gay after all. Ten years of this. Drums in my sternum + through the floor.

Next band: boy with floppy hair, same size and shape as his bass, twitching + surrounded by smoke. Beside him: dirty-blond mullet singer howling around the mic + lips touching it, is the only one who dressed up + looks like a farm boy at a school dance. The guitarist plays facing the back of the stage + looks younger than me though I can't see his face.

Smells like high school, like the Kilmarnock Street house + campfire night, safe and impermanent, cigarettes + weed + cheap beer. Girl in front of me in gold stretch satin dances like smoke + runs her hands through her hair and I wonder if maybe I'm gay after all. Cocktail dresses next to denim + leopard print + gender all over the place. Dude in black leather + bullet belt + beret holds a jug like it's a pint. Paired vintage butches stand close together. Title band lead singer has red hair + a panel necklace of child's teeth laid out in order. Get distracted wondering again if I'm actually gay. Going to leave without figuring it out. Twelve-gallon girl is back with a tutu on her head. Run into a couple of people I know, split sleeves + ears held together with safety pins. I spend the night ducking out to write things down + drive Fraser home in a borrowed car.

5. I am struggling to grow as an artist while living in cartoonish times

My barber dances around the shop as he buzzes my hair, rambling cheerfully about tattoos, his baby daughter. He and I were born two months apart, we discovered, and when did anyone last touch my face with gentle concentration? Afterwards I walk twenty-seven times around my flat then make tea and eat all the biscuits, knowing I can't afford more until Tuesday. I have written about the sharkish eye of the security camera that greets me as I come home to this building with its fire-damaged outliers and piss-stinking stairwell, the blossoming black mould that covers the central wall in overlapping circles, the rough holes where someone tried to tear away the panelling but found more spreading darkness beneath. I share this place with sixty-odd people and a fox, and the jackdaws and mourning doves who live in the roof. The building is owned by a man in London who does not know my name. I have written this poem and had it published and the stairwell still stinks and the rain comes in through the burned-out parts of the roof. I am in pursuit of artistic subtlety but I live on the floor with the worst of the black mould and all of my neighbours have children. I am lucky to be able to live here alone and so near a train station, although the trains aren't running right now because the drivers stopped working overtime they won't be paid for. I am circling a poetry of emergency policies and ten per cent inflation and my broken kitchen sink.

Day Lane is a poet and playwright who has degrees in genetics, psychology and teaching. Their poetry and short fiction has been published in *Landfall* and the art–science interface journal *SEISMA*, among other journals, and performed at events around Aotearoa. In 2022 they won the Dunedin UNESCO City of Literature Robert Burns Poetry Competition for the poem 'Uisge', part of their current project exploring ideas of home, place and immigrant identity. They now live in Glasgow.

Kate Rassie
On bushfires, blood sugars and babies

My husband and I move from Auckland to Melbourne in mid-January. Before we leave, I buy the last two N95 masks from Bunnings Warehouse in Grey Lynn and stash them in my suitcase atop silk blouses and medical textbooks. They are, of course, for the bushfire smoke.

We have briefly wondered whether we are making the right decision. Australia is burning, and on Kangaroo Island charred koalas are falling out of trees. My sister-in-law in Sydney sends through photographs of Sydney Harbour unrecognisable through smoke. She has a six-week-old baby who has never been outside without two layers of muslin over her carrier, and we discuss vitamin D supplementation.

It's over 40 degrees for the first few weeks in our new city. The shipping crate containing all our possessions is delayed at the border: because of a bushfire-related backlog, Customs are prioritising incoming relief supplies. We sleep for a month on an inflatable air mattress with a ceiling fan thwacking overhead, and cook things we can make in one saucepan.

Dust

I start work at the hospital in early February in hastily purchased new clothes. My own — along with my stethoscope — are still quarantined 20 kilometres down the road in Port Melbourne. The rain, when it falls, is brown (the product of particulate matter in the atmosphere, apparently). The queues for the local car wash go around the block after every downpour. After work, we sit at the local pub and watch the Australian Open; $2 from every pint sold is donated to the bushfire relief.

At the hospital orientation day in the first week of February, they pack us new doctors cheek-by-jowl into the auditorium. The air-conditioning is blasting so hard we can barely hear. Among other briefings, there's a short presentation by an infectious diseases nurse about what they're calling the 'novel coronavirus', with a few pictures of gown-clad doctors peering at test tubes. Ask anyone who's come from China or Iran about respiratory symptoms, they say; I jot this on the side of my orientation handout as a curiosity. We have had similar presentations over the years; none of the threats amounted to much. Mum texts a few days later: *have you heard about this new 'Kovid-19'? sounds nasty*. I correct her spelling, but tell her it's nothing to worry about.

Fridays, summer

On Fridays, I drive to an outer suburb of Melbourne to do gestational diabetes clinics at a local community centre. It's more than an hour from the CBD, and the houses are low-lying and dusty. There are 80 pregnant women each afternoon and just four doctors, but the consults are brief: review the blood sugars they've written down in their notebooks, and give brief dietary suggestions or change the insulin doses accordingly.

The community is working-class, deliciously multicultural. We talk about the carbohydrate content of dahl and chapati and string hoppers and Red Rooster. Some women are onto their fifth, seventh, ninth pregnancy; they often have a toddler in tow, and many are still breastfeeding the most recent. They're asked to annotate their blood sugar records with anything that might have caused an aberration; they write 'stress+++++', 'too much white rice', 'vomited', 'birthday cake'.

There's a nice feeling in these clinics: gestational diabetes needs to be taken seriously, but in the overwhelming majority it is a mild and easily managed condition. These babies are likely to be born healthy, their mothers have tight bellies and wide smiles and precious cargo. We laugh about reflux and swollen ankles, and the women chat among themselves in the waiting room. The clinic finishes late, at 6 p.m., and it's a nice drive back into Melbourne: a wide toll-road, fast against the traffic, the sun setting behind the cityscape, the weekend beckoning. I always leave feeling inexplicably content.

Seismology

In early March things happen with nauseating speed. There are outbreaks on the *Diamond Princess* cruise ship, in northern Italy, in Iran, in a hotel in Tenerife. Then the Louvre is closed, then all medical student electives are cancelled, then the supermarket shelves are bare of rice and tissues and toilet paper. There are a handful of cases in New Zealand, the media pores over their flight itineraries. The Pope delivers his weekly mass via video link, making history in the process. Our doctor chat-threads go all night, because none of us can sleep: we discuss asymptomatic transmission and statistical models. We are all catching up at different speeds. Most of us do highly specific subspecialities — dermatology, orthopaedic surgery — and haven't thought about viruses for years. *Sorry, but what's PPE?* one doctor asks early on, frustrated by all the three-letter acronyms.

On Friday, 13 March, I drive out to the same gestational diabetes clinic, and on the way learn that Disneyland is closed and MOMA is closed and the NBA is suspended and Coachella is cancelled and the Melbourne Comedy Festival is cancelled and the annual Pasifika Festival in Auckland is off and Norway and Denmark are in complete lockdown. I have a friend sitting a high-stakes final surgical exam the next day: cancelled. She has been studying for two years, and when she calls me, I can't understand her for the sobbing.

The clinic that day runs as normal, the waiting room heaving. I move insulin doses up and down and tell women to stop drinking orange juice. There's something there, though, moving about — vibrating — under our skins; it's like the way farmyard animals can sense an impending volcanic eruption. I need a calculator for basic calculations, and forget the name of a patient between calling her in the waiting room and sitting her to begin the consult. When I get out at 5 p.m. the United States has closed its borders and I drive home feeling like I am in a dreamscape.

We go to dinner that night at a still-bustling wine bar, and I have three glasses in very short succession. Later, I leave on my own and go to the supermarket to get milk for a pre-bed cup of tea. I walk past row after row of bare shelves, and panicked-looking people taking photographs of them. I feel a little wobbly in my heeled boots under the harsh lighting. At home I lie in bed and look at graphs of national ICU capacities and tips about being strong.

Winter

Five months later, and I haven't been out to the gestational diabetes clinic since. By the following week, we had switched indefinitely to telephone consults; we now stay in our inner-city hospital consulting rooms and work our way through a list of patients to phone. The women email through cellphone screenshots of their testing logbooks, there are endearing little smears of blood beside the figures they've recorded in ballpoint.

The afternoons of phone calls feel inexorably long; I drink instant coffee to get through. We're supposed to be chipper about how flexible we've been in adapting to this new format, but the consults have lost their texture and their light-heartedness overnight: it's hard to smile at someone over the phone, particularly behind a hospital-issue face mask. Some women just never answer — we ring them week after week, leave chirpy messages asking them to get in touch. Most don't.

We're thick into the second wave here in Melbourne, back in what we are calling 'lockdown 2.0'. It's no longer novel or bizarrely energising, just cold and relentless. Each day Daniel Andrews, the Victorian premier, issues new restrictions: we cannot leave our suburbs to exercise, we must wear masks outside the home, we have an 8 p.m. curfew. Police are stationed on every corner. I run down the streets in our city-fringe suburb and suddenly realise how desolate the buildings are looking: all the shopfronts boarded up, handwritten signs in the window, most sites vacant or for lease. Films of dust settle on the high heels in my favourite shoe shop. A handwritten sign reads: *Closed for the apocalypse*.

People walk dogs and babies, these dumb happy things dragging them out into the cold afternoon for fresh air and exercise. One lady has a black puffer jacket over her flannelette pyjamas. She wears a cloth facemask and slippers, and is the poster girl for our times.

There's guilt, too. Our extended families just think of my husband and me as doctors working in Melbourne; I know that they imagine us in intensive care, operating ventilators and suctioning airways. The reality, of course, is that we are specialists in areas that are well removed from acute medical inpatient work. Endocrinology and diabetes are important specialities, but they are office-based, subacute, nuanced; they are specialities with chronically (rather than acutely) ill patients and plenty of time and lots of blood tests. Three years ago, I could do all that fast-moving stuff; I'm now preparing to do my PhD, and spend most of my time reading research articles on the way female hormones impact breastmilk composition.

Thrown into relief by the pandemic, my work sometimes feels shameful and self-indulgent. Other days, though, it feels just as important as what the Proper Doctors are doing: I review 10, 20 patients a day, we talk about their thyroid hormones, but also their depression and their JobKeeper entitlements and their blood sugars and their progressively heavy drinking and their carb cravings and marital issues.

I think about what Rebecca Solnit would refer to as the 'tyranny of the quantifiable': the fact that the widely reported statistics do a good job of capturing R0 numbers and ICU admissions and national debt, but not the more slippery and mysterious impacts of this pandemic. I think about the way that babies in prams look at faces, and should learn to recognise facial expressions, but now just see black cloth.

It must be said, too, that some of the quantified but less reported statistics about this pandemic are the ones that terrify me most. Here in Victoria, there has been a 30 per cent reduction in reporting of cancers since lockdown began in March. This doesn't mean they're not occurring, but that patients aren't presenting to doctors with the symptoms. The cancers will be diagnosed later, by which time they'll be more advanced. Another study shows that 45 per cent of current PhD students in Australia are considering disengaging from their studies due to the financial pressure of the pandemic; 5 per cent are currently or imminently experiencing homelessness and 11 per cent skipping meals. These are, of course, the people who we're hoping to rely on to develop vaccines and rebuild our social services in the years to come.

Hubris

I think of the women I reviewed at the gestational diabetes clinic that last day in March: they will now, of course, have had their babies. Gestational diabetes usually remits after pregnancy, so they won't be testing blood sugars anymore. But they'll all still be out there with their newborns, sterilising bottle teats and entertaining toddlers and worrying.

The pandemic reinforces the size of the city — we're on to a whole new crop of pregnant women now, ones whose whole pregnancies will be defined by Covid-19. They don't attend antenatal classes, and will never make the friends there who might become a coffee group. Over the phone many describe feeling isolated or afraid, and not having left their houses for weeks. Their midwifery clinics are virtual, they attend ultrasound scans without their husbands. One woman is told over the phone that her fetus has Down's syndrome.

In the *Guardian*, Jessa Crispin writes: 'Every pregnancy is a crisis. Like all crises, they are best managed as a team and not on your own.' She could not be more accurate.

When the government locks down several public housing towers in the north of the city, we hear about a woman in forced separation from her premature baby in a nearby neonatal unit, unable to deliver her breastmilk.

Every morning — standing masked at the hospital coffee counter — I flick past the obstetric business cards in my own wallet feeling vaguely ill. Pregnancy under these circumstances now seems different, like it requires precise and deliberate action, an *in*ception rather than a *con*ception. My former practical and personal uncertainties are now eclipsed by mammoth existential concerns: is Covid-19 the first in a series of humanity's pre-terminal spasms? Are all the things we know children need (security, connection, faces, schools, grandmothers, birthday parties) going to return? How will any generation ever fix this? Is it utter hubris to create life under circumstances we know to be desperate?

Perhaps. And I do think that, most days. My husband and I have put procreation plans temporarily on the back-burner, and my Instagram algorithm has noticed. Instead of fertility clinics, I'm now offered floral cloth facemasks and wine-delivery services.

But there's this, too: the equally impressive hubris of the human foetus. The pregnant women I review have unborn babies that have increased their circulating blood volumes by 50 per cent, accelerated their heart rates, fundamentally changed the way their blood sugars respond to carbohydrate. Foetal-derived cells can still be found in the brains of child-bearing women years after the women's natural deaths. Pregnancy loosens ligaments, makes teeth fall out, can cause bizarre skin conditions and fulminant liver failure.

I sit in clinic and click past hundreds of these little sods on my screen each day. On the ultrasound scans, I look at their huge heads and their tiny cascades of fingers, their kidneys already filtering and their thyroid glands already manufacturing functional hormones.

On my good days, I think: *They'll be OK.*

Kate Rassie is an endocrinologist whose interests are in the areas of women's health and diabetes. She is a dedicated New Zealander who lives in Melbourne, Australia.

Emma Barnes
One metre

Each human is 1 metre apart in an arrangement we were not used to before this perfect vision. Each piece of you is received as something not unlike a gift. I've heard voices talking out in the hallway and understood nothing. Then I've stood across from you only able to lip-read my way through to you. It is a gentle dimming of possibility like lights through a long-distance journey at night. It is as I thought all along: we are both threats and promises. Do you know that both can be contained and restrained by the right words, by the right spelling. And both are visible even at night. You say that you say that you say. A cough hidden in a throat clearing. It's a good game to be small and to hide. An even better game is to be large and free. The best game is to see the same question in the faces of others: What are you? Never answering I just continue. I am the breeze. I have been the light, the trees and the night. I am just cells layered up like lacquer, like resin, like subcutaneous fat. You don't need to know what I am. You don't need to see anything other than what you're already looking at. You don't know what you're looking at. I am what you're looking at.

Emma Barnes studied at the University of Canterbury Te Whare Wānanga o Waitaha. Their poetry has been widely published in journals, including *Landfall, Turbine | Kapohau, Cordite* and *Ōrangahau | Best New Zealand Poems.* They are the author of the poetry collection *I Am in Bed with You* (2021) and co-editor, with Chris Tse, of *Out Here: An Anthology of Takatāpui and LGBTQIA+ Writers from Aotearoa* (2021), the first major anthology of writing by queer Aotearoa writers. They live in Aro Valley, Te Whanganui-a-Tara Wellington.

KŌRERO

José-Luis Novo
and Ruby Solly
Break the calabash |
discover and rejoice

A conversation on listening and speaking

Award-winning musicians José-Luis Novo and Ruby Solly bring their vast and varied experiences to this conversation. They explore sometimes difficult terrain, as well as common ground, encouraging us to listen to the music that underlines the written word and the greater world around us. Between the lines is a searching for reconciliation and connection. These two musicians engage each other across boundaries of space, time and discipline to sing out the power of music.

José-Luis Novo has worked with orchestras and ensembles around the world. He began his musical studies at the conservatory of Valladolid, Spain — his home town — obtaining the degree of Profesor Superior de Violín with honours in solfege, harmony and violin. His studies continued at the Royal Conservatory of Music in Brussels, where he earned a First Prize in violin. In 1988, he travelled as a Fulbright Scholar to the United States, where he graduated with degrees from Yale University and the Cleveland Institute of Music. He is the artistic director and conductor of the Annapolis Symphony Orchestra, and a keen educator of young musicians. He lives in Annapolis, Maryland.

Ruby Solly (Waitaha, Kāti Māmoe, Kāi Tahu) is a writer, music therapist, musician, composer and taonga pūoro practitioner. Her first book, *Tōku Pāpā*, which explores how culture is taught through parenting, was released in 2021. Ruby has worked with Trinity Roots, Yo-Yo Ma, Whirimako Black, French for Rabbits and the Auckland Philharmonic Orchestra. She is currently completing a PhD at Massey University Te Kunenga ki Pūrehuroa in the use of taonga pūoro, or traditional Māori sound instruments, within the field of hauora. She lives in Te Whanganui-a-Tara.

I

RS

They are speaking . . .

. . . unknown words in all the languages that this current tongue has usurped. All the words eaten up by politeness, by regiment, by I shall nots, by I shan'ts, written over and over again on the air. They are speaking in a wave of words, rising around this great auditorium. This cave-like place where story is pulled from the bottom of the lungs, from the orchestra pit, from the imagination, or deeper still, from the fibres of whakapapa.

They are whispering now . . .

Mirrors talk when the image they see is not expected. Layers of *who are you* and *why are you* and *what do your people see in you that I cannot see.* They are folding their hands in their laps as the waves settle around their waists. Cotton skirts blossoming under the water, artisan anemones billowing in general admission.

They are silent now. Waiting for us to speak.

But we do not speak like them. Under these tuxes and tulle there are tattoos; tā moko, black ink tapped into the skin. We are a young nation of an ancient peoples, we are older than ourselves and younger than our songs. I feel the waters swelling at my feet. The voices pour from open mouths; words of excess, of doubt, of a front-facing future. All the while, cradled bird-like in my hands, she waits. A gourd, a tiny calabash; Hine-pū-te-hue, the atua of peace. I bring her to a hongi to share that first breath; the breath of Tāne and Hine-tītama, the breath I will share with my children, if the water stops rising in time.

> Yes, it is the job of the children to break the calabash.
> But is that job given to us by those who have already smashed it? To those who broke the aria of the daughter of peace instead of lifting her to comfort those who have never sheltered between two beats? To those whose hearts flutter like pūrerehua above the water, spilled and sullied?

> When we were a dream in the collective imaginings of our gods, there was a war so great it nearly ripped the canvas from its frame. We were all but faded, before we had the chance to begin.

But she was there. A daughter of Tāne, able to stretch, grow, and change her form. Able to create a resonance inside herself, a resonance, an *oro*; words in the form of notes and the falls and rises between. She did not break herself, but re-formed, adapted to compose a song to soothe herself first, and then to soothe the world around her. In time, we would arrive into a world saved by song.

They are listening now. And she and I? Making music together of course

For this is how we will fix the world; with me chasing her, and her chasing me. The audience becomes outlines above the water; new land masses for a new location. Water no longer pouring from their mouths, but surging back and forth with each phrase. We create these tidal songs, and unlike these lands returning to soil and rock around us, we go with the flow; we move with the tides.

II

Music chosen in response by J-LN

'La noche de los Mayas / The night of the Mayas'
Final movement: 'Noche de encantamiento / Night of enchantment'
by Silvestre Revueltas

III

Poetry by RS
Main character sings
          With Western voice
                  and an island's curve
Hear the haka call   A rangi hung on a blue ceiling
       All drums and confusion
             For we never matched

This type of beat from before boats

Hark! Ah! At war

A horn can be a garden

A horn can be a birth

A horn can sing as well as it screams

Layer upon layer

Upon layer upon

Layer upon layer resounding

All those things we let build up

A man with a pen

Calls this song an orgy

But it sings of the forbidden

C word we hide above ground

Perfect grammar

But where is the passion

Hands crossing the centre

Chests crotchets and colonies

IV

J-LN

Voices of the past, sounds of the future. Music is a universal language that allows us to embrace ancient traditions and create new works of art. We use drums, we use strings, we use pipes. Composers draw on paper, performers decode as sounds. Audiences marvel at the abstract creation that touches their very souls, and yet it is so difficult to understand how it all happens.

There is organisation and hierarchy in music, centuries of traditions and styles that keep mutating, transforming with chameleonic qualities. The need for human expression, however, remains constant.

The Mayans, with their veneration for their land, and through their culture and habits, rooted one of the richest pre-Columbian civilisations in the Americas. Western European countries laboriously developed a sophisticated musical idiom over the centuries, and here and now these two worlds aspire to meld together, exploring each other sometimes with blind gestures, other times with explicit impulses.

Opposing the clarity of daylight, we choose the enigma of night. The perception of reality is blurred by the ambiguity of darkness, by the efforts to reach to other worlds, to the unknown . . .

The drums start to roar, the dancing begins, the conch-shell horn howls from the gut, the clashing dissonances penetrate the skin. The hypnotic effect of stubborn rhythms that impose their will paralyses us. After a few minutes of music, we find ourselves travelling back through time, joining an ancient civilisation that wants to draw us in.

The intensity gradually grows and eventually becomes overwhelming. The pressure to find a way out questions the original sense of purpose. The dancing turns unavoidable, as if our bodies are inevitably entangled in the physical rapture of the moment. And then, suddenly, we understand we are now inside a new world filled with mystery and enchantment.

Each time we play the music of a composer, or listen to poetry, we are tuning into another voice — something outside ourselves, reaching out to us. When an orchestra plays for an audience, they are interpreting the language of the composer — listening. It's a process of decoding the thoughts of the composer. There is a lot of room for subjectivity and finessing of concepts.

As a child, I was in love with the beauty of music. Now I understand its meaning at an even deeper level. As I stated in an interview once: This is where my soul is, life is not the same without music. Working in music is not working. It is doing my life.

Humankind has endured centuries of wars and colonisation crusades between different civilisations. Let's not erase, destroy, bomb, conquer but rather embrace, explore, discover, rejoice!

Music chosen in response by RS

'The Mighty Invader', by Troy Kingi

Karma strikes it strikes without fanfare
When your first contact's through the cross hair
You darn gone scorched the earth
Pushed me out of my home town
I watched it burn and burn
I can't take it just lying down

Readers can find YouTube videos of both musical compositions mentioned above: Troy Kingi & The Upperclass performing 'The Mighty Invader' live at the Vodafone NZ Music Awards, 14 November 2019, Spark Arena, Auckland; La Orquesta de París performing 'La noche de los Mayas / The night of the Mayas' — Final movement.

Vana Manasiadis
If we give up flying it doesn't
mean we can't speak to each
other as if countries or scan
our genomic sequences for
travel to the flats

φίλε μου,

it's no picnic living like a migratory bird/
adopting the godwit for resting-to-keep-
going/ the kūaka for a-rope's-pull-between
two-spurs   Ελεύθερα πουλιά Spirit
    waders/ they   submit to magnets/ field
exhaustion/ repeat routes of periphery and splice
Expats, to pine's the minor work   The real
        mahi's beak to mud   to bill
    to gut to mud   to bill   to mouth
            to mouth to belly   burial
        sand   silt

                        to   the   whenua
rearranging.   What's   θαλασσολιμάζικα
for Manukau-Pūkorokoro Μίραντα/ For sacred
                    when the migrants have settled
the carbon of their bones/   Drift and deposit
/drift   and   trade   and   sink   and
deposit   It's advice/ and tracking/
this model for translation/

                        for releasing into earth
In the gallery   we find sequel/ clip wings
    as wide as red   as blue to vein
        to torque to   tongue

307

                                                    Hotere's
over Hyde's McNeish's Frame's   We plan/
When the jets have steeped the boneyards
/χωρισμένοι απ' τ'αδέλφια μας we'll call our
godwit whānau and regroup   Kia herea mai
          kia herea mai/   our chromosomes
will go travelling till it's painless.

Vana Manasiádis | Βάνα Μανασιάδη was raised in Te Whanganui-a-Tara Wellington and Ātene Greece. She is the author of two narrative works of hybrid forms, *Ithaca Island Bay Leaves: A Mythistorima* (2009) and *The Grief Almanac: A Sequel* (2019). She also edited and translated a chapbook of contemporary Greek poetry, Ναυάγια Καταφύγια *Shipwrecks Shelters* (2016), and co-edited, with Maraea Rakuraku, *Tātai Whetū: Seven Māori Women Poets in Translation* (2018). In 2021, she was the Ursula Bethell writer in residence. She teaches creative writing at Te Whare Wānanga o Waitaha University of Canterbury.

Harry Ricketts

Lōemis song cycle: 'Epilogue'

8 p.m., 19 June 2021, St Peter's Anglican Church, Wellington: An Assemblage

The chilly June evening in St Peter's Anglican Church is made even chillier by nerves. Bracketed by lectern and pulpit, the five musicians sit or stand on the raised stage of the chancel: Dayle Jellyman (keyboard), Andrew Laking (double bass, guitar), Nigel Collins (cello, guitar), Dan Yeabsley (clarinet, bass, saxophone, tuba), Tristan Carter (violin). The two singers (Maaike Beekman, mezzo-soprano; Simon Christie, bass-baritone) are positioned slightly to the side. The five readers in order of appearance sit, flanking the stage: Nick Ascroft, Chris Tse, Rebecca Hawkes, Ruby Solly and me. Covid numbers are currently low; no one seems to be wearing a mask.

Chris Tse's email of invitation back in February had been friendly but vague. He and the musician Andrew Laking were, he explained, assembling 'a group of writers to be part of a musical performance' as part of that year's Lōemis Festival (12–21 June). Would I like to write and deliver a piece for the event?

The idea, said Chris, was to produce 'a requiem-esque song cycle', combining 'spoken word sections and musical performances'. The spoken pieces would not be set to music but be read between the musical sequences: 'Andrew is hoping that a summary / parts of each piece will get translated into Old English (or te reo Māori) and sung during the musical portions.' The project sounded more intriguing and ambitious by the second. The 'song cycle' was to have seven sections, each of which would have its 'set vibe and theme'. Chris offered as an example: '*Vibe*: General Doom. *Themes*: Transition. Eternity. Inevitability. Rest. Optimism.'

Each writer would write for a different section; the pieces did not need to marry up, but, taken together, should in some way speak to the themes and motifs of that year's festival: trees, ancestry, growth and transformation. The pieces could be in 'any style or genre' and should take 5–10 minutes to perform. First drafts were due by early April so that the translation process could begin and the musicians start to experiment. Each writer would receive a fee of $500; the performance to take place on either 19 or 20 June. I sent off my acceptance by return with no idea what I might be able to come up with, and, a little apprehensively, awaited further instructions.

These further instructions spelt out the overall schema in more detail and offered me a choice of writing for one of the final three sections:

1. Vibe: General Doom. Themes: Transition. Eternity. Inevitability. Rest. Optimism (light). Greater power. [Nick]
2. Vibe: Persistent / Unrelenting. Themes: Kindness. Mercy. [Chris]
3. Vibe: Intense / Glorious / Contrasting. Themes: The End is Nigh. [Rebecca]
4. Vibe: Constant / Optimistic? Theme: Somehow we will be saved (or save ourselves). [Ruby]
5. Vibe: General Rambling. Theme: We are Saved.
6. Vibe: Pleasant. Theme: Big thanks to whoever saved us.
7. Vibe: Brooding / Sombre. Theme: Conclusion (perhaps non-triumphant).

I opted for seven, the final slot: not feeling rambling, saved, pleasant or thankful, but definitely brooding and sombre about life, the universe and everything. Besides, coming last, you didn't have to worry about the amazing virtuoso coming after you. You either brought things to a finish, or you didn't. But what to write? W. H. Auden apparently welcomed commissions because they provided the occasion for the poem, and, like the many varied verse forms with which he experimented, the occasion went on to act as a starter-motor to his imagination. But then, he was Auden.

Now here we all are: after further emails, a couple of short, individual sessions with the musicians, but no overall run-through. The church feels quite full, but, from where we are sitting, only a few faces in the front pews of the nave are clearly visible; they float, pale and disembodied, in the blackness. Behind them hover other, more Munch-like apparitions. Up above, the eight ceiling lights hang like haloes. Candles flicker and reflect erratically off the glass doors at the rear of the church. In the silence, there is the occasional cough, shuffling of feet.

The music, listed as 'General Doom/Infinity', begins to throb, ache and fill the space. Simon's deep voice rises through it out of a great void like a world lament, the words perhaps in Old English. There is a run of organ notes. Nick slips behind the microphone, gives the title of his first poem: 'You Will Find Me Much Changed'. His voice slices into the void:

After my brain injury I felt myself at a kink with the world.
After my brain injury I was no longer in tune with the sensibilities of the age.
After my brain injury I said things like, 'Fiction is over. Tell us the truth.'
After my brain injury I no longer found wonder in the universe . . .

It's one of those poems which is at once both funny and heart-turning (a hallmark of Nick's poetry). Some later lines produce a quick flutter of (relieved?) laughter after the 'ditto':

After my brain injury I found faces difficult to recognise, which had been
the case before my brain injury.

After my brain injury I found the arts self-aggrandising, deceitful,
flavourless, which ditto . . .

The self-lacerating jokiness in his second poem, 'House, Kid, ~~Dog~~ Divorce', feels, if anything, even harder to sustain, the pain and desolation all the more palpable:

Things to file under H, K, and D, respectively, shrug one's
hunchback and roll on to the next defeat. Or the next

success, or minor success, or catastrophe framed at a
skew and a squint so as to be overlain with a success

narrative . . .

Plink-thump, plink-thump: the music slowly, inexorably, reasserts itself. Maaike's voice soars ethereally; Simon's moves to join it; the voices intertwine. Plink-thump; plink-thump. The violin sails over all; the cello earths it; the voices again intertwine, rising, falling. Fade.

Chris edges out of the pew and across to the mic. 'Persistence is futile':

In this present day when all the good in the world slips
through cracks in the light, leaving me without guidance
I am asked to choose:

    / rage or sorrow?

    / kindness or setting the world on fire?

    / mercy or cruelty?

When neither rage nor sorrow no longer serve their purpose,
when kindness and mercy have lost their sway on the world
I tell the non-believers:

    / try embracing terror as your day to day.

    / try marching for someone else's pain.

    / try ignoring the songs coming from the ruins . . .

His voice — clear, calm, incantatory — pleads to the darkness for 'kindness and mercy in this day and age', while acknowledging that the darkness is going to give nothing back.

There's a volley of repetition ('kindness is a crime / mercy is a crime / identity is a crime / fashion is a crime . . .'); a sudden burst of rhyme, the final lines spell out what seems the only possible response — to endure, dancing in the dark:

set the stars to infinity
and dance like the world will never end

The music momentarily strikes a lighter tempo, thrumming cello, ghosting the uncanny. Maaike's voice lifts — in te reo? A melancholy clarinet. Maaike again, her voice ascending and descending in arpeggios of sound, and a fading cello restore the theme, 'The End is Nigh'.

Rebecca plunges straight into the first of her three poems, the lines uncompromisingly visceral:

When we were young we kept knives in our hands
Peeling the skin from our thumbs instead of the fruit

Palms flayed like pomegranate leather or deer velvet
The bones in our fingers the shattered stems of wine glasses . . .

The imagery is surreal, often grotesque yet, because of the 'we', strangely intimate, aware of shared threat, of hunting and of being hunted. 'We' shifts to 'I', shapeshifts to venison, gun, dog, apple, moon. The overall effect is oddly reaffirming. 'Dread Weather' lives up to its title, 'doomscrolling' through a distant bushfire that becomes a metaphor for personal mayhem. 'Pink Fairy Armadillo' opens with a line — 'one of your axolotls has eaten the other' — which, I hope, becomes as disconcertingly familiar as 'The art of losing isn't hard to master' or 'There must be some way out of here'.

In a subsequent email exchange in which we shared what we had read, Rebecca described 'Pink Fairy Armadillo' as 'the new thing I was cold-sweating over through Friday and Saturday . . . axolotls, nemeses, and strategically disadvantageous fantasy armour'. Which seems to cover it:

How humiliating that I have sought
to burrow into the flesh below your chest
a pink fairy armadillo trembling for safety
the kind of paradoxically precious wild creature
that cannot even survive in captivity. is it too much to ask
to be universally adored?

Keyboard chords now, a strummed guitar: the development of an almost Mexican swing. Simon's bass; Ruby on a kōauau (a small flute): high, free-floating notes. The music takes on a quivering drone: the theme now is 'Be Saved'. Ruby sings in te reo; then she breaks into what she later self-deprecatingly dubs 'my zooming in and out Māui rope rant of saving ourselves with our past lives', which on the evening rings out loud and clear, goose-bumpy. The music in the background rasps and churns, *unheimlich*. Her voice periodically breaks out into song:

Behold! The line. The long line, the unending line. The line with no beginning. But now, look closer. Move yourself deep into the grooves of it, the structures and intricacies of it. But is it an it? No, it is alive. A gentle atomic energy flowing between strands, snippets of DNA from ancestors reaching back and back and back through time in a long . . . plait. A rope unending. Plaits within plaits binding each individual strand, each individual hair together. Fibres of flax and flesh and whakapapa. She and he and they threaded here into one, unending, undying. The taura within us, the taura that will pull us to safety . . ..

Become a tall tale to be told by all the fibres and filaments that have come this far not to break apart, but to encircle the sun, to pull it closer, so we can not only survive here in this place of uncertainty, but so that we can see who we are, so we can thrive.

The music picks up again into 'Blessed Ramblings', and Maaike sings. This time she's definitely singing in Old English, a translation of a verse or two of the poem I'm about to read, 'The Song Sings the News of the World'. There are interjections of sax; an extended keyboard solo, Bach-like runs; Maaike again. I'm worried I'll miss my musical cue, trip over invisible leads. I'll drop the poem, crunch the sheets of paper. (Probably all the others have felt the same, but you'd never have guessed it.)

My poem is a kind of sequel. A few years earlier, I'd written a poem called 'Song' about a character (ungendered) who has a small child and feels trapped by both the present and the past. The poem had seven short sections and ended: 'The black dog leads the song down long / unlovely streets. The night is eating the moon.' Much of the poem had seemed to write itself, rather the way mediums describe automatic writing — not that involuntariness is necessarily any guarantee of quality.

At some point after Chris's invitation, I'd found myself wondering what Song might think about our current world, menaced by so many threats (climate change, corporatisation, human greed, possible extinction . . .), and some lines slowly started to form themselves. The structure was simple, like a ballad, deliberately easy to follow. There was lots of rhyme and repetition, a jumble of geographies, deserted places, hopeful spaces, borrowed phrases, a stab at some sort of impersonal public utterance.

The music turns more dirge-like. There's my cue. I reach the mic without disaster, look out into the weirdly lit nave. I say the title. My voice — slightly tight — sounds as though it belongs to someone else, someone speaking in a huge echo chamber:

> the Song sings in the dark
> the Song sings near, the Song sings far
> see-where-we-are   see-where-we-are
> the Song sings in the dark
>
> the Song dreams of what has been
> the Song imagines a world of green ...
>
> the Song traces rewilding places
> Swonas of the spirit deserted apart
> the Song loiters in ghost-towns
> Tikal, Xanadu, Chernobyls of the heart ...
>
> the Song sings dust to dust
> the Song sings because it must
> the Song sings wai-ata of praise
> the Song sings for the years, the months, the days
>
> the Song dreams of a world of green
> the Song imagines what still might be

I retreat into invisibility. The music ('Ragalin') takes over; the voices lift and fall; a long, sustained sequence as various instruments come together and the music once more throbs and aches:

> Ah   Ah   Ah
>   Ah   Ah   Ah ...

Then it's over, the bubble, the tension, of performance releases itself, and, as Jordan Hamel put it in his appreciative *Poetry Shelf* review, it has overall been 'the perfect evening, poetry and music together as they should be, in a venue built for ritual'. The lights come up full glare. Audience and performers shake themselves; remember what they have to do next; return to the ordinary magic.

The performance of 'Epilogue' was broadcast in full as part of RNZ Concert's *Sound Lounge* on 6 August 2022.

Harry Ricketts is Emeritus Professor at Te Herenga Waka Victoria University of Wellington. He has published around 30 books, which include literary biographies — *The Unforgiving Minute: A Life of Rudyard Kipling* (1999) and *Strange Meetings: The Poets of the Great War* (2010) — personal essays, several anthologies of New Zealand poetry, a book of short stories and 12 collections of poems (most recently, *Selected Poems*, 2021). Among other current projects, he is working on a memoir. He lives in Te Whanganui-a-Tara Wellington.

Selina Tusitala Marsh
You send me Seneca

for PBMM

As the last plane is grounded
the last border closed

the last bag of rice
whipped away

from supermarket
shelves

you send me Seneca
he feeds me what we have:

We want
for nothing.

Our ala,
a fish kiss

beneath pool's surface,
a bare trace

till infected
by belly embrace

mutating with each
contact till

pandemic.

We started
with a single request:

One grain of rice
placed on the first

chessboard square merely
to be double on the next

square, till the last.

What could it hurt?
The Emperor said.

An oversight
he'd live to regret

when by the 64th square
18 quintillion grains

were owed.

We are seduced
by exponential love

bigger than you or me
Or Covid-19.

Selina Tusitala Marsh ONZM FRSNZ is a New Zealand poet and scholar of Samoan, Tuvaluan,
Scottish and French ancestry, and was the New Zealand Poet Laureate from 2017 to 2019. As the 2016
Commonwealth Poet, she performed her commissioned poem 'Unity' for Queen Elizabeth II. Her recent
books include *Tightrope* (2017), *Dark Sparring* (2013) and *Fast Talking Pi* (2009), and her award-
winning series for young readers, *Mophead* (2019) and *Mophead Tū* (2020); a third is in the works. She
lives on Waiheke Island.

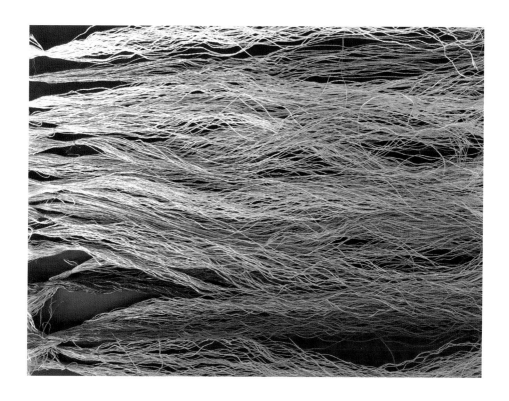

Maureen Lander, *Aho for Hinetītama*, 2020. Dyed muka thread, 900–1200 mm.

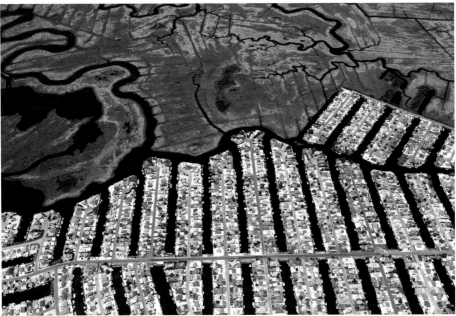

Alex MacLean, *The Star Jet Roller Coaster, Seaside Heights, New Jersey*, November 2012.

Alex MacLean, *Waterfront Wetland Properties, Mystic Island, New Jersey*, October 2010.

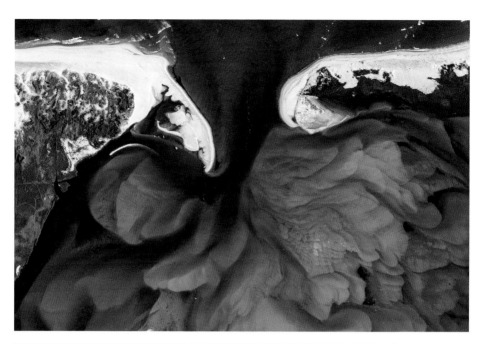

Alex MacLean, *The Wilderness Breach and Flood Delta, Fire Island, New York*, September 2018.

Alex MacLean, *Shoreline Beach Zones at Smith's Point, Nantucket, Massachusetts*, September 2018.

2/3 Red   'He Kanikani te Ora me te Mate'   von '21

Noa Noa von Bassewitz, *He Kanikani te Ora me te Mate*, from the series 'Spirit Animals', 2021.
Water-based ink on paper.

KŌRERO

Ru Freeman
and Paula Morris
On writing
humanity forward

A conversation on truth, fiction and returning to the story

Internationally acclaimed writers Ru Freeman and Paula Morris come together to talk about storytelling and humanity, and the way they travel between their own personal experiences and the idea of writing with purpose. They explore common ground and diverging viewpoints, looking for wisdom in unusual places and arriving at more questions than answers, ultimately leading to an expansion of the creative process.

Ru Freeman is a Sri Lankan-born writer and activist whose creative and political work has appeared internationally, including in the UK *Guardian*, the *Boston Globe* and the *New York Times*. She is the award-winning author of the short story collections *Sleeping Alone* (2022) and *Bon Courage: Essays* (2023); the widely translated novels *A Disobedient Girl* (2009) and *On Sal Mal Lane* (2013), a *New York Times* Editors' Choice book; and the editor of *Extraordinary Rendition: American Writers on Palestine* (2015) and *Indivisible: Global Leaders on Shared Security* (2017). She teaches creative writing worldwide and directs the Artists Network for Narrative 4. She lives in New York City.

Paula Morris MNZM (Ngāti Wai, Ngāti Manuhiri, Ngāti Whātua) is an award-winning novelist, short story writer and essayist. An Associate Professor at the University of Auckland Waipapa Taumata Rau, where she directs the Master of Creative Writing programme, she is the founder of the Academy of New Zealand Literature and Wharerangi, the Māori literature hub. She co-edited the landmark anthologies *Ko Aotearoa Tātou* (with Michelle Elvy and James Norcliffe, 2020) and *A Clear Dawn: New Asian Voices from Aotearoa New Zealand* (with Alison Wong, 2021), and she is working on an anthology of contemporary Māori short fiction.

PM: Kia ora, Ru. We're fiction writers, among other things, so perhaps our approach to exploring humanity involves more typing and daydreaming than most.

You and I are both fans of Jhumpa Lahiri's first story collection, *Interpreter of Maladies*. I often teach the title story in my undergraduate classes, and we discuss — among other things — the way the story explores cultural misunderstandings and misreadings. The characters share an ethnicity, but one is a local, and the family he drives for a day are diasporic Indians who observe India through sunglasses, visors and car windows. Misinterpretation — of behaviour, attitudes, culture, the natural world — dooms the day and its interactions.

This keeps me returning to the story, I think, not just to discuss point of view and artful use of detail: it teases out disconnection and fundamental differences. I loathe readers talking about what they can relate to or identify with, as though fiction must be about each of us in order to engage with a story and its characters. That feels both narcissistic and simplistic.

Emotions are universal; experiences, the ways we express emotion, are not.

Much of your own work seems to be about exploring the experiences of outsiders, or about people, within a family or community, who are very different from each other. Is this what draws you to a writer like Lahiri, for example?

RF: I was initially drawn to Lahiri when I was laid up in bed with 'someday' hopes of writing a book someone might want to read, and *Interpreter of Maladies*, just published, came my way. Like any aspiring writer, I thought: *Damn, this fellow South Asian wrote the stories I want to write.* Then I grew up and understood that every story is an old one, to be rewritten, that is, made new, through the particular lens and language and syntax of a new writer.

You are correct that I am drawn to this idea of difference. But I think of it more along the lines of something Stanley Kunitz says in his introduction to *The Collected Poems*: 'the most poignant of all lyric tensions stems from the awareness that we are living and dying at once. To embrace such knowledge and yet to remain compassionate and whole — that is the consumption of the endeavor of art.' For me, to live and to die is to simultaneously belong and not belong; to be very precisely different and yet complicatedly not different at all. To be outside of something is to observe more than to participate.

As writers, I feel, we are cast almost relentlessly, and despite our most strenuous efforts, into that place outside 'this' place. I can imagine that Lahiri — born in London, raised in Rhode Island, always a visitor to her origins — gifted those flawed and irritating characters the same qualities she observed in herself. Don't we all work out our own kinks in our writing, after all? For this reason, too, her writing in the book that she wrote in Italian, *In Altre Parole* (translated as *In Other Words*), is moving and

korero

323

brilliant. And by brilliant I mean as in casting a radiance, a lustre, that illuminates the act of observation and involvement in what is happening to us.

I think you were looking for similar understandings in the essay you wrote for the 'short books on big subjects' series in New Zealand, *On Coming Home*. I'm also interested in the way you shapeshift between fiction and non-fiction in your collection *False River*, which blends the genres, but also requires you to bend your own truths. What prompted that form for you?

PM: I'm stern, in person, about the separation of fiction and non-fiction. As soon as imagined elements are added to a true story, it becomes fiction. So when people tell me a given story could be one thing or the other, it suggests they don't really understand creative non-fiction, or don't grasp that adding lies or inventions drives a true story into a fictional space. Still, I'm not above submitting a piece of non-fiction in the guise of fiction, if an editor asks me for something that's a 'short story'. It works in this direction, I think, but not the other.

'Great Long Story', which appears in *False River*, is an essay I wrote about visiting sites in Mississippi associated with Robert Johnson, and exploring all the competing legends about his life and death. The fragments of Johnson that are remembered or forgotten or exaggerated are all part of his story, just as what I noted down, remembered or couldn't recall from that day in Mississippi are part of mine. The essay first appeared as a story in the fiction anthology *Black Marks on the White Page*, edited by Witi Ihimaera and Tina Makereti, and since then I've been asked if I invented parts of it.

It's my own fault. I wrote this line late in the essay: 'Everything I've written here is true, apart from the things that are wrong, and the things that are lies, and the things that are misremembered.' I didn't mean that I'd lied, but that some — or maybe much — of what's been told about Robert Johnson is a lie. Still, readers are always eager to find lies in non-fiction and uncover truth in fiction.

For me, the essays and short fiction in *False River* are discrete entities, though they reveal similar concerns or interests on my part, I suppose. And the first-person of an essay is as flawed and partial, inevitably, as the first-person narrator of a short story. You said that we all 'work out our own kinks in our writing': we also reveal our obsessions.

RF: I believe that all fiction is non-fiction. And, given the extreme subjectivity and psychological fragility of all human beings, I must then also say that all non-fiction is, to varying degrees, fiction. It is one person's accounting of things, and, as you note with regard to your own perspective on the mythologies around Robert Johnson, we are constantly remembering and forgetting things, so our non-fiction can aspire to, but never really achieve, an absolute truth.

The obsessions in my writing are always about wrestling with justice. Even if that is simply in the form of stating the details of a moment, a relationship, a war. If I cannot end the war, then I will write of it so others may hear of it. If I cannot mend a relationship, I will write of it so I may parse the details of its undoing. Et cetera.

Which brings me to this idea of universality that we sometimes speak of when we talk about creative work. I don't necessarily believe in the universality of experiences, but I do believe in an inalienable set of requirements for humanity — in ourselves, in others, in our local and global practices. What we must write to, therefore, is to advance that. The chance, however fragile it is, to live a life of dignity, seen and valued as a human being, loved in life, mourned in death: this is the sacred ground we must write toward, or write to repair and stabilise.

PM: That's an interesting (and controversial) take, both on the subject of universality and on the role of a writer, particularly a fiction writer. What about writers who have no interest in saying something, or doing anything, in their work? I remember Mohsin Hamid, some years ago, commenting on a particular very famous, much-awarded British fiction writer, saying: But is his work *about* anything?

RF: I am a big fan of Mohsin Hamid. And I have no doubt that if he made such a comment, then it came after some consideration. Hamid once said, during an NPR interview: 'I want to try to imagine a future I'd like to live in and then write books and do things that, in my own small way, make it more likely that that future will come to exist.' So that is the person, I imagine, who was making the observation about another writer. His question was whether that person was making a better future possible.

I put it slightly differently, but perhaps mean the same thing when I tell my students, year after year, 'What we write should move humanity forward'; with a close second being, 'Write the emotional truth.' The latter is what is universal, and the former is the goal. Like Hamid, I have no interest in works that don't do either. I also don't have a lot of interest in works that are pandering to what might be currently politically stylish. You can sense when someone is going there, and while those works might, arguably, be addressing perfectly laudable political objectives, it is not art. Artful, but not art.

I'm curious as to what you think of this line of reasoning.

PM: I'm in awe, really, of your commitment to a bigger, deeper aim for fiction beyond telling a story (and/or making a point, something often fumbled in less-than-deft hands). The issue you raise is the question mark that dangles — or dances — over me when I'm working on the novel I'm writing. The book has to earn its place in the world. Otherwise, why publish it? Recently I read a brilliant quote from Flaubert, cited in a *New Yorker* review that's more than 20 years old. (It's of Geoffrey Wall's biography, *Flaubert: A Life*.) Flaubert said he deplored 'sugary confections which readers swallow without realizing that they are quietly poisoning themselves'. I don't want to write poison and I don't want to write medicine.

RF: There is a balance that is required, obviously. You can't make art if you are making it with a precisely articulated intention. For instance, 'I want to argue that nobody in America should own guns', while absolutely a valid and desirable outcome, would make for a terrible piece of creative writing in any genre. I feel that the thing that drives a poet or writer should be some general way of being in the world that then translates what that world is, and turns that translation into art. The world seeps in, filters through — however you want to say it — the mind of a conscious, attentive writer, one who is deeply engaged in the world, and through the process of artistic translation the writer articulates something that is both true and aspirational. Simultaneously. We are, and we are not. We fail, and yet we hope. Both things are contained.

For me this has always taken the form of knowing one small detail — of an idea, of a story — very well, acutely, and then building the transport that can carry that to a reader. How that transport is shaped is the wild joy of writing. But what that transport is carrying is tremendously precious and delicate.

In the end, even sugar/poison can be something besides being inherently and uniformly destructive. There is a reason Nina Simone sings so longingly of wanting 'a little sugar' in her bowl. Without it, the bowl is lacking. Nothing — poison or medicine — is out of bounds for a writer. But does the poison/medicine heal? If it does, fill your work with it, I say!

PM: Thinking about detail: the scenes in *On Sal Mal Lane* where a mob maraudes through a street that's home to families of different ethnicities, heritages and religions are vivid and frightening. Neighbours hide and defend each other, but there's still a distance imposed by these differences. For example, the Nadesan family will take refuge in the Herath family's house, but because they're Indian Brahmins they 'would not eat food cooked in the Heraths' pots'. That's an example of the novel's details revealing the particulars and the complexities of the world of the story, the world of just one short street.

I'm wondering about both of us writing stories set in cities or countries that are not the perceived 'centres', and about both of us as writers who are the exception rather than the norm. At the moment I'm reading stories by an American writer I admire and enjoy, but feel disoriented by how insistently white the worlds of the stories are: only (and rarely) when a character is described as black is it clear that whiteness is the assumed norm. Also, we may never visit London or New York, but recognise them because of all the books we've read and the films and television shows we've seen. Our own cities are distorted by the lens that views them as exotic, or as not exotic enough.

Sometimes I forget how hard it is for cultures and their subtleties to travel. I just saw some copy from a UK publisher describing me as 'half Māori' and I nearly fell out of my chair. (Actually, I may be imagining the macron.) I emailed at once to say we didn't use such terms here. Of course, some New Zealanders do — some to cause offence, but most without any such motive. It seems old-fashioned to me, and loaded. We don't talk about the former Queen of England as half-German. The challenge of any humanitarian work is communication, I guess.

RF: I love how you employ *your* history in your responses. I watched you fall off that chair and I can feel the arch of your eyebrow when you imagine the Queen's heritage becoming part of any announcement about her.

You are correct that halves and quarters and percentages of this and that are very American. And in a literary scene where those who consider themselves to be 'liberals' want to separate them from anything associated with straight-up whiteness, the search for these distinctions (but not, of course, practice or familiarity with those cultures!) is a booming business.

Then again, it takes reading and curiosity to understand the preferred cadences and accoutrements of others, particularly in how they define themselves. So along with the shock and horror of being defined in bizarre ways, we also routinely define ourselves in ways that probably challenge the understanding of others. I insist on correcting people every single time they ask me where I'm from 'originally', as if by some strange psychedelia I originally came from one place, but now I'm originally from somewhere else! It takes people a few moments to understand why I insist that my origin is Sri Lanka. Forever. The end. Likewise, I had to look up 'MNZM' and 'Ngāti Wai', 'Ngāti Whātua', 'Ngāti Manuhiri', all of which are part of your bio.

What we choose to make known is, I feel, like our psychological outerwear, or maybe like a TSA PreCheck line, or even a combination of both. It's like we are saying to others 'Don't start with me on x, y and z', but also saying, 'Let's not waste time on the basics.' It is therefore equally armour and welcome. And I appreciate both when I meet people, whether through something they've written, or in person.

All of this brings us back full circle to where we began. Caring for the Earth, in very precise ways, requires understanding our roots and the places that shape our hearts, and therefore, for us writers, our words and their intent. To be attentive to those details, in our own lives, is to be acutely aware of how similar details steady the ground beneath the feet of others very different to us. To quote our reliable sage Socrates: 'To know thyself is the beginning of wisdom.' And wisdom is surely the practice of our humanity.

Chris Tse
How am I going to make it right?

before you claim your desired future / first you must destroy / every
other version you've been offered or imagined / under false pretences /

start again / with your hands pressed up against / an empty display
box / free from the knowledge of how / or with what to fill it /

then crowbar yourself / into their world / and leave your prints
everywhere / they will set the gatekeepers on you / let them

have their hunt / easy prey is easy / when a trail of clues is left
to entice and entrap / like an ultraviolet spotlight / suspended over

a pool of blood / calling out / to every wannabe detective looking
for proof in a socially constructed world / wield the crowbar

over and over / until it breaks / let it learn its own strength and how
it can ruin their fantasies / slow years have become a thing of the past /

they are another disappearing wilderness / in a world of fade-outs
and infinite crackle / to finally see beyond the end of the world / all our

once and future selves / written into an argument for preservation /
hold still / let time reveal every fracture / all the evidence of pain

and guilty pleasure / that shows us / where to bend / where to break /
where to strike / repeatedly / repeat / until nothing stays the same

---

Chris Tse was born and raised in Lower Hutt. He studied film and English literature at Te Herenga Waka
Victoria University of Wellington, where he also completed a Master of Arts in Creative Writing at the
International Institute of Modern Letters. He is the author of three collections of poetry: *How to Be
Dead in a Year of Snakes* (2014; winner of the 2016 Jessie Mackay Award for Best First Book of Poetry),
HE'S SO MASC (2018), and *Super Model Minority* (2022). He co-edited, with Emma Barnes, *Out Here:
An Anthology of Takatāpui and LGBTQIA+ Writers from Aotearoa* (2021). In 2022 he was named the
thirteenth New Zealand Poet Laureate.

Helen Rickerby

I prefer sunshine

When I realised I did not have a favourite tree, it came as a small shock. Other people, when asked, told me of magnolias, kōwhai, eucalyptus, tall trees on a grandparent's farm. Sometimes I look at ordinary middle-aged men and wonder if anyone loves them the way I love him. For two months the farthest I went was one short trip to a supermarket in the next suburb, but otherwise I was never more than 500 metres from my house, usually chasing the sun. I say that as if I am skilled in estimating measurements, but that would be a lie. There was a man with whom I had a fitful correspondence. We would send each other music. I looked for hidden messages where probably there were none. Some days, especially in mid-winter, I have to remind myself to do or have at least one nice thing a day. That day it was a hot chocolate, another day it was a compliment about my silver shoes. I started thinking of candidates: the macrocarpa on my usual walk, where I once saw someone taking or leaving a letter; the tree outside my window that always has purple flowers, whatever time of year; the walnut tree over the courtyard, which is more frienemy than friend. I can't shake the feeling that if I don't already know, it doesn't count. I would be trying to make it something it never was. When I first listen to a new song, I can barely hear anything, it hasn't yet formed a solid shape in my mind, but over subsequent listens it comes into focus. I think I am not alone in this mild synaesthesia. For weeks at a time it feels like a health risk to consider the outside world, the world beyond these borders, the world beyond this valley, the world beyond my threshold. I hold things too close. There is something special about the one and the one. There is something suffocating about the one and the one. Some things are better with your eyes closed. It is not enough, but I don't know what enough looks like. Maybe it's too much? Now I have listened to the song several times, and I am starting to see a landscape. The dawn is breaking. I can see some hills, and definitely a river. It usually takes some time to see what something is, what is wonderful about it. It was much the same with the man.

I read somewhere that being grateful changes your brain chemistry. That is a cruel thing to tell someone in a pit of despair, but I have felt it. Three things, like a plaited rope pulling me out. I feared I might drown in that river. The conclusion I came to was that I do not spend enough time contemplating trees. But perhaps these days I prefer flowers. I prefer the precise angles of his upper lip. I prefer the surprises of a new song, or an old friend. I prefer sunshine.

Helen Rickerby is a poet, editor and publisher. She has had four collections and one chapbook of her poetry published, most recently *How to Live* (2019), which won the Mary and Peter Biggs Award for Poetry at the 2020 Ockham New Zealand Book Awards. She runs Seraph Press and lives in a cliff-top tower in Aro Valley, Te Whanganui-a-Tara Wellington.

Vaughan Rapatahana
taku taiao

I love the trees	e aroha ana ahau i ngā rākau
I love the birds	e aroha ana ahau i ngā manu
I love the rivers	e aroha ana ahau i ngā awa
I love the lakes	e aroha ana ahau i ngā roto

I want to breathe

e hiahia ana ahau kia hā

taku taiao

taku taiao

taku taiao

taku taiao

taku taiao

stop the destruction! stop the decimation! stop the pollution!

kāti te whakangaro!   kāti te korehāhā!   kāti te parahanga!

Papatūānuku te matua
o te tangata

Vaughan Rapatahana (Te Ātiawa) commutes between homes in Hong Kong, the Philippines and Aotearoa New Zealand. He is published globally across several genres, including linguistic critique and poetry, in his two main languages, te reo Māori and te reo Ingarihi. In 2023 he is editing/co-editing, with Kiri Piahana-Wong, two follow-up volumes to Witi Ihimaera's seminal *Te Ao Mārama*; a collection of Oceanic-Pacific poetry, with David Eggleton and Mere Taito; and an anthology of New Zealand multilingual microfiction, with Michelle Elvy. *mō taku tama*, a collection of his poetry written in te reo Māori, was published in 2022.

Patricia Grace
Whakarongo

Since lockdown began, I haven't spoken to a living soul. I have, however, had many conversations with non-living ones.

For example, I told my non-living cousin — born on the same day as me in a different hospital — that she had no business going off like that. Told her off. After that we had a great kōrero about sea horses. We had each found one of these — non-living of course, but miraculous — among the beach stones out front of our houses. I've had mine for more than 20 years. She found hers more recently.

These souls wear their skeletons on the outside like a suit of armour, tails curled into koru shapes. Their mother-of-pearl eyes, at either side of their horsey heads, are centred by black dots. These are some of the things we chatted about. But most of our discussion was to do with how, when we were kids growing up, in all our times spent in water, we had never seen a living one. Yet here were their fossilised forms cast up on our beach. How come?

Some days I put on my walking shoes and head off to the non-livings' place of residence. As I get my feet into them, I describe my shoes like this: 'There's a white strip all the way round the base, which attaches the soles to the uppers, which are orange. These uppers are stitched behind the heels, then fold round and over the top of the foot, where they lace up. I tie double bows.'

That said and done, I step out into this world which sparkles and gleams and spins and rotates, but which now has this new added thing. I walk in the middle of the road until I come to the track leading up to their place. No one else about.

Birds are there in the trees, not many — a pair of tūī and an unseen riroriro warbling from somewhere are the ones which come to my notice.

'What's happened to the world?' I ask them.

'Oh,' they tell me, 'you stole all our homes and gave them to sheep.'

'What? Me? That's not . . . I mean . . .'

'Well, you lot. We have to pick on someone. Anyway, slow down, it's a long way to the top. You'll have a heart attack.'

So, I do, slow down. The cheeky brats.

'Anyway, this is the way we got most of you up here,' I tell the beloveds. 'Up this track, not that I had to do the carrying. Or they brought you up the road way, in four-wheel-drives if the weather was bad. And now look at you: plaques, headstones, gardens, windmills, shells, pansies, crosses, seating, carved pou, sculpted stone, words of love, photos.'

I take a seat and tell them about this unseen thing that has come to punish us, of which they know nothing. 'It's a disease,' I tell the innocent, 'mate korona', thinking the Māori term may sound less harsh. 'It's bold and deadly. It flies through the air and lands on you, or you pick it up by touch.' I describe the coloured spiky balls, the little murderers, which attack you from inside and stop your breath. 'We all have to stay home, wash our hands all day, wipe down door handles, packages, bags, anything handled by another person, and we're isolated into bubbles. Me? I'm in my own bubble. If you're old, already sick or demented, you die. It's overtaking the world. Filling hospitals. People in other countries are falling in thousands. Perhaps we will, too. Images of mass graves,' I say.

Mass graves did it. How dare I talk to them like that? I shut my running-off mouth and cry for a while.

'Never mind all that,' I say when I'm done crying. 'The weather's stunning, day after day. The world is silent, the streets are empty. There are no cars, trucks, bikes or scooters on the roads. The sea is void; that is, the surface of the sea has nothing floating on it — not a boat, surfboard or swimmer to be seen, no one fishing from its shores. There's nothing noisy in the sky except for seagulls. Schools, shops, theatres, clubs, cafés are closed. Building sites have been deserted. People, in bubbles, come out and walk in the middle of roads. Some put teddy bears in windows. Singers come to the ends of their drives and sing to their streets. On Anzac Day old soldiers or their grandkids came to stand on footpaths wearing medals, and Richie McCaw, at the end of his driveway, played bagpipes. And guess what? The cities are not polluted anymore and forest birds have come to live there. Isn't that a marvellous thing?'

As for the kids next door — and, I'd like to think, all kids — they are so happy. They are at home with *two* parents, riding their trikes and scooters, bouncing balls, jumping on tramps. Parents are playing with them or inside, probably baking. These children have not been tugged from their beds before they're ready, washed and shoved into clothes, had breakfast shoved into them, been shoved into shoes and jackets and cars to be dropped at crèche where they are looked after by strangers. Or sent to sit bunched in classrooms.

'We have new heroes, would you believe? They are the overworked and underpaid supermarket staff, deliverers of food, health providers, caregivers, drivers, volunteers. Street dwellers now have roofs over their heads. Food is being distributed to those who need it. We are reminded to be kind. What do you think of all this? Do you think mate korona has come to tell us something? Is this a wake-up call? Papatūānuku fighting back? Anyway, dearest ones, you have the best spot — safe from rising tides, swelling rivers, fire, hurricanes, tornadoes, greed, motorways, rampaging viruses. And looking out beyond, there's all this beauty. The greenstone ocean glistens, the sun strikes the mountain peaks of Ngā Tapuae o Uenuku.

'Listen to the birds.'

Patricia Grace (Ngāti Toa, Ngāti Raukawa, Te Ātiawa) is the author of seven novels, five short story collections, several children's books and a biography. Her memoir, *From the Centre*, was published in 2021. She received the Prime Minister's Award for Literary Achievement in 2006 and was made a Distinguished Companion of the New Zealand Order of Merit (DCNZM) in 2007. In 2008, she was the recipient of the Neustadt International Prize for Literature sponsored by the University of Oklahoma. She received honorary doctorates for literature from Te Herenga Waka Victoria University of Wellington in 1989 and the World Indigenous Nations University in 2016. She lives in Plimmerton, near her home marae at Hongoeka Bay.

Mohamed Hassan
Dance me to the
end of the world

I

good morning /   صباح الخير

                        I say
                            sleep a crow
                            nesting around my mouth

good night /   مساء الخير

                            the angel of your bones
                            wakes

we blink in code
satellites waltzing
around a cosmic ball

our story told in static   ستاتيك
radioed ones and zeroes
coupling in space

                          far / yes
                          flung / no
                          with eyes / yes
                          adrift / yes

we throw our wants into the sun
tulips touched by magic
or rice at a Mediterranean wedding

we practise   of longing
                                    the timbre
the way our ancestors   wanted
                                    always

                              II

Shahrzad would've whispered you   شهرزاد لهمستك
                    queen   ملكة
me a banished knight
bribing the palace guards
for parchment bathed
                    in oud
                              I text to ask
                              if I can call /

Darwish dreamt of trees
Zaoui of the moon
Dick Grace of Alice Crump

                              I map the arch
                              from Orion's arm
                                    through
                                    the bow tip
trace the arrow's path
to the Zamzam well

                              wash my feet
                              so I may pray

          bismillah   باسم الله
 and ask for wifi and ease

bismillah باسم الله

a rope to latch
to the nock

      bismillah باسم الله

for Māui's strength
and Sulaiman's hudhud

     bring me what I most desire

           or take me
           to her /

III

we have been left
to our own devices
      grounded

           and seeking flight

the internet is a vacuum   الانترنت فراغ
it robs our wilderness

         our sense
             of time

     but /

          it brings me closer to you

distance is a borderless plague   الغربة وباء بلا حدود
it robs our sense of touch

     but /

it has taught me to sing

to dervish myself
into a galaxy

spring life / نعم
from dust / نعم

it is no small miracle
to wonder
while the world   والعالم يصيح
weeps /

IV

dear sun /

I have sent
a thousand emissaries

hoping one finds
their way

through the storm /

if you are reading this
it means we are
still fighting

do / ولو
not / غبت
forget / عنك
me / زمنا

I will come find you

when the war is

done //

Mohamed Hassan, who was born in Cairo, is an award-winning poet, journalist, podcaster and producer. He won the 2015 New Zealand Poetry Slam, and the following year represented New Zealand at the Individual World Poetry Slam. His Radio New Zealand podcast *Public Enemy* won the Gold Trophy at the 2017 New York Festivals Radio Awards. In 2018 he was nominated for an Online Media award for his work covering the Israel/Palestine conflict. He is the author of *National Anthem* (2020), which was shortlisted for the 2021 Ockham New Zealand Book Awards, and the essay collection *How to Be a Bad Muslim* (2022). He lives in Tāmaki Makaurau Auckland.

Vincent O'Sullivan
Attend

It cannot help but sound imperious,
even when said nicely, as if 'I know
we have such different voices, yet
what I'm offering may be enlightening,

so isn't it better to attend?' Or that last
frayed attempt when all other excuses
fail, the final before the cliff edge
seems the only reasonable otherwise

option? Or enough to say Thank God
for as in earlier times — when the magic
works: the word itself like a distant
stream's crinkling when first heard,

then the creek broadening, you know
that, how there is only a river waiting
further on, so it's everything, give or take,
saying *listen* back, the expanses

broad enough to reflect the sky.
The past bobs along like fists of pumice
on the Waikato upstream from the Leamington
bridge. All because — no, truly — *listening*

Vincent O'Sullivan is a novelist, short story writer, poet, playwright and biographer. His awards include the
Creative New Zealand Michael King Writers' Fellowship (2004), the Montana New Zealand Book Award
for Poetry (2005) and the Prime Minister's Award for Literary Achievement (2006). He was the
New Zealand Poet Laureate from 2013 to 2015. His recent publications are the poetry collection *Things
OK with You?* (2021), the biography *The Dark is Light Enough: Ralph Hotere* (2020), which won
the General Non-Fiction Award at the 2021 Ockham New Zealand Book Awards, and the novella and
collection of short stories *Mary's Boy Jean-Jacques and Other Stories* (2022). He lives in Port Chalmers.

Poroporoaki

Where will the bellbird sing?

Hūtia te rito o te harakeke   If you pluck out the centre shoot of the flax bush
kei whea te kōmako e kō   where can the bellbird sing?

Kī mai ki ahau he aha te mea nui o te ao   And if you were to ask me
what is the most important thing in the world?
māku e kī atu   this would be my reply:

He tāngata, he tāngata, he tāngata
It is the people, it is the people, it is the people
all humankind!

Therefore, if we wish the bellbird to continue to sing:
become conservators of the planet.

And if we wish to nurture and protect the future:
look after each other.

Koia kei a ia te wā a muri, koia kei a ia te wā a mua
You who hold the present hold the past,
you who hold the past
hold the future

Select bibliography

Adam, Pip. *Audition*. Te Herenga Waka University Press, 2023; *Nothing to See*. Te Herenga Waka University Press, 2020; *The New Animals*. Te Herenga Waka University Press, 2017; *I'm Working on a Building*. Te Herenga Waka University Press, 2013; *Everything We Hoped For*. Te Herenga Waka University Press, 2010.

Baker, Hinemoana. *Funkhaus*. Te Herenga Waka University Press, 2020; *Waha | Mouth*. Te Herenga Waka University Press, 2014; *Kōiwi Kōiwi*. Te Herenga Waka University Press, 2010.

Barford, Serie. *Sleeping with Stones*. Anahera Press, 2021; *Entangled Islands*. Anahera Press 2015; *Tapa Talk*. Huia, 2007.

Barnes, Emma. *I Am in Bed with You*. Auckland University Press, 2021.

Barnes, Emma and Chris Tse, eds. *Out Here: An Anthology of Takatāpui and LGBTQIA+ Writers from Aotearoa*. Auckland University Press, 2021.

Billot, Victor. *The Sets*. Otago University Press, 2021.

Brown, Ben. *How the Fuck Did I Get Here? Soliloquies of Youth*. Read NZ Te Pou Muramura and Oranga Tamariki Youth, 2020; *A Booming in the Night*. Reed, 2006; *A Fish in the Swim of the World*. Longacre Press, 2006; *Ngā Raukura Rima Tekau Mā Rima*. Reed, 2005.

Brown, Diane. *Every Now and Then I Have Another Child*. Otago University Press, 2020; *Taking my Mother to the Opera*. Otago University Press, 2015; *Here Comes Another Vital Moment*. Godwit, 2006; *Learning to Lie Together*. Random House, 2004; *Before the Divorce We Go to Disneyland*. Tandem Press, 1997.

Cole, Gina. *Na Viro*. Huia, 2022; *Black Ice Matter*. Huia, 2016.

D'Arcy, Paul, general editor, with Ryan Tucker Jones and Matt K. Matsuda, eds. *The Cambridge History of the Pacific Ocean*. Vol. 1. Cambridge University Press, 2022.

D'Arcy, Paul, general editor, with Anne Perez Hattori and Jane Samson, eds. *The Cambridge History of the Pacific Ocean*. Vol. 2. Cambridge: Cambridge University Press, 2022.

Eggleton, David. *Respirator: A Laureate Collection 2019–2022*. Otago University Press, 2023; *The Wilder Years: Selected Poems*. Otago University Press, 2021; *The Conch Trumpet*. Otago University Press, 2015; *Time of the Icebergs*. Otago University Press, 2010.

Elder, Hinemoa. *Wawata Moon Dreaming: Daily Wisdom Guided by Hina the Māori Moon*. Penguin Random House, 2022; *Aroha: Māori Wisdom for a Contented Life Lived in Harmony with Our Planet*. Penguin Random House, 2020.

Elvy, Michelle. *the other side of better*. Ad Hoc Fiction, 2021. *the everrumble*. Ad Hoc Fiction, 2019.

Elvy, Michelle, Frankie McMillan and James Norcliffe, eds. *Bonsai: Best Small Stories from Aotearoa New Zealand*. Canterbury University Press, 2018.

Elvy, Michelle, James Norcliffe and Paula Morris, eds. *Ko Aotearoa Tātou | We Are New Zealand*. Otago University Press, 2020.

Elvy, Michelle and Marco Sonzogni, eds. *Breach of All Size: Small Stories on Ulysses, Love and Venice*. The Cuba Press, 2022.

Freegard, Janis. *Reading the Signs*. The Cuba Press, 2020; *The Glass Rooster*. Auckland University Press, 2015; *The Year of Falling*. Mākaro Press, 2015.

Freeman, Ru. *Bon Courage: Essays*. Etruscan Press, 2023; *Sleeping Alone*. Graywolf Press, 2022; *On Sal Mal Lane*. Graywolf Press, 2013; *A Disobedient Girl*. Graywolf Press, 2009.

Freeman, Ru, ed. *Extraordinary Rendition: American Writers on Palestine*. OR Books, 2015.

Freeman, Ru and Kerri Kennedy, eds. *Indivisible: Global Leaders on Shared Security*. Olive Branch Press, 2017.

Gnanalingam, Brannavan. *Slow Down, You're Here*. Lawrence & Gibson, 2022; *Sprigs*. Lawrence & Gibson, 2020; *Sodden Downstream*. Lawrence & Gibson, 2017; *A Briefcase, Two Pies and a Penthouse*. Lawrence & Gibson, 2016.

Golbakhsh, Ghazaleh. *The Girl from Revolution Road*. Allen & Unwin, 2020.

Grace, Patricia. *From the Centre: A Writer's Life*. Penguin Random House, 2021; *Ned and Katrina: A True Love Story*. Penguin, 2009; *Tū*. Penguin, 2004; *Dogside Story*. Penguin, 2001; *Baby No-eyes*. Penguin, 1998; *Cousins*. Penguin, 1992; *Pōtiki*. Penguin, 1986; *Mutuwhenua: The Moon Sleeps*. Longman Paul, 1978; *Waiariki*. Longman Paul, 1975.

Harvey, Siobhan. *Ghosts*. Otago University Press, 2021; *Cloudboy*. Otago University Press, 2014; *Lost Relatives*. Steele Roberts, 2011.

Harvey, Siobhan, James Norcliffe and Harry Ricketts. *Essential New Zealand Poems: Facing the Empty Page*. Random House, 2014.

Hassan, Mohamed. *How to Be a Bad Muslim*. Penguin Random House, 2022; *National Anthem*. Dead Bird Books, 2020.

Hereaka, Whiti. *Kurangaituku*. Huia, 2021; *Legacy*. Huia, 2018; *The Graphologist's Apprentice*. Huia, 2010.

Hereaka, Whiti and Witi Ihimaera, eds. *Purakau: Māori Myths Retold by Māori Writers*. Penguin Random House, 2019.

Ho, Ya-Wen. *last edited [insert time here]*. Tinfish Press, 2012.

Ihimaera, Witi. *Navigating the Stars: Māori Creation Myths*. Vintage, 2020; *Native Son: The Writer's Memoir*. Vintage, 2019; *Māori Boy: A Memoir of Childhood*. Random House, 2014; *The Parihaka Woman*. Random House, 2011; *The Rope of Man*. Reed, 2005; *Sky Dancer*. Penguin, 2003; *The Uncle's Story*. Penguin, 2000; *The Dream Swimmer*. Penguin, 1997; *Nights in the Gardens of Spain*. Secker & Warburg, 1995; *Bulibasha: King of the Gypsies*. Penguin, 1994; *The Whale Rider*. Heinemann, 1987; *The Matriarch*. Heinemann, 1986;

Whanau. Heinemann, 1974; *Tangi*. Heinemann, 1973; *Pounamu, Pounamu*. Heinemann, 1972.

Kennedy, Anne. *The Sea Walks into a Wall*. Auckland University Press, 2021; *Moth Hour*. Auckland University Press, 2019; *The Ice Shelf*. Te Herenga Waka University Press, 2018; *The Last Days of the National Costume*. Allen & Unwin, 2013; *The Darling North*. Auckland University Press, 2012; *The Time of the Giants*. Auckland University Press, 2005.

Kennedy, Erik. *Another Beautiful Day Indoors*. Te Herenga Waka University Press, 2022; *There's No Place Like the Internet in Springtime*. Te Herenga Waka University Press, 2018.

Kennedy, Erik, Jordan Hamel, Rebecca Hawkes and Essa Ranapiri, eds. *No Other Place to Stand: An Anthology of Climate Change Poetry from Aotearoa New Zealand*. Auckland University Press, 2022.

Liang, Renee. *Banana*. Monster Fish, 2008; *Cardiac Cycle*. Monster Fish, 2008; *Chinglish*. Soapbox Press, 2008.

Liang, Renee, ed. *New Flights: Writing from Kiwi Migrant Women*. Monster Fish, 2015.

Liang, Renee and Michele Powles. *When We Remember to Breathe: Mess, Magic and Mothering*. Magpie Pulp, 2019.

Lopesi, Lana. *Bloody Woman*. Bridget Williams Books, 2021; *False Divides*. Bridget Williams Books, 2018.

Makereti, Tina. *The Imaginary Lives of James Pōneke*. Vintage, 2018; *Where the Rēkohu Bone Sings*. Vintage, 2014; *Once Upon a Time in Aotearoa*. Huia, 2010.

Makereti, Tina, and Witi Ihimaera, eds. *Black Marks on the White Page*. Vintage, 2017.

Manasiadis, Vana. *The Grief Almanac: A Sequel*. Seraph Press, 2019; *Ithaca Island Bay Leaves*. Seraph Press, 2009.

Manasiadis, Vana and Maraea Rakuraku, eds. *Tātai Whetū: Seven Māori Women Poets In Translation*. Seraph Press, 2018.

Marsh, Selina Tusitala. *Mophead Tū*. Auckland University Press, 2020; *Mophead*. Auckland University Press, 2019; *Tightrope*. Auckland University Press, 2017; *Dark Sparring*. Auckland University Press, 2013; *Fast Talking PI*. Auckland University Press, 2009.

McKay, Laura Jean. *Gunflower*. Scribe, 2023; *The Animals in That Country*. Scribe, 2020; *Holiday in Cambodia*. Black Inc, 2013.

McNamara, Catherine. *Love Stories for Hectic People*. Reflex Press, 2021; *The Cartography of Others*. Unbound Books, 2018; *Pelt and Other Stories*. Indigo Dreams, 2013.

McQueen, Cilla. *Qualia*. Maungatua Press, 2020; *Poeta: Selected and New Poems*. Otago University Press, 2018; *In a Slant Light: A Poet's Memoir*. Otago University Press, 2016; *Edwin's Egg and Other Poetic Novellas*. University of Otago Press, 2014.

Meredith, Courtney Sina. *Tail of the Taniwha*. Beatnik, 2016; *Brown Girls in Bright Red Lipstick*. Beatnik, 2012.

Morris, Paula. *False River*. Penguin Random House, 2017; *On Coming Home*. Bridget Williams

Books, 2015; *Rangatira*. Penguin, 2011; *Forbidden Cities*. Penguin, 2008; *Trendy but Casual*. Penguin, 2007; *Hibiscus Coast*. Penguin, 2005; *Queen of Beauty*. Penguin, 2002.

Morris, Paula and Haru Sameshima. *Shining Land: Looking for Robin Hyde*. Massey University Press, 2020.

Morris, Paula and Alison Wong, eds. *A Clear Dawn: New Asian Voices from Aotearoa New Zealand*. Auckland University Press, 2021.

Neale, Emma. *The Pink Jumpsuit: Short Fictions, Tall Truths*. Quentin Wilson Publishing, 2021; *To the Occupant*. Otago University Press, 2019; *Billy Bird*. Penguin Random House, 2016; *Tender Machines*. Otago University Press, 2015.

Norcliffe, James. *The Frog Prince*. Penguin Random House, 2022; *Deadpan*. Otago University Press, 2019; *Dark Days in the Oxygen Café*. Te Herenga Waka University Press, 2016; *The Loblolly Boy*. Longacre, 2009; *Along Blueskin Road*. Canterbury University Press, 2005; *Rat Tickling*. Sudden Valley Press, 2003.

O'Brien, Gregory. *House & Contents*. Auckland University Press, 2022; *Always Song in the Water*. Auckland University Press, 2019; *Whale Years*. Auckland University Press, 2015; *Beauties of the Octagonal Pool*. Auckland University Press, 2012.

O'Sullivan, Vincent. *Mary's Boy Jean-Jacques and Other Stories*. Te Herenga Waka University Press, 2022; *Things OK with You?* Te Herenga Waka University Press, 2021; *The Dark is Light Enough: Ralph Hotere*. Penguin Random House, 2020; *And So It Is*. Te Herenga Waka University Press, 2016; *Us, Then*. Te Herenga Waka University Press, 2013.

Parkins, Wendy. *Every Morning, So Far, I'm Alive*. Otago University Press, 2019.

Perez, Craig Santos. *Habitat Threshold*. Omnidawn, 2020; *Undercurrent*. Hawaii Dub Machine, 2011.

Piahana-Wong, Kiri. *Night Swimming*. Anahera Press, 2013.

Powles, Nina Mingya. *Small Bodies of Water*. Canongate, 2021; *Magnolia* 木蘭. Seraph Press, 2020; *Tiny Moons: A Year of Eating in Shanghai*. The Emma Press, 2020.

Ranapiri, Essa. *Echidna*. Te Herenga Waka University Press, 2022; *ransack*. Te Herenga Waka University Press, 2019.

Rao, Sudha. *On Elephant's Shoulders*. The Cuba Press, 2022.

Rapatahana, Vaughan. *mō taku tama*. Kilmog Press, 2022; *ināianei/now*. Cyberwit, 2021; *ngā whakamatuatanga/interludes*. Cyberwit, 2019; *Toa*. Atuanui Press, 2012.

Rickerby, Helen. *How to Live*. Auckland University Press, 2019.

Ricketts, Harry. *Selected Poems*. Te Herenga Waka University Press, 2022; *Strange Meetings: The Poets of the Great War*. Chatto & Windus, 2010; *The Unforgiving Minute: A Life of Rudyard Kipling*. Chatto & Windus, 1999.

Robinson, Reihana. *Her Limitless Her*. Mākaro Press, 2018; *Auē Rona*. Steele Roberts, 2012.

Robinson, Reihana, Janis Freegard and Katherine Liddy. *AUP New Poets 3*. Auckland University Press, 2008.

Salmond, Anne. *Tears of Rangi: Experiments Across Worlds*. Auckland University Press, 2017; *Aphrodite's Island: The European Discovery of Tahiti*. Viking, 2009; *The Trial of the Cannibal Dog: Captain Cook in the South Seas*. Penguin, 2003.

Solly, Ruby. *Tōku Pāpā*. Te Herenga Waka University Press, 2021.

Taylor, Apirana. *Five Strings*. Anahera, 2017; *The Breathing Tree*. Canterbury University Press, 2014; *A Canoe in Midstream*. Canterbury University Press, 2009.

Te Punga Somerville, Alice. *Always Italicise: How to Write While Colonised*. Auckland University Press, 2022; *Two Hundred and Fifty Ways to Start an Essay about Captain Cook*. Bridget Williams Books, 2020; *Once Were Pacific: Māori Connections to Oceania*. University of Minnesota Press, 2012.

Tse, Chris. *Super Model Minority*. Auckland University Press, 2022; *He's so MASC*. Auckland University Press, 2018; *How to Be Dead in a Year of Snakes*. Auckland University Press, 2014.

Vilaça, Aparecida. *Paletó and Me: Memories of My Indigenous Father*. Stanford University Press, 2021; *Praying and Preying: Christianity in Indigenous Amazonia*. University of California Press, 2016; *Strange Enemies: Indigenous Agency and Scenes of Encounters in Amazonia*. Duke University Press, 2010.

Vilaça, Aparecida, Willard McCarty and Geoffrey Lloyd, eds. *Science in the Forest, Science in the Past*. Routledge, 2020.

Wedde, Ian. *The Little Ache — A German Notebook*. Te Herenga Waka University Press, 2021; *The Reed Warbler*. Te Herenga Waka University Press, 2020; *Selected Poems*. Auckland University Press, 2017; *The Lifeguard*. Auckland University Press, 2013.

Wilson, Sonya. *Spark Hunter*. AHOY!, 2021.

Wong, Alison. *As the Earth Turns Silver*. Penguin, 2009; *Cup*. Steele Roberts, 2006.

About the artists

Alex MacLean is a pilot who has flown over much of the United States documenting the landscape. Trained as an architect, he has portrayed the history and evolution of the land from vast agricultural patterns to city grids, recording changes brought about by human intervention and natural processes. His powerful and descriptive images provide clues to understanding the relationship between the natural and constructed environments. MacLean's photographs have been exhibited widely in the United States, Canada, Europe and Asia. He has won numerous awards, including the 2009 Corine International Book Award and the American Academy of Rome's Prix de Rome in Landscape Architecture for 2003–04, and has received grants from foundations such as the National Endowment for the Arts and the Pulitzer Center for Crisis Reporting. MacLean is the author of 11 books including, most recently, *Impact: The Effect of Climate Change on Coastlines* (2020). He splits his time between Vermont and the Thousand Islands region of New York.

El Anatsui is a Ghanaian sculptor who uses discarded materials such as liquor bottle caps, cassava graters and newspaper printing plates to create sculptures that defy categorisation and reflect his interest in reuse and transformation and an intrinsic desire to connect to his continent while transcending the limitations of place. His work interrogates the history of colonialism and draws connections between consumption, waste and the environment. Anatsui was born in 1944 in Anyako, Ghana, a citizen of the Ewe Nation and son of a master weaver of kente cloth. For over four decades he has been a professor in the Fine Arts Department, University of Nigeria, Nsukka, where his studio is located. His works can be found in the Metropolitan Museum of Art and the Museum of Modern Art, New York City; the National Museum of African Art; Smithsonian Institution; the British Museum; and the Vatican Museums.

Lisa Marie Reihana (Ngāpuhi, Ngāti Hine, Ngāi Tūteauru, Ngāi Tūpoto) is a multi-disciplinary artist whose practice spans film, sculpture, costume and body adornment, text and photography. Since the 1990s she has had a significant influence on the development of contemporary art and contemporary Māori art in Aotearoa. In 2017 she represented New Zealand at La Biennale di Venezia with the large-scale video installation *In Pursuit of Venus [infected]* (2015–17). Her other notable solo exhibitions include *Mai i te aroha, ko te aroha*, Museum of New Zealand Te Papa Tongarewa (2008); *Lisa Reihana: Digital Marae*, Govett-Brewster Art Gallery (2007); and *Native Portraits n.19897*, Museo Laboratorio di Arte Contemporanea, Rome (2007). Reihana has received numerous awards, including an Arts Foundation Laureate Award in 2014 and a Creative New Zealand Te Waka Toi Te Tohu Toi Kē Award in 2015. She was made a Member of the New Zealand Order of Merit in 2018.

Maureen Lander (Ngāpuhi, Te Hikutū) is a multi-media installation artist whose work has contributed significantly to the recognition of weaving in a contemporary art context. Her artwork draws inspiration from woven fibre taonga in museum collections as well as from contemporary installation art. She first learnt cloak making skills from noted Māori weaver Diggeress Te Kanawa and has spent many years researching and teaching Māori material culture at Waipapa Taumata Rau University of Auckland. As an artist, Lander is committed to innovation in a way that is deeply collaborative. Since her retirement from university teaching, she has worked with or mentored artists and weaving groups in the wider community. Lander received Ngā Tohu ā Tā Kingi Ihaka Award from Te Waka Toi in 2019 and was made a Member of the New Zealand Order of Merit in 2020. In 2022 she was made a distinguished alumna by the University of Auckland and was awarded an Arts Foundation Laureate Award.

Noa Noa von Bassewitz is an artist of Māori and German descent who lives and works between Te Whanganui-a-Tara Wellington and Te Ākau. Her primary mediums are woodblock print on paper and mixed media. Art-making is both a conduit for her creative energies and a grounding force, and relationships and the environment feature prominently as themes. Her prints weave Pacific and abstract symbolism into visual narratives, and contain creatures from the realms of the subconscious: taniwha, wild pigs and mythic creatures with teeth and claws and beaks are interwoven throughout her work.

Oliver Jeffers is a visual artist and author who works across painting, book making, illustration, collage, performance and sculpture. Themes of curiosity and humour underlie his practice as an artist and storyteller and through investigating the ways the human mind understands its world, his work functions as comic relief in the face of futility. His critically acclaimed picture books have been translated into over 50 languages and have sold over 14 million copies worldwide. His artwork has been exhibited at institutions including the Brooklyn Museum, New York; the Irish Museum of Modern Art, Dublin; the National Portrait Gallery, London; and the Palais Auersperg, Vienna.

Steve Golden, originally from Maine, arrived in Japan in 1989 with $200. Working as an academic publisher by day, he spent his free time travelling with his camera, and published photographs and articles in *The Japan Times*. In 2010, after a chance opportunity to work as an advisor for Lonely Planet, he became a travel photographer. His books include *Reflections of Tan Yeok Nee House* (2015), *Faces of Yangon* (2020) and *Heritage Shops of Singapore* (2022). He lives in Singapore and is a director at LASALLE College of the Arts.

Yuki Kihara is an interdisciplinary artist whose work seeks to challenge dominant and singular historical narratives through a wide range of mediums, including performance, sculpture, video, photography and curatorial practice, through a research-based approach. Kihara lives and works in Sāmoa, where she has been based for the past 11 years. In 2022 Kihara represented Aotearoa New Zealand at the 59th International Art Exhibition, La Biennale di Venezia, with her critically acclaimed exhibition *Paradise Camp*.

Acknowledgements

E ngā rangatira mā, tēnā koutou.

Thank you, reader, for holding this book in your hand. We hope its contents will create new spaces for all of us as we think, feel and breathe our way forward.

This book has come together with a set of people who have supported it with their various views and areas of expertise. First, the editors wish to thank Nicola Legat and her team at Massey University Press, in particular Emily Goldthorpe, for believing in this project and seeing it through with their insights and generosity. What an efficient and professional team — we could not have asked for a better working relationship.

Thanks also to Kate Stone, editor, for her sharp eye and the fast turnarounds with each round of edits — and the conversations about the views out of each of our windows of emerging springtime bird life; to Kate Barraclough, whose design work makes the book feel more complete with its flowing currents and rhythms; to Anna Jackson-Scott and Susi Bailey, who both provided essential proof reading; and to Melissa Bryant, for her expertise as our te reo Māori proof reader.

A Kind of Shelter is the culmination of a three-year project that began with Love in the Time of COVID (https://loveinthetimeofcovidchronicle.com), the online community founded in 2020 which was the space where the ideas for this anthology found their first footing. As lockdowns set in and the world went silent, it was that space or marae, established here in Aotearoa New Zealand, that created the initial ideas around connections across boundaries. The voices there proved that silence is never an option; that reaching out across the world with our many voices — in short stories, poems, songs, essays, photography, music, art, dance and video — brings solace and reassurance, and ensures the constant and deliberate asking of questions as our world faces the many perils of this century.

The title comes from a poem by Craig Santos Perez, who was one of the contributing editors of the online project. We are grateful to him, and to his fellow contributing editors Paula Morris, Catherine McNamara, Steve Golden and Vaughan Rapatahana, for providing the whakapapa link from the online project to *A Kind of Shelter*. We thank Noa Noa von Bassewitz for the print that graces the cover and speaks so beautifully to the contents.

We are so grateful to the wide range of contributors who have made this project a luminous hui surpassing any expectations. Their rich, perceptive and varied kōrero has created a further, and necessary, space to expand the kaupapa of the online project: to meet in dialogue; to sing of our pains and fears under lockdown; to make enquiries not only into a pandemic that has changed our lives but also the consequential cracks in our societies; to think about how to grasp this chance to create a better world; to examine anger and aroha; to laugh together in the small illuminating moments in which we affirm our common humanity. With vision and kaupapa they have looked out into the world that surrounds us. They are all kaitiaki.

We thank the individuals, galleries and organisations who have supported the visual artists: Imprint Gallery Tauranga and Le Petite Gallerie Raglan for Noa Noa von Bassewitz's two works; Milford Galleries Dunedin and Queenstown for Yuki Kihara's photographs; Milford Gallery, Page Galleries, Gallery Sally-Dan Cuthbert and Artprojects for Lisa Reihana's image; LASALLE College of the Arts in Singapore; Amarachi Okafor, Brandywine Workshop and Sotheby's for El Anatsui's artwork.

Hinemoa Elder crafted 'He karakia ki a Papatūānuku', a prayer that speaks of all our hopes for the safety of the planet for all of us. We pay our tribute to Moana Jackson, from whom we had hoped to commission an essay, e te rangatira, moe mai rā.

We also wish to thank Creative New Zealand for its financial support. Without it we could not have taken on this immense project with such a broad and varied set of contributors.

And finally, we thank you, the readers of this book. We hope you will enjoy the dialogue and challenges presented here, and we appreciate the way readers also play a part in an anthology such as this. You bring your care and views to these pages — and we look forward to the continuing kōrero in Aotearoa and around the world.

Nā reira, koutou, rātou, tātou, tēnā tātou katoa.

First published in 2023 by Massey University Press
Private Bag 102904, North Shore Mail Centre
Auckland 0745, New Zealand
www.masseypress.ac.nz

Design by Kate Barraclough
Cover artwork: Noa Noa von Bassewitz, *Embrace*, from the series
'The Taniwha of Te Ākau'

Extracts published with permission:
Pages 163 and 170: J. C. Sturm, 'Splitting the Stone' and 'At the museum
at Puke-ahu', courtesy of J. C. Sturm's estate; page 305: Troy Kingi, 'The
Mighty Invader', courtesy of Troy Kingi.

A catalogue record for this book is available from the
National Library of New Zealand

Printed and bound in Singapore by Markono Print Media Pte Ltd

ISBN: 978-1-99-101622-5
eISBN: 978-1-99-101623-2

The publisher gratefully acknowledges the assistance
of Creative New Zealand

ARTS COUNCIL OF NEW ZEALAND TOI AOTEAROA